## CERI LONDON

# DESTINY
# NEXUS

WAR OF AGES

Volume II

Publisher: Ceri London
United Kingdom
cerilondon.com

Cover Art © 2019 Ceri London
Book Layout © 2017 BookDesignTemplates.com

**DESTINY NEXUS/CERI LONDON** – 1st Paperback Edition
ISBN 979-8-5783632-7-6

Ceri London's

# WAR OF AGES

originally titled
*Shimmer in the Dark*

*Volume I*
Rogue Genesis

*Volume II*
Destiny Nexus

*Volume III*
Elecion Forces

*Volume IV*
To be published

This book is dedicated to my daughters.

# CHAPTER ONE

Seated in a US military installation concealed deep below the Nevada desert, Niall Kearey pushed tendrils of his consciousness into a mountain situated deep within the heart of the Middle East. He sensed a thrumming; an alteration in the magnetic flux. The UN suspected a weapons-grade uranium plant existed somewhere inside this mountain range, but without hard evidence the inspectors had been reluctant to stir up the volatile brew of politics and saber-rattling required to force an inspection.

Seemed their suspicions had been well-founded.

"Closing in on target," he said, partly to relieve his growing tension. "Think we've got something here."

He caught Jacqueline's whispered, "*Dieu soit loué.*"

Dr. Jacqueline Biron had invested a lot of hard work into this project and judging from the intensity of her aura, she needed a successful outcome from this mission as much as he did.

She glanced at him from the neighboring work station. "Need another signal, Major."

Niall leaned back in his chair. The array of visual displays blurred as his eyes glazed over with concentration. He tried to ignore the throb from the electromagnetic disruptor protecting this section of the Groom Lake base. He knew from personal experience the device obstructed remote-viewing of the immediate vicinity, but it didn't prevent him from remote-viewing out and he'd gotten used to its disorienting effect. Usually he barely noticed it.

Usually.

Just not when geomagnetic forces eleven thousand miles away chased his mind between the crystalline atomic structures making up an

1

uplift of Jurassic rock. The juncture between limestone and granite pulsated with a life of its own. Around his physical person, the underground facility pressed against his consciousness.

Sweat broke out on Niall's brow; his dual realities too close for comfort.

*Fucking rock everywhere.* Crushing him.

He flexed over-tight back muscles, took in a calming breath, and focused on forming an electromagnetic burst large enough to register on the US satellite monitoring system targeting the area. He compounded its intensity until the electromagnetic map reported a blip on the screen.

Jacqueline tapped the flat screen monitor. "Good. Locator signal identified."

Niall shifted his perspective and glanced at a screen showing the region he was remote-viewing. Jacqueline pinpointed the exact position of his electromagnetic marker. He had a couple hundred more yards to go.

*If* her calculations were right.

He raised his voice. "Someone check the air-con."

"The AC's working fine," Jacqueline said. A note of amusement softened her reply. "You can still remote-view the access tunnels."

Her original suggestion, one he should have followed.

"I'm nearly there." He could withstand a direct route through the mountain for a few more seconds. He nudged his consciousness deeper into the rock and bounced off the energy fields in the vicinity.

Relief flooded him as the oppressive rock opened into a man-made vaulted space. He scanned the lines of tall, thin centrifugal vats extending far into the huge cavern. Polished metal coiled around the cylindrical vats, which were connected to an overhead collection system by colored piping.

"Target confirmed," he reported. He differentiated between the electromagnetic fields of the illicit production machinery and the natural magnetic flux of the rock. "Good call, Doctor. This anomaly isn't obvious."

"Those new sensor modifications from your off-world friends have transformed our survey capabilities." Her voice dropped. "Do the Astereans approve of their technology being used for this kind of mission?"

"Sohan wants to maintain a neutral stance on geopolitical matters. What they don't know..." Niall didn't like deceiving the Astereans, but in this instance his loyalties sat squarely with his home country.

The door opened and General George Towden entered GBI's main lab. Niall straightened, careful not to lose his mental link to the underground uranium factory. He'd had his fill of evaluations, liaison duties, and covert intelligence gathering from a distance. He wanted action, but the general had kept a sharp eye on him, ever since the president approved Niall's return to active duty despite two long and unauthorized absences. This mission might make the difference.

"As you were, Major," Towden said. "Report when ready."

"Sir."

Niall completed his scan of the neat cascade of tall, silvery cylinders. "I estimate two thousand centrifuges, sir. No hostiles present."

"Proceed."

"Sir." Niall focused his eyes on the live satellite feed and tuned out the physical distractions around him. "Constructing magnetic engine."

Across the Red Sea and far into the Persian landscape, he gathered the magnetic flux of the mountain and created a perpetual magnetic engine. If he went a little further, he could harness the dark energy inside his spherical engine and create a bridge, a portal between Groom Lake and their target. A path existed through the shimmering quintessence of space into a dimension where space-time folded in on itself with varying degrees of predictability. However, a full-scale Special Forces invasion was unnecessary when Niall offered a more subtle solution.

Niall shifted his focus back to the GBI lab and created a second engine. Towden stepped back as a baseball-sized glowing sphere materialized in mid-air. The general eyed the vibrant ball of shifting light, his expression alive with undisguised wariness.

3

Jacqueline held out a magnetometer towards the hovering energy. "Point five Tesla. Please increase by forty percent."

Niall made the adjustment.

She checked her device again and nodded. "Can you reproduce the same field on-site?"

"No problem."

He dispersed the test engine and returned his attention halfway across the world. Deep inside the mountain, Niall increased the EM output.

"Reversing field."

He dragged his remote engine across the gas centrifuges, specifically targeting the ring magnets atop each of the rotating cylinders. The reverse magnetic field initiated a demagnetization process that would be hard to detect or stop. Niall suppressed an outright grin as he considered the damage he was inflicting on this ultra-sensitive equipment— *electromagnetic sabotage*. Add that to his resume of dirty deeds done in the name of the greater good.

"How long do you think it will take them to realize what happened and replace these magnets?" he asked.

"In theory, weeks, probably months," Towden answered him. "We anticipate a period of discovery when the uranium fails to meet the required grade, followed by arguments with the ring magnet supplier, attempts at recalibration, and then a whole new procurement process. We have scheduled dedicated satellites to monitor the above-ground facility. We'll see how long it takes them to notice. Of course, we'll prime the UN to ask some damn awkward questions. Try and get the inspectors back in. It buys time."

Niall rose to his feet and faced the general. "Reversal complete, sir."

Towden's expression relaxed. "Good job, Major." He glanced to Jacqueline. "You too, Dr. Biron. It's possible you both scratched one country off the WMD list for at least another year." His eyes darkened as his gaze rested back on Niall. "Major Kearey, your presence is requested in Washington by order of the Armed Services Senate Committee. A jet is on the runway ready for takeoff."

"Is there a problem, General?" he asked.

Towden skewered him with a stare. "You tell me, Major. Is there a problem?"

"No, sir."

"Good. You're dismissed."

Niall stood to attention, glad when an aide diverted Towden's scrutiny with a request for a signature.

Jacqueline grabbed her bag. Her face gave nothing away, but Niall detected anxiety in her aura. The emotion jumped out at him now his devious mind no longer pretended auras did not exist in the real world.

"I'll come with you," she said. "Sean's got a few days off. He's arriving this evening and my apartment's a wreck."

Niall doubted that very much. He waited until they were climbing the concrete stairs to the surface. "What is it? Don't forget the CCTV."

Jacqueline tucked errant strands of jet-black hair behind her ear. "Uncle Charles chairs the Armed Services Senate Committee. Be careful. He thinks you used me and he wants to find out who else was in on it."

Niall grimaced. He'd skirted the oily senator to deal directly with the ruling council of the Vercingetorix. The secret society had wanted Niall's data orb bad enough to pull the chain on their senatorial guard dog. Seemed their latitude might be running out.

"The Armed Services committee doesn't know about the Vercingetorix, does it?"

Jacqueline shook her head. "You can't say anything. Charles won't allow the Vercingetorix to be exposed to the American political process. They have operated international governance for centuries without anyone being the wiser. The V will cut you down if you try to compromise them. Don't go there, Major. Your family is safe. Keep it that way."

"I intend to, but if your uncle wants me to steer clear of the Vercingetorix, I can use that to avoid certain questions. If things go sideways, Jose knows the drill. I'll put him on standby. If I don't contact him after the hearing, he'll activate secondary measures. I'm not letting the V manipulate my family."

"You've made plans to disappear? Again?" Jacqueline swatted his arm. "*Merde!*"

"I went rogue. I went outside the chain of command and a data orb might not be enough to save me when my superiors discover the full story. I'm living on borrowed time and I don't know how, or when the truth will win out, or what the fallout will be." He glanced at her. "Jose's got instructions to take you, too." Her fine-boned face paled. Concern enlarged her rich-brown eyes and made him add, "I promised to protect you, Jacqueline. That hasn't changed."

He pushed open the exit door and a car engine roared to life.

"Why didn't you tell me?" she asked.

"The less you knew the better. Try not to worry. Jose and I have it covered. I'm going to have to come clean at some point, but I want to pick the moment."

A moment when his loved ones were safe and he could make a quick exit through the nearest wormhole. It might not be necessary, not if he proved his value. One thing he knew to be a dead cert. If he went down, he was dragging the whole goddamn Vercingetorix to hell with him.

# CHAPTER TWO

Niall groaned.

Should've guessed *he'd* be involved.

He walked up to Lieutenant Colonel Sam Hastor standing outside the entrance to the Russell Senate Office Building. Sam gave him a searching look that instantly set Niall's teeth on edge.

He gestured Niall inside. "We have a few minutes before they call you in."

"What happened to the forty-eight-hour notice?"

"The committee decided the issues surrounding Hideout constituted extraordinary circumstances. It's a closed session—your testimony will be confidential. You can refuse to testify, although the committee can subpoena you." Sam led the way down a corridor. "A JAG attorney's been cleared to advise you. I'll introduce you. All the attendees have clearance regarding your capabilities, the Astereans, and Operation Hideout. Nothing more, so steer clear of any mention of the Vercingetorix. Senator Biron will keep the committee within the agreed boundaries."

Niall snorted. Charles Biron would be happier plunging a dagger into Niall's back than looking out for him. Senator Biron might have telepathic ability, but the Vercingetorix's political lapdog didn't control everyone, or everything. Niall rubbed the back of his neck, sensing the presence of an EM disruptor. "You promised no charges would be brought against me. What if the committee decides otherwise? They can still refer me to a Court Martial."

"They won't. Not after today."

"I don't understand."

Sam checked no one could hear them. "Senator Biron briefed them on your intelligence gathering activity, including the magnetic scrub job you did today. He also told them the US Air Force ran interference with DruSensi's satellite sensors to screen your activity. The committee isn't interested in prosecuting an American officer fronting a government-sanctioned black-op tantamount to criminal sabotage."

"Biron knows about the satellite?"

DruSensi was a corporate arm of the Vercingetorix with a military grade satellite network that monitored electromagnetic anomalies planet-wide. They could detect every bridge and portal that Niall created. Senator Biron had significant financial interests in DruSensi. The Senator gave new depths of meaning to the term conflict of interest.

"He won't alert DruSensi to their security breach," Sam said. "President Foldane would slit his political throat."

Niall shook his head. Charles Biron's loyalties shifted faster than a slalom course.

"Trust me, Niall. You've no need to worry."

Niall's eyebrows shot up into his hairline. Rancor heated his voice. "You used my comatose wife to ensure I carried out the Vercingetorix's bidding to the letter. The moment I see your face I start to worry. Sam, I'll never trust you again."

"For God's sake! I was protecting you! And the Astereans... Jose... Jacqueline!"

"No. You should have confided in me. I didn't know if Tami was alive or dead! Imagine if you thought Linny had died, or that the Vercingetorix had taken her hostage?" Niall stopped short. The fear and panic he had felt when Sam denied him access to Tami still overwhelmed him, guilt too. With no idea where she was, if she was even alive, he had been forced to abandon his wife to protect their children.

"We were being watched." Sam's mouth pulled tight as he glanced around them. "Your reaction had to be genuine, or Biron would have suspected the truth."

"You want genuine? You got it, Sam. I genuinely do not like you. I genuinely do not trust you, Biron, or the V. It doesn't get any more genuine than that."

Niall took a desperately needed sip of water. The woman wouldn't let up.

"Major Kearey, you were granted immunity for your actions following what does appear to be an unconstitutional assault on your rights." The senator cast a disapproving glance towards Charles Biron. "However, you are obliged to answer this committee's questions."

"Yes, ma'am."

Senator Jennifer Pascale pursed her lips and flicked her pen back and forth between two fingers so fast it became a blur. Niall got ready to duck.

"I'm glad you acknowledge that fact. Now, you testified that on October 31st you were in Basque, Spain."

"Yes, ma'am."

"Basque wasn't on Dr. Biron's schedule."

"No, ma'am." The local dialect in the autonomous region had hinted at an Asterean origin and Jacqueline had suggested he check it out. "I was on the run, Senator. I hid out as a tourist for a few days."

"On the run... ah, of course... but not anymore." She treated Niall to her signature look of disapproval then tapped her pen against her papers. "Remind me. What was the population of Astereal?"

"Approximately one hundred million, including the Morrígan."

"I understand Operation Hideout saved one million Astereans from apocalypse. Is that correct?"

"Yes, ma'am."

"Thank you." The senator paused. "You also reported you helped an Asterean fleet escape their solar system."

"Yes."

"Another one million lives saved. Is that correct?"

"I hope so, ma'am. I have not made contact with the Asterean fleet."

"I see. What of the remaining population? The ninety-eight million left behind? Are there any survivors?"

For one heart-stopping second, Niall had no answer. Sweat prickled his armpit. He leaned closer to the microphone. "The others are all dead, ma'am."

Senator Pascale paled. "Are you sure? All of them?"

"Astereal was extremely volatile, ma'am."

"You haven't checked on them since?" Her shock radiated outward. "Using your mental link, I mean."

"No, Senator. As I reported, the planet Astereal was in a state of collapse."

"Yes, but..." The senator glanced around the panel of her peers. "Could you check? I mean, now?"

"I apologize, ma'am. Do you mean now as in now, this second?"

"Yes."

Niall hesitated, uncertain where this was leading, or what he would find. He extended his consciousness, hunting for a familiar sparkle that would draw him into the q-dimension, a sub-quantum level unconstrained by physical barriers. Here his mind was free to interact with the flow of energy leaking through space-time, opening up gateways to new realms, and a galaxy at the horizon of the universe, home to the planet Astereal.

The slowly disintegrating planet opened up in his mind's eye, a seething inferno of molten rock. Sorrow tightened Niall's jaw. Astereal would burn the longest death—the funeral pyre of a civilization if Earth had gotten its way. He'd saved the last of Astereal's people with moments to spare. A deep-abiding resentment uncoiled its way to the surface of his emotions.

He eyed the senators thoughtfully. "Would you like me to show you?" A stunned silence greeted his question and Niall turned to Charles Biron. "Mr. Chairman, I can safely open a small portal to view Astereal directly."

A babble of noise broke out as the panel tried to attract Biron's attention. The chairman waved them down, but it was obvious the senators wanted the demonstration. Charles Biron studied Niall with narrowed eyes. His gaze shifted over Niall's shoulder to where Colonel Hastor was sitting.

Sam stood up. "I do not anticipate a threat, Mr. Chairman, and I notice the additional security measures in place today."

Niall glanced around the guards. Additional? Hell. They really don't trust me.

"I thought Major Kearey required international authorization to create a portal," Pascale queried.

"The authorization condition requiring agreement from Hideout members applies to military operations, ma'am," Sam replied. "This committee is authorized to make a humanitarian exception."

Senator Biron nodded. "Agreed, Colonel. Yes, Major Kearey, I think a direct view of Astereal's condition would prove instructive. Please proceed."

Niall stood up, moved out from behind the table, and indicated the space between him and the panel. "With your permission?"

Biron nodded and Niall moved to the center, conscious of the security guards closing in on him, hands on their holstered weapons. The senators leaned forward. Energy sparked the air around Niall's fingertips and within seconds, he held a magnetic engine in his hands. Unseen dark matter bounced off the inside of its spherical walls releasing energy—dark energy, some converting to the visible range. Niall channeled this energy into his link, diverting the inter-dimensional strand to one point where it formed a small portal through space-time.

Astereal's chaotic forces took him by surprise and rising volcanic heat sucked air through from Earth whisking papers off the top of a desk. Senator Pascale squeaked and several of her peers jumped to their feet.

Niall controlled the energy forces this side of his portal and pulled his bridge across space-time hundreds of miles away from Astereal until a substantial portion of the planet could be seen. His audience moved around to get a better view. The planet was still intact, but the senators' shocked faces demonstrated that they understood there was no hope for Astereal, or her people.

Niall drove the point home. "Dead, Senator Pascale. Any person left on that planet after Operation Hideout is dead."

"It's like the gateway to hell," she murmured, her face ashen in color.

"We should have taken more," another senator burst out. "America absorbed nearly one million after the Vietnam war. I have met the aliens' leader here in the US. Sohan. They are like us."

"They have powers like Major Kearey's," Biron snapped with a flip of his hand towards Niall. "And look at what he can do." Distrust emerged red and hostile in his aura.

Niall met Biron's gaze with searing ferocity. A sudden welling of anger tempted him to tear up his deal with the Vercingetorix. How easy it would be to disperse the energy of his magnetic engine directly into Charles Biron's heart, or dump him into the vacuum of space to die witnessing the phenomenal cosmic event that had promised to kill an alien civilization. Senator Biron had been content to wash his hands of responsibility and let that happen.

Biron blinked then stepped back.

"Is that Bacchus, Major?" a white-haired senator asked. He pointed at a dark spot edged in pink located behind the fiery disintegrating planet.

"Yes, sir. The disk you can see is made up of gases and debris spiraling towards the black hole. Bacchus is the largest of several dark stars near Astereal's solar system. Its growing mass is what disrupted the delicate balance keeping this solar system stable for so long. The resulting stress on Astereal's core is responsible for the tectonic turbulence you can see now."

"I do see." The man turned to Senator Pascale. "I apologize for intruding, Senator, but if I may?"

"Yes, please, go ahead. I yield the floor to Senator Tyler."

Tyler inclined his head and looked at Niall. "Are you angry, Major Kearey? I detect tension between you and Senator Biron. Your family was abducted by persons unknown. Your wife was critically ill for a long time. You fought for Earth to take more Astereans and hit a brick wall. Your own government treated you with extreme prejudice."

The other senators resumed their seats. Niall dispersed the dark energy of his engine back into the q-dimension with some regret for holding back from tossing Biron out into space. The portal closed. "I was very angry, Senator. Having my family back safe is helping. I make no secret of my regard for the Astereans, but I will always be loyal to my country and to Earth."

Tyler seemed receptive to his words and Niall sensed a mood change sweep across the panel. As the senator retook his chair, Niall fought the turmoil of his emotions to express his feelings in a way that would resonate with the committee members.

He had a chance here to secure his future.

"The only crime I'm guilty of is fighting to save lives. I went outside the chain of command because my superiors did not trust my powers. I feared for the Astereans, my children, and my wife. I wanted to save them all and quickly realized I would not be allowed to do that. I escaped custody only to protect my family and help the Astereans as best I could, and then I turned myself in for Operation Hideout. I am grateful to the President for his understanding and I only ask for the chance to use my err... skills to serve my country, and Earth."

"I appreciate your candor, and the admirable sentiments you articulate with great conviction." Senator Tyler glanced down at his notes then rubbed the end of his nose. When his eyes lifted, he held the attention of everyone in the room. "I have to wonder what I am missing. Something that would explain the presence of a large mythological creature that appears to have set up home in the Amazon."

Niall's heart thumped in his chest. Shit. Macha's gryphon must have gotten loose.

# CHAPTER THREE

Niall sent Jose a text the moment he got out of the Russell building. <Hearing continues tomorrow. Stand by.> He pressed send and looked for a cab.

What a nightmare. Tyler had blindsided him. Senator Biron had called a recess to enable the committee to make inquiries. If Macha didn't get Kestra under wraps and someone identified her as a gryphon he'd be facing some difficult questions tomorrow. No chance of getting a flight home tonight. He spotted a taxi and hailed it down.

"Major Kearey. Hold up!"

Niall swore and looked back at Sam Hastor running down the steps toward him, cell phone clamped to his ear. Niall opened the cab door hoping Sam would get the message.

"Something came up, Major," Sam said, the use of Niall's rank making clear this was official. "I need to brief you."

Niall slammed the door shut and mouthed an apology to the cabbie while Sam continued a monosyllabic conversation with his phone. An official car glided up beside them. Sam motioned Niall to get in. "I'll be a couple of minutes," he said.

Niall grabbed the chance for a moment of peace. Pulling the door closed behind him, his mind surged up into space and sought out the magnetic forces that extended from the northernmost reaches of Canada to the outskirts of the South Atlantic Anomaly. Hovering somewhere over Mexico, he waited for the Morrígan Queen to sense the disturbance in Earth's grid and detected an offshoot of her consciousness riding the magnetic forces out of South America. Earth's magnetic grid was unpredictable in its effect on an individual. The grid sustained Macha's powers, unlike many of the Astereans who had discovered their gifts curtailed or simply inaccessible.

*I am sorry, Niall'Kearey. Kestra hunts at night and always returns by sunrise, but she's in season, and lonely. She's searching for a mate.*

Niall released a pent-up breath. Sadness filled him. Damn. *Pity Kestra didn't leave with the rest of her kind.*

*She didn't want to leave me,* Macha explained. *We have a connection.*

*Do you have her now?*

*Yes, she's safe. I will talk with her.*

Niall shook his head at the idea of conversing with a gryphon and noticed Sam speaking to the driver. *Hang on, Macha.*

Sam nodded to their chauffeur, got into the car and immediately slid the privacy screen shut.

"What's going on?" Niall asked.

"Senator Biron made some discreet inquiries. The Brazilian government is scoffing at the idea of a Loch Ness dragon setting up home in the Amazon. Dammit, Niall, how many aliens did you hide there?"

Niall widened his telepathic channel to Macha so she could eavesdrop. "Bit of a leap—flying birds to aliens." His tone came out more sarcastic than he'd intended and Sam flashed him an irritated glance.

"For God's sake, Niall, I'm not stupid. I'm trying to help you."

Macha poked Niall with her mind. *Use him, Niall'Kearey. Learn what he knows.*

Niall forced his personal feelings aside. "Is that what this committee hearing's really about? They think I smuggled in aliens?"

"No. Senator Tyler's a known conspiracy follower. Senator Biron pointed out he would be blaming you for Big Foot next. But I know you, and I think it's too much of a coincidence given Jacqueline made sure the Amazon was a satellite blind spot during Hideout."

Niall smoothed out a non-existent crease in his pants. Sam always knew more than Niall realized. "So where are we going? I need to book into a hotel."

"Airport. That was Senator Biron on the phone. Patrick Morgan is flying to New York for state business at the UN. He wants to meet with you. He's expected late tonight."

"No. The deal is that the V leave me and my family alone. Morgan signed it. Why does he want to see me now? Is this about the orb?"

"I don't know. Look, it's not an order, but Morgan's very influential on the Council, and President Foldane is requesting you meet with him. This is a chance to improve relations with the Vercingetorix. I don't understand why you're so worried. Morgan's at the UN representing Ireland's interests. There's no way he'd meet you there if he intended either you or your family harm." Sam raised his hands in frustration. "But, if you're saying no, I'll drop you off wherever you want."

"Good, you can drop me off at the nearest hotel, because it's never just a talk, and it amazes me you can't understand why I don't trust the Vercingetorix, or you."

Sam stared out the window, his jaw jutting out to one side. "I did what I could."

"You did squat. I gave you every opportunity to tell me about the Vercingetorix. Whatever side you were on, it was never mine."

*Don't force him to be your enemy, Niall'Kearey.*

Macha's unexpected rebuke stung.

*Sam deliberately used Tami against me. I'll never forgive him for that.*

*I am not suggesting you make peace with him, but I sense his concern for you. His loyalties may be split, but he offers a conduit to the Vercingetorix and he can speak for you with your superiors. Use him to your advantage.*

A tense silence fell. Niall moved to open the dividing window and ask the driver to stop when Sam said, "There's another matter I need to discuss with you."

Niall hesitated before sitting back. "Go on."

"That Asterean Councilor in Russia is demanding to see you. Says Earth has affected her telepathic ability. She wants to speak to someone she can trust."

Niall raised a dubious eyebrow. Trust wasn't exactly a defining characteristic of his relationship with Herecura. Interaction with her had always left Niall checking over his shoulder. "I offered to talk with her by phone."

"She's demanding to see you in person. We think the Russian group feels isolated, especially since Russia started annexing parts of the Ukraine. Senator Biron is negotiating a deal with the Russian Ambassador to allow Herecura to visit you here. Apparently, she's causing dissent over this issue. President Nobokov thinks she's a troublemaker and wants to make a swap."

"The Astereans aren't pawns on a chessboard! I'll go see her."

"Not going to happen. We're not letting you anywhere near Russia, China either for that matter. From their point of view, you're like an illegal nuclear program and you being a US military asset compounds their concerns. To be blunt, we don't trust them with you."

Niall's deepest fear lay mounted and exposed. Power came at a price. He never asked for these gifts, had viewed them as a curse from the start. Events had separated him from the rest of mankind, marked him as a threat. Now he needed the protection of his country more than ever. Standing alone against the world would set off a chain reaction he couldn't possibly control.

He would have to become the lethal weapon they feared most.

A one-man WMD.

And he knew exactly how Earth's authorities would retaliate. To force his cooperation, they would eliminate his Asterean allies and threaten his family. The Astereans' anonymity marked them as easy targets, and there were too many of them. His family was his weak spot.

He swore under his breath. Not a road he wanted to walk.

"None of this is as bad as you're thinking," Sam said. "Just don't do anything to frighten your own side. The Air Force has your back right now, but if you ever decide to leave, you'll be on your own. Why not

18

listen to what Morgan has to say? The Vercingetorix holds a lot of influence. They could be your biggest ally."

Niall's jaw tightened. Over his dead body. He'd struck a deal with the V to regain some kind of normal life for his family, but a burning desire for justice shadowed his every waking moment, haunted his dreams at night. Patrick Morgan provided a face to the organization that had nearly destroyed them all and if Morgan wanted access to the orbs, maybe he could use that.

"Okay, I'll meet with him."

In the converted cellars of an ancient chateau, Professor Etlinn Morgan entered the key code to seal her DNA scan and gain access to the Vercingetorix Library.

The new entry system had vastly improved security at the European base in the French Dordogne and DruSensi France had been quick to file the patents for this Asterean wizardry. Etlinn expected an announcement would shortly follow DruSensi's latest innovation in bio force field application while DruSensi had expressed their appreciation with a substantial investment in the French Astereans' living accommodations.

Interesting.

Who manipulated whom?

The invisible force field winked out allowing Etlinn entry as soft lighting illuminated double-height oak paneling lined with books, manuscripts, and historical treasures; a valuable collection that could pay off the national debt of more than one country. Etlinn walked across rich soft carpeting to a glass case claiming pride of place in the huge vaulted space. Inside sat an open silk-lined cedar wood box. This box had housed the Vercingetorix Orb in solitary glory for centuries.

Now it held two.

Etlinn leaned over the case, entranced by the intricate etchings scribed into the orb's silvery spherical casings. *So much promise trapped inside something so small.*

The alien and impenetrable composition of the outer casing had baffled their finest scientists, much to Nicole's amusement as Etlinn recalled. Nicole Biron had painstakingly researched the orb's provenance and her research filled the library. The Vercingetorix Orb's influence filtered through centuries of Earth's history. From ancient gods to kings and queens, Earth's rulers were depicted with the world in one hand and a scepter in the other, all probably unaware that the symbolic origin was not their home planet Earth, but a reference to a silvery orb that had somehow found its way to this world eons past.

The arrival of the Asterean Orb together with Etlinn's analysis of Asterean DNA only deepened the mystery. The Astereans and humanity shared a common ancestor. The discovery did not fully explain the conundrum presented by the American officer who traded the Asterean Orb to secure freedom for him and his family. Etlinn had studied Niall Kearey's DNA for months now, and even with the Asterean link, she still couldn't explain his abilities.

*I'm missing something vital. Searching for what I know.*

The opening elevator doors broke her reverie. Sensing her husband's mind, Etlinn strengthened her mental shielding. She detected the electromagnetic flux when the force field yielded to Patrick's DNA, but did not look around.

Patrick Morgan walked up behind her. "Research not going well?" Her husband's deep Irish voice shattered the tranquil silence.

Yielding to the gentle pressure of his hand on her shoulder, Etlinn turned. She gazed up into Patrick's penetrating eyes with their azure quality that always reminded her of his late mother. In other respects, Patrick was more like his father: tall, fierce to his enemies, and brutal when he needed to be, although he hid that side from her well.

Thank God.

Her guilty secret twisted barbs into her heart and Etlinn shook her head in answer to his question, practiced at keeping her emotions barricaded behind her shields, but not so accomplished at controlling her voice. Now was not the time to reveal the father's sins to his son, not with Kean Morgan on his deathbed.

The tightness wrapping her throat eased. "How did you know?"

"You've taken to coming down here whenever you're stuck. I came to say goodbye; the jet lands in fifteen minutes." He glanced at the orbs. "You knew Kearey would be special the moment you saw his profile."

He sounded suspicious, sensing something, but not sure what.

Etlinn gave him what he needed. "I admit I had a feeling."

"A feeling?"

"It was you and Charles Biron who discovered him."

"Aye, and he has proven to be an exceptional, if troublesome, find." He watched her carefully. "You were right about the EM pulse modification to the DRUMSI helmet, too."

She met his gaze. "What are you saying?"

Irritation flashed in his eyes. Patrick hated to be pushed.

"Are you harboring a clairvoyant talent you haven't told me about?" he asked her.

Etlinn tightened her shields. "Of course not. You're the clairvoyant around here." She smiled at his self-depreciating snort. His gift did not behave to order and her husband was not all-seeing as recent events had proven. "But you're right, I did think he was special and Charles hadn't allowed DruSensi time to properly test their modifications." She frowned. "Charles never used to be so aggressive."

"Charles resented Nicole's fascination with the orb, and this library." Patrick gestured to the treasures around them. "He hated not being the center of her attention."

"It was more than fascination. Remember the summer I stayed here after we lost Niamh? I found Nicole holding the orb in her hands. She said the orb spoke to her. I think she glimpsed a truth we're yet to discover. A pity she never got to see the Asterean Orb, but she deteriorated so fast at the end. If she'd held on a few more weeks..."

Sadness clogged Etlinn's throat. The stillbirth of their daughter had ruined their hopes for a child and Nicole's kindness had sustained Etlinn through a long, dark period in her life. She missed her friend. Patrick brushed a strand of hair from Etlinn's eyes, the concerned intimacy behind his gentle touch drawing her back.

"I'm telling you, Patrick, the existence of a second orb is monumental. Whoever created these artifacts traveled the universe long before the Vercingetorix came into being."

"Aye. I assumed the Asterean orb would be widespread knowledge among the Astereans, yet the UK and French contingents claim ignorance of its existence. So far, I believe them. They're blocking me over something, but it's not the orb."

"They must know their orb's history; how it works. Major Kearey brought the second orb back from Astereal and he could access its contents!"

"Kearey knew the orb would defeat us, that we'd have to go crawling back to him. We underestimated him from the start. I'm going to meet with him while I'm in the States."

Etlinn recoiled from him. "Meet with Kearey?" Anger mixed with concern. "Is that wise? Suppose he reads you?"

"He won't. My shields have held him off before. I want answers, Etlinn. We gave Kearey and his children up for a useless scrap of metal and I don't like being played for a fool."

"You've only yourself to blame if he works against us now. Your impatience nearly cost him his family. If his wife had died, or his children had been lost in that gorge, or on Astereal—"

"Aye, taking his family proved a disastrous mistake."

"Mistake? People died!"

"That was never the plan," he growled. "The explosions were supposed to be a distraction. Kearey alerted the police. It was bad timing."

"So now it's Major Kearey's fault?" Etlinn fumed. Sometimes she hated that she could love this mass of contradiction. Her husband was as ruthless as he could be loyal and kind.

Her husband's eyes twinkled at her. "Ach, Etlinn, still the feisty lass I married. Don't fret, my dear. I'll be careful. Kearey's a liaison for the Asterean. He's inhabited their minds and he knows the key to opening these orbs. I paid Charles a million dollars to get Kearey off charges of larceny. It's time to meet the man. Stand in the same room as him."

Patrick grabbed her hand. "Come to the States with me. I can wait while you pack a bag. Show Kearey there's a better side to the Vercingetorix. Charm him into helping us."

Butterflies erupted in Etlinn's belly. She yearned to meet the man whose abilities had jumped generations, surpassed the wildest dreams of the Vercingetorix, but how could she look Niall Kearey in the eye and keep his bloodline secret? His telepathic potential far exceeded hers. He measured off the charts in so many ways.

If she wasn't emotionally involved...

Etlinn tightened her mental shields ahead of a rising panic. Patrick revered his father, even as Kean Morgan's mind deteriorated beyond recognition. The truth of Kearey's parentage would devastate him, and however angry Patrick made her, she didn't want to hurt him. Nor would the repercussions stop there. The Council would seek an explanation for the inconsistencies between Niall Kearey's lineage and his incredible abilities.

Answers she didn't have.

"No. I must continue my research into Major Kearey's bloodline. If you insist on doing this, be very careful how you handle him. You can't buy off his anger the way you placated Charles."

Disappointment edged Patrick's expression. "If that's what you want. Perhaps you're right. Your research is crucial to understanding his abilities." His eyebrows twisted with curiosity. "So, what happened to bring you down here?"

Etlinn hesitated, unwilling to incite speculation until she had more data, but sharing her research might distract Patrick from other lines of inquiry. Her heart skipped a guilty beat. "I thought we'd identified a new chromosome in Major Kearey's DNA, but the strand disintegrated before we could run a full sequence." An inexplicable incident that kept her awake at night. "We haven't been able to isolate this chromosome since. It could be the result of a contaminated sample. I'm running more tests, but we need a complete sample set."

"A genetic mutation might explain Kearey's unusual abilities."

"At the moment, it's pure speculation."

Patrick tipped her chin up so she could not avoid his gaze. "What are you hiding, Etlinn?" His voice was soft, but his thought was loud. His thumb rubbed her cheekbone making her shiver. "Sometimes I think you hate me."

His blue eyes burrowed their way into her soul. "I don't hate you, Patrick." *I hate your father.* Her husband's inquisitive look spurred her on. "I'm worried about Kean. He's not doing well."

Patrick's expression did not alter, his thoughts suddenly closed.

"Maybe you should delay your trip to the States," she pressed him. "Go home and see your father before it's too late."

"No, I need to make this trip. I'll get a return flight back home and see him then. He has a few weeks left in him yet."

Etlinn prayed he did not. The sooner they buried Kean Morgan in the ground, the better.

# CHAPTER FOUR

Alone in her studio, Tami studied the subject of the photo displayed on her laptop screen; an old woman hunched over a grocery cart in the full shadow of a glass skyscraper that dominated the background.

Niall's familiar touch on the back of her neck made her start. Invisible fingers trailed her skin; a grazing tingle that disappeared under her blouse. She reached for her cell phone, arching her back with a slight gasp when the subtle pressure exploring every bump and curve took a decidedly erotic turn.

The phone rang and she pressed Answer. "Niall, what are you doing?"

"Having fun. That is a stunning photograph."

Blood pounded her veins as the electricity he was sparking moved towards her belly.

"It's supposed to be part of an exhibition I'm arranging."

"Supposed to be?"

"I overexposed it."

"Looks good to me."

His pleasure-giving attentions wandered and Tami got the distinct impression Niall was checking out her photo from another angle, but then his touch resumed its heavenly course.

"How's Tony doing?" he asked.

"You're asking me about your dad now? Why don't you remote-view him and find out? Oh, oh, yes, right there."

He laughed. The deep, sultry sound melted her bones.

She snapped shut her laptop, stretched out in her chair, and succumbed to the sensations he was arousing deep inside her. "This has to be illegal."

"Do you want me to stop?"

"Hell, no, but what about you?"

"I'm stepping into a cold shower right after this call. Tami, I haven't got long."

"You're kidding me."

"Don't worry. I won't leave you high and dry. I wanted to check on you all, but Tony asked me not to remote-view him while he's in rehab."

"Sheila reports that he's making good progress. She's been allowed a visit."

"That's great. Kids okay?"

"This school your mom found is amazing; no one questions that they're so advanced for their age. They moved them up a grade. I think we can be happy here."

"That's great."

"Is something wrong? You sound strange."

There was a momentary silence. His touch faltered and Tami wriggled trying to recapture the fleeting sensation.

"The politics is a little complicated right now," he said, "but I'm going to make it work."

The illicit, delicious pressure returned and Tami pushed into it. Her mouth parted and a flush warmed her cheeks. Muscles tensing, she tilted her head back and poured all her concentration into the havoc he was unleashing on her body.

"Better?"

The wicked smile in his voice pushed all thought aside. Her fingers clutched at the arms of her chair.

"Yes. Just don't stop."

Niall rested a palm on the tiled shower wall, panting heavily, focused on staying upright. The water cooled and he groped for the shower gel, starting when Pwyll jumped into his thoughts. The bottle hit his toe.

"Shit!"

*Is this a bad time, Niall'Kearey?*

A few seconds earlier could have been traumatic. He retrieved the gel. *No, I'm good. Go ahead.*

*Dr. Klotz's survey reveals that ninety percent of the Groom Lake Astereans have experienced a marked deterioration in psychic ability since arriving on Earth, but the extent varies.*

Niall squirted shampoo into his hand and scrubbed it into his hair. Thank the gods of fortune Earth had not diminished Pwyll's skills. Telepathically gifted, the kid snuck through mental shielding like a horny teenager slipping through his girlfriend's bedroom window.

Pwyll's amusement came through loud and clear.

*Dial it down, Pwyll.*

Niall met Pwyll during the defense of the Paladin sky city. Young in age and spirit, the Asterean had demonstrated an intelligent mind rooted in reality. Later, Pwyll helped Niall develop his privacy shields. Seemed he needed a few more lessons.

Pwyll's affirmative bounced around Niall's head.

*I will schedule a series of unannounced exercises for you, Niall'Kearey.*

Niall tightened up their telepathic link to exclude his private thoughts. *That would be helpful. Thanks.* He rinsed his hair under the cascading water. *What do you need, Pwyll?*

*Dr. Klotz believes that a radiation unique to this galaxy is responsible for the deterioration.*

*Worth looking into.*

*Members of the Asterean Collegiate also believe his hypothesis has merit. Dr. Klotz is pursuing his theory within GBI.*

GBI stood for Geophysical Bio Intelligence, a Department of Defense agency that had assumed responsibility for studying the Astereans located in the US. Maximus Klotz bounced around GBI's new Groom Lake base like he'd found his Holy Grail.

Niall remembered Herecura's demands to see him in person. *What about the other groups? I hear Herecura is experiencing issues.*

*My inquiries suggest that nearly one fifth of the other groups will prove immune with remaining individuals affected to varying degrees. There is geographical inconsistency. Historic data will aid our research considerably. If Asterean ancestors of the Vercingetorix suffered a loss of ability over various periods of time it might explain the general loss of Asterean culture across human history. Comparing periods of Vercingetorix emergence with the evolution of Earth's solar system might help identify the source of the radiation.*

*Max doesn't have clearance.*

*This is the problem.*

Crazy. The V had to be Earth's longest living secret and Max didn't qualify to know. Aliens knew more than those assigned to study them. *I'll see what I can do.*

*Thank you.*

*How are things generally?*

*The new village is comfortable, but our confinement to this desert is causing unrest. When will the United Nations announce our presence to your world?*

*I'm meeting with a member of the Vercingetorix Council this evening. They have a lot of influence.* Too much. *I'll try and find out what they're thinking.*

When Pwyll retreated, Niall extended his mind to locate Miach, the Asterean always quick to respond.

Niall looked out on Lake Michigan from the pillared steps to a palatial museum. *What the hell are you doing in Chicago?*

*Chicago is a big city. I can get lost here and assimilate your culture. By Lir, I love your world.*

Miach had been but a shell on Astereal, a former Councilor whose mind was gone, but whose brain retained higher order functions that made him the ideal host for Niall. In all the time Niall rode passenger in Miach's comatose body there had been no hint that its rightful owner remained intact, the consciousness of his shapeshifting doppelganger locked somewhere deep inside his brain.

Niall never imagined his last-minute decision to rescue Miach's body from the fires of Astereal would resurrect a dormant consciousness, but Earth had revived a man with a passionate soul. He and Miach had discovered an acute telepathic bond, disconcerting for them both for Miach had been consumed by grief for the loss of Astereal and the woman he loved.

Then one day he'd bounced back with a zest for life Niall envied.

*Sorry to dampen your fun, Miach, but I need you in Tampa. Jose is on his way there now. I'm meeting with the Vercingetorix. I'll contact you through the q-dimension so you can remote-view what's happening and monitor my mind. If we lose contact, or I say or think 'canasta', tell Jose to take my family and disappear.*

*I will go to the airport now.*

*Appreciate it.*

*You know how I feel about your family—your memories are mine. Jose and I will ensure their safety if trouble arises. Focus on protecting yourself.*

*Let's hope it's not necessary.*

# CHAPTER FIVE

Niall had just changed into a dark blue suit he'd purchased from the hotel shop when Sam called.

"Morgan's at the UN, Niall. Arrived fifteen minutes ago and used his diplomatic status to book a clean room. Fully secure. No personal phones or electronic devices allowed. You'll be screened before entering. A car will be waiting for you outside your hotel."

"What about the Senate hearing?"

"Scheduled for oh-eleven-hundred-hours tomorrow. You're booked on an early flight back to DC."

"Fine."

Straightening his tie, Niall grabbed his wallet and hotel key card.

His driver dropped Niall off near a colorful row of fluttering flags and a sculpture of a golden cracked sphere that lit up the entrance and reminded him of Astereal. Inside, the night security was strict, but he was screened and ushered in as if expected. A guard showed him to the room where Morgan was waiting.

As the door clicked shut behind him, Niall instantly sensed a difference, an absence of something hard to define. Sealed tight against electronic surveillance, the room felt shut off from the rest of the world, a sensation he remembered from the anechoic chamber at GBI. Niall extended his consciousness through the q-dimension and connected with Miach.

An imposing man in a sharp business suit rose from a stylish arrangement of leather sofas. Up close, the man's dark hair was shot with silver. Cold blue eyes wrinkled at the corners and managed to convey some warmth as he stretched out his hand. "Major Kearey, thank you for meeting with me. I'm Patrick Morgan."

"Of the Vercingetorix."

Morgan hesitated. "Yes."

"Good. I'm glad to meet you. 'Cos I should have done this weeks ago."

Niall pivoted on the ball of his foot and drove a thumping haymaker into Morgan's jaw, powering the blow with every callous agony and blind panic the Vercingetorix had inflicted on him and his family. Morgan's feet left the plush carpeting and he crashed down onto an elegant mahogany table that splintered under his weight.

Niall shook out his throbbing hand. *Damn I needed that.*

Morgan lay stunned in the wreckage and Niall swiftly patted him down. Satisfied, the Irish diplomat a.k.a Vercingetorix-poster-boy possessed no hidden advantages, he cased the room. A moan made him look around to see Morgan lift his head, blink a couple of times then roll over. Tenderly probing his jaw, Morgan used a nearby sofa to haul himself back onto two feet before staggering over to a drink's cabinet.

"Okay," Morgan mumbled as he loaded a handkerchief with ice from a silver bucket. "You're angry. I can accept that. But. Try that again and I will defend myself."

"I'm done. For now."

Morgan pressed the cold compress to his jowl. "Sweet Mary and Joseph, that hurts."

"So long as you give me a name." Niall's fist clenched. "I want to know who took my family. Tell me. Was it Biron?"

A darkness colored Morgan's reticent aura, quickly vanquished as Morgan strengthened his defenses. There was a trace of something familiar in the shielding protecting the man and Niall suddenly recalled the telepathic stalker intent on violating his mind in the aftermath of the kidnapping.

He stabbed a finger towards Morgan. "That was you?" Suspicion set in. What else was Patrick Morgan responsible for?

Morgan's expression turned to alarm as Niall advanced on him.

"Wasn't it?" Niall demanded. "Answer me!"

Morgan shoved out a hand. "Wait! Shit! I meant your family no harm, I swear to you!"

Niall frowned and Morgan hesitated. Then his face paled. Guilt flared in his aura and slammed Niall square between the eyes.

Stalking was the least of Morgan's crimes.

Morgan backed up a step. "Please! I swear! I didn't think anyone would get hurt!"

"Are you kidding? My wife nearly died! My children ended up across the universe! What about the car bombs? Innocent people were killed and maimed, and for what? For a distraction? That's not a distraction!" He stabbed his finger at Morgan. "That's *fucking* terrorism!"

Morgan took refuge behind a large desk. "No! Listen to me. It was supposed to be a few non-intrusive tests. That's all! I never meant your wife to get shot! For any of your family to be harmed! From what I gather, the men panicked."

"I can go one better than *gather*! I saw it all! Those men weren't the type to panic. They weren't wearing lab coats! They were armed with automatic weapons! You sent ex-military mercenaries with assault rifles into my home!"

Niall launched across the desk and Morgan stumbled backwards. Ice spilled to the wooden floor.

"No! Wait! Events escalated! Please believe me. I was horrified—"

His words cut off on a squeak as Niall's left hand gripped Morgan's suit and pinned him to the wall. Right fist clenched, Niall unleashed his fury on Morgan's face. "You planted bombs! Terrified my family! Nearly got them all killed! I'll see you burn in Hell!"

Arms raised in defense against Niall's pummeling blows, Morgan couldn't fight back. He talked fast through the blood flowing from his split lip. "I didn't authorize bombs, nothing on that scale. I contracted an independent cell, minimal communication. They were good, too good. You were supposed to be in England. When word came the police had mobilized, the cell leader triggered precautionary measures."

Niall's fist connected with Morgan's nose and he heard bone crack.

"Ow! Shit!" Morgan turned his head away, his voice barely recognizable. "The same man you sent to Astereal."

Niall paused in his attack, eyes narrowing in disgust. "So, if I hadn't been recalled from England, everything would have turned out differently?"

Morgan's shoulders sagged. "It all got out of control. Then Biron demanded names, a location. Your children disappeared."

Niall stared into Morgan's panicked eyes as fragmented pieces of a terrible, painful period in his life joined together. "You tried to breach my mental shields, in the States, and then again in Ghana."

He nodded. "When we heard they were on another planet, and what you were capable of, I didn't believe it. I tried to find out what I could. I needed to know."

"You paid Biron off in exchange for the orb. What was that? Some form of blood money?"

"Call it what you want." Morgan's chin lifted. His face swollen, he looked ready to fight back. "Nothing I say can change what happened. Kill me. Call security. It's your call."

Miach's mind blasted out a rush of caution. *This man should fear you more than he does.*

*He doesn't believe I'll kill him. Believes his power and wealth will protect him from justice.* Probably would, too. Niall studied Morgan's defiant expression. *I want to kill him.*

*I know. Think this through.*

Niall weighed his desire to beat Morgan to a pulp against the need to secure the Astereans their freedom—a future, not a life of servitude. A second ago, he'd been ready to flay the skin off Morgan's bones, but Miach's intervention made him consider the consequences. Morgan's guilt did provide a certain leverage.

He pushed away from Morgan in one easy movement, putting distance between them so he could think. "Your country will never waive your immunity from prosecution, I know that. No witnesses, a secure room, my word against yours."

Niall caught a smug flicker in Morgan's aura and wished he could wipe Morgan's brain. Then it occurred to him. He could.

"I can alter electromagnetic fields, Morgan. That opens up all sorts of possibility: a brain seizure, a heart attack, an aneurism... or maybe you make a misstep in the street one day, in front of a mack truck. Justice takes many forms." Niall drew on the surrounding electromagnetic forces and sent a short electric burst through the floor to jolt Morgan's feet. "Or maybe you just disappear into the cold vacuum of space. Saturn's rings are a sight to behold. I could arrange a one-way ticket."

A sparkling magnetic engine snapped to life between Niall's fingers.

Morgan thrust out a hand to forestall an attack. "Wait! You're angry, you want revenge. I don't blame you, but don't be hasty. I can arrange restitution for the affected families. Offer you and your family protection. Hideout exposed you. China, Russia, fear what you can do. Use your brain. You don't want the Vercingetorix against you. You don't trust us, and you have good reason, but that doesn't mean we can't reach an accommodation. We need you, you need us. Kill me and I guarantee my people will hold you responsible—whatever an autopsy says. Don't turn this into a full-scale war."

Niall shook his head at Morgan's blatant manipulation, so close to striking out and ending this right now. His engine crackled fiercely, the energy seeking a path to ground, perhaps a nice bridge into the center of the sun, vaporize the bastard before another slimy word crawled out of his mouth.

Morgan's eyes drifted to the intensifying light around Niall's hand. He cast Niall a sly glance. "You need us. More than you realize."

Niall launched a telepathic probe that boomeranged off Morgan's shielding but packed a resounding blow.

"Sweet mother of God," Morgan rasped out.

"Get to the point, Morgan!"

"You've been hiding your gifts since you were a child." He jabbed a finger in Niall's direction. "You fear exposure as much as the Vercingetorix. Society won't tolerate people like us and our numbers aren't enough to withstand the tide of insecurity that will drown us all. There's no need for us to be enemies. Let us help you."

"Did you investigate my parents?"

Morgan pressed fingers to his nose. "Wait, please." He stumbled over to the sofa and sat down. "Yes. We backed off when we discovered they weren't your natural parents. Unless they can identify your mother, they are of no interest to us."

"You asshole! You put them through hell!" A glimmer of consternation played on the visible portion of Morgan's face. Sparks crackled as Niall's energy ball flared. "What about my children? What are your intentions for them?"

"Nothing! Please. I didn't come here to make threats."

Niall held back with some effort. He believed him. Morgan was telling the truth and if Macha were here now, she'd be repeating the advice she'd given him earlier: get all the answers he could.

"What did you learn about my kids?"

"Nothing. Everything got destroyed. Look, I admit your children are of interest to us, but not as much as coming to a mutually beneficial arrangement with you."

"What did you learn about me?"

"We know you are descended from the coded lines of the Vercingetorix. You are our kin, one of us, a Vercingetorix by blood."

"And?"

"Research is ongoing. You're a genetic puzzle we haven't worked out yet."

"How did you find me?"

"A worldwide database trawl searching for coded families. Suffice it to say we analyzed military records and your name popped out as an anomaly."

"You didn't hear about me from Colonel Hastor?"

"Colonel Hastor?"

"He's known about my gifts since we were at the Academy." Morgan reacted with surprise. Niall didn't care. Sam Hastor had screwed him over royally. Hastor was due some payback. Niall flashed

Morgan a cold smile. "So, he kept that from you? Perhaps your lackey isn't as trustworthy as you think."

"Colonel Hastor's fought your corner from the start."

"Didn't stop him reporting my brush with death in Somalia."

"No, it didn't, and your data was so unusual we decided to place you in circumstances that would encourage your potential. Senator Biron helped create GBI to push forward a project we were interested in and arranged a position for you. Jacqueline Biron monitored you. You exceeded our expectations. None of our research could explain you. I got frustrated and that's when I ordered your family be secreted away and tested. The Vercingetorix Council did not authorize it and have censured me for my impatience. Then your actions to protect your children revealed the full extent of your abilities. I admit your unprecedented powers concern the Vercingetorix. Very Asterean. The puzzle deepens."

Morgan shifted in his seat. His eyes flitted to Niall's magnetic engine. The ball of light vibrated with increasing intensity and Niall diffused dark energy into the q-dimension before he blew the UN building sky high.

"You signed a deal," Niall said. "The orb and my silence for our lives back. Why did you want to meet with me?"

"We can't access the orbs."

Niall kept a neutral face. Let Morgan reveal his hand first.

Morgan's head tilted, then his eyes sharpened. "You already knew we had an orb." His voice rose. "That we wouldn't be able to resist the lure of another one. How? Jacqueline Biron shouldn't have known anything about the orb in our possession."

"Leave Dr. Biron out of this."

"Her aunt must have let it slip." Morgan rose to get more ice. He stuffed the cubes into a napkin and pressed the compress gingerly against his nose. He tested his jaw as he turned to Niall. "My wife was very fond of Nicole Biron. A powerful telepath. Her decline was exceptionally sad. Another puzzle."

Niall frowned. "What do you mean?"

37

"She didn't carry the usual markers for degenerative conditions, at least nothing we could diagnose." He paused. "I didn't think you knew Nicole."

An intense resentment from Miach washed over Niall. *Uathach was my soul mate, Niall'Kearey,* he vented. *To think this man knew her so well!*

Niall shared Miach's feelings. Uathach had been Niall's mentor on Astereal, a steadfast friend, and when she somehow escaped her dying planet through time and space, she had become his secret protector on Earth. Niall learned too late that his Uathach was Nicole Biron, the wife of Senator Charles Biron. He wished he'd met her before she died. He wanted to know what had possessed Uathach to come to Earth alone.

Maybe she wouldn't have remembered.

Morgan's brow creased and Niall reinforced his privacy shields. "I was thinking of Jacqueline. Is she at risk from whatever condition took her aunt?"

"Nicole and Jacqueline are not blood-related. Anyway, Jacqueline isn't coded."

"What, that makes her inferior somehow?"

Morgan scowled. "That isn't what I meant." He glanced again at Niall's brightly hovering ball of lethal energy. "Please put that away. Kill me and you're a marked man, you know that. No one will trust you, certainly not your country. If you care anything about the Astereans, you'll think twice about taking on the world."

Energy spat from Niall's hand and snapped Morgan on the chest.

The bastard stumbled and clawed at his chest. "Jesus!"

"Sit down and answer my goddamn questions!"

Watching Morgan slink backwards to the sofa satisfied something primal inside Niall. Finally, the man's eyes held a healthy measure of respect.

"What do you want to know?" Morgan asked after sitting down.

"How was Senator Biron involved in my children's disappearance?"

"I wish I could say he was. He suspected I was behind the kidnapping and he knew the right people to speak to. Obviously, his contacts helped you find them."

Not what Niall wanted to hear. "What *does* he do?"

"He intercedes on the Council's behalf every now and again."

Niall didn't believe a word of it. In the States, Charles Biron was like Vercingetorix glue seeping through the cracks and stopping everything from falling apart. Niall rubbed light between his thumb and forefinger together, a tingling sensation that slowly faded away. Morgan's eyes tracked his every move.

"You brought your orb back with you from Astereal?" Morgan asked.

Niall went along with the question. "Astereal's High Brighid hoped the orb would help me negotiate a truce with the Vercingetorix Council." He kept his voice casual. "Where did you get yours?"

Morgan shrugged. "Nicole traced its provenance back thirty-thousand years to the High Danube region in Germany. We suspected the artifact to be of alien origin given its unique properties. It appears impervious to the normal degradation of time. Imagine our excitement when you revealed your hand and inside it sat a second orb."

Morgan reminded Niall of Charles Biron. Charm and ruthlessness personified

"And then the orb opened and data spilled out everywhere." Morgan's fingers carved an undulating path through the air. "Beautiful. Very well played. But you kept an ace up your sleeve. Your video did not show how you opened the orb, and we assumed the Astereans could show us how."

"The High Brighid imprinted the orb to my mind. I am its key. A second safeguard if you like. And don't even think of kidnapping me, I don't care how powerful you are. I will dump you out into orbit around the sun, or I could let the US military hunt you down. No telling how far my government will go to keep me out of enemy hands."

"You don't intend to kill me then."

Niall snorted. "I'm not closing any options."

Morgan stared at him, his eyes expressing first a flash of anger, then frustration followed by a grudging admiration. "So, your mind is the key. Interesting. Cutting your finger off would have been considerably easier. I must admit at first I believed the Astereans were lying when they denied any knowledge about the Asterean orb, but their leader in France seemed genuinely unable to access either orb and even surprised by their existence." Niall kept his silence and Morgan frowned. "You walk a dangerous line, Major Kearey. Playing the interests of nations and the Vercingetorix against one another takes a political savvy I don't believe you possess, but you hold the upper hand for now. What do you propose?"

"I link to the orb and open it by arrangement."

"You don't need to be physically present?"

"No."

"The Astereans are capable of such technology?"

"Yes, but the mineral used to construct the orb is local to Astereal's galaxy. It's not an element we have discovered on Earth. The visual display is merely advanced haptic technology."

"What about the second orb?"

Niall shrugged. "I can only open the orb I gave you." Or the truth would be out. A nasty taste filled his mouth. The conversation was wandering into dangerous territory.

"Would you provide a demonstration?" Morgan asked.

"Where is the orb now?"

Morgan looked taken aback. "I can't divulge that." He frowned. "Can you locate it with your mind?"

"If I knew where to look. The sphere shields the database from outside interference and nothing can escape it, but I can sense the orb's presence. I had hoped to track it, but your couriers placed it in a secure container. Your secret location is safe. I can provide a demonstration at a place neutral to both of us. But I have conditions."

"Go on."

Niall weighed the risks of making a deal. And not making one. Hiding the truth would get harder the closer he got to the Vercingetorix.

One million Astereans knew he smuggled aliens into the past. He couldn't stay quiet much longer, but confessing the full extent of his powers scared him rigid. He needed to prove his value to his government first.

*Uathach bequeathed you the orb to help you prove your story.* Miach pointed out. *The existence of the orbs is evidence your actions did not destroy the timeline, but preserved the path of human evolution. Morgan is compromised. He will help you for your silence.*

*Morgan's a fucking terrorist!* After a moment's thought, Niall cursed under his breath. Patrick Morgan was his best chance to influence the Vercingetorix. He would have to use the man.

"I want you to go public. You can't hide the Astereans from the world forever. They are aliens, yes, but the Astereans once traveled the stars. They are our kin. The Vercingetorix must know that now. You've analyzed their DNA."

"Aye, and it explains much. Their legacy is evident within the human genome. The Astereans' ancestors must have visited Earth in the past, which explains the existence of the Vercingetorix Orb. It also lends weight to an argument that you represent an advance in human evolution enough to establish a telepathic link to our genetic cousins across a universe. But do you seriously believe Earth's populace will accept the Astereans? Perhaps have sympathy for their plight, identify with their humanity?"

"If presented to the world properly, yes."

"The Astereans speak of you as the fulfillment of a prophecy. A savior."

Blood drained from Niall's face and left him cold. *God, please. Not on Earth too.*

Morgan nodded with undisguised satisfaction. "The Catholic Church might not have a problem. The Astereans existence merely demonstrates the fullness of God's wonder. Perhaps they will canonize you. Religious fundamentalists won't like it."

"No one needs to know my identity." Niall stopped. One million Astereans knew his identity.

"You have a problem," Morgan mused. He got up and moved to the drinks cabinet where he poured two cognacs. When Niall shook his head, Morgan downed one then got more ice, this time for his swelling cheekbone. "The status quo is unsustainable. Your family is your top priority, but any illusion of living a normal life will end the moment Hideout goes public. Keeping the Astereans' existence secret forever is not an option either, I agree with you there. So many conflicting interests. We could help you, if you weren't so determined to keep us at arm's length."

"What did you expect? You attacked my family! You pitted me against the Vercingetorix and we've been at loggerheads ever since."

Morgan raised his tumbler in a mock toast and sipped his cognac. "Aye, but maybe that has to change if you are to achieve your objectives for the Astereans. Consider, Major Kearey, what contingency plans you put in place for this meeting. Can you run from the world?"

Niall's mouth set into a hard line.

Patrick Morgan's nod was thoughtful. "We have common ground that I hope will keep me alive a little longer. I will consider how we can meet your concerns about the Astereans in return for access to the orb. But let me leave you with this thought. Is it better for your family to be on the run, or to live with the restrictions that come with your country's protection? Be certain on this one point. You and your family can never be free. They lost that right when you became savior to an alien race."

Niall held up his hand and they both watched the light around his fingers fade out of sight. "I'm not worried, Morgan. Anything happens to the people I love and I'll come for you first. That's not a threat. It's a promise."

# CHAPTER SIX

The cab driver taking Niall back to his hotel turned left out of the United Nations site and eased into the steady flow of traffic. Niall reached out with his mind. *Miach?*

Miach's response was instant. *I just arrived.*

Niall settled into Miach's viewpoint and realized he was seeing the comfortable great room of their new home, the house Tami had inherited from her parents. One wall had been painted a greeny blue. He liked it.

*Where's Jose?*

Miach turned around and waved, but not at Jose. Tami was entering the room with a glass of water.

Her eyes opened wide. "Is that Niall?"

Miach nodded to her as he updated Niall. *Jose is checking the perimeter. Your children are asleep.*

Tami smiled in Miach's direction. Her unruly copper hair now reached her shoulders and her slender body had regained those gorgeous curves.

Miach gave a mental harrumph.

*Sorry. Look, I need to talk with Tami in person. Don't say anything yet—I need to get permission to use a bridge or there'll be hell to pay. Sit tight for a while.*

*I understand.*

*Tell Tami I'll be in touch very shortly. And Miach, thanks.*

Niall glanced out the window and realized he wasn't far from the hotel. Leaning forward, he caught the cab driver's eye in the rear-view mirror. "Can you drop me off here, please?"

One block closer to his hotel, Niall stopped outside a jazz club where the banshee wail of a saxophone danced on some poor soul's grave. He put one finger to his ear and called General Towden on a line so secure even the NSA didn't have clearance.

His request didn't go down well.

"Have you any idea how many calls I have to make to prevent DruSensi issuing a full portal alert?" Towden spluttered. "You've got the hearing tomorrow! What's that noise?"

"Nightclub, sir. I'm walking back to my hotel. In New York. General, I just met with a leading member of the Vercingetorix at the UN."

"Yes, Colonel Hastor briefed me." Towden fell silent.

Niall sensed the general wavering. "Sir, Patrick Morgan said some stuff. It affects my family. I need to talk to my wife in person. I'll be back in DC tomorrow for the committee hearing. I wouldn't ask if this wasn't important."

"I'll authorize the portals."

"Thank you, General."

"Don't make this a habit."

"Yes, sir."

Niall closed his cell phone and looked up at the New York skyline broken by twinkling skyscrapers. Tonight, he would see Tami. His heart thumped wildly, a mix of anticipation and anxiety. One night wasn't going to be long enough to turn her life upside down.

Niall stepped through the portal in his hotel bathroom and emerged inside his home in Tampa. Tami scrambled to her feet with a beaming smile as he dispersed the energy from his bridge back to the q-dimension.

She threw herself at him. "Oh my God, I don't believe it. How? I thought you weren't allowed to do this!"

"I'm not supposed to."

"What about the satellite?"

"General Towden authorized some downtime."

Her eyebrow arched. "Oh my God. Is this like a conjugal rights visit? Please tell me it is."

Niall closed his eyes, wished she hadn't said that then immediately changed his mind. He opened them again and stared into crystal clear blue irises smoldering with lust and blatant invitation. "Holy smoke, Tami. It wasn't. But it sure is now."

He swept her up into his arms and took the stairs two at a time. Tami nuzzled his neck the whole way. Kicking their bedroom door shut, he laid her down on the bed. Her hands unbuckled his belt as he tried and failed to unbutton her shirt. He ripped it off instead. She pulled him down on top of her, unable to wait. They were like young lovers, fumbling in the dark, desperate and needy. Stroking, kissing. Niall lifted his head for air and gazed at the roaring fire of her sparkling eyes. The passion she aroused in him left him breathless. Reducing her to a quivering bundle of nerves turned him on even more.

"I love you, Tami. There's no one like you."

"You're here to tell me something bad, aren't you?"

He nodded. She reached up and kissed him. Her lips traveled to his ear. "Then make love to me, Niall Kearey, like you never loved me before."

Placing his hand against the small of her back, Niall slid her down beneath him. She arched up, eager and responsive to his touch. An urgency overcame him. Nothing mattered more than pleasuring this woman.

When he settled his weight against her, Tami moaned. "Make it last."

Niall groaned and lowered his lips to the soft curve of her neck. "Heartless witch."

Lying in his arms afterward, Tami trailed her fingers over and around his abdominal muscles, a gentle sigh of bliss escaping her lips. Niall caught her exploring hand before she rekindled his ardor and when she protested, he rose up above her and kissed the gentle arch of her eyebrow.

"We need to talk."

"So, talk," she murmured, nestling against his chest. "I'm not going anywhere."

"I think the world is going to find out what I did."

She groaned and Niall clutched her close.

"I thought everything was settled."

"If my role in the Astereans' arrival gets out, everything will change. I need to work out the details, but if, when, that happens, I think you and the kids should go into hiding."

Tami lay frozen in his embrace for several long moments. Then she launched up dragging bedclothes with her. She wriggled around to face him, sheets covering her nakedness. "Leave our home? We just got settled! Toby and Lizzie are happy at their new school. We'd be mad to move them now."

Niall levered himself up onto his elbow as dark clouds gathered on her face.

"Please, Niall. Don't do this to us! My kids grew up without me. They needed their mom... and I couldn't be there for them." Tears filled her eyes. "I've worked so hard to get well, to give them back a semblance of normal life."

"I know." Guilt made it difficult for him to speak. He forced the words out. "I messed up. Gave you false hope. I'm sorry." She was silent for several long moments. Every second beat at his temple. "Tami? Don't. Please say something."

Tears glistened at the corners of her eyes and then she tensed at his touch. "Why are you different, Niall? What made you this way?" The words broke out from her and she gasped in a ragged breath.

Niall bit his lip. He had no answer and his heart ached for her pain.

"I need Toby and Lizzie to be safe, Niall." She hauled in more air.

"I know. Breathe easy, Tami."

He sat beside her, rubbing her back, watching the throbbing vein in her neck slow its racing beat, scared by how fragile she still was. He hadn't expected his news to receive a warm welcome, but Tami looked on the verge of a full-blown breakdown.

"Everything will work out, honey. You and the kids are my top priority."

Her eyes flashed. "Don't you patronize me, Niall Kearey!"

God, he couldn't be doing this more badly.

"I don't mean to. Okay. No one's in any immediate danger, but the world is going to find out and when they do, our lives will never be the same again. The media blitz will be intense. Not just on me. On our children as well." Damn, doing right by the Astereans was going to endanger their lives. Morgan was right on that score. "You don't need that crap. None of us do. I know you're scared, but I'm going to find a way to protect you. I promise."

Tami nodded at his every word. A tapping sound made him look closer. Her teeth were chattering. He grabbed a throw and wrapped it around her shoulders.

"Where will we go? How soon?" she asked.

"Jose has the where covered, and probably not for several weeks, maybe months, but until this hearing is over, Miach and Jose are here to keep you safe."

Tami took a deep shuddering breath. She released it slowly and he watched the tension in her body disappear. The shawl slipped off her shoulders. Her beautiful coppery hair used to fall over her breasts, but now he could see every freckle and delicate goose bump. He reached out his hand and gently traced the stretch mark crossing one side of her belly.

"Jose has his own family to look after," she whispered.

Niall didn't reply, transfixed by the erotic silhouette before him.

A finger under his chin tilted his head up. "Eyes up, mister."

And like a switch had been thrown, she was fine.

"Have I told you that you're the most amazing woman in the world?"

"Yes. Niall! Jose? He has his own family."

"It won't be for long. I'll sort something out."

She nodded, the gravity in her eyes conveying a dash of skepticism. A tremor ran through her body, a lingering vestige of her earlier distress. "You've never let us down, Niall, and whatever you decide, I'll support you. I need to know, you understand? I need to be prepared this time."

A lump gripped his vocal bands. "Tami..."
She pressed her thumb against his lips. "Everything will work out. You brought our children home from across the universe. You can do anything you want. Just don't keep me in the dark this time. I need to be ready."

# CHAPTER SEVEN

Midway through Niall's testimony, a bubble of excitement worked through the panel of senators. A door clicked shut behind him.

"Please continue, Major," Charles Biron directed before he could look around.

"Sir. Yes, I hoped the forces surrounding the magnetic North pole would allow me to extend the reach of my bridge to a planet outside the Asterean galaxy capable of sustaining life. I wanted to save as many as possible. Earth was the only suitable planet I found." He held his breath. The committee had no reason to suspect his bridge could cross time as well as space, but all the clues were there. His neck itched and an urge to dive for cover became unbearable. Niall turned his head.

"Thank you, Major Kearey," Biron said. "I see you are distracted so I will halt you there to welcome Councilor Herecura from the Asterean group in Russia."

Niall swung fully around to find Herecura walking down the central aisle towards him.

Her hand stretched out. "I am relieved to see you at last, Niall'Kearey. As you see I am learning to adopt your traditions of greeting."

"Of course, Councilor."

Niall stood up and shook her hand, but Herecura's sly smile struck him differently from her usual feline smirk. Not predatory. More triumphant. What devious thoughts ran through this woman's head? He nudged her mental shields and got nowhere. Maybe Earth had eliminated her telepathic ability, except he'd penetrated non-telepathic minds before and at least captured an image of who they were.

Herecura's mind was closed, and unlike Patrick Morgan, her aura projected a blank slate.

He studied her through narrowed eyes. "I understand you wanted to see me? Are you here to give testimony?"

Senator Biron tapped his microphone. "Councilor Herecura has agreed to testify to the committee and provide us with an invaluable insight into Operation Hideout."

Still holding her hand, Niall pierced Herecura's shields with a sliver-like probe that turned her defenses to butter. Slightly taken aback he'd gotten in, Niall rummaged through an onslaught of dark images. She gasped, snatched her hand back and rammed his mind out so hard he staggered back sending his chair crashing to the floor. Alarm spread like wildfire throughout the room. Guards stepped forward, but seemed uncertain over who was at fault.

Niall stared at his hand, grasping a sinister purpose behind her touch. He spread out his fingers then checked his palm, convinced she'd smeared him with something.

"What did you do?" He looked back at her.

She stared at him, her eyes bright with elation, but it was the feral curl of her lip that terrified him most.

"Who are you?" he demanded.

"Major Kearey! Explain yourself!" Biron barked out.

Niall glanced at the irritated senator leaning over the podium. "Councilor Herecura isn't what she seems, Mr. Chairman."

"No, Major Kearey is attempting to prevent my testimony," Herecura countered. "He has lied to you all."

*Fuck.* Niall sent out a desperate call.

When Miach answered, Niall didn't bother with explanations. He dumped his memory of the last few minutes direct into the Asterean's mind and started generating energy.

*I will warn the others, Niall'Kearey. Jose is with me now. We will be in touch.*

Movement to his left caught Niall's eye, a guard placing his hand on his holster. Grabbing Herecura's arm, Niall recognized a familiar escape route through the q-dimension, opened a portal between him and the guard and shoved the furious Asterean into the wormhole before him. They emerged in Jacqueline Biron's childhood bedroom. Sharp nails raked Niall's cheek.

"Shit." He spun Herecura around, twisted her arm behind her back, and thrust her up against the wall. She screeched wildly.

"Yell all you want. The owner's not at home."

Niall hunted for a wormhole, a bridge DruSensi would not spot and where the might of the US could not follow. Astereal shone like a beacon. Raw instinct drove him, a need to get Herecura off planet Earth.

He tightened his grip on a struggling Herecura. "Be still."

"You are too late. Kill me or not. It makes no difference."

"Shut up!" Sweat broke out on his brow. *Sohan?*

*Niall'Kearey.* His former host's telepathic ability had been erratic since arriving on Earth and he often required Pwyll's support. Today, Sohan's mind came through strong and clear before sharpening with concern. *What is wrong?*

*Astereal had a space program. Right? Spaceships? Satellites?*

*You know this.*

*Anything orbiting Astereal that could sustain life? Something that didn't go with Nantosuelta's fleet.*

*I will find out.* Sohan's mind went silent.

"You have nowhere to go, do you? DruSensi will track you down."

Niall found it hard to ignore the vindictive malice in her tone. "That presence in your mind. I've felt it before." He shuddered. "A long time ago."

"Perhaps you sense your destiny."

"What did you do to me?"

She turned her head and spat in his face. Niall pulled her back then body-slammed her back against the tulip papered wall. Her voice squealed her fury. Her mind breathed a dark foreboding that stirred up old memories.

Niall battered them down.

"I will get to the bottom of this, Herecura, and if you don't cooperate, this is going to get very unpleasant."

*Niall'Kearey?*

A wail of sirens drew his eyes to the window. *Make it quick, Pwyll.*

*There is a small observatory outpost on the third moon that may still be intact.* Pwyll's mind revealed some simple specifications.

*That will do. Gotta go.* His mind surged out into space. *Macha?*

Her silvery aura found him. *What has happened?*

*I need you to anchor me to Earth. I could be a while.*

*You are returning to Astereal?*

*Close enough.* The link between his mind and the Morrígan Queen's strengthened as his mind burst out above the disintegrating planet and searched for Astereal's outermost moon. He found the satellite at its farthest elliptical point from Astereal. The moon tracked a slow orbit at a distance far enough from Bacchus that it retained its hold on the outpost, for now. The tiny observatory had been designed to accommodate a small crew. He had a couple minutes to get life support up and running or they'd be making a quick U-turn back to Earth.

"Take a deep breath," he ordered Herecura.

A crash downstairs sounded like an armored tank had rammed down the front door. Heavy footfalls hammered the stairs. Niall fed energy to his link, filled his lungs and forced Herecura into the portal as the bedroom door smashed open. He closed his bridge behind them cutting off a shout, shoved his prisoner aside, and pushed off a wall. Niall floated in zero G to the control console as the outpost's systems detected his presence and launched haptic-style interfaces into the air. Holding his breath, he tapped into life support. The configuration was slow to respond.

*Macha?*

*Your link is strong, Niall'Kearey.*

Herecura bounced off a wall ladder and grabbed a rung, her face turning grey. She hadn't followed his instruction. Niall gritted his teeth. He spotted emergency storage, punched the release, and grabbed an oxygen capsule, a chemical oxygen generator with inbuilt carbon dioxide filter. The metal capsule would remain active for an hour. There weren't many more. Hopefully they wouldn't be there long enough to need them. He triggered the reaction.

The insane woman fought his attempt to force the attached mask over her nose and mouth. Floating back, he folded his arms and waited. Her eyes crinkled in confusion then began to close. Her floating body curled in on itself as she slid into unconsciousness and Niall held her in place as he fitted the mask in place. Her lungs autonomically dragged in the precious gas. When his eyesight blurred, he transferred the mask to his own mouth and breathed in deep. Then he returned it to Herecura. She was coming around as he discovered the outpost now had air to breathe.

"Are you crazy?" he demanded when her eyes opened.

She straightened out. "You are putting off the inevitable. The body clock doesn't stop."

"What the hell is that supposed to mean?" He studied her resolved demeanor, the churning in his stomach both a warning and a manifestation of his fear. "Why would you betray me? What did you do to me? I know you did something."

She shrugged, the movement making her drift. "You cannot stay here forever."

Anger tightened Niall's chest, a ball of pressure demanding escape. Herecura had forced his hand, his family was once more on the run, and she spouted riddles. "When I'm done shaking the answers out of you, I won't need to."

Her exultant expression snapped his self-control. He went for her throat and slammed the back of her head against the bulkhead, grabbing a fixed pipe to stop the rebound. This time her spittle reached his lips. Niall recoiled as globules floated in the air around him. Wiping his mouth with his sleeve, he pushed off a convenient fixture and aimed for the system board. Locating the gravity system, he switched it on. They dropped to the floor with a bump.

Niall climbed to his feet, dragged Herecura up by her upper arm, and dumped her on a bench molded into the wall's structure. She looked away then straightened her jacket, part of a designer-looking pants suit. In fact, she looked incredibly well-groomed despite her disheveled hair following his rough handling. Russia seemed to be treating her well.

Saliva filled his mouth. Why could he taste metal? He glanced at his sleeve then touched the cheek her nails had mauled. She'd drawn blood. Contaminated him in some way.

Spat on him.

He'd shared her oxygen mask.

Bile rose up Niall's throat, propelled by an urgent compulsion to remove every trace of her touch from his body. He rifled through storage compartments looking for the Asterean equivalent to antiseptic. When stars dazzled his eyes, he realized his mistake.

*Idiot!*

Grabbing another oxygen capsule, he took a few reviving breaths then headed for the control room. Herecura was sliding to the floor, life support icons throbbing yellow above her head. Niall stepped over her, stabilized the atmospheric systems then hunted for something to secure her with before pulling off his tie. He bound her hands, taking a cruel pleasure in her gasp of pain.

If he didn't need her alive...

He swiveled her around so her back rested against the wall then took his jacket off and sat on the floor facing her. Herecura stared back at him, sullen but apparently unfazed by her predicament.

*Why do you want to die?* He slammed her with a mental probe that boomeranged off her shields.

*Niall'Kearey,* Macha protested, their link wavering. *Whatever you are doing, please stop.*

*Sorry.* He opened his mind to the Morrígan Queen and replayed events since Herecura entered the Senate committee room.

*She is possessed,* Macha stated.

*What?*

Herecura's expression clouded. "Who are you talking to?"

"Someone more powerful than you."

She laughed and Niall fought an urge to slap her. Herecura hid a dangerous secret. That darkness in her mind frightened him, its familiarity disturbing.

*What makes you think she's possessed?* he asked.

*Your impression of her mind from when she touched you. There is a core of innocence at the heart of the evil inflicting her, the innocence of a child. Something attacked her mind when she was young and it twisted and defiled her, something that has lain in wait for this moment. Something truly evil.*

*Wow. You're better at this than Uathach.*

He studied Herecura, leaned forward and examined the crow's feet around her eyes that he didn't remember noticing before. He reclined back before she spat at him again. "You're ageing," he said with a frown.

Her smug expression spoke volumes and Niall snapped his fingers. "No, you're dying. You're on some kind of countdown. Something's killing you but you can't wait. Why the rush?"

"Natural death is painful. Organs break down. Functions fail." Her eyes slid to his throbbing cheek.

"You bitch! You have infected me!" His hand shot out and wrapped fingers around her neck.

Her eyes blazed defiance as a volcano of anger and fear from deep inside him squeezed the living breath from her.

"What. Did. You. Do?"

Her lips moved, but no sound emerged. He loosened his grip enough to catch her gargled plea. "Finish this. Kill me now."

Niall released his choking stranglehold fast and launched to his feet. Breathing harshly, he stepped out of temptation's reach and watched a white impression of cruel fingers assume a bluish tint around her neck. "No, I've got a better idea."

# CHAPTER EIGHT

President Robert Foldane slammed his palm down on his desk. Roosevelt's desk. "He's got a guilty conscience over something, Charles. He prepared for this. His family is in hiding. He's somewhere DruSensi cannot detect. It's clear he believes himself above the chain of command, and the way I see it, he's right!"

Senator Biron raised placating hands. "Mr. President, I sponsored Councilor Herecura to visit the US. She promised to give evidence regarding Major Kearey's activity on Astereal after he escaped custody. You know I have little inclination to support Kearey's cause, but I've studied the visual recording several times and I'm convinced this Asterean threatened him in some way. Kearey accused Herecura of doing something to him. Then he asked her, 'Who are you?' I don't think we should jump to conclusions."

Before Foldane could reply, the door to the Oval Office opened and his secretary announced General Towden.

"When did you get here?" Foldane asked as Towden walked in.

"Thirty minutes ago. Major Kearey met with Patrick Morgan last night, Mr. President. I spoke to him afterwards and he sounded shaken, anxious about his family, so I decided to meet with him after the hearing. Sir, Councilor Sohan contacted me. He's requested to speak to you. Given the circumstances, I agreed to make his request in person. A visual link has been set up to your office."

Foldane grunted his approval. He liked Sohan. Quiet, scholarly, and reasonable, the Asterean leader of the US contingent inspired trust. He glanced at a winking light and pressed it. They all turned to the wall screen displaying Sohan's face.

Foldane waved Charles and the general to take seats. "Councilor Sohan, I take it you have information regarding this unexpected turn of events."

"Yes, Mr. President. Thank you for speaking with me. Major Kearey has contacted me. He wants me to inform you he has removed Herecura to an abandoned moon observatory inside Astereal's solar system."

"That explains why DruSensi didn't detect the other end of his bridge," Charles murmured.

"Did he say why?" Foldane asked.

"Herecura appears to be dying. Not only that, she is actively trying to take her own life. Niall'Kearey probed her mind and found evidence of an alien entity he has encountered before. He described this entity as evil. His exact words were 'makes aliens look like Barney'."

"Barney?"

Towden rumbled low in his throat. "I believe Major Kearey is referencing both the film *Aliens* and the kids show *Barney*."

Foldane exchanged a glance with the general. "That doesn't sound good."

"Excuse me, Councilor," Charles jumped in. "Is Astereal in alignment with Earth? Can Major Kearey get back?"

"Astereal's time flow is currently in close alignment with Earth, Senator. Niall'Kearey assured me he can create a bridge back anytime. His concern is to keep Herecura alive. He requests your government permit us to construct a cryogenic pod."

Towden stood up. "You have consistently refused to divulge this technology, Councilor."

"Circumstances force us to reverse this decision."

Foldane held back a snort of irritation. The Astereans treated mankind like unruly children, but when Kearey wanted something, they jumped. How much could he trust Major Kearey's assertions? Suppose Herecura had been about to give evidence damaging to Kearey and this was his way to silence her. His heart pounded in his chest and he gripped the edge of the desk. Who should he believe? Kearey? Or this Herecura?

"Are you alright, Mr. President?"

Foldane stared at Charles, confused. "What do you mean?"

Charles winced, glanced at Towden. "My apologies. For a moment..."

Foldane waved him to silence. "Councilor, how long will it take you to construct this cryogenic pod?"

"We can provide Niall'Kearey with a temporary solution within a week. To match the cryogenic pods used by our High Brighid and Niall'Kearey's host, Miach, I estimate at least four Earth weeks."

Foldane glanced at Towden and understood the gleam in the general's eyes. The military was desperate for any technology the Astereans were willing to share. Charles offered a discreet nod.

"Very well, Sohan. General Towden will ensure you are provided with the requisite materials, but your work will be supervised. Please inform Major Kearey that I want an immediate explanation of his actions."

Sohan nodded his agreement. "Pwyll will act as liaison between Niall'Kearey and General Towden, if that is acceptable."

"Pwyll is young, but an exceptionally gifted telepath, Mr. President," Charles explained.

Towden caught Foldane's eye. "I'll get work underway at Area 51 by this evening, Mr. President."

"Good. Councilor Sohan, I am grateful for Asterean cooperation in this matter."

"I am pleased we are able to assist, Mr. President." The screen went blank.

Towden stood up. "Mr. President, with your permission?"

"Yes, go. Thank you, General."

Foldane studied a relieved Senator Biron. "Your political antenna's slipping, Charles. I think you've been right from the start. Kearey's hiding something and this Herecura knows what that something is. I want them back on Earth, both of them."

"I agree, but what then? Kearey does what he wants, chain of command be damned. He hoodwinked us all when he turned himself in

59

for Operation Hideout right down to forcing the Vercingetorix into a deal. He can step off the planet whenever he feels like. We need to find a way to control him before the other Hideout members get DruSensi's report."

"We've tried that before. No, find his family, but discreetly. I don't want to spook him, the man's too resourceful and I suspect we haven't begun to tap his potential. His family is his weakness, and while his loyalties are in doubt, I need rapid access to whatever influence we can muster. Nothing more, you understand?"

Biron tilted his head and smacked his ear twice. "I'm sorry, Mr. President, but are you asking me to use my contacts?"

Foldane glared at him. "Yes, I am, but warn Morgan I've had enough of being sidestepped and manipulated by his goddamn Vercingetorix Council. I'm warning you, Charles. If the Vercingetorix double cross me on this, we will be at war. I want cards on the table, a full deck of them, because Kearey's an unexploded bomb and if he blows, he'll incinerate us all."

"Matre?"

Herecura's whispered call for her mother caught Niall's ear. Something about the manic brilliance to her eyes gave him pause. He took a knee beside the pale woman lying awkwardly on the floor and ran a quick exam, then moved to the command console and upped the oxygen level point two percent. Their oxygen supply was limited, but he could take shallow breaths to compensate.

Hunkering down beside Herecura, he touched her lips with the pipe of a water pouch. "Here, drink this."

She shook her head, dazed, her earlier venom evaporated like a mist at dawn. A tempest hovered over the horizon instead. Niall rested the back of his hand against her burning forehead and she jerked at his touch then struggled to free her hands bound tightly behind her.

Tears welled. "*Hubi esmi? Matre?*" She spoke Asterean. Where am I?

Niall dredged up what he remembered of the language. "What age are you, Herecura?"

Glazed eyes searched for him. "I'm scared."

The tremble in her voice cracked Niall's guard. Something inside him relented and he put aside his resentment and fears enough to soften his voice. "What is it? What scares you?"

Her tears spilled over. "Why can't I move?"

She sounded so helpless. Niall probed her mind and discovered no obstruction. She read like an open book, the innocent mind of a child.

Niall pursed his lips as he debated the risk. "I'm going to sit you up, Herecura, so I can untie you."

Her confusion reassured him. She let him lift her body. She was so hot, her fever spiking. When her hands were free, he managed to persuade her to sip some water then he reduced the environmental temperature.

*Pwyll?* he called.

*I am here, Niall'Kearey.*

*Herecura doesn't look too good. She's delirious and her mind is wide open. I want you and Macha to scan her.*

Niall sensed Pwyll's mind retreat from his. A moment later, Herecura stirred. Her face contorted into an expression of pure horror and then her head began to thrash from side to side.

Niall grabbed her head. *What's happening?*

Pwyll's mind surged back on a wave of shock. *Niall'Kearey. Do not bring her back to Earth.*

Herecura's back arched.

*What? Why? Shit! Can you calm her down?*

*I believe you should see the problem for yourself.*

Niall shuffled into a more comfortable position to hold Herecura still. To his relief, her struggles abated. *Okay, I got this. Go.*

Pwyll directed Niall into Herecura's mind. There was a slight pause before Pwyll thought, *Herecura, tell us about Balor.*

An older Herecura burst out of the shadows. *Balor is all-powerful! The ruler of worlds.*

Silent, maniacal laughter flooded Niall's mind with filth and debris. He slammed up his shields, leaving the smallest of gaps to filter her thoughts.

Her taunt seeped through. *My memories will lead him to you.*

Niall flinched. *To me?*

Irrational dread fractured his defenses. His dread. That same mind-bending terror he had shrank from as a child searching the universe with his mind, and then in training on Astereal, when the touch of an alien malignance had reduced him to a shivering wreck. Her own shields down, Herecura transmitted Balor's soul-destroying aura into the deepest corners of Niall's mind. A wave of nausea left him cold and shaking.

He forced his mind to frame the question. *How?*

*You are Niall'Kearey, a beacon to your world. You always have been, but I did not understand. Before. No matter. When I die, Balor will find you.*

*What the hell is she talking about?* Niall asked Pwyll. *Who's this Balor?*

*Wait, Niall'Kearey. Sohan is joining us.*

Niall felt his former host pressing his mind for access via Pwyll's link. He opened a tiny channel that let Sohan in, but kept Herecura on the fringes of their shared awareness.

*Balor is a name that predates the Great Divide,* Sohan informed him. *Legend depicts Balor as a monster, a devourer of minds and creator of abominations. The gryphon are believed to be an early product of genetic engineering by the highest ranks of Balor's servants.*

Niall sensed Macha flinch in the background.

*But this Balor must be dead, right? You said it predates the Great Divide.*

*I can only tell you what I remember from my studies.*

*Morrigan legends remember a Balor from before the Great Divide,* Macha concurred.

*Herecura's Balor is very much alive,* Pwyll asserted. *She remembers her early childhood with longing. Something entered her mind when she was young, and it has influenced her ever since. Her memories are constructed differently.* He showed them a visual image.

Sohan expressed it best. *Her memories are stored, like a data bank ready for transmission.*

Niall stared at the Asterean woman so eager to die. *She sees death as a release.* An urgent debate erupted between Pwyll and Sohan, too fast for him to follow. *Could someone fill me in, please?*

Pwyll responded first. *Niall'Kearey, Herecura has been searching for you for a very long time.*

*She met me cycles ago on Astereal.* Niall smacked the bridge above his nose making Herecura jump. *Damn! She needed to touch me! That's why she said I was a beacon to Earth, and, whatever this Balor is, I know it's evil.* A strange noise caught his attention. *Hang on a sec.*

He leaned down and caught the soft rattle coming from between Herecura's lips. Her hair had shriveled white in the short time they had been trapped on the outpost, and yet she still possessed that unnerving feral beauty.

"Herecura, can you hear me?"

Her head fell forward. *Balor comes for me.*

*She is lost,* Pwyll stated. *Her mind is rambling and I fear her time is short. We will not construct a working cryogenic pod in time.*

*So how do we stop this transmission?* Niall asked.

*Uathach's pod...* Sohan's thought was uncompleted, an idea still in formation.

*The one buried under lava?* Niall paused to think as Sohan's suggestion took proper shape. *Is that possible? The timeflows are aligned and—*

Niall stopped, remembering a porthole through time, one created by Succellos to help him understand his dual existence on two worlds. Resting a quieter Herecura on the floor, Niall rose and crossed to the observatory's domed porthole. He looked out on a glowing Astereal. Farther beyond lay the dark star that spelled her doom.

If that temporal link still existed...

He opened his memory to the others. *Succellos once viewed the future, but he didn't create enough energy to form a bridge. Is there anyone else who could fold time and space?*

*Yes,* Sohan answered him. *Miach.*

A wry smile caught Niall's lips. His former host had been selected for his natural ability. Hell, the Asterean shape-shifted at will, much to Lizzie and Toby's delight. Miach's higher brain function had supported a link across the universe to Ancient Africa. It stood to reason he could bridge time, at least from Astereal.

# CHAPTER NINE

Niall double triple-checked he could see the shimmering path that would lead him home to Earth. Once he broke his link with the Morrígan Queen he would be on his own with a raving madwoman.

*I always thought my bridge crossed time by accident,* he said. *Nantosuelta explained it as a side-effect of Alignment.*

His former host on Astereal mentally shrugged. *Alignment undoubtedly affected the fold in time and space, adjusted the broader parameters if you will, but you manipulated the precise moment of locking a bridge in place. The link to Earth has been constant, at least for your lifetime. Constructing a local bridge takes a more precise skill.*

Niall nodded although no one but Herecura could actually see him. He winced at the sight of the former Asterean Councilor clutching her head in her hands as she rocked back and forth. The contagion killing her did not offer a peaceful death.

*Niall 'Kearey?* Miach prompted.

*Yes. Okay, I need to do this. Stand by.*

Niall cleared his mind and focused on a link into Astereal's past, aiming to reach right into the city, but unable to get any closer than the Fel. He narrowed in on a single location and suddenly his mind was once again encased in rock, black rock that burned red before melting to an angry, gold-red viscous liquid that simmered and boiled. His heart pounded; the visual effect so real he could feel the searing heat sucking the breath from his lungs. The link slipped away.

Miach's mind broke through his confusion. *Check your oxygen level!*

Niall staggered over to the environmental system and increased the oxygen percentage. Within seconds his lungs began to draw breath more easily and, as his head cleared, the backwards flow of time brought a series of changes to the landscape. Lava transformed into the Fel overlooking a dried-up riverbed. A falc'hun stood where Sohan had parked it just before stepping through the portal to Earth. Niall adjusted his link until he caught a glimpse of the portal closing. Any farther back in time and he risked meeting himself.

*Good,* Miach approved. *Not much point lecturing you on the dangers of creating a paradox, seeing as you have already broken every Shileky principle I know, but you should try to avoid further indiscriminate acts of mayhem.*

Miach's criticism stung. Niall hadn't realized Miach had such reservations. *Hey, buddy! Couldn't have done it without you.*

*I do not recall having a say in the matter. It surprised me to learn the High Brighid endorsed you taking such a risk with Earth's timeline.*

Niall detected a tinge of concern behind Miach's acerbic riposte as the Asterean dimmed his tide of disapproval.

*The universe always finds a way to redress the balance,* Miach warned. *Do not stay in the past for long.*

*Copy that.*

Damn. Now his mouth felt dry as sawdust. On the other side of his link to the past, lava swept across Navan, the grounded city that had once graced Astereal's lilac sky. A city he remembered from his childhood, and one of many sky cities he had later fought the Morrígan to defend. Sweat trickled down between Niall's shoulder blades. Sipping water from a pouch, his mind tuned in to the Morrígan Queen.

*Macha, you know where to look for me?*

*Kestra and I will find you, Niall'Kearey.*

*Miach, if...*

*I care for your family as if they were my own, Niall'Kearey. I will protect them with my dying breath.*

*If I get lost, tell Tami never to give up hope. I'll never stop fighting to get back. Tell her—*

"What are you doing?"

Niall spun around, startled to find Herecura listing over, but standing on her own two feet. She pointed at the shimmering portal. "Is that the Fel?" Her voice rasped, her eyes glittering with fever. "I do not understand."

"You're going home, Herecura."

She swayed, started to keel sideways. "No..."

Niall grabbed the last oxygen capsule, strode over to her and swept her into his arms, her feeble struggles pitiful to see. This once innocent child, had been corrupted, her life robbed by this Balor for some evil purpose Niall did not understand, but feared absolutely. Instinct drove him onward.

Tightening his grip on Herecura, he cut his link to Macha and strode through the portal onto the Fel. Once moving, he didn't stop. He loaded her into the falc'hun, found filter masks and fitted one with the oxygen capsule to a now semi-conscious Herecura before clipping the other over his nose. Flying into Navan was akin to dropping into a firepit. Toxic gases stung his eyes. He could barely see for the black sooty cloud swirling through the city. Unwilling to risk landing, with time his enemy, Niall flew the falc'hun straight through a large, stained glass window directly into Uathach's personal chambers.

The falc'hun skidded across the floor, Niall braced, and they crashed into the far wall with a jarring jolt, the falc'hun's nose shooting back into the cockpit. Niall did not move for several long seconds. When he finally pulled his head out of the console that had come close to decapitating him, red blood filled his vision. His body doused in sweat, he crawled out of his mangled chair.

Safely strapped into the chair behind him, Herecura focused on him briefly before her eyes tracked away. He unbuckled her from the seat and she let him lift her out without protest. She clung to him, her arms winding around his neck as he kicked open the door and jumped out.

"Balor will be pleased," she whispered.

"I don't think so."

The stone floor burned through the soles of his shoes and Niall picked up speed. When he kicked open the door to the room he'd awoken in too many times over numerous generations, the ancient wooden panels splintered to ash. Niall didn't stop to reminisce. He carried a still unwitting Herecura to Miach's open pod and laid her inside. She looked around her and then her hand shot out and gripped Niall's wrist as dawning comprehension twisted to panic.

"No!" Her talons dug into his skin. Her other hand scraped at her face, pulling the oxygen tube out of the filter. "You cannot do this! Do not do this to me!" Tears of frustration and terror tracked down the thin layer of soot covering her skin.

Niall wrenched his wrist free. "You won't feel anything," he said. Vomit climbed up his esophagus. "You'll be asleep." Inspiration struck. "The pod won't survive the lava. I'm just buying time, Herecura."

"No! I can see the truth in your eyes. Please, do not do this!" Her face screwed up in a paroxysm of madness. Curses and obscenities spilled from her mouth and then she screamed—a haunting, shrieking wail of devastation that tore a gaping chasm through his conscience.

Niall slammed the lid down on the spitting, snarling creature before she found the wit to climb out. Choked with horror at what he was doing, he hesitated. A screeching scrape of nails against the inside of the pod chilled his blood and then Herecura's mind ripped through his shields.

*I hate you!*

Forcing his emotions aside, Niall forced his trembling fingers to program the pod to cryogenic stasis, stopping to wipe the blood from his eyes so he could work out what the hell he was pressing. *God, don't throw up.* Dammit! No time for this shit! The temperature shot skyward. He couldn't breathe and Herecura had the oxygen capsule with her in the pod. Her pleas for mercy ceased. Too late to retrieve it now. The stasis had come online. A large cracking noise made him jump. The lava had breached the huge arched doors to the Council Chamber. He didn't have long.

Getting control of his rattled thoughts, unable to fully eradicate the echo of Herecura's torment, Niall formed a new link in his mind, one that led directly into the bowels of Bacchus. The black hole opened up in his mind and he focused on the swirling vortex of gases drifting towards its heavy stillness. Energy shot from his fingertips, played at the edge of his growing portal and disappeared inside. He locked his bridge into place and then put his shoulder against the foot of Herecura's living tomb.

He grunted and groaned as he pushed that pod into the heart of a black hole, his mind accelerating its speed until it matched the detritus of space spiraling slowly towards the dark star's event horizon.

The enormity of what he was doing gnawed at his insides, a black stain seeping into his soul. The Astereans built cryogenic pods to last. The atomic power source on Uathach's pod had lasted the equivalent of centuries. Miach's was brand new. The gravity of a black hole slowed time down. Thousands of years could pass by on Earth.

She might never die.

*God forgive me.*

# CHAPTER TEN

Niall heard the clap of Kestra's massive wingspan slapping aside the massive tree canopy blocking out the stars. Branches rained down on his head and he darted behind the reassuring thickness of a tree trunk to give the huge beast plenty of room to land. Gryphon took a perverse pleasure in plummeting to earth from the sky, unnerving both their rider and anyone foolish enough to get in their way.

He stepped out with caution as a snorting Kestra settled in the clearing with great sweeps of her head. "I don't think she likes me."

Macha jumped off Kestra's lion-like back. "She is very happy to see you."

"Could have fooled me."

Kestra ruffled her jet-black feathers before tucking her wings against her furry flanks.

Macha laughed and flung her arms around Niall's neck in greeting, her warmth setting off a fresh burst of guilt. He had killed her mother the Queen Nuada in a battle of medieval savagery and his remorse hovered constantly in the background. He returned Macha's hug wishing he could just accept the generous forgiveness she radiated, although relieving one stain on his soul wouldn't erase the haunting memory of Herecura's last moments of lucidity.

Macha stood back and then offered a greeting more befitting of a Morrígan Queen. Their foreheads moved closer until her silvery aura touched his with an explosive sparkle.

"I sense your pain," Macha murmured, her mind open. "Show me."

Shadows darkened the night as Niall replayed his actions on Astereal before his return to the observatory outpost where her mind had been waiting to guide him home. She absorbed every macabre detail, her aura weeping for the woman he had sentenced to a living death. Niall shrank from her expression of sorrow and Macha caught his wrist.

"You did what had to be done, Niall'Kearey. The Morrígan retain ancestral memories of the atrocities committed in Balor's name. Your instincts have always proved sound. Don't doubt yourself now." Her aura dulled with sorrow. "I was a small child when my mother died. I witnessed that terrible day through your memory. You fought for your people and I felt your pain at her death. Nuada allowed her bitterness for the injustices done to the Morrígan to fuel her grievance with the Asterean. She would have killed your host, not you, and Sohan is a gentle Asterean who did not deserve to die at her hand. Our two cultures had diverged until we no longer remember what tore us apart. I cannot hold you responsible for this."

Niall held still. Macha never talked about her mother. She *had* told him to let his guilt go, and trust his instincts, but the guilt kept him grounded.

Macha chased his thought. *You are a stubborn and complex man, Niall'Kearey.* "The man who risks his life to save others is at war with the warrior, the general who defended the Asterean way of life for generations. The man who killed my mother, the man who ambushed Yerit and his kin on Kalyasyian Ridge, the man who killed hundreds of my people defending Paladin, this man did not hesitate, and yet every death weighs on your conscience. You are not without compassion and mercy. Your heart is honorable. My people did not die on Astereal. You brought them to Earth and we evolved."

His lungs still burning, his brain aching from the blow to his head, Niall dragged in a ragged breath.

"No. I treated Astereal like a fantasy world, made decisions I now regret, and judged your people unfairly for too long. I can't rely on instinct. I need information. This Balor threat is real. Herecura did something to me. I sensed something in her touch, a connection. I'm certain that's why she insisted on seeing me in person. She required the physical contact. With me." He paused, thinking through his options.

"We need to get away from here. DruSensi's satellites will detect my portal and Kestra has already brought too much attention to the Amazon."

"We are close to a well-traveled section of this great river and a considerable distance from our settlement. However, there is a cave a night's journey to the east. Kestra found it." Niall shook his head at the gryphon's dark bulk. "Do not blame her," Macha added, her tone defensive. "I wanted to explore my new world, too. We were careful to fly at night. The cave makes a natural nesting spot and Kestra returns to it often. I think she hopes a mate will find her there."

"I'm sorry her kind did not survive here on Earth. She's going to be lonely."

"Her season will pass. She is the last of her kind, an abomination from another galaxy." Her voice came out gruff.

"Sohan didn't intend—"

"I know," she said, her hand touching his arm. "Come, we will talk on the way."

She approached Kestra who lowered her head allowing Macha to pet her nose and Niall wondered if Kestra would bite his fingers off if he attempted to do the same. *Why the heck would I want to find out?*

The gryphon settled onto her belly and Macha mounted Kestra's expansive back then extended a hand from her perch.

Niall's pulse took off. Flying a gryphon on the other hand...

He settled into place behind Macha. His heart pounded as the jet-black gryphon rocked to her feet and looked heavenward. Powerful wings flapped the air and then Kestra shot through the trees like they didn't exist. Niall ducked, narrowly avoiding a branch that would have taken out an eye. They broke through the leaves into a cloudless sky twinkling with the light of galaxies.

He had never seen the Milky Way so bright.

Tami refolded Lizzie's sweater for the third time then stuffed it in a drawer. Every time Niall went on a mission she succumbed to this sick nervous tension. The second she relaxed her guard something would happen, from a knock on the door to announce Niall had been injured to armed mercenaries invading their home. Now that something involved going into hiding.

She grabbed a pink polka dotted sock hiding under the bed, straightened the sheets, then stared out the window at the sun glinting over a pine-forested slope. She couldn't believe this cozy mountain cabin Jose had rented for them, in a spot so secluded Jose had dropped them off by helicopter. The well-stocked kitchen had the most enormous freezer she'd ever seen. Her eyes welled with tears. The sheer level of preparation lifted the hairs on her head.

The door opened and Miach walked in. "Tami. He's back. He's with Macha."

She burst into tears. "Is he—?"

Miach crossed the room in four strides and wrapped her in his arms. "He's fine."

He held her up as relief and fear collided in a maelstrom of emotion with only one way out. She let the tears flow, his chin resting atop her head.

"He told me to say he loves you and not to worry. He has a few things to resolve with your president before he sees you."

She sniffled and a second later he was pressing a wad of tissues into her hands. "Thank you. I'm sorry. I shouldn't be blubbering all over you like this."

"You love him. Your reaction is natural."

Relief turned to anger, unexpected and powerful. "What Niall does isn't natural though, is it? Crossing a universe and drawing energy out of thin air isn't natural."

Miach grabbed her flailing hands. "For me it is very natural. The brain holds so much potential and it is true that your husband has greater command of his gifts than most, but you should not fear this."

Tami blinked. Miach radiated calm, his physical touch a balm that soothed her frazzled nerves. "You're so much like Niall. Are you sure he didn't leave something of him behind in you?"

74

Miach's grizzly eyebrows knitted over coal-black eyes that twinkled with sudden humor. Releasing her hands, he stepped back. "I retain his memories, memories Niall'Kearey accessed when I hosted him. The emotions those memories inspired are imprinted here." He thumped his heart. "They help me to read you, and your children. I hope you do not consider this an intrusion. It is not something I can change."

Tami thought about that. The connection explained much. Miach had slotted into their extended family so easily she forgot he was an alien from another world. "It's not an intrusion and I'm glad you're here. Toby and Lizzie love having you with us."

He smiled, a wide generous smile that created a dimple in his right cheek. She wished he'd smile more. Despite Miach's passion for life, she often noticed a sadness wash over him. She bit her lip. She still had Niall. Miach had lost the love of his life.

He gave her a penetrating look. "Tell me. What scares you the most about Niall'Kearey's gifts?"

"I'm not sure." His eyebrows raised and she flung her hands up. "We knew each other so well before everything changed. Niall had this sixth sense that kept him out of trouble, but also led him into it. I just knew things I shouldn't. I knew we'd get married the moment I laid eyes on him. I saw it. Niall calls me his witch. I glimpsed danger that day we were taken." She shuddered, the ugly memory a nightmare she'd never forget. "I shouted at Lizzie to hide. I don't even remember grabbing that knife. Before I could call for help, they were in the house. I couldn't find Toby!" She forced the words past the tightness constricting her throat. "My second sight wasn't there for us that day, not soon enough to count. Maybe Niall sparks it off in me, and when he's not there I become normal. Since the shooting, it's not been the same, and Niall is something else altogether."

Something unnatural. She shook her head.

"You feel he's leaving you behind?"

His words crystallized the fear eating her. She nodded. "I'm not sure I'm enough for Niall anymore." She looked away from the shocked concern in Miach's eyes. "I'm worried I'll hold him back."

Foldane closed his mouth, absorbed the sudden change of surroundings from his private living room to prehistoric cave, and then laid into the arrogant moron who had just bodily snatched him *out of the White House for Christ's sake!*

"Are you crazy?" he yelled at Major Kearey who was backing up a step, hands raised as if to ward him off. "Have you any idea what you've unleashed? You can't kidnap the goddamn President of the United States and get away with it!"

Kearey grimaced. "Nothing compared to what I have to tell you, sir."

"That I can well believe," Foldane snapped, the adrenalin rush testing his usual control. Hell. This was going to play havoc with his blood pressure, although Kearey's sheepish response didn't suggest an immediate threat of danger, and there was even a roaring fire—his eyebrows lifted—being tended to by a strange woman in a tribal-looking shift dress that was both clean and modest. Almost Amazonian... if she wasn't so petite. As his heart calmed to a steady beat, snippets of information fell into place. He looked back at Kearey. "DruSensi reported a portal in the Amazon. Of course, you'd disappeared by the time the retrieval team got to its location. I assume this is where you've been hiding out. I give you two hours before we're surrounded."

"We'll be gone before then, and I've had enough of being stalked by satellite—" Kearey stopped short as his voice began to rise.

Foldane glimpsed the strain the man was under. More than that, Kearey seemed edgy. Fearful. The notion threw a huge rock into the president's anger. When Kearey took a deep breath, the president made ready to listen.

"I believe Earth to be facing an alien threat, Mr. President."

"You don't say," Foldane couldn't resist. He regretted the dig when Kearey slung him a contemptuous glare. "Okay, let's be precise about this," he said more reasonably. "When you say alien, do you mean the Astereans, Herecura, or this Balor?"

"Balor. Herecura is in cryogenic stasis."

"She is? I didn't think the pod was ready. Where?"

Kearey didn't answer at first. When he spoke, he delivered his words carefully. "I left her in Astereal's solar system. I didn't want to bring her back to Earth."

"I see." Foldane grasped he was going to have to drag the information out of the man. "Could you elaborate?"

"I need to explain a couple of things first, but the Senate Armed Forces Committee isn't the appropriate forum. That's why I brought you here, to prepare the ground. Plus, there's someone I need to introduce to you."

Foldane turned towards the woman. She rose to her feet and he barely held back a gasp as the firelight revealed squared pupils and a slightly ridged brow. He could also make out a thickening around her neck where, if he recalled correctly, he would see spikes if she intended to attack him. His eyes traveled to her hands. No thumbs. "You're Morrígan, aren't you?"

The incline of her head confirmed his hunch.

Kearey beckoned her to join them. "Mr. President, this is Macha, the Morrígan Queen."

Foldane believed it. The woman's every movement spoke of nobility. He straightened when she stepped forward, her arm outstretched. Somewhat bemused, he shook her hand in greeting.

Her smile was polite, her tone modest. "A queen displaced from her people, with the exception of two companions. But I have been warmly welcomed by descendants of the people I once ruled."

Her English was excellent.

"I understand," Foldane began, before realizing he hadn't a clue what she was talking about. "I'm sorry, but you have me at a disadvantage. How are you here?" He glanced at Kearey's guilt-ridden grimace and groaned. "*Goddammit!* Senator Biron had it right all along. You smuggled aliens onto Earth! You idiot!" He reeled back from the ramifications, the late dinner he had finished minutes earlier now sitting a little too heavily. He turned on Kearey. "How many? And where?"

"Mr. President. Enough."

Foldane blinked, startled by Macha's quiet but commanding tone. Standing there under her expectant gaze he felt suddenly crass and bullish. "Forgive me, um..."

"Macha, is fine. My kind does not stand on ceremony."

Foldane winced. "Earth thrives on ceremony."

She smiled, amused, and his tension lessened. He glanced at Major Kearey and suddenly recognized a man on the brink of exhaustion. The president narrowed his eyes. Kearey looked thinner, his face drawn, and Foldane could make out a closed cut just below Kearey's hairline. The last few days on the Asterean outpost had knocked the vitality out of the man, and this Morrígan, Macha, knew it too. Her rebuke had been a protective warning.

He expelled air through his nostrils. "Okay, I guess I'm here, the circumstances are unquestionably exceptional, and so I'm prepared to listen. Not that you've given me much choice. However, right now, all hell will be breaking loose back home. Someone's bound to think of asking the Astereans what they might know about my sudden disappearance."

"No one knows you disappeared, sir. Not yet, anyway."

"What?"

"I'm keeping an eye on things. You were upstairs alone in your residence, just retired for the night. Most of your staff have left for the evening, and DruSensi's satellite network is probably rebooting. I kinda boosted a solar flare and knocked it offline. That's what they'll blame. No point hiding it from you, the timing is obvious, but this is important."

"You can't remote-view the White House. It's protected."

"I shorted out the disruptor while I was there."

Foldane cursed. "You're hoping I'll cover for you."

"Yes, sir."

"Taking one hell of a risk." He kept his voice casual. Kearey may have miscalculated. DruSensi International produced parts for military satellites worldwide. Stood to reason they'd hardened their own network against electromagnetic and radiation attack. He made a mental note to check whether they'd suffered any downtime. Encouraged a solar flare? Damn. "Secret Service check in regularly."

"Yes. It will be a minute before they realize you're not in the bathroom, or your bedroom. Then they'll panic."

"So we should get back there, quickly, before anyone notices," Foldane suggested.

"With apologies, sir, I first need your word that no harm will befall Macha."

Foldane looked at the tiny alien queen and went with his gut. "You have it. What about you?"

"I'm hoping that after you've heard me out, you will understand my actions and let this particular incident slide."

Foldane mulled that one over. It sounded like Kearey had more serious crimes to answer. "We can't locate your family," he told Kearey. "You must have done something very bad."

"Not bad, sir. Big. I did something very big, but I had my reasons."

"And you're willing to confess all."

"To you, sir. I need to explain to you. And I want Patrick Morgan there too." Kearey's tone dripped with distaste. "The Vercingetorix need to hear the truth and Morgan represents the Council. He's en route to the White House now, with the expectation that you will see him."

Foldane considered Kearey's demands, curiosity burning up his reservations. "Okay, we'll do it your way, but I want General Towden present to even up the numbers. He likes you. He'll give you a fair hearing."

"He's in DC?"

"Gave me a personal briefing this afternoon. On this cryogenic pod you have us building."

Kearey winced a second time. "Ah, I see. Thank you, sir. General Towden will be fine." His fingers began to pull filaments of energy out of nowhere.

Foldane watched mesmerized as a portal opened revealing the Oval Office on the other side. He stepped through before Kearey changed his mind, or Secret Service burst in, guns blazing.

# CHAPTER ELEVEN

In the Oval Office, Niall watched Macha explore the silk-lined drapes and objects d'art on display, her obvious fascination relieving the undercurrent of tension permeating the room. A bronzed sculpture caught her eye and she dropped down on bended knee to view the rearing horse at eye level.

"This horse is an Appaloosa, a rare Spanish breed," Towden said, joining her.

The general's reticence towards the Morrígan Queen had thawed quickly while Niall's nerves twanged a discordant chorus that kept him pacing back and forth by the tall glass window overlooking the garden. He sensed Morgan's arrival just before the inner door opened. Macha turned around slowly, both her expression and aura betraying her mistrust of the new arrival.

"You're late," President Foldane snapped, but then his eyes bulged out. "What the hell happened to you?"

Morgan removed tinted glasses revealing the full severity of the yellow blue bruising on his face. A swollen bottom lip vied with his nose for top billing and a white plaster looked to be holding his right cheekbone together.

Niall rubbed his knuckles.

"Short argument with a sidewalk," Morgan replied, not even looking Niall's way, although Towden threw Niall an accusing glance. "Teach me to be more careful," Morgan added. "My apologies, Mr. President, I had an urgent call. My father died fifteen minutes ago."

Foldane's impatience collapsed and the president strode forward offering Morgan his hand. "Patrick, I'm sorry, Kean was a good friend of my father's. My condolences. Can I get you a drink? Whisky?"

"Tea, if you would be so kind. I suspect I'll need a clear head." He glanced around, barely acknowledged Towden, nodded at Niall, and then his eyes fell upon Macha. Confusion shifted his bruises around. "Damn, woman, that's a powerful aura you have there."

Macha's eyes blasted a chill across them all. "Your aura hides so many secrets I am impressed it shows at all."

Morgan shot Niall a dawning look of comprehension before looking down at himself. His mouth thinned. Too late he dimmed the irritation he now radiated out. "Feisty little thing, isn't she?"

"Watch your tongue, Morgan," Niall snarled, prompting a surprised frown from Foldane. "This is Macha, ruler of the Morrígan of Astereal."

"Correct me if I'm wrong, Major, but I don't recall Operation Hideout agreeing to any Morrígan for her to rule."

A thumping fury let loose in Niall's temples. "And why was that? Morrígan too alien for the Vercingetorix, perhaps?"

General Towden stepped between them. "Major, stand down. Mr. Morgan, I suggest you sit over there." He glared at them both.

Morgan shrugged then dropped into the designated chair.

Foldane stepped forward. "Macha, please accept my apologies for Mr. Morgan's rudeness. His father just died."

"He shields his grief well, Mr. President."

*I take it there isn't much love lost between Morgan and his father,* Niall asked Macha as the president ushered her to the sofa.

*The relationship appears complex. Morgan is baiting you, Niall Kearey. I assume you have a reason for not dismembering him.*

*That's what I want you to help me decide. I need to know if he's being honest with me, and his intentions for my family.*

*I understand.*

"Okay, Major," Foldane said as he handed Morgan his tea. "This is your show. I suggest you get started."

"Thank you, sir." Shit. Niall couldn't remember how he'd intended to start. He took a moment. Imagined Morgan centered in the cross hairs of his scope, his finger on the trigger. Aim... "Okay, it's no secret I was against the one million cap imposed on Hideout, and I argued for more Astereans to be saved, but then I discovered something, well, several somethings, that changed everything. First, Jacqueline Biron confided to me the existence of the Vercingetorix." Fire... "And her belief that the Vercingetorix lay behind my family's kidnapping."

Morgan placed his tea on a side table and uncrossed his legs. "If you've brought me here to rehash unsupported accusations..."

*I hope you're getting a read on this asshole,* Niall thought to Macha. *Yes.*

"Does he have reason to make accusations, Patrick?" Foldane asked sharply. The president's glance shifted to Niall. "Major?"

"I do, but that's not what this meeting is about." Justice for the victims of the Vercingetorix would be handled vigilante style, when the time was right. "Jacqueline believed my children to be truly lost. She was distraught and she believed the Vercingetorix to be responsible. She told me everything, and that's when I told her about Astereal. She agreed to help me, act as an inside source of information on the Vercingetorix."

"We know this," Morgan dismissed.

"Please, let Major Kearey confess his sins in his own way," Foldane intervened.

Patrick Morgan subsided with a low mutter.

Niall took a calming breath. "What you don't know is that I asked Jacqueline to research the possibility that Astereans had visited Earth in the past. Jacqueline's research uncovered archaeological evidence suggesting that both Asterean and Morrígan had at several points visited Earth in the distant past. I then discovered that although I could not lock my bridge from Astereal to Earth into the present—not until Astereal reached Alignment—I could lock onto Earth's past."

Morgan laughed. "What are you saying? That you smuggled aliens into Earth's past?"

Niall met and held his gaze.

The Irishman glanced nervously from Niall to a serene-looking Macha, and then Morgan jumped up gesturing wildly. "Sweet Jesus, Mary and Joseph, you did! You smuggled aliens into the goddamn past! Fecking hell, man, did you let the hard stuff go to your head?"

President Foldane stared at Morgan bewildered. "Into the past?"

Towden perched on the edge of his chair, his face blotchy and looking fit to burst.

Niall raised his hand and focused on Morgan. "Remember the driver of the car that ended up on Astereal? Well, his DNA proved he was descended from both Asterean and Morrígan."

Morgan paled. "What about your children? Did the Asterean test them, too?"

"Yes. The evidence was conclusive."

"Are you telling us you tampered with Earth's timeline?" Towden growled, his jowls quivering with barely suppressed rage.

Niall broke out in a cold sweat. "I am not certain it's possible to tamper with it. I merely discovered that it had already happened. Think about it. Nothing changed in our world from the moment I began evacuating the people of Astereal into our past. And why? Because it had already been done! Humanity as we know it is the result of my actions, but those actions came into effect thousands of years ago. I simply fulfilled what the archeological records of Earth show to be true."

He ran a shaking hand through his hair. "Shit. I know that sounds like god-complex stuff, but it's not. It's a massive paradox in reverse, where doing nothing would have changed everything! Imagine the consequences if I hadn't followed through, if humanity never evolved with the Asterean and Morrígan influences we now know existed. Imagine our entire world unmade by my inaction."

Damn, that last hadn't gone down well. Foldane had assumed his poker face, the same one he'd presented when Niall told him he'd dumped Lizzie and Toby on an alien planet somewhere across the universe, Morgan had turned pale despite his bruises, and Towden looked ready to disembowel Niall and feed his entrails to Somalian pirates as a peace offering.

Macha rose to her feet. "My people and the Astereans are your ancestors," she said. Her quiet statement sunk in slowly. "So, your presence today suggests that Niall'Kearey preserved your timeline, as he was meant to do. He had a simple choice. Ignore the evidence, do nothing, and see mankind wiped out of existence. Or accept the destiny his powers bestowed on him and preserve the path of human evolution."

General Towden shook his head. "That wasn't his place to decide."

Niall leapt to his feet. "My place?" Stress stockpiled during months of deciding what was best for Earth, the people of Astereal, and his family, ruptured. "I possessed this power, no one else. That *made* it my place! My responsibility!" He batted away the doubting voice that tortured him at night and eyeballed his commanding officer. "I made my choice from the perspective of two galaxies and two different timeflows. Two different civilizations required that I do what was in my power to do. It was my duty. Senator Biron would have buried me in ferrite tiles and," he turned on Foldane, "you would have let him! There were millions of people on Astereal and you were prepared to let them die. By then I didn't know who I could trust. Senator Biron was messing with my chain of command, using my best friend against me, both of them with connections to the same secret society responsible for kidnapping my family and putting my wife in a coma!"

"It was never that cut and dried," Foldane protested.

Niall stabbed a finger at Morgan. "This man instigated carnage on my hometown, and now he sits here protected by *diplomatic immunity* knowing anyone who could finger him is dead!"

"I never ordered a hit on your hometown," Morgan barked back, his hands gripping his chair as if he expected Niall to shoot him down any second. He was right to worry. The desire to gather energy sizzled the tips of Niall's fingers.

"But you ordered the kidnap of his family?" Towden's condemnation hit home.

Morgan launched to his feet. "I'm admitting nothing, and you, General Towden, should be more concerned that a man under your command deceived the entire US military and altered the course of human evolution on your watch!" He stopped on a sharp intake of breath, his head swung back to Niall, the fight in his eyes shifting to astonishment. "The orbs! You smuggled both orbs to Earth, didn't you?"

It was impossible to deny the man's razor-sharp intellect and Niall regrouped his thoughts, the question sooner than expected. "Yes. There are seven data orbs in total. They were supposed to have been hidden in the past. The Asterean group who brought yours over can't have hidden it well enough. Uathach brought my orb to Earth."

"Uathach? The High Brighid?" Foldane pounced on the name. "I thought she perished on Astereal?"

"No, she made her own way into Earth's past." Niall watched Morgan's face closely. "She married Senator Charles Biron and helped collate the Vercingetorix library."

Patrick Morgan's jaw dropped. He sat back down heavily. "Well, I'll be fucked," he drawled with a thick Irish brogue. Then the man groaned. "Etlinn will be lovin' that. She'll be bending me ear for years to come." He shook his head. "Why, Nicole Biron, you sweet bonny lass! Will the senator be after knowing this gem?"

"No," Niall replied.

Morgan rubbed his hands together. "Even better."

"How long have you known this, Major?" President Foldane asked, his voice so soft that Niall nearly missed the question, too busy pondering over Morgan's angle with Senator Biron.

"About Uathach? Not until well after Hideout. Nicole Biron left me the second orb, and a letter, in a codicil to her will. Jacqueline passed them to me."

"I see. I have not heard of these orbs until now. What are they?"

"There are seven data orbs containing the sum of Asterean knowledge. Imagine a highly advanced time capsule. The Vercingetorix already possessed one orb, and I gave mine to the Vercingetorix in a deal to protect my family from further terrorist attacks." Niall enjoyed Morgan's flinch. "It was either that or tear up the world hunting every last member of the Vercingetorix until I could be sure my wife and children would be safe. Jacqueline got protection from any reprisals, too."

A tic in Foldane's jaw betrayed the president's irritation.

"He neglected to mention that only his mind can open the orb," Morgan added. "Both orbs, I guess. A little insurance policy the High Brighid took out on your behalf, I assume."

Niall nodded. "Uathach's letter indicated she had gathered proof of Asterean settlements on Earth. I suspect these will provide clues to the other five orbs, but I need access to the Vercingetorix library to find them."

Morgan leaned forward. "The orbs are suddenly important to you, Major. Something to do with this Herecura business, I wager. Where is she, exactly?"

"Herecura has been..." Niall's heart pounded loud in his ears, "... contained." Pacing up and down, he explained his decision to incarcerate Herecura in cryogenic stasis, and how. The tension in the room increased, and when his story reached the point when he'd sent the pod spiraling into a black hole, it felt like the horror on Herecura's face had sucked the oxygen out of the room.

Macha's melodic voice broke the memory's hold on him. "The name Balor has survived hundreds of thousands of Earth years. It predates the Great Divide on Astereal. Morrígan legend describes a..." She paused and flashed Niall an image.

"An exodus," he supplied.

"Thank you. Yes... an exodus across the galaxies."

"Is that when the Astereans and Morrígan settled on Astereal?" Niall asked.

Macha inclined her head. "I believe so. Legend does not describe Balor, only the atrocities carried out in its name. These are stories of worlds reduced to rubble, whole races subverted to slavery, or annihilated."

"It," Towden mused. "Not he, or she." Niall expelled a breath of relief. The general had focused on the real threat here. "Do we know what galaxy this Balor inhabits?" Towden asked.

Macha looked to Niall for the answer. His jaw clenched, an instinctive reaction to the pervasive fear that took hold whenever he recalled that brief encounter with overwhelming mindless aggression.

"Major?" Foldane prompted.

"I don't know where it comes from, but I think I once stumbled upon Balor as a child, and again more recently in a link from Astereal during my training with Nantosuelta."

Foldane shifted his bulk. "Nantosuelta. She was your mentor who left with the Asterean fleet?"

"Yes, sir. Nantosuelta is one of the few Astereans gifted enough to bridge space, and a fine drill sergeant." His lips twitched at the idea of those bouncing curls marching up and down a parade ground. "She wanted me to explore holes throughout Astereal's solar system, mainly to help me develop finer control over my ability, but she also hoped I might find an alternative planet to Earth. I didn't find a planet capable of supporting life, but I did encounter something wild…" Mind-freezing panic erupted deep inside him, coagulating his thoughts. "Total madness..." He stopped, struggling to breathe. The room warped in and out. He dragged in a sharp breath and then another, but the walls disappeared. Holes shimmered all around him. "Crap." He grabbed for his chair.

*Niall'Kearey, slow your breathing, release the memory.*

Someone pushed him into his seat and slowly the room returned to normal. Niall cringed to find Macha crouched in front of him, her hands on his knees. Towden was offering him a glass of water. Niall accepted it with shaking hands. He caught Foldane's concerned appraisal, Morgan's considered frown.

"I'm fine," he said to Macha. *Thank you.*

She nodded and stepped away.

"Are you able to continue?" Foldane asked him.

Niall sipped the water so he could reply. "Yes, sir. I think my reaction just now demonstrates why I avoid thinking about this... encounter. It terrified me as a child. My parents thought I was either possessed or our home was haunted. We moved home, but by then I'd found Astereal and stopped exploring anywhere else. When I had the same experience during my training with Nantosuelta we agreed there were some things best left undiscovered. If I did encounter Balor, sir, then it is the most dangerous threat to Earth that I can imagine. I couldn't risk Herecura's death releasing her memories of me and somehow guiding this Balor to Earth. I couldn't risk that." His voice hardened. "I did what had to be done to protect Earth, and I'd do it again."

Foldane raised a hand. "Easy, Major. I admit I was shocked by your story, but based on what I've heard—and seen—I'm willing to concede your actions were justified. My concern right now is the suggestion that Herecura targeted you. My question is why?"

Niall swallowed. "Assuming Balor is the same entity I've encountered before—"

"Aghh," Morgan uttered. The strangled groan hung in the air as the Vercingetorix Councilor found the words he needed. He pointed an accusing finger at Niall. "It noticed you. When you were a child. You spiked its curiosity and it came looking for you. Holy Mother of God, Herecura was its agent."

Niall listened to Morgan's tirade with a detached sense of impending doom as the man jumped from one conclusion to the next.

"You need the orbs to research this Balor. Discover who or what is hunting you down. No, more than that, you're looking for a way to defend Earth. You're the most powerful, gifted product of human evolution and this thing terrifies you!" Morgan turned to Foldane. "This man," Morgan's finger stabbed towards Niall, "isn't the exclusive property of the US any longer. He is answerable to the world."

"Property?" Niall jumped to his feet. "That's been the problem right down the line. You and the Vercingetorix see everyone as your personal property to be used as you see fit! Goddammit! I barely recognize this world anymore!"

Macha was standing right beside him. "Is this how you treat the man who saved your race?" she railed at Morgan. "Your prized Vercingetorix bloodline exists because of his actions! You would not sit in these fine chairs but for Niall'Kearey. You would not have been born. He has done nothing wrong to be treated this way!"

"Perhaps we should all calm down," Foldane murmured.

Morgan stabbed a finger at Niall. "If you've brought Earth to the attention of this Balor—"

"Then I'll deal with it—"

"No!" Macha snapped, taking Niall by surprise. She glared at him. "You were a boy when Balor noticed you, *if* it noticed you. Pwyll believes Herecura's mind was poisoned when she was a child. That is long before you explored the universe with Nantosuelta, and do not forget the timeflows. Your childhood encounter with something evil occurred many generations ago when seen from Astereal's timeline. If Balor is hunting for you, then it has been hunting for a very long time." She drew breath, and her aggressive stance softened. "You assume too much responsibility."

She turned to Morgan. "This is not a time to throw accusations and make claims on a free man." Her voice dripped with her disgust. "Mr. Morgan, you say Niall'Kearey must open the orbs and search for knowledge of Balor, but you miss the key point." The conspicuous silence became uncomfortable and Macha lifted a regal eyebrow. "Five orbs are missing in the past."

Towden snapped his fingers. "Major Kearey can time travel."

"I need to check that's possible on Earth," Niall warned.

"You smuggled aliens into the past for months," Foldane pointed out.

"That was more to do with the timeflows being out of step. I could manipulate the bridge lock from Astereal to a certain extent, but stepping back into Astereal's past required me to merge a hole in space with a hole in time and I used a link I knew existed."

"Essentially it's the same principle that allows people to predict the future, clairvoyance and premonition," Morgan mused. "We have many families coded with such talents, but none able to combine it with kinesis." Morgan studied Niall with unnerving focus. "Sometimes I get the impression you don't quite understand your own gifts. You realize of course you are coded for premonition. Your uncanny capacity for survival is all due to the ability to shortcut time. You predicted the earthquake at Sedona. I suspect that every time you remote-viewed Astereal you were one step from manipulating time, and your subconscious filled the gap for you. Now you can consciously control this aspect."

He paused for a moment in thought. "Nicole Biron—Uathach—is bound to have left clues in her library pointing to the other orbs' locations. Jacqueline Biron helped identify where to insert our ancestors and she knew her aunt better than anyone. She'll be a good person to search the library for these clues."

Niall started. His premonition hadn't spotted that one coming. "Now wait a minute—"

"No, *you* wait," Morgan overrode him. "Stop with the suspicion. No harm will come to Jacqueline. She worked against us for a time, but with good reason. Now we need her. The Vercingetorix can be ruthless, Major, but contrary to belief, we are not vindictive."

"Yeah, well, try explaining that to my wife," Niall snarled.

Morgan fell silent. He studied his hands for a few moments. When he looked up all sign of irritation had been erased. He pointedly turned to Foldane. "Mr. President, I have offered Major Kearey's family protection and I personally guarantee the offer comes condition free. They would be shielded from political interference from the Vercingetorix Council, from their government, and other governments who might resent all this coded power residing in a Western civilization, and from the public at large."

Foldane rubbed his chin, eyes narrowed. "You're willing to guarantee that with your holdings?"

Morgan winced then looked at Niall. His back straightened. "I think I can go a long way to alleviating any concerns."

"Mr. President!" Towden objected.

Foldane held up his hand. "Hold up, General." He turned to Niall. "Actually, Major, I think you would be wise to consider this offer. Your family can't hide forever."

Niall nudged Macha's mind. *What do you think?*

*Morgan's aura is sincere in this one regard, Niall'Kearey. He did order your family's abduction, but the scale of the attack on your hometown grieves him. I do not like the man, but he regrets what he did to your family and genuinely fears for their safety. In this instance, his objective is aligned with yours.*

Niall nodded. "I'll consider Morgan's offer, Mr. President, but I have a few conditions of my own."

"I wouldn't expect anything less." Foldane rose to his feet and Towden and Niall automatically followed. The president stepped up to Niall, his eyes stern. "I once promised you the resources of a nation. I had no idea who I was dealing with. I still can't decide if you are the all-time American hero your record suggested, or a wild card with the potential to destroy us all. The fact you are here now tells me you recognize you can't do this alone. However, I will not countenance you operating outside the chain of command again. Is that clear?"

Niall straightened to attention. "Sir."

"Is there anything else you haven't told us?"

Niall wracked his brains then mentally groaned. "Yes, sir." He hesitated. "My children's Morrígan guardians accompanied them to Earth. And I brought back my host from Astereal. Earth revived him, and his shift-shaping talent is intact. Oh, and," Niall glanced at Macha's wincing expression, but it was now or never, "that dragon reported in the Amazon is a gryphon from Astereal." Foldane's head jerked back. "She's the last of her species and she's linked to Macha, sir."

# CHAPTER TWELVE

Niall grinned as arms wrapped around his waist from behind him. He looked out across the crashing blue surf of the Pacific Ocean as Tami's head rested against his naked back. So much had changed in less than a week. When a powerful member of the Vercingetorix joined forces with the US President, obstacles melted away. Morgan had signed up to every condition that didn't involve admitting any wrongdoing.

"I can't believe you're here," she said.

He clasped her hand in his. "It feels strange. No more lies and hiding what I did. DruSensi's filtering out the island's location from its reports to the Hideout members. It means I won't need to ask General Towden for authorization to bridge to the island."

Only the undefined threat of Balor marred Niall's relief at being reunited with his family on a beautiful island offering refuge from the world.

Pwyll snorted in his mind and Niall ramped up his shields.

*Better,* Pwyll commented, *but too late. I already read your thoughts.*

Heck. Pwyll was probably Uathach's secret weapon for keeping the Vercingetorix in line.

Tami's breath tickled Niall's spine. "I'll expect you home for dinner every night from now on."

Niall grunted a noncommittal reply as he asked Pwyll, *What did you read?*

*The thought of working with the Vercingetorix irritates you. It is distractions like this that create weaknesses in your shielding.*

Tami's chin nudged the edge of his shoulder blade. "Who are you talking to?"

Pwyll chuckled, but then his mind turned serious. *Contact me when you are free. We are being interviewed.*

Before Niall could answer him, Pwyll's mind withdrew. Niall turned to draw Tami beside him. "No hiding anything from you. Sorry. Pwyll breached my shields. He's gone now."

"Pwyll?"

"An Asterean who's made it his mission to make my shields invincible." His answer was distracted. Why were the Astereans being interviewed?

"So what, at any time Pwyll could drop in on us?"

Tami's tetchy question grabbed Niall's attention. "No. The idea is to prevent that."

She didn't look convinced. "If he can reach you, does that mean he knows where we are?"

"Maybe." Niall frowned. He'd known Miach was in Chicago, but Miach hadn't been hiding. Uathach hadn't been able to find Niall on Astereal when he went looking for his children. He'd deliberately shut her out. The island was protected from remote-viewing, but it didn't prevent telepathy. Pwyll could only see what Niall allowed him to see. "I don't think so."

"What about the people living here? Anyone with a sextant and a brain could work out where this island is located."

Niall tightened his grip around her waist. He didn't want her worrying over this stuff.

"You're right. Nothing's foolproof. Foldane, Towden, and the Vercingetorix Council know where we are, but the Vercingetorix is very careful who they allow here. This is their safe place." He took out his cell phone and showed her the dud GPS reading. "DruSensi supplies software to GPS and there's an encrypted layer of coding to convert any signal from this area to a false location. Wi-fi uses a similar principle. The island has access to advanced military and covert technology that disrupts any unauthorized signals. This place is well hidden from the rest of the world."

Tami relaxed and snuggled closer. "This place *is* amazing," she admitted.

Unbelievably amazing. Tami had an aura here, light and full of interesting promise. The island's magnetic flux drew out the latent potential of its inhabitants and Niall sensed Tami could heal here.

Enjoy living.

Their bungalow extended like a dhoni boat over the ocean. Water lapped the supports beneath the slatted planking of their deck. Steps and a walkway led back to white-gold sand. An oasis of trees offered shelter and privacy. Patrick Morgan seemed determined to purchase Niall's cooperation. The Vercingetorix wanted the data contained within the orbs. They all wanted more information on Balor and an increasing urgency scratching at Niall's mind stopped him from balking at the constant demands for every conceivable detail of his timeline tampering.

Foldane granting him a few days leave to settle his family on the island had surprised him. But not if they wanted time to corroborate his reports with the Astereans.

That made sense of the interviews. He would check in with Pwyll later. Make sure.

Niall spotted his parents walking along the beach, deep in conversation. "Macha believes she can help Tony manage his alcoholism."

Tami followed his gaze. "I think you explaining everything to them has made a big difference already. How did you get them clearance?"

"Foldane decided the cloak and dagger routine was making my life impossible—too many conflicting lies and loyalties. Maybe I should have come clean earlier."

An excited cry was followed by the sound of running feet. "Daddy!"

Niall swung around and caught Lizzie up in a bear hug until she squealed. "God, you've grown," he moaned, setting her back on her feet. Lizzie wrapped her arms around his waist. She wore a swimsuit under her shorts and sunshine-yellow vest top, her hair scraped back into an untidy knot at the back of her head. Freckles dotted her nose.

Toby ambled around the corner of the bungalow and offered them a grin. "Dad! This place has everything. Mom, I signed up for a climbing expedition."

"With the school?"

He rolled his eyes. "No, Mom. With the sharks." He grinned at Niall then disappeared into the house.

Tami laughed, her nose scrunching up. "That boy will be the death of me. I blame Yerit."

"Yerit has pitons for nails and this cool ability to create a cushion of air if he falls," Niall said.

Lizzie giggled. "Choluu's a way better climber than Yerit. She doesn't need to show off like the men, is all."

Niall winked at his daughter, but it was Tami's relief that held his attention. "I haven't seen you laugh like that in ages. Do you think you can be happy here? You won't feel trapped?"

"No more than I felt hiding out at the lodge Jose found us. At least here we're not confined to the house and the island is huge. The kids can go to a school suited to their abilities. Niall, I haven't seen Toby so excited since we left the Morrígan. He's really missed Yerit and Choluu and the friends he made, but the other kids here make him feel normal. That's helping." She surveyed their new domain. "And the light is magical." Her eye stopped on Lizzie. "What about you, honey? Are you happy? I know you left new friends behind in Tampa."

"Mom, I compared auras with a girl called Sheldon from Perth. Her accent is crazy! Pure Aussie. The teachers are great, except for Mr. Galke who's got a bat up his—" Lizzie's eyes shifted to Niall and she changed tack. "He's knows some interesting stuff, though." She grabbed a beach towel from a chair and moved towards the diving deck protruding over the clear blue waters. "What's for dinner?"

"Grilled rockfish with shrimp," Niall called after her. He caught Tami's fingers and brought them up to his lips. "How old do you think they are? Ten, or sixteen?"

"I'm calling it ten. They've just experienced more than most their age. Niall, I wanted to ask you about Miach. Where is he?"

Niall caught a strained note in her voice he didn't understand. "Miach's undergoing tests at GBI. Why?"

"I was wondering if he'd have to join the Astereans in Nevada, now they know about him."

"I've asked for him to be assigned here. I need people I trust close at hand. The Vercingetorix intend to offer him a teaching post at the school." That was the official story. General Towden had worried that a shape shifting alien with Niall's memories and knowledge posed a security risk at Area 51, while Niall trusted Miach with his life and his family's lives. Patrick Morgan had suggested the compromise given Miach's abilities hadn't exhibited the ability to form bridges through space-time and airline and hotel records of his falsified passport tallied with Miach's statement detailing his travels around the States. Niall suspected that might change as Miach acclimated to Earth's magnetic field, but said nothing. For now, the island offered a secure hideout and Miach had raised no objection.

A smile softened Tami's lips. "Good. The kids like him. They think of him as family." She blushed under his quizzical gaze. "Miach helped me through a rough patch. I get jittery when you're away and he has this link direct to you. He's become a good friend. I'm thankful he'll be around. What about Yerit and Choluu?"

Niall grimaced. He worried over the twins' former guardians. The Morrígan couple had cared for Toby and Lizzie on Astereal as if they were their own. It had been Sam's treacherous actions that had ultimately separated Yerit and Choluu from their tribe back in Earth's past. He wanted them to be happy, but like Macha they would always be different. Alien. The last surviving members of a race destined for extinction.

"Niall?" Tami's fingers reached up and smoothed the worry frown forming on his brow. "You okay?"

"Yes." He smiled at her. "I did talk with them, but they feel at home in the Amazon, and someone needs to keep an eye on Kestra. The Vercingetorix has influential contacts in the Brazilian government and they've arranged that entire sector to be designated a protected nature and indigenous reserve. Still, I'm worried. The Morrígan descendants are accepted by other tribes in the area, but if the authorities decide to study them, their physical characteristics will stand out. Yerit's smart, though. He and Choluu can disappear if they have to."

"And Jose?"

Niall looked down the road leading to their bungalow and then waggled his eyebrows. "Look."

Tami glanced over her shoulder, did a hop-jump then ran to meet the man limping down the road preceded by several children. A woman carrying a baby in a shoulder sling beamed and waved in their direction. Niall rested his elbows on the wood railing running around the perimeter of their bungalow and watched his former second-in-command swing Tami around, set her back on her feet then introduce her to his wife, Luisa. When they reached the bungalow, Niall walked down to greet the new arrivals.

"Mano!" Jose Pérez Navas opened his arms.

"Swing me around like you did my wife and I'll shoot you," Niall warned before his face relaxed into a wide grin.

They exchanged a manly hug but then Jose grabbed Niall's head and smacked kisses on both his cheeks. "Mano, you saved my bacon. Luisa was at her wits end coping with the kids on her own. How did you get President Foldane to give me immunity? Thought I was done for when the Feds arrived at the lodge."

"Persuaded him you helped save humanity."

"Perhaps you could convince Luisa, too."

Escaping Jose's clutches, Niall greeted Luisa with a warm hug. "I'm sorry I kept dragging him away from you. I couldn't have entrusted my family's safety to anyone else."

Luisa chucked his cheek and then gestured around them. "You are forgiven. This job for Jose could not come at a better time. The children will get an education we could never afford. How did you manage it?"

"Jose managed it. This island employs top-notch security and the Feds told the president that Jose ran the best witness protection they'd ever seen." He didn't say Foldane had told Patrick Morgan. Or that

Niall had refused to give his family's location up unless Jose remained part of their security team.

"Well, I am very happy," Luisa said. "Our bungalow is *soo* big! Every child has their own room!"

Niall's throat closed. He had jeopardized Luisa's security selfishly protecting his family. "You deserve it," he managed to say.

Tami threw Niall a perceptive look then put an arm around Luisa's waist and guided her towards the veranda. "Let's get that baby out of the sun and get you all a cold drink. Niall's parents are joining us. And Macha. She's alien! You'll love her."

As kids disappeared in every direction—Jose hollering at the older ones to watch the younger children—Niall took the opportunity to gaze around him.

"Quite the paradise you found," Jose said, but his sharp eyes spoke another story. "Why do I get the feeling you're not digging the vibe?"

Niall exhaled then pointed at a dark cloud gathering on the horizon. "There's a storm brewing, Jose. Alien. Deadly. And it's coming for me."

"What can I say? Poke a *culebro*, snake bites back. I warned you not to play on Capitol Hill."

Jacqueline gravitated to a bookcase stuffed with documents and archaeological reports. She moved quietly, half-convinced someone would discover her in the Vercingetorix Library and throw her out.

The shelf index referenced the Tiahuanaco civilization and she gestured Sohan over.

The Asterean pursed his lips in concentration as he scanned the collection of historical information. Picking out a journal, Sohan flicked through its pages. "The High Brighid," he glanced at her, "your aunt, questioned the reasons behind the fall of this particular civilization. I suspect she liked the idea of an ancient city remaining undisturbed for thousands of years beneath a lake, and it does make an ideal hiding place." Putting the book back, he plucked out a folder of papers and started reading where he stood.

Jacqueline took her selection of reading material to a table and sat down. An old grandfather clock chimed the hour, reminding her of the one in her uncle's house in Washington, DC. Looking around, she could see her aunt's hand in the decor of the Vercingetorix Library.

"Jacqueline, look." Sohan sat opposite her and placed an historic parchment on the table between them.

She pointed at the circle notation drawn at the top. "You think this is a reference to an orb?"

"Read."

Jacqueline skimmed the handwritten report of a Spanish diving expedition describing a collection of ancient ruins buried in sediment. "I researched Lake Titicaca before." An addendum written in her aunt's hand listed several papers. Jacqueline tapped an entry with her fingernail. "Another crackpot theory claiming prehistoric sea fossils have been discovered in the sediment. Just not true, but Tante Nicole could not have known that when she wrote this."

"We chose Titicaca because the carvings on stone artifacts there are reminiscent of the Paladin culture. Paladin was one of our oldest sky cities."

"I remember." Jacqueline read the inventory of treasure and stopped at an intricate sketch of the carved inner lining of a wooden chest. "This pattern is very similar to my aunt's orb." She looked up in astonishment. "It says the curved wood lining has a diameter of ten point three centimeters."

"According to their report, the Spaniards broke into an empty box they found buried four feet deep in sediment."

"We know the lake's level has varied considerably over the last twenty-five thousand years. So the orb must have been removed before that area flooded. I need to research when that might have happened."

Sohan's eyes took on a speculative slant. "The orb could be missing because Niall'Kearey went back to retrieve it."

Jacqueline splayed her fingers on the table and pushed back, a little freaked out by the idea. "Okay, say that's true, where is the orb right now?"

"In effect it sits outside the timeline, ceasing to exist in this dimension. It exists in a different timeline in what you refer to as the q-dimension. Call it the q-timeline. The q-dimension exists by its own rules. Its timeline barely moves, at least relative to the thousands of years passing here." Jacqueline widened her eyes and Sohan gave her a wry smile. "A simplistic explanation, but one I understand."

She chuckled. "General Towden will hate it."

A shimmering pinpoint of light caught her eye. It bloomed into a portal six-foot high and they both jumped to their feet. A tall man she recognized stepped through and she backed up, bumping her calf on her chair. *Merde*, Patrick Morgan looked like he'd been in a boxing ring. Major Kearey followed after him.

"A warning would have been nice," Jacqueline said as the portal winked out behind them.

Kearey smiled an apology, looking tanned in a dark, casual suit and white shirt. "I was aiming for the chateau grounds, but locked on your aura instead."

Goose bumps chilled her skin.

Morgan stepped forward. "A pleasure to meet you again, Dr. Biron. You were a child the last time I saw you."

Heart thumping, Jacqueline shook his outstretched hand. With his facial features showing the effects of a beating, Patrick Morgan looked every bit as terrifying as she remembered him to be.

"I dined with your uncle last night," he said.

Jacqueline opened her mouth to reply, but the stern set to Morgan's eyes scrambled her brains. This man could destroy her career—her whole life—with a single word.

"I smoothed things over for you, Jacqueline. May I call you Jacqueline?" He didn't wait for a reply. "Good. A friendly word of advice, my dear." His gaze nailed her to the wall. Her heart hammered hard in her chest. "Don't fuck with us again."

A fist shot across her vision and smashed Morgan's face aside.

The blanket of intimidation lifted and Morgan crashed to the floor. The huge man sat stunned for a moment then gingerly felt his jaw.

Kearey stared down on one of the most powerful men in the world. "Reality check, Morgan. If it weren't for Dr. Biron here, your tin-pot empire wouldn't exist at all."

Morgan climbed to his feet and returned Kearey's glower with a furious glare of his own. "That's the last one you get away with, Major. You need our protection. Dr. Biron needs our forgiveness. And the Astereans need our influence to keep their hosts from succumbing to paranoia. Here's a reality check of your own. We're on the same side, and if I didn't believe that," he gestured to the library surrounding them, "you wouldn't get within a hundred miles of this place."

Jacqueline struggled to draw breath, this time for fear Major Kearey's deep seated loathing for the Vercingetorix wouldn't know when to stop. There were few men her Uncle Charles respected and Patrick Morgan had always been one of them, an uneasy regard founded on an ancestral alliance that had lasted centuries.

Patrick Morgan took this Balor threat very seriously to allow them access to this Vercingetorix vault of knowledge.

Kearey looked ready to eviscerate the man.

# CHAPTER THIRTEEN

Niall scrubbed at his hair, the idyllic days spent with his family a fading memory. Pacing the corridor waiting for admittance to some pompous Orb sub-committee with an agitated Jacqueline did nothing to calm him down. This whole chateau was protected, the outer walls probably stuffed with ferrite insulation, but the Vercingetorix opened their doors to their secret sanctum like he'd joined them in some devilish truce. His nostrils curled with disgust as he remembered Morgan's words.

He had.

Jacqueline plonked herself down on a cushioned bench. "It was a stupid thing to do," she said.

"Stop worrying. He deserved it."

"I can defend myself."

"I couldn't resist. He's a bully. Gets what he wants, anyway he can, at any cost, and then manipulates people regardless."

"Well, unless you're about to blast the Council into the q-dimension in a bid for world domination, you need to work with the likes of Patrick Morgan."

He looked at her long and hard. How much better would the world be without the menace of shadow governments like the Vercingetorix? Damn tempting.

"The Vercingetorix has resources and influence you're going to need," she continued.

"I know the score, Jacqueline. But men like Morgan understand power, force and fear. He must respect me, respect the power I hold. He put my family through hell and he needs to know I haven't forgotten."

Her glance was sharp, inquisitive, the cogs of realization turning. "You *know* that? Morgan did that?"

"Yes."

Her brow creased. "I see."

Before she could say any more, the door to the Council Room opened and the subject of their conversation stepped out. Patrick Morgan looked to be in shock, distracted.

"There's been a development." His voice came out gruff. "The meeting has been postponed, but there's someone you need to meet, Major Kearey." He stood aside and gestured Niall to go through before turning to Jacqueline. "Dr. Biron, I apologize, but I think you should return to the library."

Niall frowned, but a weariness in Morgan's demeanor persuaded him no threat or disrespect was intended. He nodded to Jacqueline. "Go. Make sure Sohan's behaving himself. I'll fill you in later."

Her eyes reflected her unease, but she inclined her head and left in the direction of the basement elevator. Niall waited until she had passed the chateau's sweeping oak stairs with its gargoyle newel posts. "Problem?" he asked Morgan.

A flickering anger shot through Morgan's aura. "I'm not sure. Follow me."

Niall's subconscious mind surged through the open door, sensing the layout, assessing potential threats. He found an attractive-looking woman wearing a cream designer dress standing by a grouping of cream-colored sofas in a large ballroom.

Niall followed Morgan in, their footsteps resounding on the wooden floor. An intricately painted ceiling depicted a variety of celestial bodies. Light pouring through a large arched window picked out a touch of silver in the woman's brunette hair. She walked towards him, a soft smile giving her a natural charm, but Niall read nervousness in her aura, mixed with a steely resolve.

Morgan grunted. "Major Kearey, allow me to introduce you to my wife, Etlinn Morgan. Etlinn has been your advocate on the Vercingetorix Council. Turns out there's a reason why."

"Hello, Niall," she greeted him.

The use of his first name confused him. "Have we met before?" he asked. Close up, caught by the mesmerizing quality of her grey-green eyes, he sensed a portent of something momentous awaiting him.

"Yes, but you were far too young to remember." Her eyes softened. "I'm your mother, Niall, your birth mother, and I have waited for this moment for a very long time."

Her revelation slugged him straight in the stomach. His raging emotions made it hard to think. Shock robbed him of speech long enough for one overriding concern to bury all other considerations.

His throat closed and he had to force the words out. "Tell me that Morgan isn't my father."

She blanched. "No, dear God, Patrick isn't your father. It's... it's more complicated than that."

"Complicated?" Morgan snapped, blood suffusing his face. "Sweet Mother of God, Etlinn!" The pain in his voice was raw. New.

"You didn't know?" Niall asked Morgan.

"No."

Etlinn turned to her husband. "I wanted to tell you, Patrick, but I made a pact... with your father."

Morgan flinched and the drumbeat in Niall's ears got louder. Faster. This life-defining revelation didn't affect only him—Etlinn and Patrick were stumbling in the rubble of a matrimonial bomb blast.

"What's it got to do with his father?" Niall demanded. "Do you even *know* who my father is? Hell! Give me one good reason why I should believe a single word you say."

Etlinn stared at him with appalled eyes then appealed to her husband. "I think I need to sit down."

Morgan grabbed a chair and gently pressed his wife into the seat. "We need a drink," he muttered, moving to a side table holding a decanter of golden liquid. He poured out three generous glasses and downed his in one gulp before bringing Kearey and Etlinn a glass each.

Niall didn't consider refusing. He inhaled the honeyed aroma and knocked back the whiskey in similar fashion. Etlinn sipped hers, grimaced and handed her glass to Morgan, who was clearly expecting its return.

"I'm sorry to spring this on you, both of you," she began, "but I've kept my secret for over thirty-five years. There's no pleasant way to break this news, so I will say it plainly. Your father is Kean Morgan, Patrick's father."

Niall reeled back, glad for the whiskey warming his gut.

Morgan waved his glass at Niall. "Yeah, got a good idea what you're going through. I gained a brother and stepson in the space of seconds. Your children are my blood-line—pretty much guarantees their safety. The Morgan line continues. You'd think the fecking bastard planned it this way."

Etlinn flashed him a furious look and Morgan shut up, but his words careened around in Niall's mind. Brother. Stepson? The whiskey burn curdled. He remembered Sheila telling him how young his mother was.

"How old were you?" he asked.

Shame leaked from every pore of her aura. "Barely seventeen," she whispered. She took a deep breath. "Kean raped me. He swore he would ruin my family if I said a word. Kean practically owned my father. He owned the world with holdings in every major bank. He was impossible to fight. I hated him. Then I discovered he'd made me pregnant."

"Christ," Niall whispered. Murderous bile washed up his throat. Morgan handed him another whiskey. Niall slugged it down and slammed the empty glass on a nearby table. Miraculously, the crystal held intact.

"I hid my pregnancy," Etlinn continued. "Kean helped without even realizing it. He sent my parents abroad on business. The bastard effectively isolated me in a vast house with a housekeeper who didn't care what I did. I gave birth to you in my bathroom, alone."

Morgan growled and flung his glass at the nearest wall. Shards of crystal scattered everywhere. "Stupid! You could have died!"

Etlinn glared at her husband. "I was having a child out of wedlock! You know what Ireland was like in those days. I was young and very scared."

Niall stared at the defiant woman, horrified at the risk she had taken, stunned by her fortitude. "How did you find my parents?" His voice choked. "Tony and Sheila. Why them?"

Her eyes glistened. An anguished flood of remembered pain bombed his mind's shields head on. Morgan must have felt it too, because he moaned. Niall thought the man would go to his wife, but then he turned away.

Etlinn tracked his retreat with an expression of indescribable sorrow. She turned to face Niall. "I wanted you well away from Kean Morgan, so I resolved to find you a family." Her shoulders lifted in an expressive shrug. "The Vercingetorix has always been at the forefront of I.T. Well, long before intranets were even discussed, my father had the best that DruSensi could offer including remote access to a main server holding the Vercingetorix core database of genealogy."

"What, you hacked into your father's computer? You were a kid!"

Morgan straightened, his movements stiff. "The best hackers start young, but as it happens, Etlinn showed a natural aptitude for genetic engineering from an early age. She carried out basic research for her father over the holidays. She didn't have to hack into anything."

Etlinn nodded. "I expanded my research parameters to include uncoded families with fertility problems and found Sheila. A good friend did some investigating for me, found out that Sheila was a nurse, that she and Tony were good people, and desperate to adopt. You arrived early. No one was home. I thought to take you to a hospital, but I couldn't be sure what would happen to you. I was learning to drive, so I wrapped you in a towel, put you in my father's car and drove to their town."

"Sheila was wonderful, after the initial shock. Of course, she wanted to take me to the hospital, but I said I'd get sent to the mother and baby home. Sheila knew exactly what would happen there. I told them I lived locally and heard they were hoping to adopt a baby. I begged them to help me. She took charge, examined you first, then me. Helped me feed you. I knew she'd make a wonderful mother. Then you grabbed Tony's finger and wouldn't let go. I think his mind was made up from that moment. I could tell they wanted you. She had baby clothes in a cupboard; that made me cry. We talked for a long time. She wanted me to be sure. She's a genuinely good person. A rare thing in this world."

A lump clogged Niall's throat. "You made a good choice." He refused to think about Tony's alcoholism, his moods that eventually drove Niall to enlist. Sheila and Tony hadn't been perfect parents; terrified when his telepathic powers opened up worlds he and they couldn't possibly understand. The young girl who gave him up never took account of the needs of a child with psychic powers.

"So what now?" he demanded, his voice harsher than he'd intended. "The Vercingetorix claim me as a coded member? We play happy families? Not gonna happen. I'm here to fulfill the terms we agreed. Why tell me now? After all this time?"

"Kean's dead," Etlinn said.

"So what? He's dead. He raped a kid. My father raped a kid and watched her marry his son. *Fuck!*"

Morgan kicked a chair. "My father wasn't always like that. He became ill. Disturbed."

Niall recoiled. "What? You're excusing him? He raped your wife! Made her pregnant at seventeen!"

"That wasn't the man I knew. Not then." His head shook with denial as he turned on Etlinn. "What made him do such a thing? Did you lead him on?"

Etlinn leapt to her feet. "Damn you, Patrick! Think about what you're saying. Kean's older than my father! But you're right about him being ill. He was *sick*, depraved, and the Council came to realize it."

Morgan's face paled. "Shit, Etlinn, I'm sorry. But he wasn't always like that. I..." He swallowed. "I'm not helping. Finish your story. We'll talk later." Turning, he stalked out, not sparing Niall a glance.

Silence fell, loud and awkward. Etlinn stood looking after her husband, flinching as the door slammed shut.

Niall's brain slowly began to make connections. "You helped him steal my family."

She uttered a sound of disgust. "No. Toby and Lizzie are my grandchildren. I could never harm them. I learned what had happened with the rest of the Council. None of us believed what we were hearing. Discovering the extent of your powers, discovering that your children were on an alien planet—each new revelation stunned us all. You need to understand that you frighten the Council. The extent of your powers makes no sense to us, even with the knowledge of your parentage."

"I thought being the product of two coded families would explain everything." Distaste threaded his tone and Etlinn winced.

"I've been researching your ancestry ever since the earthquake at Sedona. There's nothing in my line or Kean Morgan's to explain such a wide span of powers. You integrate kinesis and telepathy in a way beyond anything recorded over ten thousand years. I've been analyzing the Asterean's DNA since their arrival, and the initial results from my tests of Macha's blood sample confirm the Morrigan are also integral to our human genome. You have strong markers from both races, as do all coded members of the Vercingetorix." She hesitated.

"What?" he demanded.

"Despite this evidence, not every member of the Council is happy about the decisions you made. They think you assumed too much autonomy. Very few people know what you did. It might be better for you if it stayed that way."

Niall's jaw tightened, unsure what she was saying. "The Astereans can't stay hidden forever."

"Patrick has been arguing for a motion to release them into society, but this business with Herecura hasn't helped your cause."

"That woman did something to me."

Etlinn nodded. "I'm analyzing samples of her blood taken during Hideout. Maybe her DNA will reveal something." She bit her lip with a grimace and Niall tensed, waiting for the next hammer blow. "There's something more you need to know, about your father. Patrick is correct when he said his father changed. I think it might be something caused by an unstable chromosome attached to his DNA... a chromosome I found in your blood samples."

A chill ran down Niall's spine, a sixth sense warning that whatever Etlinn had discovered, it was important.

"Sometimes these things are better left unknown," she said softly, "but not in your case."

"You're worried I'll go the same way as Kean Morgan?" Revulsion built inside him, the very suggestion vile and repugnant, a new fear he wasn't prepared to handle. "No, I'm not him. I am not my father."

She put out a hand. "It is not my intention to distress you. I'm going to work out the function of this chromosome and make sure whatever ailed Kean Morgan doesn't happen to you."

The door burst open making them jump. Patrick Morgan stood on the threshold, his face red with fury. "Maximus fecking Klotz!"

Niall frowned. "What about him?"

"The fecking idjit just blew the whistle on Operation Hideout is what. Now 'Aliens in Secret Locations' is breaking news worldwide!"

Niall's cell phone vibrated in his pocket. He took it out and checked the message. Max.

<I didn't do it. Suits here. Please help>

The words gripped Niall by the throat and didn't let go. A map gave his location as Washington, DC. Niall hesitated. Max had deceived him before. He should check with General Towden for orders. He might not like those orders. Max's message glowed bright and desperate.

<I didn't do it.>

Niall looked at Etlinn. Member of the Vercingetorix Council. His mother. Her face clouded with questions and concern as he searched her eyes, but Max's plea created a vortex of urgency he couldn't ignore.

He made his decision. "I gotta go."

# CHAPTER FOURTEEN

Niall scanned the desolate alley on the other side of his portal and stepped through. He verified his GPS position on his phone, his breath fogging the chill air. Max's apartment was farther than he'd hoped. Max didn't project a very distinctive aura or Niall might have locked onto him. Instead, he set off down the alley at a run, narrowly avoiding some cardboard boxes, and a vagrant's foot poking out that he didn't see until he was on top of it.

He burst onto the street and shifted gear into a full sprint. He didn't have long before DruSensi's satellite tracked him and alerted General Towden to his change of location. This part of Washington was quiet, well clear of the early morning commute to work. He detected huddled groups squatting behind boarded up windows, but nothing specific caught his attention. Why Max chose to live surrounded by abandoned rental slums Niall couldn't imagine.

Sweat slid down between his shoulder blades as he slowed to a jog near Max's block. He cast out his mind, surfing for anything out of place, like the black suits climbing into a black 4x4 that pulled away before all the doors were shut. A nasty inkling that he might be too late accelerated him back to a sprint. He dodged a startled couple by a whisker and jumped their dog setting off a furious barking behind him.

His cell phone went off. He whipped it out and glanced at the caller id. Towden.

"Shit."

He stopped at the end of a street in time to avoid being knocked down by the same 4x4 and mentally noted the license plate. He jogged down the street, checking the names of every building as he answered his phone. "Yes sir."

"Report your location, Major."

"Outside 215b Rainer Apartments, General." He prayed his superior didn't command him to stand down.

"Stand by." *Good enough.*

"Sir."

Niall pressed every button on the entry panel until the door buzzed open. He rushed up the stairs to the second floor, reached door 15b, raised his right foot and kicked the door clean off its hinges.

Max Klotz jerked at the end of a noose. Strung up from the top of a closet, his twitching body hit the wooden door with dull thuds, hairy toes dancing a foot above the carpet. A dark-colored patch stained the crotch of his pants. Beady eyes bulged in panic and his fat fingers grappled for purchase on the rope noose embedded in the folds of his neck.

Niall grabbed a toppled chair and shoved it under Max's feet so the man could take his own weight. "Gotta get you fit, Max."

He got out the knife strapped to the back of his calf and sliced through the rope above Max's head, catching the asphyxiated man as Max fell forward. They collapsed on the floor in a disorderly heap. Niall fought to undo the noose. Max's thick beard tickled the back of his hand. His cell phone vibrated. Shit. Towden. He levered the knot loose. *Come on!* He managed to introduce some wriggle room and Max dragged in a gargled breath.

He patted Niall on the arm and mouthed, "Deal," on the end of a wheeze.

Niall got some decent slack into the rope then pulled his foot out from under Max's legs, all the while trying to support Max's head. "I want you to lie still, Max."

Max stared at the ceiling, his acquiescence as unnerving as his rattling breath. Niall pulled out his phone which had gone silent. He pressed call back. "General?" and climbed to his feet.

"Where the hell have you been?" Towden demanded as Niall rapidly checked the rest of the apartment.

"NSA types strung Dr. Klotz up by his neck." He glanced out the window from behind a curtain. The roofline and the windows overlooking the building looked clear.

There was a brief pause. "And?"

"I reached him in time and the situation's under control. He needs medical treatment." He wondered at the NSA walking away before the job was done, if it was the NSA. This job didn't fit their usual MO. "I assume you want this kept low key."

"You assume right. President Foldane ordered Dr. Klotz's arrest for treason. An FBI team is en route to take him into custody. I'm on a private line with the Director now."

"Can't see anyone, sir, but someone beat them here." He gave a quick description of the 4x4 and license plate.

Max wriggled his fingers. Niall cast another look out of the window. "Putting you on speaker, General." He moved back to crouch behind Max's head, placing his phone on the floor beside him. Klotz stared up at him, his breathing shallow and hissing. Vivid rope marks adorned his neck.

"Help's on the way, Max. Try to relax." *Shit.* He didn't want to intubate. He had a knife, and there was a collection of ball point pens on a desk. "Just tell me one thing. Without moving your head. Did you talk to anyone about the Astereans?"

Max raised a finger in the general direction of his desk. Satisfied Max's breathing had calmed, Niall got up and discovered a suicide letter. He scanned the note without touching it.

"What did he say?" Towden asked.

"Stand by, General, sending you a picture." Niall grabbed his phone, snapped a picture of the letter then sent it to the general.

"Did you write the letter?" he asked Max.

Max mouthed no, raised a finger and pointed it to his temple.

"Max is indicating he was coerced, sir."

"FBI report they are entering the building. EMTs on site," Towden informed him. "Hand over to Special Agent Fricklan, he should arrive in the next minute, and then report to the Pentagon. The FBI will provide an escort."

"Sir."

Towden's call terminated at the same time two agents appeared in the doorway, their weapons drawn. "Place is clear," Niall said. One of the agents checked the apartment anyway. The other studied Niall and then checked his phone. Putting it away, he stepped over.

"Major Kearey, I'm Special Agent Fricklan."

Two EMTs appeared and Fricklan beckoned them in. Niall gave them a quick medical update then stepped back. He looked at his watch as the medics put an oxygen mask over Max's face and checked his blood pressure.

Ten minutes ago, he'd been across the Atlantic, immersed in his own personal crisis in a chateau in the Dordogne region of France. But for his intervention, Dr. Maximus Klotz would be dead. A conspiracy had leaked the presence of aliens on Earth to the press setting Max up as their cover, except he didn't believe the Vercingetorix were responsible.

Not this time.

Senator Charles Biron leaned back in a faded, brown leather chair and studied the cold, grey eyes returning his gaze from the silver screen propped up on Charles' desk.

"Je t'avais prévenu, Emile ! Kearey's a law unto himself." Charles lapsed back into French, his first and preferred language. "You need to clear up your mess. The FBI doesn't care for foreign agencies assassinating US citizens on its own turf."

"This is not necessary. Use your considerable influence."

Emile Fitzroy behaved like he held the upper hand, an arrogance that had settled on him since his appointment to the European Commission. Charles preferred Emile when the man had been Minister of Foreign Affairs. Certainly, more useful. He shielded his annoyance—he needed Emile's cooperation.

"I got the investigation into the Kearey kidnapping and related car bombs closed down. I can't get involved in this as well. Inform your people that Kearey got visuals and the car plate. It's time to disappear."

"What about Klotz? Major Kearey applied for clearance to tell the man all about the Vercingetorix. Next Klotz is leaking stories about aliens. He needs to be silenced."

"I'm working on that. We have another problem." Charles glowered at his wife's portrait sitting on the floor while he decided how to trash it. Nicole, his devoted, brilliant wife, struck down in her prime by some mysterious disease, had shown him up as the biggest fool of all. He reached for his cognac, something sweet to drown the bitter taste in his mouth. Uathach, High Brighid of Astereal, had used him to gain access to the Vercingetorix. A woman with extraordinary gifts, an anomaly that centuries of Vercingetorix records could not explain.

She'd been his inspiration to find others like her.

He'd found Niall Kearey.

Son of Kean Morgan and Etlinn Cavanagh. The Morgan lineage survived. Interesting.

"Kearey has too much influence with the Morgans," Charles said. "Patrick is lobbying the Council to accelerate the Astereans' integration. When did you last speak with your Russian contact?"

"A week ago. Why?"

"Russia upgraded their satellites to detect energy portals. They picked up Kearey's return to the Amazon and realized DruSensi had not. President Nobokov demanded an explanation and Foldane was forced to provide a full briefing. Now Nobokov is withholding authorization on a portal mission to recover operatives trapped in Afghanistan. He wants a guarantee of equal access to Kearey's abilities and we can't agree to that."

Fitzroy harrumphed, jowls quivering. "Don't pretend the US military hasn't used Kearey in a black ops capacity by now."

"I'm not pretending anything, but now we know Russia can independently monitor portal activity. Just let your Russian contact know that Kearey's recent bridge to Washington, DC was unauthorized.

Nobokov is bound to increase pressure on Foldane to control Kearey, and I happen to know DruSensi has a solution that will satisfy all the Hideout countries."

"I'll call my contact now. I'll be in touch." Emile's hand reached out and the screen went dark.

Charles raised his glass towards his late wife. "Made a big mistake there, Nicole. Can't protect your precious Kearey if you're dead." Looking into her intelligent eyes, Biron considered all the angles. He was missing a contingency plan. He didn't trust Colonel Hastor anymore. Or Patrick Morgan...

Picking up the phone, he called his aide. "I need the personnel files of all the candidates General Towden is considering for the Special Ops attachment to GBI. Yes, one hour. I'll be at the house." He terminated the call then redialed. "I have another job for you... Yes. Get me a report on Kean Morgan's will. I'm particularly interested in any legal provision for illegitimate children."

# CHAPTER FIFTEEN

Niall stepped back, but the officer leaving General Towden's office paused then stood to attention despite Niall being out of uniform.

"Major," the younger man said.

"Captain."

Pale blue eyes briefly met Niall's, eager and curious, but then General Towden waved Niall into his Pentagon office. Nodding politely, Niall went in.

Towden's eyes were glued to a wall screen. Niall glanced over, saw his own image taking up half the screen, and froze.

Towden looked across to him, his mouth set in a thin line, his bushy eyebrows meeting in a ferocious frown. "You made the news."

Niall racked his brains trying to think how. "No one saw me, certainly not long enough to ID me."

"This isn't about Klotz, not directly. This is about you smuggling aliens into facilities across the world. President Foldane is buried in calls from member countries of Operation Hideout."

Niall swallowed the nasty taste in his mouth. A whooshing sound filled his ears. Sparkly dots danced at the edge of his vision. It didn't matter that Astereal was dying and lifeless. It shone like a beacon in his mind's eye; a bolt hole as the judgment of the world weighed upon him. He'd always known a day like this would come, but the magnitude of the reality made his knees weak and threatened to upturn his stomach.

"Can't we shut it down?" he asked. A croak filled his voice.

Towden clicked through several news channels: CNN, CBS, Fox News, BBC World, Reuters. Niall's face flashed on all of them, the story world-wide breaking news. His family was tucked away on a remote island few people knew existed. Would it be enough to keep them safe now? The twisting knots of truth tightened until Niall could hardly breathe.

Towden upped the volume.

On screen, the anchorman was milking his moment of glory for all it was worth. "So, Carol, GBI stands for Geophysical Bio Intelligence. Leaked reports suggest this agency provides cover for an operation called Hideout involving an invasion of aliens. Has anyone seen these purported aliens?"

His co-anchor tittered. Apparently, the idea of aliens was a little far-fetched to be taken seriously.

"No mention of the Vercingetorix," Towden grumbled. "Slippery buggers. Can't even get hold of the president because he's consulting with that Irish bastard."

"Morgan?"

"Know any other?" Towden scratched his head. "I always thought America pulled Europe's strings."

Niall opened his mouth to reject the idea but then closed it again. A new reality hung uncomfortably between them.

"Bet they hate that we have you," the general added. He looked rattled, kept glancing at the phone.

Niall didn't remind the general that he was Irish born. Now with Vercingetorix parents. *Damn. I'm supposed to be done with secrets.* "General, there's—"

A loud buzz diverted Towden's attention. Towden muted the TV and snatched up the phone.

"Towden, here... yes, sir. He's with me now." The general frowned. He accessed his laptop while muttering a series of "yes sirs."

Niall kept one eye on Towden, the other on the text flowing across the CNN screen. The anchor was looking increasingly animated. The reason seemed to be a UN press announcement scheduled for later that day.

*Niall'Kearey?*

*Miach, go ahead.*

*I'm with Tami. She's watching the news. She's very upset.*

Miach's thought colored Niall's mind with disapproval. Niall turned his head away from Towden's penetrating gaze and pretended to read the breaking news text bar while tension mangled his insides.

*Tell her I'm safe.*

*She knows that. I have reassured her. You should be with your family.*

*Shit, Miach. This job isn't nine-to-five. I just had a week off.*

*No, but you are so much more than a simple man who made an oath to God and country. Assert your authority. Now is the time for the world to learn respect for Niall'Kearey.*

*And that's exactly the kind of thinking that will alienate me from my own kind. My powers never scared your people. On Earth I need to prove I'm still human.*

*You have nothing to prove and humanity is descended from us. We are your kind.*

Niall rubbed at his eyebrow. Towden was looking at him strangely. Damn it. It would be so easy to build a portal. He could be with Tami within seconds. Hold her in his arms. Hide from the world.

Except the world wouldn't hide from him, Vercingetorix would surround them, and there was nowhere else they could go. Even the Amazon was compromised.

*She needs you, Niall'Kearey.*

A twinge of impatience caught Niall. *Tell Tami I'll be there as soon as I can. Tell her I love her.*

*She needs to hear this from you.*

"Major!"

Niall snapped to attention. The general was glaring at him, his hand covering the mouthpiece of the phone he was holding out to him. "The president wants to speak to you."

"Yes, of course." Niall stepped up and took the phone. "Mr. President?"

Foldane's voice boomed in his ear. "I have a job that requires your talents, and then I think it would be best if you were unavailable for a few days. You can resume your visit with the Vercingetorix. Let the press furor die down."

Niall raised an eyebrow. It would take more than a few days.

"I just got off the phone with Patrick Morgan," the president continued. "I understand there are some family matters that need to be resolved. DNA samples to be taken. We need to understand this Herecura issue, but I've insisted any medical procedures will be carried out by us. You can take the samples with you."

More medical tests.

"Sir. What about the Astereans? I'm their liaison."

"Then I suggest you make good use of your time in France."

Damn. "Yes, sir." A door slammed shut in his head, Miach cutting off their link. "Sir, permission to visit my family first. This news leak has come as a shock to my wife and—"

"I'm sorry, Major. This other job is a matter of life and death and vital to national security. General Towden will explain. One last thing. No more unauthorized trips. You will report to Colonel Hastor. Do I make myself clear?"

Niall's mouth went dry. Foldane was punishing him. "Sir, Dr. Klotz's situation was—"

"Enough. When you unilaterally took matters into your own hands you didn't know Dr. Klotz's situation, did you? Now, if you'll excuse me, *Major*," his voice cut into Niall with undisguised sarcasm, "I have damage control to do. I'll consult with you on the Asterean situation when you get back." The president hung up.

The door opened to reveal Sam Hastor dressed in civvies. "Colonel Hastor reporting—"

"Yes, yes, I know who you are," Towden snapped. He turned his laptop around.

Niall studied the image. GPS coordinates put it in Afghanistan. Sam stepped up to get a closer look. Towden tapped a dark shadow. "Can you remote-view this outbuilding? We have two friendlies inside that need an urgent evac."

Niall threw the general a sharp look then let instinct guide him. His mind explored several links before he found one close enough to remote-view the region. As he zoomed in on the building, he pointed out the positions of several Taliban snipers, although none seemed overly interested in his target.

"No one's getting near that building without being spotted," Sam commented.

"Right now, they're focused on a downed Black Hawk," Niall said, pointing at a mountainous area one quarter mile west.

"Special Tactics can focus on retrieving their rescue team," Towden said. "They have a bird holding position waiting for a go. We'll coordinate timings to divert enemy attention away from a direct rescue of the operatives."

Passing through crumbling stone walls ridden with bullet holes, Niall rapidly assessed the condition of the dark-skinned men inside, both dressed in Afghan clothing. One had a wad of material stuffed under a blood-stained shirt. The hand holding his weapon shook dangerously.

"Chest wound. Short breaths. Suspected hemopneumothorax. Armed."

The second man was limping across to a window. Blood matted his hair. More blood trailed down his arm to his fingertips before dripping to the floor. The man swayed and fell against the wall. His eyes looked glazed. Adrenalin fueled Niall's focus. The Taliban were playing a waiting game. No point getting shot when your targets were bound to bleed out. "The other has a head wound, possible leg fracture, and a gunshot wound to one arm. He's in a bad way." He wanted to go now. This was the work he'd trained for and those men didn't have long.

"Can you get Colonel Hastor in without drawing enemy fire?" Towden asked.

Sam? Alarm sharpened Niall's voice. "Yes, sir, but that chest wound needs stabilizing before he's moved. He needs a stretcher."

"Got that in hand," Sam advised.

Niall's aggravation increased. Sam had clearly been briefed already, always one step ahead of the game. "This isn't a one-man job. You want me to just open a portal?"

Towden nodded. "Can't risk you in the field, Major."

Agitation weakened Niall's link. Shit. He searched for a return link back. "I can get Colonel Hastor in, and I can see a link to Groom Lake, but I need be there to create the bridge back, just like I needed a host on Astereal to create a bridge to Earth, sir. General, Colonel Hastor hasn't the medical training. I'm the best chance these men have."

There was a knock on the door. "Colonel, your requisitions are here," the general's aide reported.

Towden narrowed his eyes.

Did the general doubt his word?

"Very well, Major. In and out. No heroics. Do not get involved with the other rescue mission. Understood?"

"Sir."

"I'll have a medical team standing by at GBI," Towden said.

Sam straightened. "Okay, we gear up and head out."

Niall pushed aside his irritation and focused on the two men. "Yeah, but they're gonna think they're under attack. Can we warn them we're coming?"

Towden picked up his phone. "Torkham Base can warn them. Get ready. You have a go the moment I confirm contact and the diversion's in place."

Niall watched Sam step through the portal, chafing at the delay.

On the other side, Sam was shouting, "Friendlies! United States Air Force! Do not fire!"

The wounded operative still on his feet blinked in confusion. As the muzzle of his weapon drifted downwards, the man followed it.

Sam grabbed the weapon then disarmed the second man. "Target clear."

Niall stepped through and remote-viewed the surrounding area. The second rescue helicopter was taking heavy fire. Niall contained his frustration. In and out. "Perimeter clear."

He headed for the agent leaning against a wall, his breath short. The man had a faint aura, angry and reserved. Up close, Niall recognized the face under the beard. CIA. The man's eyes sharpened with recognition.

"Okay, let's see what we have." Niall snapped on sterile gloves then peered in behind the blood-soaked T-shirt. The bullet hole bubbled and the lower chest yielded to Niall's fingers.

"How's your one doing?" he asked Sam without looking back.

"I think a bullet clipped his head, but didn't penetrate. Gunshot wound to the upper arm. Dressings secured."

"Check his leg for any strange protrusions," Niall ordered as he massaged the wound area on his man to release any trapped air, but to no avail.

"Nothing," Sam replied after a few seconds. His man groaned. "Sorry, buddy."

Niall closed the wound with a dressing and took the man's pulse. Too rapid, and under the grime his lips and skin around the eyes were blue. Neck veins visible. He felt the man's throat. Shifted windpipe. He sensed Pwyll attempting to breach his mind as his patient's breathing reduced further.

*Not now.*

Niall whipped out antiseptic wipes and a decompression needle. He located the correct rib space with his fingers, placed the needle and pressed it in. Air hissed out. Taping a catheter in place, he watched his patient's breathing improve. Good enough. Niall applied padding to the wound. "Try to stay still."

He explored the q-dimension, recognized the link he needed to reach GBI and formed a bridge, keeping his glowing hand out of sight. His patient's eyes shifted to the shimmering portal devouring the back wall then back at Niall. Niall had to bend down to hear him.

"You my guardian angel now?"

Niall chuckled. "Nah, that's the latest black art from the farm." He glanced at Sam. "How you doing, Colonel?"

"Think this one's in shock," Sam said, gently slapping the man's cheek and getting no reaction. "Perimeter check."

Niall assembled the stretcher as his mind scanned the area. "All clear. Help me get this one on the litter then take yours through. I'll be right behind you."

Sam didn't argue, but then he never pulled rank when it came to command in the field. Niall had more training, and the experience.

Pulling the stretcher holding his patient, Niall stepped into the GBI event room reserved for his portals and was swamped by medics. Letting go of his bridge, he rattled off a handover, and had followed the medics into the hallway when Sam grabbed his arm. "Our job's done."

His lips thinning, Niall shook Sam off. "I should have been doing more of this all along," he hissed.

Sam glanced at a passing lab technician. She scurried past, a wary look on her face. He waited until she was out of earshot. "You know the other Hideout members don't like you using your powers." He grimaced and Niall braced for the unwelcome reminder. "We're expected back at the Pentagon for these DNA samples." Sam raised placating hands. "President Foldane updated me. I know Etlinn Morgan being your mother is heavy stuff, but it explains a lot and she is a genetics expert on coded bloodlines. She'll want to help you. Anyway, I thought you were intent on finding out what the orbs contain on this Balor?"

"I am." Niall fumed in silence, more annoyed because Sam was right. He also needed to know the Vercingetorix position on the Astereans now the news of aliens had gone public.

Pwyll nudged his mind.

*What is it, Pwyll?*

*I could not breach your shields when you and Colonel Hastor were rescuing those two men.*

*So?*

*On a mission you isolate your concerns. They do not distract you from the pressing priority.*

Niall took in a deep, calming breath. This he needed to know, and before he faced the Vercingetorix Council. He compared his thinking on an op with his turbulent emotions now. Out in the field, doing the job he was trained to do, he felt calm. Clear-headed. Focused. Distractions packaged up and put away for later. He could even tolerate Sam.

*Gotcha, Pwyll. Thanks.*

Pwyll's mind retreated.

Niall fixed Sam with a steady look. To hell with tolerance. "A few minutes delay so I can check on my patient won't hurt. So, unless you want a public demonstration of exactly what I can do, you'll meet me back here in fifteen, *Colonel.*"

# CHAPTER SIXTEEN

The needle entered Niall's vein with barely a scratch; the doctor's movements quick and sure. Red blood filled the vial. The beak-nosed, spectacled doctor was thorough and professional; nothing to justify the uneasiness that had Niall itching to scratch the back of his neck.

He forced himself to submit to these tests. When Herecura touched him, there had been a connection of some sort. He had a genetics specialist for a mother. The Vercingetorix had the most advanced DNA database and testing facility in the world, their prime tool for controlling the psychically coded families they called 'clans' in deference to their Celtic roots. There was no better place to find out what Herecura had done to him.

Colonel Sam Hastor leaned against the wall, arms folded, looking like he was trying to blend into his surroundings and failing miserably.

Suffocating.

"Go take a walk or something," Niall snapped. A buccal swab moved towards his face. He opened his mouth so the doctor could take scrapings from inside his cheeks.

"Don't tempt me," Sam replied, his mild tone in stark contrast to Niall's snarly frustration.

Niall winced as the man plucked several hairs out of his scalp.

"I'll need a sperm sample too," the doctor said, possibly the third sentence he'd uttered. "Just a couple of questions first."

"You're kidding me."

"No." The doctor glanced at Sam. "It might help if you weren't here."

"Yeah, 'cos we're close, but not that close." Niall laced his words with a heavy sarcasm even Sam couldn't ignore.

Sam unfolded his arms and straightened. "I'll be outside."

The doctor pushed his spectacles above the prominent ridge on his nose, but said nothing as he took several nail clippings.

"I'll also need a bone sample," he said conversationally.

"Biopsy?" Niall asked, feeling again that sense of unease.

"We take it from the pelvic bone, less intrusive than anywhere else." He studied his notes. "Your records indicate no allergy to anesthetic. Is that correct?"

"Yes."

The doctor finishing labeling his samples, asked Niall some personal questions, then handed over a sterile sample pot and indicated a door. It led to a small bathroom. Niall eyed the rouged, bare-breasted woman draped across a Suzuki adorning the top magazine and was hit by a pang of guilt. Once he got to France, he would ring Tami. The rest of the world could go on pause for a few minutes so he could check how his wife was coping with her husband's unwelcome fame.

Jacqueline read Max's email and frowned. Scrolling back up the screen, a horrid sick feeling grew inside her. She checked the recipients and groaned.

"Max, you idiot," she murmured. Throwing her head back, she studied the library's stone barreled ceiling and expelled her despair with a long sigh. Sam Hastor appeared at her shoulder making her jump.

"You found something?" he asked.

"When did you arrive?"

"A few minutes ago."

"The system let you in?"

"My DNA's on record here."

"Where's Major Kearey?"

"Security's escorting him to Etlinn's lab, he wanted to drop off some test samples in person. Then he wants to call Tami. I'm giving him some privacy before he bites my head off."

Jacqueline glanced down the room and found Sohan browsing the news channels on a TV inset into an oak-paneled wall section, far enough away that he wouldn't hear them. She flicked her laptop with a fingernail. "I think I know how the leak happened. Max emailed a research paper to DruSensi and copied it to ENCODE, the human genome research project."

"How do you know?"

"He copied me in. I just opened it. GBI's been collaborating with ENCODE for a while now and Max was firing off reports all over the place. I doubt he even realized." Poor Max. The mistake could cost him everything. She shuddered. It nearly cost him his life.

"So, it's possible someone there leaked the information to a whistle-blowing group," Sam said.

"The email attached a schedule of test appointments with Hideout facilities in each of the member countries." She scanned through the detail and grimaced. "Max mentions that Major Kearey is overseeing the security arrangements."

"Linking Niall to both GBI and Hideout. The disappearance of his family made the headlines last year. I'll report this to General Towden. Not sure it will help Dr. Klotz, but it explains why the Vercingetorix weren't mentioned. His clearance only extends to Hideout and the Astereans. What did his paper cover?"

"A geo-mapped comparison of EM-induced experience by cultural origin. The US settlement includes representatives from across Astereal. Max wants to establish the degree the Asterean's cultural origin and current location factors into their response to Earth's magnetic field. It's a good hypothesis; many of the cities were distinct and Astereal's magnetic grid varied dramatically more so than Earth's."

"It says 'Asterean'?"

Jacqueline ran a quick search on 'Astereal'. "No, 'alien'."

Her cell phone beeped and Jacqueline's heart leapt. Sean! She'd been expecting his call since the news of 'aliens' broke. Sean knew she worked for GBI. She unlocked the slide bar and winced to see her uncle's name. The text read, <Call me.>

"Dr. Biron? Colonel Hastor," Sohan called them.

Jacqueline paused with her thumb over the call icon. *What now?*

Sohan turned up the TV volume as she and Sam joined him. Jacqueline settled into a comfy sofa. On screen, reporters were clamoring for the best spot inside the UN building in front of a huge white screen. The CNN anchor was making it sound like Earth had been invaded when the news cut to the White House Press Room where President Foldane stood on the podium.

"He's early. I thought he was making a statement at the UN," Jacqueline said, glancing at Sam. He stood to one side, arms folded, his expression giving little away, but Jacqueline had known him since childhood and that jumping tic in his cheek told her something was troubling him.

She narrowed her eyes. Later.

On the TV screen, President Foldane smiled genially. "There are no aliens," he stated boldly. The press erupted with questions and the president waved his hand. The room fell silent. A tight band constricted Jacqueline's tummy. She felt adrift on an ocean—Foldane appeared so genuine. If she didn't know better... "At least not the ET kind," the president continued. "Unless anyone captured pictures of purple creatures running around Earth and hasn't thought to tell me." One of the reporters snickered. Foldane smiled. "Seriously, I do need to announce an alien exchange program between several countries signed up to an operation named Hideout.

"Hideout is the recently classified program leaked by an intelligence agency investigating psychic phenomena linked to areas of magnetic anomalies. Alien of course means visitors to a country in which they are non-citizens. I can confirm these aliens are very much human. Dr. Maximus Klotz hypothesized a theory that psychic responses are affected by exposure to an alien magnetic environment. This exchange program was devised to test that theory. It is one of many projects the US military and government agencies have funded over many years. I'm sure many of you remember the SCANATE project. This is a natural extension of many similar projects that the US military routinely investigate with varying degrees of success."

"Mr. President?"

"Go ahead, Weston, good to see you today."

"Quite the performer, isn't he?" Jacqueline said. Her mouth felt dry as cameras panned to a cheery silver-haired veteran of the President's press conferences. She felt a little breathless, pent up tension nowhere to go.

"This sounds like another expensive geeky project better suited for a prime-time sci-fi show," Weston commented. A ripple of laughter broke out and the reporter grinned. "Aren't there better ways to spend the American taxpayer's hard-earned money? Reducing the national debt? A Halloween-themed National Park in the Nevada Desert maybe? Lots of UFO sightings there."

"The Armed Services Senate Committee provides oversight and the—"

"Excuse me, Mr. President," Weston interrupted, "but Senator Biron chairs the Armed Services Senate Committee and is well known for his interest in geomagnetic research."

"And the reason Senator Biron's interest is well-known is that he meticulously states his interest in related items at every committee meeting. It's a matter of record. As for hard-earned money, the research into human interaction with electromagnetism is at the forefront of new developments in stealth technology and military communication in the field to better protect our brave men and women who put their lives at risk to protect this great country of ours."

Jacqueline looked across to Sam as Foldane pulled out the patriotic card guaranteed to fell all opposition. "What now for the Astereans?"

"I don't know." Sam's voice was low, strained. The disapproval set in his down-turned mouth surprised her. He shook his head. "Foldane didn't actually lie. Wanna bet your uncle had something to do with that?"

Jacqueline gasped. "*Merde*! He wanted me to call him." She stabbed the call button, and put the phone to her ear.

Her uncle answered immediately. "I assume you watched the press conference?"

Once, Charles' caustic tone would have put her immediately on the defensive. Not anymore. She was barely able to keep relations civil between them; she didn't think she could ever forgive him for his indifference towards her dying aunt. Tante Nicole had the last laugh though. Discovering Nicole was the Astereans' High Brighid must have given Charles an emotional apoplexy. She hadn't hung around to find out.

"Jacqueline?"

"*Oui, je suis ici.* So, tell me, *Oncle.* Is Foldane's speech what you'd call an honest lie?"

A silence followed. When Charles spoke again, he delivered his words slowly. "The world isn't ready for the truth, Jacqueline. Major Kearey needs to understand—"

Anger made her jump up. "Oh no! You're not using me to justify this total crock of bullshit!"

Sam's head snapped around from the TV, his eyes questioning. Jacqueline shook her head at him and walked out of earshot.

"I thought you and Kearey were friends," Charles said.

"What's that supposed to mean?" She noticed a new text message come in. Sean. Her tummy jumped. Her pulse beat faster.

Her uncle explained. "Major Kearey may have negotiated some goodwill with the Vercingetorix, but no one, including the Council, believes the world is ready for aliens that make the rest of mankind look like throwbacks on the evolutionary scale. The Astereans are being well-treated in all the countries. Ask Sohan. Exposing their presence will only turn them into targets. Religious groups will see their presence as a threat to their beliefs and society, the uneducated will resent their abilities, and neo-fascists resent anything that makes them feel inferior."

Jacqueline slumped into a chair.

"Think about it," he continued. "Each new group of Astereans in our past—our ancestors—faced this exact dilemma. Each group found their own way to integrate into Earth's society. Most formed civilizations that lived in isolation and then died out. Later groups formed druid orders. Others explored their world in a nomadic existence. But this is a different age, a technological age."

Damn. "Okay, I get your point."

She noticed Sam's shoulders relax and guessed he'd heard her. *Zut*, Sam had known exactly why her uncle had called. She threw him a disapproving frown.

"This is the right way," Charles labored on, "for mankind and for the Astereans. Over time they will integrate into our society."

It made sense. She wanted to believe him. She just didn't trust his motives. And something this big should be far beyond Charles' manipulations. It sickened her to think he might be twisting the fate of a million Astereans to serve his agenda.

Charles continued to press his point. "Major Kearey and his family are better off this way."

Jacqueline sat there, stewing in indecision. She glanced at Sohan who was watching Foldane answer questions.

"Did you discuss this decision with the Astereans?" she asked. "Because I know you didn't discuss it with Major Kearey."

Charles didn't reply. He didn't need to. His heavy silence said it all.

"A gilded cage is still a prison," she pointed out, her voice snippy.

"Don't let idealism lead you astray; that is the prerogative of young fools," Charles said softly. "Now Sam will handle Major Kearey, and Sohan is a student of culture. He will understand. Don't go making enemies, Jacqueline." He paused. "I have to go. I'll speak to you later."

Jacqueline blinked. Charles had terminated the call before she could ask about Max. "That was weird." She stared at the phone. "I'm not sure why he called me."

"He's worried about you," Sam said. "He wants you to understand."

Her mouth dropped open. She pointed an accusing finger at him. "You knew Foldane was going to do this, didn't you?"

Sam's gaze shifted away. He looked like he was struggling with himself.

"What?" She punched his arm, angry now.

Sam's head lifted, a frown framing eyes full of doubt and worry. He pulled Jacqueline farther down the library where Sohan couldn't possibly overhear them. "Foldane's speech is only the half of it, Jacqueline. And I'm the convenient punching bag when Niall finds out the rest."

# CHAPTER SEVENTEEN

Niall made his call to Tami in the garden he'd seen earlier from the ballroom. The fresh air would clear his head. He discovered Foldane's charade had jolted her out of her earlier insecurity.

"They lied!"

Her outrage made Niall want to laugh. "I know."

Sohan had telepathically fed him Foldane's speech complete with Asterean commentary via the q-dimension. He rubbed the numb area in his back, probing the puncture site just above his right pelvis. It was going to ache like hell, he knew it. Bone biopsies officially sucked.

"In a way, it's a relief," she said. "I just can't believe President Foldane would lie like that. I want to call someone."

"Shit, don't do that."

"Where have you been? I wanted to call you..."

"Why didn't you?"

"The same reason I never call you when you're working."

The reproachful note to her voice warned Niall he'd wandered into dangerous territory. Tami never called him at work. It was an unwritten rule. He always called her, when it was safe to call, when his job deemed it to be a convenient moment, and it was a rare occasion that Tami wasn't available to chat, catch up, and tell him the latest news.

"You're amazing, Tami. And I'm sorry. You and the kids mean everything to me. I know my job sometimes gets in the way."

"Sometimes?"

He grinned, liking the way Tami always made the blood rush to his head, and his groin. He pitched his voice low. "I was thinking of you earlier."

"You were?" And suddenly he was on the phone to a seductress. "What was I wearing?"

"Not very much."

"Where was I?"

"There was water, and bubbles." He remembered the bath salts on the shelf. "And the smell of pink grapefruit."

"Hmmm, sounds like heaven. Who was I with?"

"A sex god; an Adonis-like figure."

She laughed softly. "Sounds like you need some loving attention."

He remembered a plastic pot and a porn magazine. "More than you know."

"When will we see you?"

"I'll try to work something out as soon as I'm finished here. Miach mentioned my news appearance upset you. Don't let it worry you. You and the kids are in a safe place." He tried to keep his voice light. "And I suspect I'm going to be keeping a low profile for quite a while."

Damn Foldane. How long did he think he could keep the Astereans in isolation? Like industrial rats under the Nevada desert, or the Siberian tundra. Uathach had mentioned her people would be able to deal with Earth's authorities. Had she meant because of the orbs? Maybe she'd thought he'd make better use of them.

"Are you happy on the island, Tami?"

There was the tiniest hesitation. "Yes, of course."

"What is it?"

"The island's perfect, Niall. We live in the lap of luxury. The kids are thriving in school. Tony is doing well, Sheila's more excited than I've ever seen her, and Jose's family love living here. Luisa and I have become close."

He noticed she didn't mention Miach. "But?"

"You're not here, and when you are, you seem distracted. Something's troubling you. I thought we were past all the secrets."

Niall grimaced. He looked back at the ancient chateau that hid the best technology this world had to offer. He didn't want Tami worrying over Balor. Not until he knew what to tell her. "I met my mother earlier today. My birth mother."

"You did? Oh my God! Why didn't you say?"

"A lot happened very quickly. My mother turns out to be a genetics expert. While Foldane was getting ready to airbrush out the Astereans, I was giving DNA samples."

"Damn it, Niall. Why? They have your blood. They tried to steal mine and our children's! Is it because of your mother? Oh my God! She's Vercingetorix, isn't she?" Her voice began to rise. "Did she know? When those bastards came for us? Did she know?"

Niall rubbed his face. Shit. Mistake to tell her over the phone. She needed to know the whole sordid story; that his father had raped a seventeen-year old girl; and that the man behind their abduction was his elder brother. He couldn't do that over the phone. On the other end of the line, Tami started to cry.

*Lir's breath, Niall'Kearey.* Miach's displeasure rattled Niall's brain. *This isn't what I had in mind. I can sense her distress from here.*

*Where are you?*

*Reaching the bungalow now. I just walked Lizzie to her friend's home. She is worried about her mother.*

*Okay, I'm on my way.*

He heard a gasp. A clatter. "Tami? I'm coming home."

There was no reply.

*Hell!* Niall hunted for a hole. He'd bridged to the island before and he quickly found a link. His fingers started to form the quantum engine he needed to extract dark energy from the space around him, but nothing happened. He frowned then tried again. The same unease he'd felt earlier slammed him right in the solar plexus.

*Miach, I can't build an engine.*

Mind-numbing panic scrambled his brains. He glanced back at the sun-dappled chateau. Fury chased the panic away and his mind chased the sequence of events. He rubbed the numb area at his back. "Bastards! Fucking, stupid bastards!"

*I have her,* Miach thought to him. *Fix whatever the problem is and return to your wife. What in Lir's name did you say to her? I contacted Macha. She will be here soon.* His thought was cold. Angry. Miach broke their connection just as his phone went dead.

"Goddammit!"

Niall stormed towards the chateau. Sam met him at the door, a peculiar expression on his face. He held his ground as Niall stalked right into his face, fists ready to lash out, one still holding his phone. He shoved the cell phone into Sam's nose, hard enough to rock Sam onto his heels.

"What the fuck did they do to me?" Niall yelled.

Sam waved off the security guards descending on them with their weapons drawn. "I came out to explain... I never thought you'd try to leave so soon." Blood dripped to his lip. He pulled out a handkerchief and pressed it to his nose. Red blossomed across the white crumpled material. "Shit."

Niall threw his hands up. "Goddammit, Sam!" Somewhere, deep inside of him, he found the ability to think. "What is it? How does it work?"

Sam paused in his mopping up operation. "It's a bio-chemical nano chip. It was in the local for the biopsy. If it detects an energy build up consistent with a portal it projects a counter-polarizing field. Don't worry, nothing like the EM pulse before. DruSensi learned their lesson."

Beads of sweat appeared on Sam's brow as Niall absorbed his words.

DruSensi. Again.

Did Morgan have a death wish? No, the procedure had been carried out at the pentagon. But why? He thought Foldane trusted him? Was this because of Klotz? Dammit, he saved the man's life! Theories spun around in Niall's head, his rampaging emotions adding to the confusion.

Violation. Betrayal. Fear.

"Tami needs me," he spat out. "I think she's suffering some aftershock from the abduction and I need to get to her. Now!"

Sam's jaw tightened. He pulled out his phone and pressed a number. "This is Colonel Hastor," he said almost immediately, his voice nasally. "Authorization for portal granted." He looked at Niall. "It'll take a couple minutes before you're good to go."

Niall blinked. With a single call, Sam had demonstrated who ran the show. The government and the Vercingetorix had lied, cajoled and manipulated him all along, since the moment they knew of his abilities. The last time they tried to control him they'd roasted his brain with an EMP pulse resulting in a collapsed bridge on Astereal. Hundreds of evacuees had died. Now, they could simply shut off his ability whenever he didn't beg hard enough for authorization. He thought the mission to Afghanistan had been his chance. He'd been deluding himself. All this time, DruSensi had been working on an alternative method to contain him.

"I'm not the *enemy* here!" Niall ground out.

"No, but what you can do is terrifying," Sam replied. "What you did, smuggling aliens into Earth's past, tampering with human evolution, is beyond terrifying. A couple of weeks ago, you ported to another planet, stepped back into the past, put a woman into a cryogenic freezer, and left her in timeless stasis at the edge of a black hole!"

Niall swallowed, remembering Herecura's lips frozen in an everlasting scream. The image wouldn't shift. Sam spoke through the handkerchief stuffed against his nose. "You kidnapped the President, your Commander-in-Chief, right out of the White House!"

"I explained why I had to do that. Every step of the way, I've made the hard decisions. No one else could make the calls I made. No one else knew what I knew. No one else could have done what needed to be done. So, no one else has the right to judge me for the things I did to preserve the existence of the human race."

"Listen to yourself." Anger sparked in Sam's eyes. "You consulted with no one!"

Niall took a deep breath. "I've done this already! With the goddamn President of the United States. I don't need to do it with you!"

"These gifts of yours don't give you the right to act unilaterally. I know this chip seems extreme, but nothing about this situation is normal. This chip secures the chain of command, the way it should have been from the beginning."

"*Bullshit!* Foldane could have led the world into offering asylum to all of Astereal—it could have been done! Asterean technology could have helped Earth absorb their entire population. Instead the *chain of command's* lack of vision and *humanity* forced me underground. And maybe that's how it was supposed to be, and in the last few days, I thought my country recognized that. I thought Foldane was ready to use my gifts to do stuff like saving those men today, protecting Earth, but this chip—" Words failed him.

"None of this is as bad as you're thinking. I meant to explain this properly..." He stopped at Niall's glare and ran his fingers through his hair, his expression a quagmire of indecision. "The initial consensus behind Hideout is faltering, Niall. The world hasn't stopped. Conflict is escalating, across the Middle East, Ukraine, Korea. Member countries are considering their national interests and your abilities are a major source of dissent. You know this! It's why you agreed to the restrictions on creating a bridge. Well, Russia has implemented its own satellite portal detection system to monitor US cooperation and it detected unauthorized output over the Middle East, Washington DC, the Amazon, and most recently your trip to rescue Dr. Klotz."

Niall took a deep breath. "Okay. That's not good."

"While you were on the island, President Foldane was briefing Heads of State on the Balor threat and what really happened to the Asterean population. He ended up fighting demands to have you arrested and investigated. We could explain everything, but the black op. China supplied the magnetic rings and revealing the degradation you set off would spark a diplomatic crisis. Fortunately, the energy reading turned out to be minimal and we think China will link it to the existence of a uranium plant in the vicinity and keep quiet. Russia's not sure. President Nobokov can't be sure the blip wasn't natural, but he suspects you've interfered with DruSensi's satellite more than once. He's threatening to move to full combat readiness if one of its satellites ever gets hit by a solar flare."

Niall felt suddenly nauseous. "Someone could have just told me this!"

"The government's official position is that none of this activity was authorized, and we will take all steps necessary to prevent it happening again. Somehow, Russia knew DruSensi had been developing this nano-bio technology and insisted we deploy the chip as security. China backed them up. In return for full disclosure, they would support missions like the Afghanistan one, but now with this Balor threat, they're concerned for your safety. Foldane's agreed to assign you a Special Ops team to accompany you on high risk missions, under your field command, but with a primary objective to protect you. They're getting clearance and being briefed as we speak. I've been authorized to approve any portals and liaise with all parties." His phone beeped and Sam checked the message. "We're good to go."

"We're? The island's supposed to be a secure location. Wait. Does Russia know where it is?"

"They never mentioned the Pacific. It's possible the island's defenses concealed the portal's energy signature, but we can't be sure. And I spent two years at school on that island. I already know its location."

Niall took a deep breath, grappling with the dark resentment establishing a foothold at the back of his mind. Concern for Tami spiraled with a growing realization that his family might never be safe, and now this chip would stop him from being able to protect them. A quiet fury gripped him. His government had sold him out. He couldn't trust any of them. For now, he put all his anger on hold. "Fine," he spat out.

He tested out Sam's words and a second later an engine hung in the air between them, a glowing ball of energy. Finding the link he needed, Niall built his bridge across a continent and an ocean, senses alert to the slightest trace of an electromagnetic signature emanating from a tiny chip that had no business in his body. He detected nothing. At the last moment he said, "Don't mention anything about this Russian satellite."

Sam gave him a tight nod and a second later they stepped onto the decked veranda projecting over the lapping waves below. The stars were bright in the sky and a full moon cast its silvery light across the water. Niall ignored the beauty and marched into the bungalow, Sam following close behind.

Miach appeared and indicated the living area. "She's in here. Macha will arrive shortly."

Niall entered the room and crouched down beside Tami who was curled into a tight trembling ball in an armchair. Her vacant eyes stared into nowhere, her aura practically non-existent. "I'm here, honey," he said, touching her knee. His voice projected nothing of the turmoil consuming him.

Her head lifted and then her lips parted at the sight of him. Tears spilled over and Niall gathered her up in his arms.

Her hands stole around his neck and clung on for dear life. "I... thought they were... dead, Niall."

"When?" He carried her to their bedroom, away from prying eyes.

She spoke into his shirt, muffling her reply. "On the plane... they were so still."

Niall knew that sick fear. For a terrible, heart wrenching moment, seeing the satellite image of Toby and Lizzie limp in their captors' arms, he'd believed them dead, too. "They're fine now."

He kicked the door shut behind them. It slammed into the frame with a bang. Tami started then struggled in his arms, her bid for freedom escalating quickly. He set her down and she backed away from him, a shaking finger pointed at his chest.

"You used our daughter to stop me!" Anger blazed from her every pore. "Stand down? Stand down? There were men with guns in our house, Niall! They wanted our kids! They threatened to kill me!" Lost for words, defenseless against her anger, Niall stood and let her fury batter him. "I was fighting to protect my children. Me! Because you weren't there! You're always there for everyone else, but you're never here for us." The accusation turned Niall cold as Tami paled. Her hand covered a ragged gasp. "Oh God," she backed away from him, "I'm sorry, I don't know where that came from."

He reached out a calming hand. "It's okay." Guilt roughened his words. "When you needed me most, I wasn't there. You went through the most terrifying experience alone. Then I go off saving aliens you've never heard of messing our lives up even more. Your whole world's been turned inside out. I'm so sorry."

"Miach said something very similar."

Niall held back a sigh. His once time doppelganger knew him too well.

Tami tilted her head, regarding him with a look he didn't quite understand. "You're very alike," she added.

Niall could feel a frown forming. "What do you mean?"

"He always knows what to say."

"My mind was part of him for a long time." Irritation made his voice harsher than he'd intended and he lightened his words with a smile that Tami returned.

"I'm okay," she said. "I think I've been bottling that up for too long." When Niall stepped forward, she flew into his arms. Grasping his face in both hands, she studied him through red-rimmed eyes. "I can't believe you're here." He tried to capture her lips, but she held him off. "Something's happened, and not just your birth mother. What is it? Tell me!"

"I'm gonna need a drink. You too."

Half a bottle of Glenmorangie helped dull Niall's outrage as he updated her on the day's events, with the exception of the Russian satellite. When he told her about the chip, Tami pulled out his shirt and probed the puncture site on his back.

"Careful, it's a little sore."

She let him go and sat back. "How could they do that?" Red blotches tinged her cheekbones as new tears sprang to her eyes. "That's like branding you! Or locking on one of those awful curfew things to stop you leaving the house. This is horrible, Niall. They can't do this!"

"Yeah, I feel like I'm wearing one of those electric collars people use to control their dog."

"Why don't they trust you?"

"For all the reasons Sam said. They've been preparing for this; waiting for me to slip up, looking for an excuse."

"Why didn't he warn you?"

"Because Sam's an ass-licking bastard. When will you realize he's not who we thought he was?"

"Don't say that. Sam and Linny are our friends."

Niall swallowed the last of his whiskey. Sam was about as innocent as a rattlesnake in the grass. "Sam's got me on a fucking leash, and Linny lives in happily-medicated Stepford land."

He reached for the whiskey bottle, but Tami grabbed a fistful of shirt and tugged him back. She eyeballed him with a serious glint in her eye. "Don't." When he frowned, she added, "Tony just got clean. I know you're angry and upset, but enough."

Niall stared at her. "Even if it's genetic, Tony isn't my father! Wish he was, 'cos from what I've heard, my real father's a crazy sicko—"

Her fingers on his lips stole all the fight from him. "Don't," she whispered, but this time the word carried a sexy promise way more interesting than whiskey.

Her lips opened to his searching tongue. She tasted of sweet Madeira and blood rushed to his loins. He adjusted his position to ease his weight off her and let his fingers pull out her T-shirt. She arched beneath him as his hand crept up her belly to a lace-covered breast. Her responding moan sent him wild. Succumbing to the wiles of the temptress beneath him, Niall focused on the one addiction he would never give up. His wife was 100 proof intoxicating in every way that counted. Balor, nano chips, and the whole fucked up world filled with people he no longer trusted faded into the background when he was in her arms.

Miach shook with a consuming outrage as his mind explored the intricate device inserted into Niall'Kearey's body. He closed his eyes and focused on the minute traces of bio-inconsistencies betraying its presence. Heated indignation washed through him. His mouth thinned. "This would never happen on Astereal. Our higher-level abilities are a natural part of who we are. What they have done here is akin to controlling someone's sight or their hearing. It is an abomination."

"Welcome to Earth," Niall'Kearey replied, his voice laced with contempt.

Miach opened his eyes and followed Niall'Kearey's gaze down to the beach where Colonel Hastor was deep in conversation with Tami. Miach didn't need to sense her fury. It was written in the rigid line of her body, and the jerking motion of her pointed finger in the colonel's face.

Niall'Kearey's thunderous expression hardened. "Hope she's giving him hell." Then he switched his penetrating gaze to Miach. "I need to know exactly what this nano device can do. Can it record or transmit what I'm saying?"

"I am not detecting any response to vibrational energy. It is broadcasting a constant output more consistent with a tracking signal."

"I don't detect anything."

Miach directed Niall'Kearey's mind to the low frequency output.

"Okay, I've got it now. Damn! I need to get rid of this thing, Miach. Can't you blast it with an EM pulse or something?"

"The device is protected, much like your satellites."

"You mean hardened. Yeah, I expected that."

"A pulse strong enough to disrupt this chip could cause massive damage to the surrounding organs. I do not advise this. Surgical removal would have a greater chance of success, but the chip is attached to bone."

"So, extract it with another needle biopsy."

Miach monitored the chemical interactions between the device and the surrounding tissue. "It is not easily accessible. There is a self-replicating organic component. I suspect a fail-safe mechanism that could trigger an alert if the chip is attacked. We need to be careful. An electrical shock this close to your central nervous system could cause transient paralysis or lesions leading to neural damage."

Miach detected a sudden elevation of adrenalin followed by a rapid increase in oxygen and falling sugar levels, the chemical expression of a furious emotional response. He shielded his mind against the burst of energy flooding Niall'Kearey's systems and withdrew.

Outwardly, a slight tic in his temple betrayed Niall'Kearey's anger, his aura volatile. "The bastards designed it to be impregnable. They knew I would try to get rid of it, neutralize it, do something."

"I will consult with Sohan. We have several healers across your world with the ability to defeat a foreign body like this. It is like any disease. Once it is fully understood, it can be treated."

Niall'Kearey nodded, the muscles in his neck thickly corded with his emotion. Their eyes drifted to Tami who was walking back to the bungalow. Colonel Hastor trailed behind her, his eyes cast to the sand.

A chilling determination radiated towards Miach.

I'm going to lull them into a false sense of security, Niall'Kearey communicated to him. Let them think I'm beaten. His searing gaze rested on Miach. Work with Pwyll. Find a way to get this thing out of me, because God help them, they're going to regret doing this to me.

# CHAPTER EIGHTEEN

The Vercingetorix Council circled him like vultures. Niall knew they were there, he just couldn't see them. He stood beneath a directed pool of light that exposed him and left most of the seated council members in shadow.

Cowards.

Only Patrick and Etlinn allowed themselves to be seen through the simple use of a diffused light inset into the floor. The huge ballroom had proven to be a foyer leading to a high-tech purpose-built suite. A low hum at his feet made Niall step back from a podium emerging out of the floor, its glass lid folding back on a hinge as it rose. It was a neat piece of engineering.

Two orbs sat cushioned on velvet inside. Niall recognized the one Nicole Biron had left him in her will from its engraving. He picked up the second orb. The silvery casing opened at his touch and he removed the top half inciting a murmur of disgruntled awe. Touching the shimmering surface of tingling luminescence released a stream of Asterean symbols that settled into a colorful light show around his head. Niall explored a series of airborne buttons, cascading paths of information across the room like a spider's cobweb. Both council members and security guards reacted far too slowly as he swiveled on his heel and committed each and every face to memory.

"God almighty," Morgan said, gesturing the guards to back off. "What did you have to go and do that for?"

"*Cette situation est inacceptable*," snapped a sharp-suited man with a familiar face.

"Got the EU tied up, I see," Niall observed, searching his memory for the commissioner's name and coming up blank. He turned to

Morgan. "My government put a DruSensi manufactured chip inside me, a development the Vercingetorix must have commissioned. Treat a man like an animal and see how fast and hard he bites back." He pressed a symbol and the threads of data flowed back to the orb, plunging the members back into darkness. He snapped the lid back on and placed the inactive orb in its box.

Morgan folded his arms. "Then we have a stalemate. I'm told the chip has a failsafe mechanism. We can't remove it without harming you even if we wanted to."

Niall looked at Etlinn who flushed under his scrutiny.

"Patrick speaks the truth, Niall." The use of his name struck a jangling chord and he nearly missed her next words. "... access to these orbs as much as we want to discover what's in them. It is our hope that the information you seek on Balor will be in one of the two already in our possession. If not, then we must identify possible locations for the others. The Vercingetorix is the only organization that can invoke the cooperation of authorities in any part of the world. You need us. We can protect your family—"

"I could protect my family until this chip got put inside me! For all I know the Russian government and the whole of DruSensi know the location of this secret island of yours. I don't trust a damn thing any of you say!"

Etlinn's eyes narrowed, perhaps in shock, or disapproval, but then her expression softened. "I understand your anger, but I suggest we all carry a measure of guilt. You tampered with our past, created the origins of the Vercingetorix, and attracted a monstrous threat we can only take your word for. We need each other."

Niall ground his jaw, wanting to counter Etlinn's words, reading nothing but truth in her aura. Conflicted, he held her gaze, searching for a weakness in her argument. The tension snapped when Morgan leaned forward and pressed a button flooding the room with light and causing the other council members to shield their eyes.

"Morgan, *avez-vous devenu fou?*" yelled the European Commissioner.

148

"It's not been a good week, so, yes, maybe I have gone a little crazy, but, Emile, don't you feel a little stupid hiding in the dark?"

The rest of the man's name fell into place. Emile Fitzroy.

"I do," answered a tiny Asian woman with a Malay accent. She nodded to Niall. "Your government agreed to the chip under international pressure not of our making. DruSensi's American arm manufactured the device and your government implanted it. The Council was not party to this decision, although I suspect none here would have had issue with the suggestion, with the possible exception of your mother."

The woman's tone conveyed a gentle censure and Niall's eyes shot to Etlinn. However, Etlinn's aura and expression betrayed no reaction.

"She objected to altering the DRUMSI to emit an EM pulse," Fitzroy said. "Insisted on testing it out in this very room."

"Should have guessed there was more to her concern than pious moralizing," Patrick Morgan sniped.

Etlinn's shielding cracked and, for a brief second, Niall glimpsed hurt, and regret.

"Forgive our apparent indifference," the petite black-haired Asian continued. "We do understand this infringement on your liberty antagonizes you, but I personally respect your president's dilemma." She leaned forward, her sari a splash of turquoise against the black leather of her chair. "My name is Sharifah, Major Kearey. In the country of my birth, my influence must be wielded through others. Our religion does not allow for women to be so," she paused, making her point, "gifted. It is an interpretation of scripture that I resented growing up, but I observed my country's traditions, the restrictions on my liberty, for a greater purpose. Now women in my country are well-educated and flourishing in business and I am one of three women in government."

"Your culture is not mine," Niall pointed out.

"But respecting the orders of your command should be." Kohl-lined eyes challenged him and her flawless olive complexion displayed an expression of honesty. Sharifah's mind opened and filled the room, gentle but with a backbone of steel. "This council does not mix sentiment with our aim to shepherd humanity to its full potential. There are those among us who will stop at almost nothing to achieve our objectives, yet we are not all monsters. It is not our desire to curtail your abilities, but by your admission you have brought Earth to the attention of something deadly, an evil that outstrips our feeble manipulation, and although you undoubtedly have the potential to be Earth's best defense, you have given us little cause to trust you. So, whether you work with us or against us, the Council will deal with your choice."

Niall hesitated. In one way, Sharifah was right. Balor changed everything and her honesty clarified his situation. He couldn't think in terms of friend or enemy anymore, the lines were too blurred. He needed to pick his battles, create a new strategy, forge alliances where he needed them and dump past illusions of loyalty. This chip wasn't going to disappear fast and he had a job to do.

"What's your plan for the Astereans?" he asked.

When the council members turned as one to Fitzroy, the European Commissioner waved a hand like he was batting away a pesky wasp.

"Answer him," Morgan growled.

Fitzroy's eyes flared, his disapproval plain. "Our plans haven't changed. We will assess the Asterean's capabilities and integrate them into the culture and society of the country that has provided them with asylum." Niall listened carefully. Fitzroy's heavy accent was hard to follow despite his excellent English. "In due course they will receive detailed cover stories, passports, paid employment and references, after they sign non-disclosure agreements in both their given and newly assumed names. They will be required to attend assessment centers on a monthly basis, at least to start with. Some, like Sohan, will be free to work internationally and act as representatives for the group. If an Asterean cannot be accounted for they will be tracked down, arrested, and returned for assessment."

"Tracked down how?"

"It will be a condition of their release that they agree to an injection of nanites disguised as blood cells. These nanites will emit a tracking signal detectable from space. No doubt this research is the source of the chip inside you."

"The Astereans aren't criminals. It's wrong to treat them like they are."

Etlinn leaned forward. "Niall, you're too close to the Astereans. Use your professional judgment. These restrictions on their freedom are minor ones, a reasonable compromise to both ensure Earth's security and prevent the hysterical reaction we witnessed after Dr. Klotz's unfortunate leak. We've talked with the Astereans. They came here knowing that Earth was not going to welcome them with open arms— you made sure of that."

"Who will employ them?" Niall asked. "Vercingetorix-owned industries? Or will they be free to seek employment as they see fit—"

"Set up a competing business?" Patrick Morgan shook his head. "No, we've invested considerable money to save the Astereans from a terrible fate. This is a deal favorable to all sides."

Morgan's babble drifted over Niall's head. Etlinn's final comment tumbled around in his mind. He *had* warned the Astereans. He'd known right from the start that Earth would struggle to accept an influx of advanced aliens. There was another battle to fight, an entity that threatened human and Asterean alike.

Balor. The name whispered to him constantly, the moniker of a terrifying specter that had connected with him then sent agents out hunting for him. Niall wished he could write Herecura off as a mad woman, delusional and sick, but she had tripped off a childhood paranoia that was undermining all his intentions to do his best for the Astereans.

Reaching out he touched Nicole's orb. Silence reigned as Niall scanned the data threads, searching for the connections he needed. "Sohan should be doing this," he said. "He might need help, too, Asterean help."

"Not a problem," Morgan replied. "You open them and we'll arrange for the rest."

Niall didn't answer, too busy following up a message he hadn't spotted before. It was a coded file that required his mind's touch to unlock the contents. He experimented, nudging the air around it. A timer unveiled and he hid a smile. Uathach had built a failsafe into the orb's mechanism.

# CHAPTER NINETEEN

*Niall Kearey?*

Niall slowed his run around the Vercingetorix estate. *Sohan. Found a way to get rid of this chip inside me?*

*No. Pwyll has a healer in China working on the problem. I am contacting you, because I found a reference to Balor.*

Niall jogged to a stop. Bending over, he rested hands on knees and took a second to catch his breath. Ten miles more and he would be done. *Go on.*

*The reference mentions the Ancient Prophecy, but I cannot find details on the Ancient Prophecy in either orb.*

*We need to find another orb. Any ideas on where?*

*Excuse me while I consult with Dr. Biron.*

Niall straightened and continued his run. The Vercingetorix estate inhabited a beautiful but isolated area in the Dordogne region. He still hadn't established its boundaries; natural vegetation made parts of the estate almost impenetrable without resorting to a machete. He wasn't even sure there was an entry way in and out. As far as he could tell, the only way to know this place existed was to fly directly over it, or consult an aerial map, although he doubted one ancient chateau would generate much excitement when the Dordogne boasted so many.

Sohan's mind nudged his. *We have a few possibilities. Dr. Biron thinks the GBI database might prove a useful way to catalog and map possibilities against areas of recorded psychic phenomena.*

*Because those areas might indicate an Asterean settlement?*

*Yes.*

*Have you mentioned this to Colonel Hastor?*

*He is in a conference call.*

Niall decided to cut his run short. *I'll be back in an hour.*

Sohan's mind peeled away and Niall put out a call to Miach.

*I am teaching,* Miach answered him. *Is it urgent?*

*No. Just checking on Tami and the kids.*

*Toby is showing signs of kinesis talent, but I don't see the potential you demonstrate. Lizzie has inherited your telepathic skills and her mother's empathy.*

*I wasn't asking for a school report. Are they okay? How's Tami?*

*Your children are happy and Tami is visiting Luisa. She told me she has decided to teach a photography class. Your wife has an eye for the unusual.*

Pride underscored Miach's words and Niall swerved to avoid a root. *I'll let you get back to your class.*

*Thank you.*

Niall tried Macha instead and found her strangely distracted. Then her thought sharpened.

*Kestra's in trouble. Men have her trapped in a cave and Yerit has gone after her. Alone.* There was a pause, then, *Niall'Kearey, she is distressed. I must get to her.*

Niall picked up his pace as Macha's mind opened showing him a second hand remote-view of men steadily climbing rocks towards Kestra's lair. Kestra poked her beaked head out and a shot rang out. Dirt sprayed around her and with an angry screech the gryphon darted back inside the false security of its cave.

Niall pulled out his cell phone and hit speed dial. Sam answered within seconds.

"We're going to the Amazon," Niall said.

"What? Why?"

"Macha's gryphon's in trouble. Yerit's gone solo and it's going to be a gunfight."

"How do you know?"

Niall kept it simple. "Macha has this telepathic connection with Kestra."

There was silence, then, "I need to get higher authorization for this one."

"If news of a gryphon gets out it will make headlines. Add a Morrígan into the mix..."

"I'm aware of the ramifications. What's your ETA back here?"

"One hour. Too long. Get me authorization and I'll be back quicker. You did it before. We're going to need weapons. Is that Special Ops team in place?"

"Stand by."

The line disconnected. Niall tested if he had bridging capabilities as he ran. Nothing. He swore and pounded his rage into the ground as he ran. Trees raced by him in the other direction. If anything happened to Yerit... or suppose Yerit decimated the loggers and precipitated an investigation? What the fuck was Sam doing? He tried again and the crackle of energy caught him by surprise. His mind dived through the nearest hole into the q-dimension and searched for a shortcut to the chateau, but he couldn't find the one that had got him there from the States, or from the anonymous island his family now lived on. He was too close. Heart pounding, he picked up speed, eyes scanning the path ahead, his mind searching for another option.

*Macha?*

The Morrígan Queen was listening for him and he used her mind like a homing beacon. His bridge shimmered in front of him. He ran straight through the portal opening onto the beach and skidded to a halt in front of her, sand clumping around his feet. "This is shit!"

Macha scrambled to her feet. "I am sorry..."

"No, not you. Look, we need to get back to pick up Sam. Now, before he realizes I've gone and raises the alarm. This isn't the moment to test out what this chip can do." His fingers built another bridge, the distance allowing him to nudge his link into a direct connection to the chateau. He'd shave off at least forty-five minutes.

"My presence will alert him to the truth," she pointed out.

"I'll handle Sam, if he hasn't reported me missing already."

They stepped through to find Sam talking into the phone. Sam narrowed his eyes at the sight of Macha. "General, Major Kearey just arrived. He took a shortcut."

"Thought it would be quicker." Niall couldn't keep the note of insolence out of his tone.

Sam's jaw tightened, anger radiating off him like porcupine spines and Niall knew DruSensi had detected his side trip to collect Macha.

*Why do you aggravate him this way?* Macha asked.

*He's like this stone in my shoe.*

Sam eyed his attire. "We're picking up your Special Ops team from Cannon Air Force Base. You can gear up there. An EM marker has been set up in a hangar. Can you link directly there?"

Niall nodded then thought he'd better check. The tiny holes that sparkled in the periphery of his mind's eye weren't conduits linking two points, but sub-particle sized access points to something else, a dimension outside the normal parameters of space-time, open to energy and linking all points. The super-pathways to other galaxies stood out to his inner eye, but he was searching for routes across Earth. He let instinct guide him to where he needed to go. When his subconscious mind emerged over Cannon AFB, the marker drew him like a magnet, just as Macha's mind and Jacqueline's aura had.

"I see it."

He spotted the Special Ops team inside the huge hangar, adjusted his link and started to build his engine. Sam shook his head as a door-sized portal materialized before them. Startled faces looked their way. Sam stepped through first, closely followed by Macha. Niall closed the bridge behind him, dispersing the harnessed energy safely into the q-dimension they had just traversed.

A man jogged over to greet them and Niall recognized the officer from outside Towden's office.

He came to a halt before Hastor. "Captain Whelan reporting as ordered, Colonel. Major."

Whelan nodded to Niall and then Macha. Surprise widened his eyes as he took in her gold-flecked square pupils. Macha smiled at him and after a stunned moment he returned the gesture, his cheeks coloring.

"This is Macha, Captain," Sam said. "And you obviously recognize Major Kearey."

"Yes sir. Honor to serve with you, Major. There's gear for you both. We weren't expecting..." He indicated Macha dressed in sun top, shorts and sneakers. She made an odd mix with her alien features and Western clothing.

"I will be fine as I am, Captain," Macha assured Whelan.

Niall shook his head. "We'll find you some body armor."

Whelan nodded.

Approaching the team, Niall realized he'd trained two of them. He exchanged high fives and a back slap before changing into fatigues. Jester, whose thickset appearance belied his nimble fighting skills, handed him an assault rifle. Jester lived for the action. Niall's confidence in the team grew. As Niall added ammo to his belt, Macha snatched up a knife and holster, which she fixed around her thigh. Whelan gestured to comm-units and goggles then drew back to take a call.

"Macha, tell us what you know," Sam said. "You can speak freely. This team has been assigned to GBI as a tactical unit attached to the Asterean compound in Nevada. They've been fully briefed."

Macha inclined her head then addressed the group like a seasoned pro. "Kestra is a gryphon. She's alien to your world and she's looking for a mate. These caves are a natural habitat for her kind, but they are outside a protected zone your government has negotiated with Brazil. Workers destroying the forest have spotted her and tracked her to her cave."

"What's your information source, ma'am?" Whelan asked, rejoining them.

"We have a source on the ground," Niall replied, wanting to avoid a discussion on Macha and Kestra's telepathic bond. "His name's Yerit, and he has features like Macha here, except his pupils are black, and he's about my build. He's a friendly. Captain, you've got C4 here. We got any explosive experts, too?"

The only other female present raised a hand. She had a nose slightly bent out of shape and sharp intelligent eyes. "Sir, Sergeant Draper."

"Otherwise known as TomTom, and don't you go looking at her skinny white ass or she'll cut your eyes out," Jester added.

Niall nodded to the woman. "Once we've secured Kestra, I want to create a similar cave formation near a waterfall not far from Yerit's village. See if we can persuade her to settle there."

"Yes, sir."

"What about the men hunting Kestra? Won't they look for her?" Macha asked.

Niall caught a deadly glint in Whelan's eye. "Captain?"

"Sir. CIA just confirmed these men are no loggers. They're members of a drugs cartel. Deadly force has been authorized."

Macha's aura darkened. "These men have done nothing yet to deserve execution," she said.

Niall took her aside. "These men will hunt Kestra down. If not today, then in a week. Or a month. If they find Yerit, they will kill him without a second's thought. Then they will look for the place he came from and destroy it. Our job is to neutralize them before they contact the outside world. Before they talk. They don't deserve your pity, Macha." Her shock filled his mind, but Niall sensed Whelan's team growing impatient. He turned to the others. "Give me a second to scout ahead."

He extended his mind up into space, practiced at catching the weakening magnetic field extending from the north down towards Brazil. Dipping under the edge of the radiation belt, he stabbed deep into the Serro do Araca extending south from Venezuela. Starting from the Morrígan settlement he surfed east until he found Kestra. Her cave extended into the cliff face for some distance.

"I can open a bridge directly into the cavern Kestra's commandeered. Macha, you'll need to keep her calm."

"I understand."

"The targets will have no idea we're there," Niall continued. "There's enough cover to slip out and flank them from both sides. Take them out one by one in a pincer movement." When no one objected to his plan, Colonel Hastor nodded. "You have a go. Major." The Special Ops team watched a silvery globe form in the palm of Niall's hand.

Jester stepped sharply out of the way as a portal sprang into existence, its luminous edge defining an empty darkened space beyond it that wasn't supposed to exist in a Cannon AFB hangar. "Jeeping creepers! If that's what Special Tactics is teaching nowadays, I'm applying for a transfer."

"You need to be in tune with nature, Jester," Niall said. "Too big a reach for a knuckleduster like you."

Jester gave him a finger while Whelan scanned the cave beyond.

The captain told Niall what he already knew. "Okay, it's clear, except for this gryphon." His head shook from side to side in disbelief and then he raised his weapon. "Jester, take point."

There was a general shift into readiness. Comm links and NV goggles were thrown in place and weapons checked. The thrill of action raised Niall's pulse rate—he had missed this, the camaraderie of a real-life mission, a shared determination to get the job done, bring their man back alive. Kestra might not be human, but her perilous situation was as real as any rescue mission he'd been involved in.

"Go, go, go!" he ordered, his voice focused and controlled.

Jester shot through closely followed by the colonel, Whelan, and the remaining members of the assault team. Macha went last. A rattle of gunfire from outside greeted Niall as he stepped into the cave. An inhuman shriek assaulted his ear drums.

"Shit!"

The terrified gryphon stood ten feet tall on its hind legs blocking the Special Ops team from reaching the entrance. Its huge talons raked the air as Kestra's scream filled the vaulted roof space. A large wing thrashed the air, but the other hung limp and useless. Kestra screamed

159

again. The portal closed, plunging the cave into darkness that the daylight outside could not reach. Niall switched to night vision and caught a glimpse of Macha slipping past the men, her mind fixated on reaching the wounded creature.

Niall charged after her. "Macha, stop!" He bulldozed Whelan and Sam aside. *She's too stressed. Give her time to recognize you.*

Macha pulled back the hand reaching up to Kestra.

"Look out!" Sam yelled. He raised his weapon as Kestra's razor sharp beak shot down on the Morrígan Queen.

"Hold fire! She's been shot," Niall ordered as he shoved Macha towards the rock wall. White fire raked his left shoulder dropping Niall to his knee. His vision tunneled down to a red dot and he clamped his good hand to the arterial spray of blood jetting out from his arm. His brain couldn't quite work out what Kestra had just done to him. He had been stabbed before, but this fire went up his arm, around his shoulder, under his body armor and into his back. He couldn't feel his hand. He sensed Kestra rear up again.

"Hold fire," he growled out. "Give her a moment."

"Confirmed," Sam snapped.

For a brief moment, silence reigned as Kestra ceased her screeching. Niall caught a whiff of what smelled like horse dung. He knew Macha stood beside him, silent and still; partly recovering from being bounced off rock, mostly concentrating on extending a calming aura around the angry, wounded gryphon. Someone was taking in short rapid breaths. When Niall realized that someone was him, he took a deep lungful of air, pushed the debilitating pain to the back of his mind, and vowed he would not vomit.

Kestra suddenly dropped onto all four paws and sprawled on her belly like a big cat chilling in the African savannah. Her huge feathered head lowered to the rock floor. One wing hung limp and useless, the other twitched angrily. Macha walked towards her.

"Go, go, go," Whelan ordered quietly. "Carefully. I'll stay with the major."

The men gave Kestra a wide berth as they filed past, their mission off to a shaky start, but back under control. There was a second burst of gunfire, rifle shots, the hunters probably testing their prey. Kestra jerked at the sound, but this time her response was to crawl closer to the Morrígan Queen; the proud, majestic gryphon seeking a place of comfort to lick its wounds. Blood glistened on her black eagle-like beak. Macha crouched down and ran exploring fingers through Kestra's feathery mane.

While Whelan took up a position covering Kestra, Sam dropped his backpack down beside Niall. "Try not to move."

Niall twisted his head to see the damage then hissed. White bone glistened through red blood and torn flesh in the light from Sam's helmet. He didn't dare move his hand, but he was beginning to feel shaky. "Help me sit down."

Sam maneuvered him into a sitting position where Niall could rest his good side against the wall, except he couldn't while his hand clamped whatever damage Kestra had inflicted on him. Maybe he would throw up after all.

"Hell," he whispered. The nausea passed. "Find a pack of hemostats. You need to clamp off the main bleed. Then pack the wound with gauze. Damp the gauze with sterile water."

Sam nodded.

Niall stared at him, unsure if it was the night vision goggles or if Sam had turned green. Sam directed the flashlight on his helmet directly over Niall's fingers. He had the clamps ready. "On three. One, two, three." Niall let go. Blood spurted out in a jet stream. Sam swore. His hand shot forward and he clamped something. "Got it."

Niall swallowed a scream. The earthy metallic smell of blood filled his nostrils. "Find the other end."

Sam peered closely. "God, what a mess... yes, I see it." He clamped something lower in Niall's arm and then poured water onto a pack of gauze and shoved it inside the wound.

Tears blurred Niall's vision. His good hand formed a fist until he felt the pain from his nails digging into the palm of his hand. He stared down at the hazy weapon laid across his lap. *Did I take the safety off?*

"Usually you're doing this to me," Sam said.

Niall swore the walls of the cave were caving in. "Gonna take more than first aid to make up for what you did."

Sam didn't reply. He continued to wet gauze and stuff it in until Niall began to wonder if he had any arm left. After he'd wrapped a bandage around the extensive mess, Sam pulled out a pain syrette.

"No," Niall said. "Got to keep my head clear."

"What about a tetanus shot? God knows what that creature's carrying."

"Later." Niall glanced at Macha inspecting Kestra's wing. "Check my weapon, then help me up."

"Shit. Really?" Sam shone the light onto Niall's assault weapon. "No, you're good." He heaved Niall onto his feet by his good arm then gestured to Kestra. "She gonna be able to fly?"

"Ask Macha."

She looked over. "Not for several days, Colonel. The bullet went through muscle, but she will recover with rest." Kestra's bloodied beak was nuzzling her arm; her usual independence abandoned. Macha represented a place of haven amid the insanity of warfare. Macha's gaze shifted to Niall. "I am sorry, Niall'Kearey. She was terrified."

"Trust me, I know."

"I thank you." She had no need to say more. Kestra could easily have killed her.

"She can walk though, yes?" Sam asked. "She can walk through a portal?" When Macha nodded, he turned to Niall. "Question is, can you form a bridge? Would pain meds help?"

"No." Niall willed away a new onslaught of nausea. "No meds." As the sensation faded, Niall searched for a link to the Morrígan village. Kestra could stay with Macha until she was ready to fly. Give them a chance to fix her up with a permanent home. Damn, his mind was wandering. He felt a little light-headed. "Hang on."

Prickly heat broke in waves across his body. God knew what alien bugs crawled through him. First Herecura, now Kestra. He broke out in a sweat. His knees buckled.

Sam grabbed him. "Careful. You'd better sit down before you do any more damage."

# CHAPTER TWENTY

Yerit crept up behind the evil stench desecrating this beautiful forest. The human tendency to destroy its habitat clashed with every tenet of Morrígan philosophy. His leather-hide boots made no sound as he stalked his next victim, giving Yerit a moment of satisfaction that was immediately eclipsed by a fierce thirst for vengeance.

He had both sensed his queen's arrival and heard Kestra's screech of pain. He allowed himself a moment of pleasure as he sliced the man's jugular from left to right in one eye-blurring move. He managed to avoid touching any part of the animal's body or clothing. The human dropped silently to the ground, falling face first into the forest debris.

A spider scuttled across the dead man's splayed hands. Yerit carefully avoided the tiny creature as he side-stepped the body. The smaller the bite, the more it stung. On Astereal, he could walk bare-foot in the forest. Here, Niall'Kearey had advised his immune system might react badly to the insect venom found in these parts. After sweating for five days and nights following a mosquito bite, Yerit had decided Niall'Kearey's words to be wise. It was either wear boots or endure Choluu boxing his ears. He had even begun to like his new footwear.

He crouched down to study the clearing ahead. Through the leaves he could see a pale-skinned man resting his rifle on the rock. The hunter was eyeing a cave in the cliff above, awaiting another opportunity to shoot down his prey. Yerit narrowed his eyes on the man, noting details like his wide-brimmed hat, his grizzled beard and the smoking stick in his mouth. These men thought they were on a simple hunt, oblivious to the enemy closing in on them.

The man straightened and Yerit followed the man's gaze towards the dropping sun. They both caught a glimpse of something slipping from the shelter of the rocks at the mouth of the cave into the vegetation clinging to the cliff. The man studied the area for a long time, oblivious no longer. Minutes passed as the hunter watched and listened.

Yerit remained perfectly still.

He would let the hunter make the first move.

Movement from the rock prompted a reaction. The hunter swung his rifle up to his eye and aimed at an emerging head. Yerit raised his arm and threw his knife. The sharp blade hit the man square in the back of the neck as a shot rang out. The hunter flew sideways. He did not move. Yerit bared his teeth. He watched the tall shooter creep out of the bushes and stoop over the man, noting with interest that the warrior's skin tone was much darker than the members of other tribes Yerit had seen in the forest. When the new arrival noticed the knife protruding from the man's neck, he swung around to sweep the bushes with a searching eye.

"I Niall'Kearey friend," Yerit said, preferring to deter this warrior from shooting at him. The stranger met his eyes through the undergrowth.

"Me too," the man replied, his voice low. "And you are?"

"Yerit."

"Nice. Good to see you're okay, Yerit. You can call me Jester. Think I'll give you this one." Jester nodded to the dead hunter. "Did you notice any others?"

Yerit turned and pointed behind him. "Two dead. Four more near the cave."

Jester nodded and tapped his mike. "Spider Two here." His voice stayed low. "Friendly identified and with me. Three dead. At least four more closing in on target. Over."

Yerit's sharp ears caught the sound of a voice in Jester's ear. Jester nodded as if the speaker was in eyesight. "Copy that." He looked at Yerit. "We're gonna make sure no one slips through the net. You okay with that?"

For answer, Yerit approached the body, bent down and extracted his knife from the man's neck. Wiping the blood off on the hunter's clothing, he nodded towards the distant rock where he and the dead hunter had spotted movement. "Bait?"

"Yeah, decoy. Thought we'd draw them out."

Yerit looked at the body laid out on the ground. Bloody brain tissue oozed out of the star-shaped hole centered on the dead man's temple. The human's weapons were effective. He slipped his knife into the sheath around his calf. "Okay."

Jester looked momentarily confused and then his face cleared. "Okay! Cool. We'll split and circle around. No one gets away."

Yerit took the outer perimeter. His warrior blood sang through his veins. He would need Choluu in their bed tonight.

Macha knelt at Niall's side; she had a natural fragrance he liked. The back of her hand against his forehead felt good. Warm.

Niall opened his eyes. "Any Morrígan voodoo you got would be good right now."

Her slightly ridged brows scrunched together. "Voodoo?"

"He means alien magic," Sam said.

Her face cleared. "He's too cold," she decided.

"Shock," Niall mumbled. "Kestra alien."

Sam rummaged through the med kit. "We should give you whatever shots we've got here."

"Might not help."

"We need Miach," Macha decided, rocking back on her heels. Her eyes glazed over. "Take deep breaths, Niall'Kearey. Increase your heart rate. If you can open a link to the island then Miach will be able to assist you."

Sam's head shot around to stare at her. "Miach can form a bridge, too?"

*Shit.* Niall's heart thudded up a gear, enough for him to send her a tight warning. *Macha. Careful.*

Macha shook her head. "The High Brighid selected Miach to be Niall'Kearey's host for a reason, Colonel, but Earth does not suit all his abilities."

"He might be able to help me out a little," Niall added. *If he could even reach Miach.*

He remembered hanging from a rope off Bell Rock in Sedona, Uathach badgering him to increase the oxygen flow to his brain. *That's what he needed to do now.* He took a deep breath and focused, forcing aside the needle-like pain hacking away his left side. *Thank God Kestra hadn't taken out his right arm.* His heart jumped at the thought. Adrenalin kicked in and sparkly little holes sprang up around him. His consciousness shot through one of them and instantly drove towards Miach's mind searching for him.

*I have you,* Miach reported as Niall began to form a magnetic engine.

Dark energy built up inside the spherical glowing ball. They had done this on Astereal so many times, the process felt so natural, Miach's mind open and familiar.

Miach stopped him from taking full control. *No. Your mind is unstable. Use me to create the bridge to you, but do not bind with me.*

Niall screwed his eyes up in concentration. *What am I doing?*

*I see the link. Focus on the bridge.*

A glowing portal formed behind Sam. Miach shot into the cave so fast that Sam swiveled around, his weapon raised ready to fire.

"You're frightening Kestra, Colonel," Whelan warned.

Miach showed the palms of his hands as shadows reclaimed the perimeter of the cave. The focused beam from Sam's flashlight lit up the Asterean's face. "My apology. Niall'Kearey's link was unsteady. I feared his bridge might collapse."

Sam lowered his rifle. "My government does not know you can build a bridge." His voice was tight.

"He can't. He helped me focus is all," Niall muttered. He drew in a raggedy breath. Even with Miach contributing much of the energy, stabilizing the bridge through another had exhausted him. He could feel his body weight sinking into the cave floor. He didn't need Sam going homeland defensive on him.

"Perhaps we could discuss your concerns later, Colonel," Macha said. She gestured Miach towards Niall. "Can you help him?"

"How? How can he help?" Sam demanded.

Miach dropped to his haunches beside Niall. His fingers hovered over but did not touch Niall's dressed shoulder and arm. Niall sensed his former host's mind expand then invade his body.

"I am what you humans term a shape-shifter," Miach said to Sam, his voice calm, matter-of-fact. "The manipulation of microorganisms underlies the ability to heal. Reconfiguring DNA is the next step."

Sam relaxed his defensive stance. "That actually makes sense."

Miach grunted with a half-nod. "Niall'Kearey lacks the antibodies required to fight off a common but aggressive bacterium carried by gryphons. Previous contact with Kestra has caused his body to build up an immune response and it has gone into overdrive in response to an overdose."

"Like an allergic response," Niall mumbled.

Sam turned to his bag. "I saw anti-histamines."

"No, I need adrenalin." *Why didn't I think of that before?* "There should be some in the med kit."

Miach was silent, his mind working on something. Then he nodded. "Your body is responding as it should, but it will take time. I have increased the protein required to jumpstart antibody production and adrenalin."

Niall's mind was clearing already, enough to feel he had back control of his body, and the chemical buzz was dulling the excruciating pain. He stretched out his good hand and realized his weapon had been taken off him. Miach rose effortlessly, caught his hand and hauled him up. "Since you're here, you can help," Niall said. "I want to get Macha and Kestra out of here."

"Of course."

Niall found the link he needed to a spot far enough from the Morrígan settlement it wouldn't alarm the villagers. His mind scanned the clearing. Overhead an overlapping canopy of trees filtered sun to the ground and screened the forest floor from view by satellite or air traffic. He opened his mind fully to Miach as he began to form a bridge. Miach fed him enough dark energy to stabilize a much larger portal whose dimensions reached into the vaulted space above them. Niall fashioned it to look like the entrance to the cave. Macha stepped through to the forest on the other side and then looked back. They could not hear what Macha said, but Kestra suddenly lurched to her feet and slunk after her, her damaged wing making her movements lop-sided. Whelan's rifle tracked her every step.

For a split second the huge beast straddled the portal before forces beyond Kestra's control sucked her through.

Sam heaved an audible sigh of relief. "Thank God for that."

Niall let Miach help close the portal, more concerned with Sam's newfound suspicion regarding Miach's abilities. "I can return you now," he said to Miach as his mind thought, *If they think you can leave the island, they will lock you down.*

"I would like to visit the Morrígan, if that is acceptable to the Colonel," Miach said. "I do not know when I will get another opportunity."

"Be my guest," Sam said, gesturing to the space the portal had just occupied.

Miach's confusion was well done. He turned to Niall. "Major Kearey should rest before making the attempt again."

Sam tapped his comms-link, but his eyes stayed fixed on the Asterean. "Report."

"Our friendly has taken out the last runner. All identified targets neutralized. Heat sensors detecting a lot of smaller-sized creatures," Jester reported in Niall's ear.

"Conduct a final sweep," Whelan ordered. "Return to the cave when clear. Over. Shouldn't take long, Colonel." He glanced at Niall. "Suggest you rest while you can, Major."

Niall sank to the ground before his shaky knees gave way again. Miach slowed his descent by grabbing his good arm.

His brow furrowed, Sam squatted beside him. "How about those pain meds now?"

"No. Water would be good."

Sam found a bottle, wrenched off the lid and handed it to Niall. The cool liquid soothed Niall's throat but not his severed nerves. The whole left side of his body burned a searing crevasse in his ability to think.

As his mind drifted, he caught a ticking noise, a steady beat thrumming through his body. For a moment, he couldn't work out where it came from, but then Senator Biron's sinister face warped in and out, his mouth constantly moving, an implied threat behind every syllable.

Niall shivered. A hand touched his brow. He looked up and Sam's face morphed into the bearded visage of Biron's interrogator. He dug his heels into ground that did not give and tried to escape into the rock at his shoulder. A mountain surrounded him. He couldn't get a breath.

*Niall'Kearey.* Niall mentally swatted the voice away but Miach bounced back. *Niall'Kearey. Your fever has broken and your body has regained control. It is time to make a move.*

Niall nodded inside his head and Miach withdrew. Opening his eyes was like fighting a blindfold. Exhaustion pinned him to the ground. Despite his body's reluctance to cooperate, his mind cleared with every passing second. He banished fragmenting nightmares into the deep recesses of his mind and tested his ability to explore a dimension outside of space and time. For a brief moment, his subconscious grasped an insight of existence beyond the physical realms their bodies inhabited. The second of comprehension skittered away as his mind locked onto Macha's just a few hundred miles distant.

He could hear TomTom giving a running report.

Niall frowned. "Drug runners got too close."

His voice came out scratchy and someone pressed a water bottle against his lips. He took it with his good hand, the movement setting off that fiery burn in his shoulder. When his eyes finally opened, he found Captain Whelan studying him, his expression serious. Hard.

"We got them all, Major."

Niall understood. Whelan wanted the mission back on track and Niall was their transport, either that or a couple of days hike through rainforest. Whelan's team would enjoy the walk. Niall might not survive it.

"Captain, check the meds for adrenalin." The man rose to his feet and raided the med kit. Niall looked around for the Morrígan warrior. "Where's Yerit?"

"With Jester; they've been on clean up. They should be here any minute now." Whelan's eyes met Niall's. The captain indicated the epipen he'd found. "Is this wise, sir?"

"Pain meds dull my head too much. I just need a shot to get us to the village. Then you can shoot me up with every antitoxin and antibiotic we've got. I can rest up while you blast Kestra a new home."

Whelan didn't look convinced. He glanced at Sam who nodded.

"If Major Kearey says he can handle it..."

"Sir." Whelan pushed the tip firmly against Niall's outer thigh, waited several seconds then pulled the needle out. If there was a slight sting, Niall didn't feel it. Niall rubbed his thigh and within seconds his heart was racing.

"Get Jester and Yerit," he growled. "Gear up to go." His team grabbed loose backpacks, torches and lined up ready to move out. Niall's lock on the Morrígan Queen tightened. Miach helped him to his feet. The dark shadows of the cave glittered with holes. Sweat beading on his brow, Niall picked one, established a link and let his fingers automatically create an engine.

He sensed Miach monitoring the soundness of his bridge, but with Sam watching every move, the Asterean did not offer any assistance other than to keep him standing upright. On a chemical high, Niall formed a human-sized portal in seconds.

"Go, go, go," he ordered when Jester and Yerit arrived.

Miach half-carried Niall through the portal with Sam holding up his other side. It closed with an explosive flash as excess adrenalin surged through his system and hit him with palpitations. Jester and TomTom, who were nearest, ducked for cover.

"Sorry, couldn't control it there at the end," Niall mumbled. An agonizing swathe of pain cut him to his knees. Only Miach's arm around his waist stopped him from toppling over. Everything went dark.

# CHAPTER TWENTY-ONE

Macha squinted up at the cliff-face.

"Here," Captain Whelan said offering her his sunglasses.

With her eyes protected from the harsh rays of Earth's sun, Macha studied the proposed spot for Kestra's new home.

"If it's too low there's another section of sandstone that looks good." TomTom pointed out horizontal layers of rock twenty feet higher. "I thought that slight outcrop would make a good landing pad."

Yerit stood with Jester on TomTom's other side. "That is good," he approved.

The foliage-covered plateau stretched for miles towards the main central basin, abutting up against a sedimentary clay and sand valley carved into a deep ravine by a waterfall one mile distant. High enough to deter predators, a cave would be partially protected by the jutting vertical section farther along. Kestra would love it.

"Ma'am?" Captain Whelan asked.

Macha studied the man. Whelan radiated anxiety, his jaw tight. The captain wanted to get Niall'Kearey home. "It will make a fine home for Kestra."

"Okay! TomTom, you have a go."

"We'll climb up and check for cracks," TomTom said. She grinned. "If it looks good, I'll bore a hole and set up a test charge. Pound of C4 should do it. Don't want to risk that ledge."

Jester clapped Yerit on his back. "Okay, dude, do your stuff. I've been waiting to see this."

Yerit tilted his head, gave a glimmer of a smile then unsheathed a set of talons so sharp the Special Forces man stepped back, hands raised.

Jester shot his gaze to the spikes either side of Yerit's neck then seemed to relax on finding them soft and unthreatening.

Macha caught a glint of amusement in Yerit's aura, although his expression conveyed his usual stoic severity.

TomTom's eyes balled out to the white. "Hallelujah, that's serious weaponry you have there." She presented her neatly cut and shiny nails for comparison then gestured to the coil of rope on Yerit's shoulder. "I'll stick with the rope, if you don't mind."

"Well that's sorted out Yerit's call-sign," Jester said, his voice full of admiration and a touch of envy. "Scissors!"

Yerit ignored them both, stepped up to the rock face and started to climb. Jester chuckled softly, pointing in genuine amazement before starting to call out advice on where Yerit should hammer in the pitons hanging off his belt.

Macha nodded to Whelan and left them to it.

Outside her people's tiny settlement, village children screeched with laughter as they kicked a ball around with the rest of the Special Ops team. Her tribe had brought out a protective streak in these toughened soldiers. Earlier she had witnessed Jester's eyes soften as tiny hands pulled him around the camp. The children were fascinated with his dark skin and short curly hair, constantly turning his hands over and chatting nonstop with words he should not understand. The big man responded anyway with intuitive nods, grunts, and the odd smile. It had been the same for Macha and Niall'Kearey's children when they had arrived from Astereal. Macha smiled, remembering how one little girl had offered her mud to cover her own pale-colored skin.

Earth had changed her people, but not their hearts.

She had missed them.

Entering Yerit and Choluu's hut she moved across to where Niall'Kearey lay on a pallet. A cushion wedged against the small of his back tilted him onto his good side so that his injured shoulder remained free of pressure. Choluu knelt beside him, trying to tempt him to drink.

Macha didn't need to see Niall'Kearey's eyes dulled with pain he refused to admit. His aura had dimmed to a fragility she had not seen from this man before. His pain stabbed her heart. His suffering was her fault. She'd trusted Kestra to recognize her. If she'd been more cautious in her approach...

"Where's Miach?" she asked in her own language.

"I bade him to sleep," Choluu explained. "His concentration was waning."

"That is sensible. Good. Have his efforts made a difference?"

Choluu peeled back the thin cover. A sling strapped Niall'Kearey's hand to his naked chest. "His fingers are a good color now. The blood flows well."

"I won't lose my hand," Niall'Kearey said in a rasping voice.

Macha's eyebrow shot up. "I did not know you knew our language."

"I know a few words, and Choluu nagged Miach to fix my *foil* and she's been checking my hand all night. Wasn't hard to work out."

"*Fuil*," Macha corrected automatically.

"Whatever." His eyes closed.

Choluu put down the cup of water. "His shoulder is inflamed, but that is natural for the healing process. Miach believes Niall'Kearey's body is fighting the infection well."

"Hey, speak English," her patient protested without opening his eyes.

Choluu ignored him. "He tries to hide his pain, but—" Her aura colored with agitation.

Macha shared her concern. "I will ask Colonel Hastor to make him accept some pain medicine. It will allow Miach to focus on healing. He will be here at least another few hours." She studied Choluu's aura, struck by a new tint she hadn't seen before.

The Morrígan female turned her head and met Macha's assessing gaze with a shy smile. Macha's eyes dropped to Choluu's belly and her mouth dropped open. Choluu had always been barren. She took a quick intake of breath. Barren on Astereal. But this was Earth. Macha beamed and the new mother's smile widened. Macha wondered if Yerit knew.

Niall'Kearey raised his good hand. "What about Colonel Hastor?" he muttered.

"Yes, what about Colonel Hastor?" the colonel's voice echoed behind them.

Sam Hastor needed no persuading of the need for intervention. When he got out a morphine syrette the major rallied enough to demand a fentanyl lollipop instead. With Niall'Kearey settled, Macha addressed the main question on her mind.

"Colonel, I wish to stay with my kinsfolk for a while. Kestra will need me until she is recovered enough to fly and I want to make sure she settles in her new home." And she missed her people. She expected Choluu would welcome her presence too.

*Macha?* Niall'Kearey's thought was dull and Macha glimpsed the reason behind his reluctance to use pain medication.

*I wanted to help Tami settle on the island and reassure your government at the same time, Niall'Kearey. But Miach will be with her and my place is with my people.*

His mind withdrew, but the tense line of his jaw betrayed his unhappiness. Was it her leaving his family that upset him, or her mention of Miach? He had no need for concern. Miach was a source of great comfort to Tami Kearey. Macha wished Niall'Kearey could see the way his wife's aura lit up at the mention of her husband's name. They had a connection, an empathic sense for each other's feelings, but Tami's mind did not have the same telepathic promise her daughter showed. If Tami and Niall'Kearey could share each other's thoughts perhaps they wouldn't feel so far apart, although Macha had seen Tami's aura strengthen in the weeks since living on the island.

Perhaps with more time...

A distant explosion broke her chain of thought.

Colonel Hastor turned towards her. "Yerit told me the tribe can extend Kestra's cave over the next few days while she's recovering on the ground. We just need to give them a good start." He indicated Niall. "I want to get the major back to the Asterean village at Nevada as soon as possible. Miach says they have healers more skilled than he at repairing the cellular damage to his arm and shoulder. I'll inform my superiors of your decision to stay. We're going to put in place security measures to better protect this whole area from unwanted attention anyway."

"I understand. Please tell your president that while I regret the injury to Niall'Kearey, I am grateful you and your team have spent time with my people." She tilted her head to gaze up at him. "Perhaps we are not so alien, after all?"

The colonel's smile held warmth. "I definitely like the eyes." His mouth pursed up in thought. "We should start a new craze for weird shaped contact lenses. My children would love the idea."

A chill made Macha shiver. She glanced down. A glittering anger lit up Niall'Kearey's eyes, and disapproval streaked his aura. A deep anger for the colonel seared her mind.

*Don't trust him, Macha. Sam Hastor will turn on you in an instant.*

# CHAPTER TWENTY-TWO

Pwyll shoved his long hair out of his eyes and surveyed the cedar-tree lined curves spiraling up to a glass-topped ceiling in a series of interconnecting layers. He and Niall'Kearey occupied a balcony overlooking a stunning vista of glass, crystalline elevators, and arboretums. Fountains and a water sidewalk led the eye through what was becoming a popular air-conditioned mall for the small community.

A group of Astereans lounged on chairs outside Saltside Café, chatting and laughing. The café was one of several new eateries. The number and range of facilities had recently exploded. A hot desert lay above the subterranean structure, but a newly constructed tunnel led into the mountains, allowing his people to experience the Nevada landscape.

Life on Earth was unquestioningly better than death.

"Yeah, well enjoy the gilding while it lasts," Niall'Kearey muttered.

Pwyll understood the weariness in the Earth human's voice, but he couldn't help but wonder if Niall'Kearey had taken his cynicism towards his own people to an unwarranted level.

"The facility here has always been very comfortable," he said, "and since you made your government aware of the blood ties between your people and mine there has been a change in attitude. I feel we are treated as valued allies." He noted how his mentor carefully flexed the newly-created muscle in his shoulder. Their mental exercises had achieved their objective and the strength of Niall'Kearey's shielding forced Pwyll to ask, "Does it hurt?"

"Not really. It feels strange, like it doesn't quite belong to me yet. It will be fine. Your healers have saved me months of recovery."

181

Niall'Kearey cast Pwyll a sidelong look. "You don't want to break out of here? You know, see the outside world?"

Pwyll grinned. "Yes, and we discussed that with the base commander. He proposed some guided tours of the US to start with. I put my name down to visit the Grand Canyon."

Niall'Kearey's lips twitched. His head bobbed up and down a few times. "A good choice. I have to admit I'm surprised. The tours, I mean."

Pwyll chose his words carefully. "Maybe you should have trusted your government with the truth sooner."

Niall'Kearey grimaced. "Maybe." He looked into the distance. "Don't forget my government has exactly what they want. Civilized aliens willing to assist Earth develop technological advances that would have taken us decades, even centuries, on our own. Even better, those aliens view humankind like a distant cousin, and this integration is just the last of many such cycles."

"Your mind is so full of cynicism you view your own kind as an enemy."

"My people abandoned the vast majority of your race, Pwyll. Have you forgotten that? Uathach understood. She told me the Hideout groups were prepared to deal with Earth." He massaged his healing shoulder with his good hand then waved at their surroundings. "Or perhaps you have been dealing and I've been too busy to notice."

Pwyll hadn't expected such an astute observation. Hiding his surprise, he went for a diversionary tactic. "What if your government hadn't abandoned my race? Maybe you would not have been here to save us. The Morrígan and my people would have perished on Astereal, and no one here might exist to know it."

Niall'Kearey let out a defeated sigh. "Thinking like that always gives me a headache. So, what you're saying is to let sleeping dogs lie."

Pwyll stalled. Sometimes Niall'Kearey used strange expressions, but if Pwyll thought them over long enough they acquired a semblance of sense. When Niall'Kearey went to open his mind to explain, Pwyll waved his fingers to stop him. "You are saying some things are best left undisturbed. I agree."

Niall'Kearey's head snapped around. Sharp, intelligent eyes studied Pwyll then narrowed. "Okay, so you're all happy. Everyone's super-dandy getting along and I'm wasting my time arguing for your rights. Where the hell's Sohan?"

*I am here, Niall'Kearey.* The scholar acknowledged Pwyll's presence through their open telepathic link. *I have news. Jacqueline and I believe we have determined the last known location of one of the orbs.*

Pwyll monitored the stream of information Sohan sent their way, but used a private channel to update Sohan on his conversation with Niall'Kearey.

Sohan's mind rippled with concern. *Be careful, Pwyll. Niall'Kearey walks a fine line between his loyalty to us and his duty to his superiors. Uathach wanted to protect him from yet another conflict of interests.*

*Induco is how the Vercingetorix have forced their will on others for centuries,* Pwyll pointed out while, on their shared thread of communication, Sohan reminded Niall'Kearey of his trip to Lake Titicaca. *I suspect Niall'Kearey would approve. We are evidently more skilled in the art of persuasion, as Herecura proved when Senator Biron arranged her passage to this country's capital.*

*Herecura was agent to an entity we are yet to fully understand. And our influence is limited. The Vercingetorix Council is stronger than we anticipated so I have been circumspect with my activities in France. Macha experienced more success with President Foldane, but I do not foresee another opportunity for them to meet.*

*Should we be assisting in the search for the remaining orbs? The High Brighid argued that full access to our knowledge could accelerate human development beyond their maturity.*

*Uathach had no knowledge of Balor. Macha shared her experience of Niall'Kearey's fear with me. There is something demented out there and it threatens both Niall'Kearey and Earth. I am convinced one of the orbs contains the ancient legend relating to Balor and its minions.*

Niall'Kearey had finished reviewing Sohan's memories of his research into the underwater city at Lake Titicaca and Sohan snapped off his private link with Pwyll.

*We need to acquire the orb before it goes missing*, Niall concluded.

Sohan's thought sharpened. *It may be that you are the reason the orb went missing in the first place*, he replied.

Niall'Kearey's face assumed the pallor coloring his thoughts. The man who had saved an entire civilization worked his jaw back and forth while his eyes looked to an unseen horizon through time and space. How far back are we talking?

Dr. Biron estimates fifteen thousand years.

Niall'Kearey's knuckles whitened where he gripped the railing. That doesn't sound good.

# CHAPTER TWENTY-THREE

Tami bit into her lower lip with growing unease. Niall had forced his healing shoulder through a series of weightlifting exercises that morning. Now he dripped sweat onto the deck as he shifted through a series of one-arm push-ups. His fierce determination to rebuild the strength Kestra had torn out of him made his mood volatile, and her jittery. She was supposed to be selecting photos for a website gallery, but the rampaging bear outside her window had put a stop to that.

She shook her head as Niall's arm broke into a trembling spasm under his bodyweight, almost couldn't watch as his face contorted with frustration but did, and then winced when he crashed to the wooden boards.

He snapped out a curse, rolled over and put a hand to his jaw.

Tami filled a glass with water, grabbed some tissues, and went outside. Niall sat on the wooden decking with his knees pulled up in front of him. He mopped his forehead with a towel. Anger and frustration rolled off him like the surf crashing on the silver-white beach.

She sank down beside him cross-legged and handed him the water. "You're pushing yourself too hard."

He slung the towel around his neck. "Not hard enough. I fell."

Tami caught his chin in her hand. He tilted his head to let her mop up a trickle of blood with a wad of tissue. "Serve you right if you broke your nose."

"I wouldn't dare. You'd have my hide."

"And then some, my handsome stud. There, you'll live." She put away the used tissue and waited. Something was rattling him and she was past doing the dutiful wife at home routine. As the seconds ticked by, she sensed the cool water soothe more than his thirst.

His hand covered hers. "Thank you."

Tami tilted her head and studied him until a wary expression stole over his face. "I don't think I've seen a mission scare you more."

His eyebrows knitted together giving him a boyish look of puzzlement. "Scared? Over a little treasure hunt? Nah."

Okay, if that strain in his voice wasn't about the pending mission to Bolivia there had to be something else. She narrowed her eyes at him. A mistake. His melting chocolate eyes held her gaze, the intense glint in his eyes making her tummy quiver. Damn it, he had this knack of turning her giddy. She could drown in Niall Kearey's sea of charm. "So, what's worrying you?" she persisted. "What aren't you telling me?"

Niall put his glass down on the deck, an easy excuse to look away.

Tami grabbed his wrist. "You can't keep protecting me like this. Not knowing is worse. I get tied up in knots imagining what you might be facing. You don't know what it's like... waiting all the time."

He spun around, a haunted expression in his eyes she recognized. "I do know. When you and the children were abducted, not knowing where you were, if you were okay—" His voice grated on the shards of remembered pain.

Tami shivered. She could smell his fear, almost feel his agonizing failure when he hadn't been there to protect his family, but even as her heart ached for him, resentment spurred her on. "Niall, for every second you risked your life on tour, I spent hours ignorant of every second you were perfectly safe. You knew that you were on base, or asleep in your bunk, eating a meal, or just messing around." She snatched back her hand from his fingers. "I didn't."

"I'm sorry—"

"I don't want apologies! What you experienced that day was my every day. I can't do that again. I need to know. I need to know so I don't have to imagine something worse."

"I tell you everything I can." His eyes closed. When they opened and slid away, she knew nothing had changed. "There's just so much. You need to trust me."

Tami tensed with frustration. "And you need to trust me! You chat with Miach and Macha all the time!" She tapped his head. "In there. They always know what's going on. Why can't you do that with me? You managed it with Lizzie."

A deep crevasse spanned his brow. "That was a brief connection. Adrenalin sparked off her latent telepathic talent; her mind was open—"

"Okay, what about the others? You told me you've possessed strangers before—people with no obvious talent, but," she drew angry curves in the air, "on your wavelength."

"That was before. I have more control now." Niall shook his head, his hands parting in a question. "Where are you going with this, Tami?"

"Aghhh... I don't know." Tami frowned at her toes, painted blue with yellow flowers, courtesy of Lizzie. She marshaled her thoughts, determined to verbalize the source of her anger, help him understand. "Okay, we've always had this connection, right? I usually have a good idea what you're feeling." He nodded. "And sometimes I see stuff. But all the empathy and clairvoyance in the world won't open your mind to me. You can reach across continents and play the air against my skin; step through space and time; possess alien minds across the universe, share your innermost thoughts with Macha and Miach, and one day, your daughter, but not with me. Your wife." Hot tears sprang up from nowhere and she wiped them away, embarrassed.

Niall's face cleared. "Honey, what we have has nothing to do with any of that." Tension formed a hollow pit below Tami's ribs as he continued, "And we do share a wavelength, I can see your aura now, but your gifts don't involve the right kind of telepathy so—"

Tami leaned away from him. "The right kind of telepathy! Are you even listening to me? I don't need a science lecture! Don't you see? I'm your wife and others know you better than I do!"

"That's not true—"

Tami slapped a hand over his mouth.

His eyes widened then and reaching up, he pulled her hand down. "I'm sorry. Obviously, I'm making a mess of this. Look, you have the floor. Just tell me exactly what the problem is."

"Niall, I'm your wife. I used to be a good military wife, but I don't care about all that classified claptrap anymore. And I don't like others knowing more than I do just because they don't need to use words. You need to talk to me. Include me in your plans. Share your fears. I don't want to be scared every second you're not with me. Not ever again."

He took in a deep breath then released it slowly and looked her straight in the eyes. She could see her reflection bouncing off his retinas.

"Okay. What do you want to know?"

Tami raked in every ounce of patience she could muster. "I want to know what's scaring you so bad."

He stilled. Hell! She actually saw the shutters drop down. Her mouth opened in disbelief. Hurt wrapped around her like a rope. Scrambling to her feet, she stumbled to the steps and ran down them, her vision blurred by tears.

Sea water was curling around her sandals when a hand clamped around her elbow. Niall spun her around in the shallows and gripped her upper arms. "I'm sorry!"

She smacked his chest, furious with him.

He let her go. "Just give me a chance here, Tami." His mouth grimaced. "The full truth is I need to look for another Asterean data orb... in the past... fifteen thousand years into the past. Maybe."

She stared at him for several long seconds. "That's like pre-biblical times."

"It's all guesswork at this point. And I didn't say anything because I don't want you worrying over guesswork!"

Grabbing her hand, he began to walk through the water lapping their ankles, pulling her along with him. Tami kicked back her feet one at a time to pull off her sandals with her free hand. Silky sand squelched between her bare toes.

Niall tucked her in close to his side. "Our first educated guess is that a group I settled in Bolivia became the ancestors of the Tiahuanaco civilization. I didn't have a geological clock. I worked by instinct. God, it sounds crazy now. I get sick thinking about what I did, but I was caught in a spinning wheel I couldn't escape. In the end, stopping became the more terrifying choice and when everything here on Earth carried on as before, it got easier."

Tami scrunched up her face. "I hear you say these things, and I stepped through your portal to this island, but when you talk about settling people in the past my brain wants to shut down."

Niall barked out a hollow laugh. "I don't think President Foldane quite believes it either, except that the Astereans have verified my story, and they can't deny the genetic evidence. It helps that I'm the only one that can open an orb that has been handed down through the Vercingetorix generations for thousands of years."

"Why fifteen thousand years?"

"There's a record of a box Sohan believes once held a data orb. It was found in sediment dating back to a time when the land there was flooded. I need to go back to a time before the flood and see if I can locate the box and hopefully find the orb inside it. Fifteen thousand years is Jacqueline's educated guess."

"What if she's wrong?"

"Back to square one."

"Can't you use your remote-view? The same way you did when you placed the Astereans and Morrígan into the past?"

"That's what I'm arguing for. But Sohan and Jacqueline think I might be the reason the orb went missing in the first place. The Vercingetorix want me to bind with someone, make them take the orb and hide it nearby, somewhere that's been undisturbed for thousands of years. Then an archaeological team will be sent to discover it."

The fluttering in Tami's tummy eased. "That sounds kinda okay to me."

"Yeah, but how long until the Vercingetorix or the government realize they have a time traveling weapon at their disposal."

"Say you can't do it. That it's too dangerous."

"Can't do that. I need to find these orbs." Something dark misted her mind and she glanced across at him. Exasperation clouded Niall's features as he caught her look. His jaw tensed. "There's something out there."

"What something?"

"It's complicated. The orbs may be the key to understanding it." He kicked the water sending up a salty spray.

"Complicated? Like discovering your mind can possess the bodies of our ancestors on the other side of the universe complicated?" Anger took her voice hostage. "Or deciding your wife can't be trusted to know her husband is learning to build wormhole bridge things through space because an alien species wants to come to Earth?"

He grabbed her shoulders and spun her around to face him. "I couldn't put all that on you. I could barely cope with it myself!"

Her mouth dropped open. She raised her hands up between them and sprung them apart dislodging his grip. "It affected us! The whole family! You didn't have the right to decide! And you still don't. Dammit, Niall, you make me so mad. You take everything on your shoulders. I guess when you're superhuman you begin to think the little people don't matter. Bit too much like the Vercingetorix, don't you think? Bet that's how our proud and great leaders think, too. Don't need to tell the general public we're spying on them for their own good. What they don't know won't harm them. Everything's fine as long as the right people are in charge!"

She stabbed a finger in his face, stopping a centimeter short off his nose. "You should have told me, Niall. Maybe I could have been better prepared! Have you any idea what it felt like to have men with weapons come into your home and take your children?"

"Shit, Tami—"

She shoved him hard and taken by surprise he staggered back. "Just leave me alone! If you won't tell me what's really going on, then nothing has changed at all. And I can't live that way anymore." Heart thudding in her chest, Tami turned and stumbled through the water back to the bungalow, hardly able to see through her tears.

A terrible ache filled a rift in her heart. This wasn't what she wanted. She loved Niall so much, but he was changing. She'd always believed that push came to shove he would be there for her and his children, before everything else. Now she wasn't so sure.

Niall watched Tami run from him through a blur. He swiped at his eye. Every word she said was true. He had played Russian roulette with their lives, understanding the dangers, thinking he could contain the situation, discovering his mistake only after it was too late.

Spinning around, he punched the air and yelled out his self-loathing to the sky. "Fuck!"

Tami had the right to know what was going on inside his head. Herecura's Balor had resurrected dark memories, given substance to an old nightmare he couldn't ignore, and it was driving him forward. He owed her the truth. Anything less would destroy them.

Okay, go for a walk. Give her a chance to calm down, and him time to figure out how to tell her he believed the orbs held information about an evil ghost from his childhood coming to get him.

No, not ghosts. *Aliens.*

An evil alien coming to Earth. To find him.

Dammit! This was going to be a long walk.

His cell phone rang as he neared home an hour later. He looked at the caller ID and smacked his forehead. He'd forgotten to check on Max.

"Max, hi. How'ya doing?"

"I'm alive, Major, thanks to you. I screwed up bad. Jacqueline worked out what happened and I've been given a formal warning, this time." Niall heard an audible gulp. "Err… this is a secure line, isn't it?"

"Yes, but possibly not as secure as you'd like. I can guess what's worrying you, though. I know the general's investigating the circumstances I found you in." Although Niall doubted Towden would ever identify the thugs who strung Max up to die.

"Oh. I wondered," Max cleared a glitch in his voice, "if you knew anything more."

"I don't." Niall hesitated. Not a single curse had crossed Max's lips. His close call with death had shaken him. Not surprising given black-suited agent types had invaded his home and set up a suicide that should have gone off like clockwork. "You back at work yet, Max?"

"Yeah, today. Why?"

"I was interested in your theory about our sensitives' erratic response to Earth's magnetic grid."

"Actually, DruSensi has been pulling overtime on my request so I'm guessing some high-up's interested in the results. Gotta run a batch of bio-chemistry tests. Hope you don't mind my using your blood results as a benchmark."

Niall sighed. "Go ahead, my blood's public property nowadays. But I appreciate you telling me."

"Least I can do. You ever need any help—that doesn't involve me breaking any non-disclosure agreement—you just ask."

"Sure, Max. Good to hear you're okay."

He terminated the call just as he reached home. Tami greeted him on the deck, dressed in a low-cut vest-top, jean cut-offs, and holding a glass of whiskey. No ice.

He stopped with one foot on the top step. "Is it safe? No ninja assassin waiting to jump out on me?"

She leaned her hip against the railing and leaned forward so he got a really good view of her cleavage and a good whiff of his favorite Scotch. "Depends. Do you come bearing promises of make-up sex, or honesty?"

Niall took the glass, put it on the railing, and backed his wife up against the bungalow wall. "I'll make you a deal. The longer the honesty, the longer the make-up sex."

Tami looked up at him from under her dark, thick lashes. She smelled great, an exotic mix of pineapple and vanilla. She projected a siren aura that captured his full attention. Her hand crushed his hard-on making his muscles tense with anticipation.

"Better start talking, boyo. Got a long night ahead of you."

# CHAPTER TWENTY-FOUR

GBI Headquarters extended two kilometers under Groom Lake and had been upgraded to oversee the search for the data orb in Earth's past. The place had sprouted so much hi-tech Niall wondered if the US-Asterean facility hid a hitherto undisclosed time-machine. He wandered around, his presence all but ignored by the busy technicians checking... stuff.

Sohan was in the control room, his head bent over a table. Niall walked over and scanned the data scrolling across the flat screen built into the counter top. Most seemed related to the Inca civilization. "You're monitoring Earth history?"

The Asterean straightened. "I am outside your timeline. I have memorized a number of key events in South American history since you settled the Paladins at Lake Titicaca. At the first sign of deviation, Pwyll will advise you to reverse your actions."

"Actions? If this works, I'm going to look around. That's all."

Sam Hastor joined them and Niall forced out a civil, "Colonel."

"Major. How's the family?"

"Fine... sir." He returned Sam's irritated glare with a questioning eyebrow. Sam's uniform guaranteed he held on to his pristine white teeth, nothing more.

Sam scowled. "Good, well, the Event Unit's ready for you."

Event Unit? Dear God, they were determined to turn a simple trial run into a SWAT team drama. He followed Sam to the large bullet-proof glass cylinder dominating the room. Someone had gone to a lot of trouble to provide a blast-proof cage for him. A comfortable chair sat in its center. All very different from last year when he skulked around Earth planting alien groups into Earth's history, and it wasn't just the setting. This time he had the experience of stepping back into Astereal's timeline to force Herecura into a cryogenic pod.

Could he do the same here? On Earth?

Although he'd no intention of physically stepping through time to anywhere, all he wanted to do was look.

Feeling the pressure of several pairs of eyes turning towards him, Niall stepped into his new domain and tested the chair. As he sat down the lights dimmed and the activity outside became less distracting; a movie sequence of shadowy figures.

"Ready when you are, Major," someone said.

Niall waved a hand, tuned the peripheral noise out, and focused on finding his way to South America, more specifically, the border between Bolivia and Peru.

An inner world replaced the physical one around him. He could feel his heartbeat accelerate as his mental faculties shifted into the higher order required to astral project across to another continent. He had done this joy ride since childhood, whether subconsciously surfing Earth or surfing the solar system and landscape of Astereal through a tiny hole in the fabric of space-time. The gradual Alignment of Astereal's timeflow with Earth's had forced him to recognize his ability. First, he had remote-viewed Washington, DC from Ghana, then South America from South Africa, and later the Amazon from the magnetic North Pole.

The more he did, the easier it got, but whether surfing the geomagnetic field or shortcutting space through the q-dimension, his sense of wonder remained undiminished. Even now, as he homed in on the northern Andes Mountains and then Lake Titicaca, his mind's eye admired the stunning waters that seemed to stretch on forever. He could make out the infamous causeway that crept out of the lake to nowhere, a throwback to an era when this whole region formed some huge lake port. An earlier time when the Paladins might have been caretakers to a data orb, and a time presently beyond his reach.

"Damn," he muttered.

"Major?"

He recognized General Towden's voice. "I'm remote-viewing Lake Titicaca, General, and I can see the link to Astereal just like before, but nothing much local to Earth. Nothing to help me reach the past. Stand by, sir."

Niall sent out a call to the only man who might be able to help. *Miach?*

*I am here.*

Niall shared his problem. *Any suggestions?*

*Maybe recreate the link you used to settle the Paladin group. The slight discrepancy between timeflows might help you to manipulate the time component of your lock.*

He could return to the observatory where he'd holed up with Herecura. Take oxygen with him.

*Alignment helped you create a link to the past from Astereal,* Miach observed. *The timeflows are closer now. It might not work.*

*Could you do it? Create a bridge to a different point on the timeline?*

*No. I could not pull in the energy requirement, but what you are attempting now is akin to a vision, whether forward or backward in time. Often a residual time memory in an object helps to find that link. Perhaps you should return to the lake. The effort of projecting your mind to a different location from your physical one is adding complexity to your task.*

Towden wasn't going to like that suggestion, although the idea would be considerably more attractive than him returning to Astereal's timeline.

Niall broke the link he had formed to remote-view Bolivia and waved his hand. "Lights, please."

"Report, Major."

"I can't see a link into the past from here, General, but it's possible I will have better luck if I'm physically onsite."

"Luck?"

Sohan stepped forward. "If I may, General, that is a good suggestion."

Towden looked around the expensive control room, his craggy eyebrows forming a deep V. Then he sighed. "Personally, I'm not surprised. Traveling into the past shouldn't be easy. I have another suggestion. Try to go back in time here. Five years. Report back what you see."

Niall settled back into the chair. The link to Astereal shone as bright as ever, but he focused on the other pinpricks of light in his mind, looking for one that would take him directly to the center of Groom Lake. The local holes were the hardest to find but the surrounding flux helped. His mind's eye studied the low-slung buildings dotted around Area 51, the source of an electromagnetic intensity that added to the natural anomaly emanating from Death Valley.

He studied one link more carefully, drawing his focus out until the control room began to thin and he could see through the whole underground complex to the sky above. He thought back to the observatory outpost on Astereal's third moon. There he had increased his heart rate, focused on rock, felt the panic of being trapped, and then had burst out onto the Fel.

He tried the same here, burrowing his mind into Groom Lake's salt bed. A second passed. He could hear the rush of blood in his ears. His lock nudged back and then he could sense time racing back faster and faster. Towden had said five years. He looked for the buildings and found empty desert. Movement caught his attention. He locked on an army vehicle bouncing across the white lake bed.

Yes! He had what he needed.

Breaking the link, he opened his eyes.

"I went back to a time before Nellis Air Force Base existed, sir. I did see an army car though. Got the license plate. Twenty-five, nineteen, Nevada 1932."

Towden rubbed his hands together. "Nellis was McCarren Field back then. That car could have been a survey team. I'll see what we can check out. Meanwhile, work on improving your accuracy, Major. Try conducting a visual survey of the area at five-year intervals. Details we can verify."

Niall inwardly groaned. "Yes sir."

"Colonel Hastor."

"General?"

"Contact Captain Whelan. I want his team ready to accompany you and Major Kearey to Bolivia in twelve hours. Secure communications with GBI."

With arrangements set in motion to explore the past, it was the future that concerned Niall more. The potential for abusing his skills would escalate dramatically the moment he found the orb and proved that he could indeed reach into Earth's past. The Vercingetorix weren't going to stand for anyone but their Council controlling his ability to remote-view the past, and possibly manipulate the future. He was headed into a dirty political battle, but overriding every instinct to leave the past well alone, a visceral dread of a bigger threat kept Niall silent.

The data orbs presented their best hope for understanding Balor.

# CHAPTER TWENTY-FIVE

Niall placed his hand against the huge block of granite holding up the Gate of the Sun at Tiahuanaco in Bolivia and this time managed not to jump out of his skin. God, his brain was practically humming. He lifted his fingers clear then touched the artifact again. He recognized the sensation, but he'd never fully understood it before. This gateway was different, ancient. Now he perceived the residual memory Miach had mentioned, a sense of ages pining to be revealed.

He let go before his head spun away or he fell over. He needed to build up some resistance to its effect, learn to manage its potency.

Jester was walking around the huge monument staring up at carved squares decorating the entire upper mantle of the gateway. "You sure those ones are condors? Looks more like a Kestra to me."

Sam Hastor joined him. "Damn, I think you're right. That's amazing. How old is this thing?"

Niall recalled the brief facts he had memorized in preparation for settling Asterean groups across Earth. "At least twelve thousand years according to some studies, but I settled the Paladins here about eighteen thousand years before that."

Whelan lowered his binoculars. "How can you be so precise?"

"I can't. But there was no lake here at the time. I don't remember the mountains being so close either." Niall pointed to a strange animal etched into the stone. "That is supposed to be a toxodon, extinct over ten, maybe sixteen, thousand years ago. But Jester's right. The condor symbol is actually a representation of the gryphon as depicted on several structures in the city of Paladin. It's partly why we settled the Paladins here."

"Your report said you knew the city would be destroyed by flooding. Why didn't the Paladins evacuate their city?"

"They probably did. They certainly had fair warning. But the original settlers knew they had thousands of years before it would affect them. This would have been an amazing home for them."

"The Inca civilization may have originated from Lake Titicaca," Jester said. They all stared at him with undisguised surprise. The former Marine grinned broadly. "PhD in Latin American History."

Niall's jaw dropped. "You're kidding."

"I kid you not. Not everyone wants to join the officer ranks. It's entirely possible that the people who lived here migrated north and became ancestors to the Inca civilization. Unless you settled Astereans at Machu Picchu too?"

"We looked at Machu Picchu, but the Inca culture diverged too much from the Astereans," Niall explained. "But you could well be right."

"Fascinating as this is," Sam said, "we have a job to do. Major?"

Niall placed his hand on the monument, this time prepared for his body's reaction. He searched for a link that would take him back to the past. His eyes glazed over as his mind swept down the ages, faster and faster. He fought for breath and when the world began to spiral out of control, he sank to the ground and rested his back against the hard granite.

Green cloudy water surrounded him.

*Must keep breathing! I'm not really here.*

He felt his lungs expand with air and everything went dark. Sediment. Which made sense, the gateway was discovered half-buried in sediment. He began to control his journey—scary how easily his mind extended its ability.

Could he have done this earlier? Uathach had warned him off tampering with the past. Now his fear of Balor pushed him to explore every potential facet of his capabilities. Instead of fighting him, his government prodded him forward. He didn't know which was worse. With time his superiors, and the Vercingetorix, would grow more confident; expect more and more until their demands turned into a feeding frenzy.

Caught up in his thoughts, he nearly missed the moment he emerged into sunshine. He locked on to the moment, unwilling to go back farther than necessary. To his surprise the palace and pyramid in all its former glory was deserted and he could hear the crashing of waves in the distance. His mind surfed towards the sound and discovered an ocean. Puzzlement tinged his thoughts as he scanned the sea out to the horizon, then checked out the port and causeway.

After a few moments he followed a trail of increasing activity to a city several miles distant. An outer plaza was busy, a throng of people engaged in everyday activity. A woman mended fishing nets. Men sorted out sacks of corn. Niall passed through the city walls and found a market in full swing. A boy ran in and out of legs and stalls, laughing joyfully whenever chaos erupted behind him. He was a little younger than Toby and Niall instinctively knew this boy would love baseball, too.

As Niall explored the market, getting a feel for the place, his inner eye tracked the boy's antics. He noticed the kid kept stopping to look around him. A penciled frown pulled his huge black eyes together.

Niall stayed with him, listening to the raucous chatter around him, catching several words he understood from a lifetime of visiting Astereal. He was particularly drawn to one wizened woman who sat cross-legged on the ground with a wooden box containing fish buried in a generous layer of white salt. Her black hair was shot with silver and coiled around her head in plaits. She wore a simple brown-shift dress and she was studying the boy with interest.

Eventually she beckoned him over. "Venac," she said. "Venac."

The boy walked over to her. She lectured him for a few moments. He answered her, gesturing wildly around him, scuffing the ground with his toe in a circular motion. Then he glanced around him again, a wary expression crossing his face.

*Can he sense me?*

Niall blasted a wave of reassurance towards the boy. The kid yelped and broke into a proverbial run for the hills. He disappeared around a stone wall. Niall let him go. Chasing him would only scare the kid further.

The old woman muttered into her chest then climbed to her feet. She picked up her box, looked around and said to no one in particular, "Venac."

Niall followed her out of the city and into the surrounding hills. After a mile, the woman arrived at a stone-hut. She went inside. Niall scanned the room. It was simply furnished with a cot in one corner. The woman placed her box of fish down and turned around, eyes alert and attentive.

Niall sensed her mind reach out. She had a settled aura, wise and gentle after a lifetime of experience. He sensed sadness. Loss. She lived alone, but this hut had once been home to two. Loneliness enveloped him. Grief filled his heart. So lonely. Should he respond? He dared not open his mind, but surely a respectful touch couldn't do much harm.

He reached out. The woman stilled.

Then she nodded and moved the fish into a clay-lined hole sunk into the ground. She dipped a cloth into a pot of water, wrung it out and laid it over the hole. When she picked up a broom and began to sweep, Niall sensed he had outstayed his welcome.

He drifted back to the city.

Sam scrunched his face in a pensive frown. This wasn't good. Niall had always had part of his mind on Earth even while the rest of his mind was on Astereal. Perhaps going back to the past worked differently.

Crouching down, he waved fingers in front of Niall's nose. Nothing. No reaction whatsoever. He looked up at Whelan. "He's completely gone."

"Check his pupils, Colonel."

Sam took out a penlight, peeled back one of Niall's eyelids then passed the beam across his pupils. The pupil contracted. That had to be good.

"Err, Colonel?" There was a clear uh-oh note in Whelan's voice.

Sam released Niall's head and looked up. Whelan gestured down the trail. A police car bumped down the half-made road towards them. Damn. Sam stood up, pocketed his flashlight, and stretched his neck to ease the growing tension between his shoulders.

"Hope they got the memo," Whelan commented. He tapped a mike by his ear. "Keep weapons out of sight. Jester, contact base and get someone to call the authorities in Puno."

Jester moved back several yards.

The car pulled up. Two burly officers got out and walked over to them. Then they saw Niall. Sam winced. With his chin practically on his chest, Niall looked either hung over or like he was suffering from heat exhaustion.

An animated conversation broke out in stilted Spanish as Whelan tried to show them documentation and passports. The policemen just kept gesturing at Niall.

Sam frowned. Maybe he should try to rouse Niall, except he had no idea what the consequences might be. Then Jester stepped forward with some impressive arm waving and rolling of eyes, interspersed with broken Spanish, until one of the policemen laughed. Shaking his head with wry amusement, he got out his radio and called his station.

There was more rapid talk, gesticulation, frowning before the perplexed officer started to listen to the authority speaking on the other end of the line. Finally, he shrugged and terminated the call.

"Okay, okay," he said, scratching his head. He nodded at Jester and shook his hand. Then with one yelling "Crazy gringos," they returned to their car and drove away in a cloud of dust.

Sam looked down at an unmoving Niall. He had no idea how long this would take. He glanced at Whelan. "Set up camp. We'll take watch in pairs."

The market was closing down. Used to the Asterean blend of sophisticated technology, higher order skills, and medieval living, Niall was fascinated to discover the Tiahuanaco civilization felt familiar.

205

Granted, in several thousand years they had not ventured far from their home, falc'huns and airborne visuals were not in evidence, and power relied on consumable natural resources, but the city had a clean, well-ordered look about it.

The Astereans retained their genetic capacity for telepathy, but it was weak and sporadic in nature. When Niall connected with the odd aura some responded to his presence. He had startled more than a few. A binding with another was outside the parameters of this mission, the potential for interference too high, but he had seen no sign of the orb, and General Towden would want to know if binding was an option.

He decided to surf some extensive catacombs underground, but found little evidence of sun-god worship or a secret tomb perfect for hiding an orb.

Emerging into the evening light he spotted the same boy kicking a stone down a side street. Niall shielded his mind, but the youngster spun around, his eyes full of fear.

"Queca?"

*Amigo.* Niall made the thought more a nudge than anything else. The boy yelped, grabbed his head, "Aiya, aiya! Veta, veta."

*Shit.*

A voice called from shadows. "Venac, ven conmika!"

The old woman's wrinkled face shifted into the light cast by a fire lamp. She grabbed the boy's arm in a fierce grip then peered into the gloom. "Queca."

A thought shot towards him. *Parec!* Its tone was angry; demanded an answer.

This was the best chance he would get. *I seek the orb.*

He projected a mental image and she gasped.

*Queca?*

He sensed her mind opening to him.

*I am Niall'Kearey.*

Shock crossed her aura. Then awe. Excitement. She clapped her hands causing the boy to look back at her with a questioning look. "Samsara," she said to him with a hint of command. "Samsara."

Niall had no clue what that meant, although he thought he'd heard the word before.

The woman bent down, whispered in the boy's ear for several seconds, and pushed him forward. The kid looked perplexed, but resigned. He patted his ear as if he had water inside.

The old lady cackled then boxed it.

"Aiya!" he protested. A mutinous expression on his face, the boy's mind reached out, a tendril of consciousness extending in greeting. Their minds touched and Niall showed him his children playing with a Frisbee on the beach. The boy's eyes lit up.

*Me llamo Niall.*

*Si, Niall'Kearey! Niall.* The boy thumped his own chest. "Tupac."

*Tupac,* Niall thought back.

The boy beamed, his earlier fear forgotten. "Venac."

"Si. Shoo. Shoo." The woman moved to hit his rear, but the boy skipped out of reach laughing uproariously and vanished into the darkness.

Niall followed Tupac's aura back to the palace. Perhaps the orb was hidden in the pyramid. In a secret tomb. Or maybe the boy was leading him on a wild goose chase. How long should he stay? It had been several hours now. He focused on trying to see his own time and sensed the team settled close by.

Tupac stopped at the same gateway Niall had used to access the past and pointed at the Sun god.

*You're kidding me.*

The boy shrugged expressively and Niall mentally grinned, wishing he could explain the joke. Before he could reply, the boy's eyes widened. Niall's own attention was caught by a massive disturbance in the forces around them, something in the sky. He followed Tupac's pointing finger and caught sight of a shooting star. A wave of nausea sent his mind tumbling.

Then the boy screamed, pointing again up to the sky. Still reeling, Niall caught the briefest glimpse of a dark-ridged shiny shape headed toward the ocean. An object so large the supersonic vibration caused the earth to tremble, and rock to splinter.

Niall saw the boy scramble out from under the falling gateway, a sheer look of terror on his face. "Samsara!" he screamed.

More words followed Niall could not catch, but the boy's mind revealed his conviction that Niall'Kearey had brought death upon them all.

*No!* Niall shouted as Tupac ran out into the wilderness. He chased after the boy but then all Armageddon broke out; a massive explosion that rent the air and rocked the ground. Niall sensed a catastrophe beyond the imagination. For a few minutes there was silence, an eerie, wind-tearing silence. Certainty filled him. This was the moment a civilization ended. He heard the ocean thundering across the plain.

*Run! Tupac! Run!*

Niall searched for Tupac's aura. The palace began to fall, the very earth moving beneath the solid stone foundations. Another sonic boom scrambled his mind. He sensed his link closing, an irresistible force hauling him out of there.

It was a blazing white light that sent his consciousness spinning into the darkness.

Niall opened his eyes and gasped. Twisting sideways, he threw up on the dirt. Hot tears sprang to his eyes. "Shit! Oh my God, shit!"

Someone grabbed his arm. "Major, you're back. It's okay. You're safe. Colonel Hastor! Over here!"

Niall shook Whelan off, scrambled to his feet, and staggered sideways. His legs gave way and he hit the ground on hands and knees. A second bout of nausea swept through him and he emptied his guts, the vile smell filling his nostrils.

"What happened?" Sam demanded.

Niall shook his head, unable to speak.

"Not sure, Colonel," Whelan said. "Bad trip by the look of it."

Niall retched up more bile. The foul taste mixed with his tears and streamed from his nose. His head pounded. He had never reacted this way before. He should never have gone back in time. This was the payback.

He'd disturbed something.

That huge shape thundering across the night sky filled his mind. He groaned. Had his presence wiped out a civilization? Pulled a meteorite down to Earth?

"I did it," he croaked. "I did this."

"Did what?"

He moaned. "There was a little boy." A handkerchief was pressed into his hand. Niall wiped his mouth and fell onto his backside. "Goddammit! He was just a little boy!"

Whelan handed him a bottle of water. Niall swished his mouth with water and spat it out to one side.

Sam dropped to a knee beside him. "What did you do?"

Niall waved at the ruins around them. "This. All this. A meteor shower. Huge meteorite. You know like that meteorite that cruised over Russia. The one that destroyed windows across entire blocks. Earthquakes. But much, much bigger. Couldn't see it all. Disaster."

"But what did *you* do?"

Niall blinked. "Don't you understand? It can't be coincidence. Going back in time disturbed something. I shouldn't have been there."

Silence greeted his words.

Then Sam rose to his feet and scanned the city ruins. "Even if your link—not a full-blown bridge, note, a link—caused this, you couldn't have changed it. I mean, nothing's changed this end. Everything is as it was before."

Except the inevitability of it all didn't help. In the short time his mind had been there, he had connected with the people who had inhabited this place. He had witnessed a thriving civilization destroyed in a single night.

"There was a boy. A little kid. He didn't stand a chance."

"However, he died, he died a long time ago," Sam pointed out.

Niall stared at the dark outline of Sam's face. Then he turned away. A lump blocked any possible response. Tupac died a very long time ago.

He took another swig of water and rinsed out his mouth again. Then he tested his limbs capacity for holding him up. When he wobbled, he rested his hand on the granite and felt again that connection to the past. He looked up at the Sun god and shook his head.

"Unbelievable."

"What?"

"I think I know where they hid the orb."

# CHAPTER TWENTY-SIX

In her office, deep under Groom Lake, Jacqueline growled at the words on her screen. Pathetic. Totally lame. Sounded like she was begging for the job. Resisting the temptation to delete the lot, she saved a draft. Tomorrow. She'd finish it in the morning. Anyway, she was hungry and Sohan was meeting her at the Saltside Café.

Grabbing her bag, she logged out, switched off her laptop and the lights and locked up. Glancing down the corridor she saw a vertical strip of light pouring out from Kearey's office doorway. The tapping of keys told her that Major Kearey was still hard at work. A pang of guilt made her walk down and look in. He looked tired.

When he looked up and smiled, she leaned against the door frame. "I thought you wanted to get home."

"General Towden wants a full report for his meeting with Foldane tomorrow. Then I'm authorized to go home."

He sounded bitter. Her guilt deepened. "Almost nine to five."

"Almost." His brown eyes studied her until she squirmed. "Something wrong, Jacqueline?"

She winced, straightened, and walked in. He always had been able to see right through her. She had to tell him. She'd hate him to hear it from anyone else. "I'm leaving, Major."

He frowned. "For the night? Or?"

"Resigning. From GBI. From all this. I'm moving in with Sean."

His head tilted as he digested this information. "Wow. That is... unexpected." He paused. "And great, too. I mean, that's wonderful news. I hadn't realized you two had gotten so close."

"I need to get away."

"Ah. Your uncle?"

"He keeps trying to use me. To manipulate you. I need to make my own life. And this job is killing my relationship with Sean. I love him, Major. I can be happy with him." She wanted to be happy. She wanted what Kearey enjoyed with his wife. "I'm applying for a teaching post in Oregon."

He leaned back in his chair. "I wish you'd call me Niall."

She wanted to, but saying his name felt so intimate. She needed to keep a distance. Major Niall Kearey stirred up all the wrong feelings— illicit feelings. Her heart thumped too hard and fast. *Merde*, she'd been here thirty seconds. She turned to go, but something about his demeanor struck her. "Are you going to be okay?"

A dark shadow crossed his face. "It was a hard day. A little boy died."

Jacqueline covered her mouth. "Oh, God, I'm sorry. And here I am blabbing on about Sean and resigning and—" Tears welled. "How old was he?"

"Eight or nine."

"I see."

"I'll be fine. Once I get home. Hug my children."

"Yes." God, she could hardly speak. "I'd better go." Before she started blubbering. "I'm meeting Sohan."

He nodded and then looked down at his report. "Sure. I'll see you tomorrow. At nine."

She smiled, gave him a little wave, and fled. Walking down the corridor, she smacked her forehead. What the hell was that? The man had just gone through hell and all she cared about was making sure he didn't see how chewed up inside she was over him. God, the sooner she got back to Sean the better.

He had a way of making her forget about everything.

"Jacqueline?"

Surprised, she turned back to find Major Kearey standing in the doorway to his office. "Yes?"

"There was an ocean."

"Excuse me."

"In the past. At Lake Titicaca. And a sea port. A whole fishing industry."

"Lake Titicaca is massive."

"Jacqueline. There was an ocean."

Blood pounded through her veins, strong and invigorating. Scientific curiosity needed to know more. "How far back did you go?"

"I don't know exactly, but the people I saw were descendants of the Astereans I settled there, I'm certain of that. A meteorite hitting the ocean would explain how the place got flooded though, don't you think?"

"Wow." She remembered the papers her aunt... Uathach... had collected in the Vercingetorix library and embarrassment warmed her cheeks. "I think I need to do some more research. I may have overlooked something."

Niall stepped onto his deck. The instant his portal closed he tested his ability to create an engine.

Nothing. His lips thinned. Barring an emergency there wouldn't be any portals authorized until seven a.m. tomorrow when he was expected back at GBI. He should go see Jacqueline first thing. If Charles Biron was pressuring her, he needed to know why and how. He should have pressed her tonight, but thoughts of Tupac cluttered his head.

Toby ran out, wrapped his arms around Niall's waist, and gave Niall the biggest hug he could ever remember getting from his son. His son squeezed all the pain and hurt right out of his mind. He laughed and ruffled Toby's wild hair. "Has Lizzie been talking?" he asked.

Toby looked up at him and grinned, his nose wrinkling up as he worked out whether to break rank with his twin. "Yes," he whispered. "She says you're feeling sad."

"I've only been here a few seconds."

"She's known since we got back from school."

Lizzie slammed open the door. "You are such a sneak, Toby Kearey." Hands on hips his daughter was a force to be reckoned with.

213

"Did you hear him say that? Or were you spying on us?" Niall questioned, eyes narrowed.

She blushed. "I might have been spying."

Niall reached out with a simple thought.

Her immature mind responded. *Hi, Daddy.*

Niall stepped back in awe. Her thought sparkled like morning dew on a petal.

*Hi, sweet pea. Good day at school?*

She grinned and ran forward to give him a kiss. "The best," she whispered. "Could you help me with some math? Mom's forbidden me to ask Miach. She says I pester him too much."

Tami's voice answered her. "That's because you trick him into doing it for you!" She stepped out onto the deck, her lovely blue eyes lifting from Lizzie to Niall. "You okay?"

"I will be." He walked over and kissed her. "Now I'm fine."

"It all went okay?"

He rubbed the worry line from her forehead with his thumb. "I'll tell you everything. Later."

She nodded then rose up on her toes to plant her lips on his. "Jose and Luisa are coming to dinner. If it's too much..."

"No, that's great. I could do with the diversion. And they're already on their way over."

She poked him gently in the ribs. "I hate that you can do that and I can't."

He caught her hand and brought it up to his lips. She stilled as he softly kissed the inside of her wrist. Toby groaned and ran off to meet their guests. Lizzie sighed happily. Niall only cared that Tami knew he was okay.

Her eyes dilated and her neck relaxed. "Just tell me. Did you find the orb?"

"Yes. A team's already working on what's inside."

"Balor?"

"Too early to say. Tami, worrying over what's in the orb won't make them find it any faster."

"I know." She took a deep breath. "I've cooked a traditional island dinner. Fish soup followed by chicken coconut creole. Dessert is a surprise."

"Can't wait," he whispered. His head swam as he savored her scent. On a slight Tami-high, he let her go to greet a beaming Jose. They shook hands and exchanged a manly hug. Niall wrapped Luisa in a warm embrace then kissed her on both cheeks. "Good to see you, Luisa. I hope Jose's behaving himself."

She rolled his eyes. "I can't get rid of him. He comes home for siesta then tells me about all the little inlets and beaches this island has. Far as I can tell, he spends his day sunbathing on a boat!"

"He does look well-tanned," Niall admitted.

Jose smirked. "That will be from the stick she beats me with."

"Dad, Jose, watch!" Toby yelled.

They all leaned on the deck railing and watched as Toby juggled five balls. The balls jumped in intricate patterns from one hand to the other, impossible to track them properly.

Luisa clapped her hands. "*Bien cocido*, Toby!"

"Do it without using your mind," Lizzie shouted. "I dare you." She grinned at Luisa. "Watch and weep!"

Toby kept the balls moving for several more seconds before they dropped one by one into the sand. He stared up at his audience sheepishly then collected the balls. "I wasn't cheating. The point is to use my mind," he grumbled.

Niall laughed and walked down to help him. "You need to teach me your trick, Toby. That's a really useful skill."

Toby's eyes grew round. "Yeah, you know how those ninja people in films lift their finger up and the bullet misses them by a millimeter! This is how they do it."

Niall's heart pumped with excitement. "Show me what to do."

Toby went pink. He started throwing balls at Niall. "These balls have magnets inside them. It helps you see the air flow."

Niall's memory flashed back to Baffin Island when Sam had tried to sneak up on him with a gun. The change to the magnetic field had alerted Niall to his presence. This was the exact same thing. What if they used rubber bullets? Or 3D printers started churning out plastic weapons?

Every skill could be neutralized with the right understanding of how it worked. EM disruptors could block an external remote-view. A nano-sized implant could disrupt his brain's EM output. The right force field could take him to the edge of madness. Ferrite tiles could block his telepathy. An EM pulse could fry his brain as easily as the next person.

A real bullet could kill him in an instant.

Not everyone could bat it aside with a mental flick of a finger. He needed every advantage available to him.

A ball hit him in the face.

"Ow!"

"Concentrate, Dad!"

Niall focused on the airflow of the next ball thundering his way. Fortunately, he knew someone who understood his abilities better than anyone. *Miach?*

*Yes.*

*We need to talk.*

Jacqueline knocked on Max's door. "Max, you awake?"

She heard a grunt and then the door opened. A shiny, flushed, tousle-haired Max, slimmer than she'd ever seen him, opened the door. The smell of sweat permeated the room. For a moment she thought she'd called at a really awkward moment and then she spotted the cross-trainer set up in the middle of the room. "Wow, Max, you're taking this really seriously."

He nodded, beckoned her in then disappeared into a small kitchenette for water. Jacqueline paused at the air-conditioning unit by the door and increased the flow of air.

She heard the tap flowing and the sound of splashing. When Max reappeared, he was toweling his hair and face dry.

"Sorry about that. Had a life-changing experience recently," he said.

Her eyes watered. "I'm proud of you, Max."

He smiled. "Bet that's not why you came."

"In a way it is. I wrote my resignation letter today."

His head jolted back. "Resign? Shit. You can't."

Jacqueline frowned. "Why not?"

"We're a team. We need you."

"You don't." She waved her hand. "Anyway, I wrote to the university in Oregon offering a five-year term teaching post. They emailed me to thank me for my application, but that my application hadn't been successful."

He blinked. "Really?"

"Is it conceited of me to think I'd be a catch for a university?"

"No. I'd have thought they'd jump at you."

"I think my application was intercepted."

"Undoubtedly. Jacqueline, the only thing keeping us alive is cooperation. I've spent my life rebelling, but when black suits can drop round and string you up, and the authorities claim they've drawn a blank identifying the perpetrators, but not to worry, good behavior will keep charges of treason being filed against you for a stupid fucking mistake, you soon focus on basic survival 101."

She paled. "Is that what you're doing?"

He dropped down into a huge sofa. It sagged under his still considerable bulk. "The work's interesting. I'm getting paid really well. And the Asterean village is a really nice place to live now we can get out a bit more. Just wish it wasn't so hot."

"That's not what I asked."

"No." He sighed. "You think your uncle's behind your application getting scrubbed?"

"Can't think who else would be so vindictive. General Towden would probably write me a reference if I asked him."

"This isn't Towden's style. And you haven't betrayed your country or upset the powers that be, so you really shouldn't pay my cynical view any attention."

Ouch. Max had hit the nail on the head. She had revealed the existence of the Vercingetorix to Kearey and then aided and abetted him in his secret mission to smuggle aliens to Earth. She looked around Max's quarters. "Max, if you had the choice, not threats hanging over your head, what would you want to do with your life now?"

"Truth?" At her nod he leaned over and grabbed a magazine and flicked it open to a page of yacht ads. "I would get fit, learn how to sail, buy a boat, and go deep sea fishing."

Jacqueline looked at pictures of blue sky, blue ocean, and sleek white sailing boats battling the waves.

"That's a fine dream," she whispered. "You can do it, Max. You are doing it."

"CIA operatives get to retire," he said. "Presidents change, and your uncle won't be a senator forever. I'm playing a waiting game. I'm going to save my money and at the right time, I'll quietly retire and buy a boat. Then I'll disappear."

"I want to marry Sean."

Max belched. "Shit. Marry? The guy at Crater Lake. I didn't expect that."

"Why not?

"I always thought you had the hots for Kearey. God, couldn't have got that more wrong."

A prickly heat attacked the nape of Jacqueline's neck. Was she so obvious? New determination fueled her need to get away. GBI, working with the Astereans—at the cutting edge of electromagnetic science— was amazing for her career, but her personal life was stagnating. A man she loved and who she could make her very happy lived in an amazing place and if she didn't make the move now, she knew she would regret it for the rest of her life. Charles could go to hell.

"Thanks, Max, you helped me make my mind up."

"I did?"

"I don't need a job. I don't need money. I need to make the jump. Now. The rest will fall into place." His crestfallen face made her feel guilty. "You keep thinking of that big fish you're going to land one day. They only own you if you let them."

"Shit, Jacqueline, you can't go yet. I need you to go through a catalog of satellite images DruSensi sent me. You know how they discovered the lost city of Tanis in Egypt. I think the Asterean groups Kearey settled may have gravitated to areas with significant geomagnetic anomalies. I don't want the ancient sites. I want to find the prehistoric settlements buried under the sand."

Jacqueline stared at him open-mouthed. "Max, that's brilliant!"

A most un-Maximus blush suffused his face. He shifted his large buttocks on the seat. "Really?"

"Yes. I studied those Tanis images six months ago." She pounced on his laptop. "There was another site in Syria I noticed. Of course, the political tension made an expedition out of the question, even more so at the moment, but—"

She stopped, remembering Max wasn't cleared yet to know about the Vercingetorix, but there were references to ancient Syria in the Vercingetorix Library. Tante Nicole didn't have the satellite images, but if she was right... "I think we might have our next lead."

Niall chucked a beer to Jose leaning against the railing and handed another to Miach who sat on the lounger beside him. Picking up his own bottle Niall took a swig, sighed and rested back. The Milky Way twinkled overhead.

"I want to see these hops," Miach said, his nose wrinkling with distaste.

"Keep drinking," Jose told him. "You always like it after a few bottles."

"I prefer green tea."

Niall and Jose shuddered as one. Niall waved his bottle at the Asterean. "You need to drink beer to fit in on Earth. It's a rule."

"You only drank water on Astereal," Miach pointed out.

Niall snorted. "Asterean beer tastes like dishwater."

"Coño! I've either drunk too much or you need to break out the hard stuff." Jose plumped his butt down on a low bench. "Okay, *amigo, qué paso*? What are these *cabrones* up to now?"

"Not so much what they've done, but what they might do next."
Niall gave Jose a quick rundown of his trip into the past.

A glower settled on Jose's face. "They're gonna tear you apart."

Niall sat forward and the others subconsciously leaned in, too.
Elbows resting on his knees, bottle in hand, Niall directed his gaze to
Miach. "I've got to find a way around this implant, a backup plan."

Jose's expression headed south. "Don't play games with those *mama
bichos!* Shove an anti-satellite missile where the sun don't shine! *En el
culo!*"

Niall cracked a smile. "Not enough missiles."

"I've been monitoring the implant and we're investigating ways to
neutralize it," Miach said. "The problem is the tracking signal."

"I don't want to invite stronger measures."

"Could you switch it on and off?" Jose asked. "Use a dummy
signal."

Miach shook his head. "The signal changes frequency and output."

"They've encrypted it," Niall stated.

"Yes."

"I kinda expected that. Forget tampering with the thing for the
moment. I need to develop skills that don't involve the use of dark
energy. I can remote-view, communicate telepathically, interact with the
geomagnetic field, explore the q-dimension."

Jose stabbed a finger at him. "*Ah si es!* You need to become Toby's
ninja!"

"Yerit survived a fall of thousands of feet using a form of
levitation."

"This ability manipulates dark energy," Miach replied. "Falc'huns
and sky cities work on the same principle. Pwyll informs me the project
to replicate a falc'hun is making progress, but Earth's mass is proving
an obstacle. You will need to overcome the same problem."

"They're calling it a Falcon," Niall said. "Can't wait to test it."

Jose slapped his thigh. "Green Hornet to Top Gun!"

Miach shook his head. "There are several skilled Asterean pilots in
the US."

"You think our top brass will let aliens loose on millions of dollars' worth of advanced technology?" Jose countered. "They'll have our boys up to speed in no time."

"You think of us as aliens?" Miach asked.

"It's not a question of what I think. It's what the establishment thinks that counts." Jose thrust his beer towards Niall. "They don't even trust him."

Niall grimaced. "Which is why I need to be better prepared. I'll be here most evenings for the next few days at least." He looked at Miach. "Will you teach me? Whatever you know?"

A gleam lit up Miach's aura. "We will experiment, see what this implant permits, but do not give up on us neutralizing the implant. We will break this code."

Niall grinned. Leaning forward, he reached across his knees and snagged a beer from the cooler. Jose whipped it out of his hand.

Niall's jaw dropped. "Hey!"

"Major, you're gonna need more than magic tricks. You need to get back into fighting condition. That shoulder ain't right. Miach can teach you the fancy stuff. You and I are going into full-on training. No more beer, no more Scotch, no more deluxe cheeseburgers." Jose punched him in his weak arm and grinned as Niall winced. "See? You ain't there yet. But don't worry, the Juggernaut's gonna fix you up right!"

One look at the wicked twinkle in Jose's eye, and Niall knew the Juggernaut was gonna pummel him into the ground.

# CHAPTER TWENTY-SEVEN

Foldane moved from his study to the Oval Office to read Sohan's report on the Bolivian Orb. He preferred to receive Senator Biron there. The man respected the Office of the President, just not its incumbent. He sat down and scanned the introductory comments and was immediately hit by a foreboding sense of deja vu—this newest orb contained minimal reference to Balor.

Suppose Balor was all a myth. Kearey had kidnapped and unilaterally imprisoned a senate witness out of a closed hearing then abducted the President of the United States out of his bedroom in the White House. If Foldane hadn't witnessed Major Niall Kearey's terror with his own eyes, hadn't stuck by his instincts, Kearey would be contained by Biron's obscene force fields in a high-security prison pending trial.

The president scrolled down the orb's vast and incredible contents, and quickly succumbed to a building excitement. The more he learned about the Asterean civilization, the more he appreciated mankind's true potential.

Niall Kearey presented him with the biggest dilemma of his life. The idea might sound whimsical to Foldane's usual pragmatic thinking, but when Kearey brought the people of Astereal to Earth, he fulfilled the equivalent of some momentous destiny. The genetic evidence was indisputable. If Earth had shifted into an alternate reality—a new timeline consequential to Kearey's actions—Foldane didn't feel the new paradigm. Earth was in a good place. Niall Kearey proved that humanity had the genetic potential to outreach their alien cousins. The Astereans offered new solutions to managing Earth's climate crisis and the technological knowledge to expand mankind into space.

Kearey's actions since were the fly in the ointment.

His fear of this 'Balor' cast doubt on his legacy, and Foldane's blood pressure rose every time he considered the man's ability to sidestep space and time. Foldane reached for his medication. The thought that Kearey's personality was dysfunctional in some way, psychotic, seeing monsters that didn't exist, terrified him. Senator Biron once presented Kearey as an anomaly that needed explaining. Now that anomaly was bigger than ever, increasingly complex, and inciting friction between the Hideout countries with the Vercingetorix stirring up rival national interests to get their own way.

A knock on the door made him look up. He dry-swallowed a pill quickly as his secretary popped her head around the door.

"Senator Biron, Mr. President."

Foldane rose to greet the man. "Charles. Punctual to the second."

"Mr. President." They shook hands. "I won't preamble, Robert. I've just learned that Etlinn Morgan's research has uncovered evidence that supports Major Kearey's story regarding Councilor Herecura and the existence of this Balor."

Foldane's heart quickened. "So Major Kearey's actions were warranted?"

"It would seem so. Patrick Morgan informs me the UN has been notified of the significance of Professor Morgan's discovery. The Secretary-General is convening a closed meeting of the Hideout members to agree what steps should be taken to protect Earth. Expect his call. Special envoys in attendance will be allowed direct communication with their country's leader. I respectfully urge you to attend in person. The meeting's decision will be binding."

"What has Major Kearey been told?"

"Nothing at this point. The Vercingetorix refuses to release any data until the meeting. Mr. President, if Balor does exist, and Herecura is an agent for an alien aggressor, then we need to assume one of the orbs holds the historic data we need for a proper threat assessment." Biron was positively slathering at the mouth. "We have a lead for a fourth orb."

If the senator puffed up any more Foldane would need to call housekeeping. "Go on."

"My niece, Jacqueline, identified this new site and Patrick Morgan is insisting we give Major Kearey the chance to investigate so members have all information available to them."

"Insisting, is he?" It stuck in Foldane's craw. Morgan's impatience had resulted in bloodshed on American soil, but without any connecting evidence, he couldn't risk going after a diplomat whose international banks owned a substantial portion of the US economy.

"Kean's death has undoubtedly increased Patrick's influence, Mr. President," Biron acknowledged, "but Councilor Sohan is very optimistic about the chances for success. The settlement is laid out in an ancient symbol of the Mesopotamian god, Shamash—a star and sun. Sohan believes the sun represents the location of the orb. You might conjecture that the Astereans placed a message to the future, for this lost settlement could never have been discovered before the emergence of satellite technology."

"Where is this lost settlement?"

Biron grimaced. "Syria."

Foldane groaned. "Why couldn't Kearey smuggle the orbs into the US? Or France? Even China. Anywhere but a Muslim country in civil uproar. Do you know I spent a whole hour placating the Bolivian president over the destruction of their Gate of the Sun? I don't know where to start with Syria."

"First, we need to establish if the orb is even present. We know Kearey can remote-view the Middle East from Groom Lake. It's possible he will be able to remote-view the past. General Towden will be calling you shortly to report. He cannot know about the UN meeting or Etlinn's research. Morgan detected Macha probing his mind when they met here. She is a very powerful telepath. So is the Asterean, Pwyll. We need to be careful when meeting with the Astereans."

"More cloak and dagger shenanigans?"

Biron hesitated. "There's more. I have arranged for some precautionary measures to be put in place."

Foldane remembered why he disliked this man so much. "Sometimes, Charles, I think you're just waiting for an excuse to take Niall Kearey down."

"Not at all. Major Kearey is like an architect of history. I want to make sure he doesn't end up defining our future. That right belongs to the people."

"How magnanimous, Senator, given your Vercingetorix masters act like they are the only people that matter."

His Chief of Staff burst into the room preventing Biron's reply. "The Director of the CIA is on line four, sir."

His urgent expression forestalled any questions and Foldane picked up the handset.

"Amy? Go ahead."

"Mr. President. I understand Senator Biron is with you."

"Yes, that's correct."

"Good. Senator Biron needs to hear this."

"I'm putting you on visual, Amy."

"Thank you."

"Amy," Biron said, nodding to the woman who appeared on the wall screen.

Silvery white hair cropped short hinted at a woman who kept up with the latest fashion, while her lined face spoke of hard experience in the field. Foldane had never seen Amy Tighbuck smile, so her expression gave little away, except she wouldn't have called unless it was serious. Her eyes tracked left.

"Senator, a few months ago you tasked us with monitoring Commander Muhuza. This followed the terrorist attack on the town of Crestfall and the abduction of a military family."

Concern spread across Biron's face as Foldane raised questioning eyebrows. The senator leaned forward. "One moment, Amy. Mr. President, Commander Constantin Muhuza was the Rwandan militia commander who lost his son in a rescue operation of one of our agents, a rescue operation led by Major Kearey. When his family was kidnapped, the major expressed concern that the media coverage might alert his personal enemies to his family's situation."

Amy's voice spoke up. "I understand Major Kearey is one of the officers who got our two operatives out of Afghanistan?"

"That's classified information, Amy," Foldane warned. "I'd appreciate you putting a lid on any chatter."

The CIA director raised a delicate eyebrow. "Sir. Well, we knew Muhuza had put a bounty on Kearey's head and the intelligence services managed to keep Major Kearey's image out of the public arena, but when the alien story broke his face was all over the news. We subsequently increased our surveillance of Muhuza's activities and have been monitoring communications between Muhuza and terrorist groups in the US. They're searching for his family and getting increasingly frustrated by their inability to locate them or Major Kearey. We're picking up hints of a new plot. They intend to target a political figure in the hope they can torture the information out of them."

Apprehension shifted into alarm. "Who?" Foldane asked.

"Senator Biron is an obvious target," the CIA director replied.

"What? How?" Biron demanded.

"Excuse my bluntness, Mr. President," Amy said, her voice too professional to be genuinely apologetic, "but during your press conference you identified Senator Biron as having oversight of GBI activities."

Charles Biron fumbled for something in his suit pocket. "Oh my God." His face whitened.

Foldane had never seen the senator so distraught. Angry, cold, alarmed, yes, but suddenly the man looked about to collapse. He jumped to his feet. "Charles, are you alright?"

Charles pulled out his cell phone. "Jacqueline. My niece," he replied, but his attention was on accessing his phone. "I got a call earlier." He put the device to his ear. "Dr. Dayton? This is Senator Biron. Has my niece arrived yet?" Biron swallowed. "She hasn't? No... Please call me if she arrives." He paused. "I'm sure everything's fine.

Thank you." He shut down his phone, his eyes strained. "She was expected at Crater Lake four hours ago. Her boyfriend can't get hold of her. He texted me earlier. I was angry. I ignored the call."

Foldane glanced at the CIA Director. If Jacqueline Biron had been taken, she could be out of the country in four hours. "Amy?"

"Already on it. Alerts are being sent to all egress points, the Coast Guard, airports, FBI, police. I have to say, sir, we haven't picked up a whisper of any suspect activity. If she's already been taken, it's been done very quietly."

Biron dropped into the nearest seat and buried his head in his hands. Foldane knew why. 'Quiet' meant efficient. Professional. 'Quiet' meant that Jacqueline Biron was going to be very hard to find. Then Charles shot up straight, his eyes bright and piercing. He looked revitalized.

"Kearey. Major Kearey will find her. They have a connection. You need to call him now."

# CHAPTER TWENTY-EIGHT

Niall drew his mind back to a more distant perspective and studied the indentations in the landscape matching the circular shapes in DruSensi's satellite image of the Syrian Desert. It took a while to tune his inner eye in to what he was seeing but eventually new lines began to jump out at him.

"I can see the outline of a buried settlement, General," he reported. He searched for something, anything that would explain the deep unease that had tortured him all morning.

"Can you access the past?"

Niall connected to the sandy desert and traced the stone outline. He sensed the passage of time moving backwards, the sun rising from the west and setting in the east. The shifting landscape remained a barren rocky desert. No city alive with an ancient civilization. No hint of the events that had brought it down. His journey into the past slowed, became sluggish. "Maybe a hundred years. Nothing of interest." Niall wondered what he was doing wrong. "Maybe I need to be physically present to go back farther. At Tiahuanaco, I was connected to the orb, I just didn't realize it."

No one answered him.

Niall opened his eyes and tracked Towden's darkened figure pacing outside his bulletproof glass cylinder, the Event Unit a security measure designed to contain any adverse reaction resulting from his tampering with time. Every gizmo in GBI's newest facility was designed to monitor him, his EM and EEG output, his heartbeat, or the surrounding geomagnetic environment. It wasn't unreasonable. He had created seismic disturbances before.

229

At least Max no longer strapped him down under a magnetometer scanner.

"Stand by, Major," Towden said. He moved away. A small glow from a cell phone lit up the hand by his ear.

Niall sat up. Whatever was wrong, it couldn't be happening in Syria, at least he hadn't sensed anything going on. The creeping anxiety dragged at him. The glow winked out.

"Lights on," Towden ordered, his voice grave. He met Niall's eyes through the glass. "Dr. Biron is missing. They think it's Muhuza."

The name punched the air from Niall's lungs.

Max swung around in his chair, his eyes wide with alarm. "She left to catch an early morning flight."

"She never checked in at the airport," Towden replied.

Niall clenched a fist as a sick dread filled him. On the other side of the glass surrounding him, alarms registered his emotional output. He'd known! He'd fucking known and his psychic sixth sense hadn't been enough to save her!

"Can you find her?" Towden asked him. "Senator Biron seems to think you can."

"Maybe. I mean, I've fixed on her aura before. If I knew where to look, she would stand out."

Towden frowned. "Then until we get better information, I suggest you start with Las Vegas."

"Sir."

Towden stepped away, his body merging into the shadows. "Turn those alarms to visual."

Heart still thumping loud in his ears, Niall settled back in his chair. He remembered this feeling. The need to race out across the world and snatch his family from danger. When his wife and children had been taken, he'd no idea what his mind was truly capable of. Now he did, and it still wasn't enough, but he hadn't lost the insight of experience. Wherever Jacqueline was now, she wasn't in Las Vegas. They would have moved her. One person knew where she was.

Commander Constantin Muhuza.

Fortunately, unlike South America, Earth's geomagnetic grid put the African continent within easy reach. The lights went out and he settled back against the leather upholstery and let his mind soar then zero in on the Congo like a guided missile. He'd start in the Nord Kivu province, a constant source of instability. Trouble followed Muhuza around like a bad smell. The warlord switched allegiances with every change of wind and took his loyal followers with him.

"Major? What are you doing?" Towden asked.

Niall shifted part of his mind's attention back to GBI. "Sir?"

"Your brain activity is unusually high for local surveillance."

"She won't be in Las Vegas, sir. I was checking if I could find Muhuza." Towden didn't respond, but Niall sensed the general struggling to contain his anger. "I apologize, General. I thought Las Vegas was a suggestion."

"This isn't a one-man team, Major. You're part of a command structure. Communication flows two ways."

"Yes sir."

"But tracking Muhuza's a good idea. I'll get you the latest intelligence on his movements."

"Thank you, sir."

The invisible leash of command tightened around Niall's neck. Not for the first time, his desire to be accepted in the Air Force he loved was at odds with the person he had become. He wanted the freedom to travel at will, to act on his own recognizance. He'd taken decisions that had determined history, commanded wars across the universe, saved entire civilizations.

He was Earth's best chance of defending mankind against an unknown threat searching the universe.

For him.

Niall shivered. A familiar dread wrapped around his gut. He had faced all manner of terrors in his life. Nothing chilled his blood more than the thought of that inhuman mind crawling through his thoughts and dreams.

"Major," Max spoke up. "Your vitals are looking a little spooked."

Niall steadied his breathing and forced all thought of Balor aside. His focus had to be Jacqueline. "I'm fine. I'm surfing north west of Goma." He paused. Several auras were merged into one. He zoomed in on the group and discovered kids ferreting around a rubbish tip in the dark. Movement between two towns caught his attention. Armed rebels on the move. They were headed towards Sake, huddled together in an open bedded truck with dipped headlights. Perhaps hoping to retake lost territory. "Anything happening in Sake, General?"

"Stand by."

Niall followed the road. More trucks. Mount Nyiragongo spewed lava in the distance.

"Rebel forces are attacking the Congolese army in Sake," Towden reported. "Muhuza has been sighted in Goma."

"Copy that." Niall moved on from the developing conflict to the city that was divided by a ridge of hardened lava left by a previous eruption. Residents moved normally around the streets on bicycles and motorbikes, broken up by the occasional vehicle. The headlights of a covered armored truck headed west caught his attention. Sake lay twenty-seven kilometers to the west. Muhuza could be sending in reinforcements. His concentration slipped, the geomagnetic output from the whole area distracting him. Niall let his mind drift, searching the artificial electromagnetic radiation for a signature. Signals overwhelmed him. Television. Radio. Satellite.

"The situation is escalating. The UN team is under orders to evacuate," Towden advised.

Niall's mind picked up the sonic vibrations of a firefight. He followed the source, spotted a building on fire. A UN vehicle hurtled down the street. People were scattering from its path, the town waking up to imminent trouble. Terror covered the UN jeep like a cloud. Bullets kicked up dust around its rear tires. The UN team was under attack on all sides. The road to Rwanda traveled east just a thousand meters distant. Too easy a target for the ambush he sensed waiting to take them out.

"UN vehicle under attack, General. Muhuza's escalating the conflict."

"How many?"

"Seven, maybe eight."

"Can you open a portal to the area," Towden asked. "I'm seeking authorization to send an assault team to assist the evacuation."

"It will be too late. Sir, I might be able to hide them."

Silence.

Then, "Do it."

Niall's mind surged down towards the UN jeep. He had once created the equivalent of an electromagnetic shield to deter a lightning strike hitting the water around him. Electromagnetic forces might nudge a bullet aside, but he had a better idea. The shield he formed around the rut-bouncing jeep scattered light radiation in all directions. To the naked eye the car just disappeared. A few seconds later the rattle of machine gunfire emanating from the surrounding buildings stopped. He imagined the rebel's confusion. He stayed with the UN vehicle until it reached the open road to Rwanda. Congolese units were descending on the town from the east. Residents who had taken refuge inside had emerged and were fleeing the town on foot, bike or vehicle. Pandemonium was breaking out.

"UN team clear of immediate hot zone," he reported.

Rebels were gesticulating and arguing in the street where the UN jeep had vanished into thin air. Niall recognized one of Muhuza's lieutenants.

"Let's use the confusion to our advantage," Towden said. "Captain Whelan and his team are gearing up. Be ready to depart from the event room in five. Major," a deadly note entered the General's voice, "intelligence suggests Muhuza has stepped up his hunt for you over the last few years. Now your identity has been made public, no one close to you is safe. The president has authorized any and all deadly measures. Do whatever is necessary to find Muhuza, retrieve Dr. Biron, and neutralize an ongoing threat to national security."

Niall's mouth dried. "Sir," he nodded. Keeping part of his mind firmly fixed on Goma, he jumped up as the curving door to the cylindrical viewing platform swung open.

"Good luck, Major," Towden offered. "We'll monitor your activities from here. Goma only. Check in for orders before you bridge anywhere else." He glared at Niall from under his bushy eyebrows. "That's an order, Major."

"Understood, sir."

Towden's voice stopped him at the door. "Major."

Niall looked back, his hand on the doorknob, his body straining to get moving.

The general frowned at him. "This is your chance."

A chill ran up Niall's spine. Towden's message was clear. Prove he played for a team.

# CHAPTER TWENTY-NINE

The geomagnetic upheaval thudded up through the soles of Niall's feet and tingled in his teeth. The confusion made it difficult to separate out radio signals and other stuff hitting his EM radar, but gave him plenty for an engine.

"That volcano's not just puffing," he said.

Whelan shot him a questioning glance from his position by the window.

"It's messing with my head," Niall explained. "I'm not getting a clear visual."

The captain nodded his understanding and resumed his surveillance of the street. They had emerged from the portal into an empty warehouse situated behind the source of significant radio traffic. A shift in Whelan's stance alerted them they were about to leave their temporary place of safety. "Clear," Whelan announced. "Go, go, go."

The team moved instinctively. As TomTom took point and negotiated a shadowed path down the deserted street, the others covered her with their HK-416 assault weapons. Niall hefted his rifle in his arm, his jaw tensing at a slight reluctance in his shoulder to bear the weight. Jester went next. They all made it to the far end without detection. The rebels were headed out to Sake. No one seemed interested in scaling the lava rubble left over following the last eruption to reach Goma.

Heart pumping adrenalin-fueled blood, Niall sensed a thought. A rebel with telepathic potential. He touched Jester's shoulder. "Stand by," he ordered.

"What is it?" Jester hissed, searching around them for the problem.

Niall tapped his head and the Marine rolled his eyes. Niall jumped into the open mind, not bothering to attempt a binding, solely interested in locating the man's command post. He pulled out and surfed past the suburb of Giyensi to a lakeside plantation with white beaches and a rich man's house. The communications array drew Niall to the exact location. A thick menacing aura filled Niall's thoughts.

"Found Muhuza."

"How the fuck?" Jester demanded, looking around them again.

Muhuza sat in a thrown together communications hut moving toy soldiers on a map. He looked way too busy to be masterminding the abduction of a woman on the other side of the world. Niall isolated a link that would get them close to Muhuza's position. He nodded to a travel agent's office.

Jester busted the door down with an easy kick. Niall was spinning his engine before TomTom who had been covering their rear joined them. A portal emerged in the center of the small room. Jester bent down and snuck through first. By the time Niall crept through, Whelan had organized his team into a watch.

Niall did a quick recon and shorted out the satellite box in passing. "There are ten guards," he reported quietly. Jester cracked his knuckles. "Muhuza has heat sensors. I'm sending them noise."

"Communications?" Whelan asked.

Niall nodded to the satellite dish. "Suddenly not working."

The captain shared a look with TomTom. The explosives expert hefted her weapon up. "You been working out, sir?" she murmured.

Niall wished he'd had this fine control last year. "A few tricks I thought might come in handy. No one knows we're here. Let's keep it that way. I might need that dish working again."

TomTom nodded. "Sir."

It was a silent massacre. Niall choked his chosen target into unconsciousness, but the man's nails dug into his arms, fighting him every step of the way. Niall increased the pressure until his shoulder gave out. Cursing his body, he gathered dark energy and shot it inside the man's heart. As his victim went into cardiac arrest, Niall laid the man out on the ground, peeled back the man's eyelids and checked his pupils with his flashlight. Nothing. Dead.

He swallowed. Another life gone at his hands.

Niall's thoughts turned to Muhuza. The warlord had a lot to answer for and his death might bring an abrupt end to the night's uprising as his forces fell into chaos without their commander to direct them.

Jester met Niall and Whelan at the hut door. Niall could hear Muhuza yelling at some unfortunate, something about the communication network's mysterious failure.

Their goggle's heat vision negated any need for remote-viewing, but Niall spied in on them anyway. "The one under the table's buried in wire cabling, trying to fix the comms link," Niall whispered. "Muhuza's in the middle. Another target to the right."

"On three," Whelan whispered.

Jester put his hand on the knob. They burst in, Whelan low, Niall heading to the left and Jester covering the right. The two Africans spun around, mouths open. The one under the table hit his head trying to pull out. The guard to the right went for his weapon. Jester landed a knife straight into his throat.

Muhuza's aura turned red, his black eyes fixed on Niall. "Kearey!"

"Hands in the air," Whelan barked at him, as Niall grabbed the ankles of the man under the table and pulled. The man pivoted as he came out, Uzi, in hand. Jester killed him with one blow to the head with his weapon. Muhuza raised his hands, the sole survivor. Not a single shot had been fired.

"Where's the woman you took? Jacqueline Biron?" Niall demanded once Whelan had checked Muhuza for weapons.

A manic gleam in Muhuza's eyes betrayed his responsibility for Jacqueline's abduction. "Nowhere you'll ever find her." His accent gave away his English schooling. "Kill me and you will never get her back. What will your superiors say to that?"

Niall glared into coal eyes full of hatred and loathing. Behind Muhuza, Jester recovered his knife from the other dead man then took up a position behind the warlord. Baring his teeth in a grin, Niall casually lit a web of electric filaments between his fingers, a minuscule magnetic engine where the energy bouncing off the inside of its spherical walls was visible to the naked eye.

Muhuza's pupils reflected the moving light. "What trickery is this?"

Niall fed the energy to the link he'd located, growing a portal well in the floor, prepared for erratic forces this time. Molten lava spewed hot into the air, hissing as it hit the other side of the transparent portal membrane, an effect Niall hadn't seen before. "One-way portal," he postulated conversationally.

Jester obligingly thrust Muhuza's head over the edge so he could get a good look down. "Tell us where the woman is," he demanded. "Tell us the truth and I won't drop you in."

The rebel commander stared into the fiery bowels of the earth. He shook his head. Niall read disbelief in his aura and he stepped forward and bent down close to Muhuza's ear.

"It's real," he said softly.

Muhuza spat into the portal. Globules of spit evaporated just below floor level and the commander jerked back, getting nowhere with Jester behind him.

"I'm going to keep watch outside. Do what you got to do," Whelan said meaningfully, tapping his communicator with an exaggerated gesture.

Muhuza's eyes grew large; the warlord clearly thinking Whelan had tapped off his mike.

"You got this?" Whelan added to Jester.

"Love throwing scum into a good hot bath," Jester boasted.

"You can't do this," Muhuza snarled. "You are American!"

"You're looking to hurt my family, Muhuza. I can do anything I want," Niall retorted, his voice colder than ice.

Whelan emphasized Niall's point by walking out without a backwards glance and Muhuza went wild in Jester's arm hold, but with his arm twisted up into the hollow of his back the tough wily warlord was no match for Jester's iron grip.

Niall peered down the hole. "That looks hot. Good thing we can't feel it. We need something to test it properly."

He looked around and spotted a jacket. He picked it up and dangled it over the edge, holding it by its sleeve. Niall braced his feet on the floor, conscious of the pull he'd once experienced passing a camera through a portal to Astereal. He let the jacket go. The jacket smoldered the moment it passed through the event horizon of the portal then burst into flame when it touched the boiling pit below.

Jester edged the commander closer.

"Go to hell!" Muhuza spat.

His aura reddened and Niall sent a stabbing probe into Muhuza's mind. A vicious fury and bitter hatred blasted him back out. The Rwandan had latent telepathic ability, but not a wavelength that allowed Niall to jump in and take possession. Frustrated, Niall moved over to the table and rifled through the paperwork. A shipping invoice caught his attention. He thumbed through the printout portraying a three-way exchange of diamonds, drugs and AK-47s heading south from the US into Mexico.

Whelan's voice spoke out of his ear piece. "Confirmation received, Major. Any and all means necessary."

Niall and Jester exchanged glances. Jester shrugged, a deadly glint in his eye. Niall checked the invoice address on the letterhead and anxiety threaded through Muhuza, a dead giveaway.

"She's in Tampico?" Niall demanded.

The militia commander growled at him. Froth leaked from the corner of Muhuza's mouth. A sick madness leeched his aura, a darkness no light could penetrate. "You will not find her. She is a dead woman. Unimportant. Worry about your family instead. I have men closing in on your hometown as we speak. You will learn what it means to lose family and I will laugh in your face!"

Niall froze and then white-hot fury surged through him. Dark energy pounded to his fingertips and intensified to a laser beam. He would have taken Muhuza's hand, but Jester was in the way so Niall lanced off Muhuza's foot instead; shearing off the ankle and cauterizing the wound in one. The man's eyes bulged. Jester swore and adjusted his hold on Muhuza as the man's leg slowly slid off its usual support. Momentary shock brought a brief moment of silence.

Then Muhuza screamed a cry to wake the living dead.

Niall picked up the man's leather boot containing the severed foot. He gripped Muhuza's hair, shoved the Commander's stricken face into the bloody mess, and yelled at him. "Tell me where she is or I'll feed you limb by limb to a lake of fire, even if it means tying your rotting torso to this chair!" He stepped up to his portal, held the booted foot over his makeshift grill to BBQ heaven and dropped the meat into the coals.

Muhuza's pale shocked face contorted into spasms of protestations and pleas. Niall clicked his fingers sending sparks into the air.

Muhuza screamed as Niall eyed a point just below Muhuza's knee. "She's in Tampico! I have a shipment waiting to be loaded." His aura glowed with desperate honesty.

Niall moved to the phone. "I need that satellite back. And authorization to Tampico."

"Copy that," Whelan responded in his ear-piece.

"Okay, Muhuza," Niall said, pulling over a chair. "I want the address."

"Satellite should be back," TomTom said.

"But first, call off your men in Crestfall. My family aren't there. They're wasting their time."

Jester thrust the commander towards the desk, plonked Muhuza in the chair, and put a knife to the man's throat. Almost crying, his eyes constantly moving to his missing foot, Muhuza grabbed the phone. He stabbed the number and mis-dialed. They all heard the dead tone.

"Don't piss me off," Niall warned.

The broken man scowled at him with undisguised hatred. "You killed my son. I have done nothing to you."

"Your son was scum," Niall snapped back. "He tortured and raped a defenseless woman, and just for the record, it was him or me. And you? You send men to attack an innocent woman so you can target my family, my wife and children. You twist people's minds and get them to wage your insane war, killing innocents along the way while you call the shots safely from your hut. You're a coward, Muhuza."

Jester leaned forward. "The man has a point. Do what he says or I'll fucking rip off your ear!"

"Rip it off, anyway," Niall ordered.

"No!" Muhuza screamed, stabbing the handset buttons again. Niall leaned forward and put it on speaker so Whelan could hear. Towden might be able to trace the call.

"You," answered a gruff voice.

"This is Muhuza. Abort the mission, the family isn't there."

There was silence. "What about our money?"

"I'll pay you double for the inconvenience."

There was a long pause, the sound of heavy breathing, then, "You're the boss." The man hung up.

Niall's hand shot out and stopped Muhuza disconnecting his end. "Leave it."

Jester dragged Muhuza on his chair out of reach, the blade never changing pressure against the man's throat. The commander perspired, his face contorted with agony, his severed ankle a cruel reminder that Niall meant business.

"Where's the woman?" Niall demanded pacing up and down between Muhuza and the portal to Earth's mantle.

"She's in a shipping container. End of Reformat."

Niall took out his phone and accessed a map of Tampico. He stretched another part of his mind, determined not to lose the hold his portal gave him over Muhuza. Jacqueline's aura drew him in. It was thready, terrified. Niall's throat thickened. She felt violated. Shamed.

There were others with her. He didn't have time to mess about.

"Bastard," he whispered, anger thinning his eyes to a slit.

Muhuza seemed to recognize something had just changed. "I gave you the address."

"Jester?"

"Sir?"

"Stand back."

Jester raised his eyebrows in query, but he did let go. Niall backed away too. Muhuza sat in his chair, partly unsure, half-relieved, sweating and shaking with his pain.

Niall beckoned with his finger.

Muhuza pointed to his own chest, but then the slivering portal of fire shot across the floor under Muhuza's chair. It and its occupant dropped like a stone. A dawning horror contorted the commander's face as he plummeted into the thick viscous lava. He didn't sink straight away, buoyed up by his chair. At first, he sat silent in shock. Then he screamed, loud and long as his skin burned off to bone before his whole body incinerated into flame. Niall closed the portal over the horrific sight and studied Jester's dumbstruck face.

The marine shrugged. "Kind of poetic really." His eyes didn't quite meet Niall's.

Jester hadn't seen inside Muhuza's mind. Muhuza met the end he deserved.

Niall started building his bridge to Tampico. "We're going," he announced.

Jester nodded. "Egress in formation at my location now," he said into his mike.

Whelan and the rest of the team burst in seconds later. TomTom glanced around the room, her wary eyes narrowing, but no one mentioned the missing prisoner. When Niall outlined his rescue plan, they readied arms without a word.

As he made his lock inside the shipping container holding Jacqueline, opening his portal right on top of the positions of two armed guards, Niall spared a final thought for Muhuza's fate. The man had brought it on himself and, for the first time in his life, the need to inflict death stirred not a shred of remorse.

Niall caught the key Whelan threw him and inserted it into the handcuffs chaining Jacqueline to a bolt in the iron wall. He was sweating already, the rusted container like an oven, and it was getting hotter with the team cramped inside with TomTom on watch. Jester supervised confirming that the guards were definitely dead.

"I knew you would come," Jacqueline whispered.

Niall turned the key. "I'm sorry we didn't realize sooner you were missing."

The cuffs parted and her hands dropped into her lap. Her knees were firmly clasped together and she immediately smoothed the remnants of her tattered skirt over her exposed thighs. She shivered violently despite the warm temperature.

Niall took off his jacket and wrapped it around her bare shoulders covering up the cigarette burns marking her skin. His mouth tightened. Her left eye was completely closed, black and blue. He bottled up his anger at finding her bruised and cut up like this.

Harder to deal with the guilt swamping him—*his* enemy had done this to her.

*Should've hacked Muhuza to pieces.*

Niall crouched beside Jacqueline, giving her time to come to terms with the idea that her ordeal was over. Her hand plucked at her skirt. "I had to tell them something," she confided. "My uncle says if you need to lie, stick close to the truth."

Niall shifted uncomfortably. "We know about Crestfall. You did the right thing. You probably saved your life."

Her quivering chin wobbled a face already twisted and misshapen. "What about the people that moved into your house? I didn't think. I was so scared. I told them it wasn't true, but they didn't believe me." She gasped, running out of air.

"They're fine. We got it all called off."

"You did?"

Niall nodded. He gestured for the med-kit, gave her a fentanyl lollipop then moved around to gently probe her swollen ankle. She sucked in a hiss. A nasty sprain he decided.

"Sorry. I'm going to put your ankle in a support, and then we'll go. Get you fixed up back at base. We can be there in a moment."

"I've always wanted to go through one of your portals." Tears welled in her eyes.

Niall smiled at her. "You could have just asked."

She snorted, damp seeping between swollen eyelids on one side. Patting her shoulder, he put her ankle in a splint. Signaling to Jester, he began to work out a link back to GBI.

The Marine stepped forward. "Begging your pardon, ma'am, I'll be real gentle."

She wiped her nose with the back of her hand and nodded. Jester hoisted her into up his arms like she weighed nothing at all.

"Back behind me, Sergeant," Niall said.

Jester moved out of the way.

"Ready to move out," Whelan barked into his mike to TomTom.

The portal materialized just in front of the rear wall where Jacqueline had been chained up, the GBI event room on the other side. Jester and Jacqueline went first, followed rapidly by the rest of the team. Niall shot the pile of bodies in the shipping container one last filthy look, then stepped through.

# CHAPTER THIRTY

George Towden gently replaced the phone when he really wanted to slam it down. The president had barely given him one minute, palmed him off to the CIA director, unmindful of the fact that Amy had been monitoring the situation from Langley. Fortunately, he respected Amy Tighbuck. The Director had alerted the appropriate authorities to an impending eruption of Mount Nyiragongo and would monitor the fallout in Goma as Muhuza's forces discovered they no longer had a leader.

Looking out his internal window into GBI's main lab, Towden spotted Colonel Hastor newly arrived from Washington DC and beckoned him in.

"What's going on in New York?" Towden snapped at the man.

Hastor stood briefly to attention then shut the door. "Some big UN security meeting, sir. To discuss the Asterean situation, I think. Senator Biron didn't say. He was too worried about his niece."

Towden's eyebrows shot skyward. He hadn't imagined Senator Biron possessed a heart. He leaned back in his chair and loosened his collar. He hated this underground facility. The place suffocated him, despite the cool air from the AC. He noticed Sohan hovering outside. The Asterean straightened as their eyes met. He had an expectant air about him.

Towden rose to his feet. "Very well, Colonel. You're scheduled to leave for Syria at nineteen hundred hours. This mission needs to be low key, so try and keep Kearey out of mischief. Please show Councilor Sohan in on your way out."

He watched Hastor and Sohan exchange a few brief words before the councilor entered Towden's office. They shook hands; Towden knew the Asterean councilor liked to adopt Earth custom at every opportunity. The US drew the long straw with Sohan. He was a sensible guy, discreet, and always willing to progress Asterean relations with Earth.

"How can I help you, Councilor," Towden asked. He offered Sohan the Asterean's preferred choice of water over the 'shot in the arm' coffee Towden kept on heat.

"No, thank you. General, I have new information regarding the buried settlement in Syria."

Towden waved him to a seat. "Go on."

"I thought the orb would be found at the center, but I have learned that during this era of Earth's history your moon deities were considered ascendant to gods representing the sun."

Towden chuckled at Sohan's perplexed expression. "The Mesopotamians thought the Earth was flat, too. A lotta knowledge must have got lost in those early Asterean settlements. Okay, how does the moon fit into things?"

"There is a satellite circle indicating buried settlements five kilometers to the west."

"Okay, if the first settlement offers nothing, we'll check it out. Captain Whelan's team is gearing up to leave for Syria in two hours. I want an initial assessment carried out while it's dark."

"Thank you. How is Dr. Biron?"

Towden scowled. "Badly shaken."

"I would like to see her. She has been very kind."

A warmth in Sohan's voice soothed Towden's rattled nerves. Jacqueline might welcome a friend. "I don't see why not. I'll check if she's willing to receive visitors and let you know."

"Thank you, General."

After Sohan left, Towden accessed his laptop and opened the threat assessment to Major Kearey. Muhuza may have been eliminated, but the chatter from conspiracy theorists over alien visitors continued to mention Kearey's name. The president made a good call when he assigned Kearey a Special Forces escort, but in Syria, the roving radical units sweeping the country presented the biggest threat, especially if Kearey blanked out like he had at Lake Titicaca.

He buzzed his aide. "Get me the projected satellite coverage for the Syria op. I need to adjust the parameters. And alert Colonel Hastor and Major Kearey to a possible change in target site."

He'd let Kearey choose between the sun and its moon.

"Well?" Niall asked Pwyll.

The young Asterean dragged his cup of herbal tea towards him. He'd cut and spiked his blond hair since the last time Niall had seen him. In blue jeans and black t-shirt, Pwyll looked the image of a young American, his slight stubble adding a hint of experience to his youthful appearance.

Pwyll's sharp hazel eyes glanced to the corridor linking the Asterean village with GBI. "Sohan is on his way back." *General Towden is angry over the injury done to Dr. Biron and anxious about the mission to Syria. Nothing else.* His thought switched back to Niall's bio-chip. *Do you still have access to the dark energy?*

*I'm fighting the urge to drop in on Tami and the kids, but I don't want to spook anyone.* Niall was finding it hard to hide his relief. The more minutes that passed and no security descended on him, the more confident he felt that the deception had gone unnoticed. He wanted to do a victory dance, yank Foldane out of the Oval Office, blast DruSensi's satellite network into the moon, and obliterate the Russian satellite along the way. *How did you manage it?*

*We broke the encryption key and transmitted the code to the bio chip we inserted into your shoulder bone. In simplistic terms, when the DruSensi chip receives a transmission to switch on, preventing your ability to harvest energy, the bio chip we inserted emits the correctly encrypted transmission to switch off. We haven't a solution to the tracking emission, yet, but you gave us an idea when you cloaked the vehicle in Goma. We will work on a way to cloak the energy signature of a bridge.*

*It's a good start and I can access dark energy if I need it.* He thought the Asterean's strategy through. *If you can cloak the tracking emission, then I could use a decoy emitter to fool the satellites.*

*I will suggest this.*

"Thank you," Niall said, injecting the words with a ton of gratitude before adding, "for the tea."

Pwyll grinned. "I am glad we could be of assistance."

Niall stifled a yawn. "I'm going to grab forty winks before we head out to Syria. Let's hope one of these settlements is hiding the orb. I have a real bad feeling about this Balor, like something's about to happen soon." A foreboding terror continued to eat at his insides even after Jacqueline's rescue. "We have to find that orb."

"It might not be the right orb, if one exists at all," Pwyll pointed out.

"So we find the rest."

Niall had left Saltside Cafe when Sohan's mind nudged his.

*I will continue to search for possible sites. China is a distinct possibility. Maybe Tibet?*

Niall considered the possibility. The Himalayas had been one of his favorite settlements for the Morrígan and he remembered Uathach had been present at one of his insertions of Macha's people into Asia. Would she have hidden an orb with the Morrígan?

*Anything's possible, Sohan.* He opened the door to his quarters. *Right now, I'm getting some shut eye. I'll catch you later.*

He closed the door and headed for the bathroom, desperate to scrub the stench of Muhuza out of his skin. Wash away the sight of Jacqueline chained to a wall. Getting rid of the vengeful warlord solved one security problem. Morgan and Senator Biron were irritants he might have to live with, but at least he knew where to find them.

Chucking off his clothes, he stepped into the shower. Hot water hit his face. He lathered shampoo into his hair as steam filled the small cubicle.

But who ordered the attack on Max? Morgan accepted responsibility for his family's abduction, but denied knowledge of anything more and Niall believed him. The Vercingetorix was bigger than Patrick Morgan.

That woman, Sharifah, held considerable influence, and Emile Fitzroy would stamp on a kitten.

He rinsed his hair and turned the shower off.

The only one who inspired his trust was Etlinn, his mother, and he couldn't be sure that wasn't wishful thinking.

His cell phone rang. Wrapping a towel around his waist, Niall noted the caller id. Towden. "Sir?"

"I'm bringing forward the op, Major. There's movement into the area and the target sites could be crawling with some sort of military action by morning. The sooner you go, the longer you have to look around."

"I can be there in ten, General."

Niall hung up, sent his bed a longing look then grabbed some fresh BDUs. Syria's ancient past could hold the key to understanding Balor. A sudden adrenalin rush set his body buzzing.

Niall made a three-sixty-degree turn, letting his mind expand across the buried settlement. Jacqueline's notes made clear she believed these settlements predated the Natufian village of Abu Hureyra submerged under Lake Assad. He could be searching back ten thousand years or more.

"Anything?" Sam asked.

Niall grimaced. "Yes, a warplane approaching us from Aleppo."

Sam Hastor frowned. "Damn. Captain, report."

"Confirmed, sir," Whelan said, his fingers pressed to his ear piece. "Intel's coming through now."

"We're standing in the center of the outline Sohan described," Niall said. "I'm getting something, but nothing like the reaction I got at the Gate of the Sun."

"We've got ten minutes," Whelan called. "Then we're out of here. Stay close to the major! It's going to be a fast exfil."

"Can you reach the past, without getting lost in it?" Sam asked.

Niall dropped to one knee and rested the palm of his hand on the sand. "Stand by." Slowly the landscape whirled around him. The roving desert drowned under water. The River Khabur flooded the surrounding wadi before retreating. A settlement grew, but no big city, a simple village then dismantled. A force pulled at him. Drew him in. No, not a force. A mind. Familiar. Strong. Inexplicable anger choked Niall's thoughts until he had to know who this person was that pulled his attention from his mission. The shifting sands of time slowed in response to his interest. He locked on an old, wizened man in tattered robes walking across the desert. A long, scraggly beard hid his features. His eyes though were familiar. The old man's gaze sharpened and his body stilled.

"Ogmios," Niall whispered. *How in hell did you get there?*

Ogmios recoiled. He turned around and then stiffened. Niall watched as indigenous hunters charged down from a nearby hillside. The murdering Asterean Councilor hobbled away on a stick, his eyes tearing, stumbling on a rock. He didn't stand a chance.

Succellos' murderer didn't deserve a chance.

"Major! We have to go. Now!"

The scene whizzed away. Niall blinked, his mind back in the present.

"Are you okay?" Sam asked him.

Niall drew in a breath. The fighter plane approached, two miles out. He felt normal. No sickness this time.

"Good." He began to gather the energy for the trip back to GBI.

"Did you find the orb?" Sam said.

Niall looked around him for Whelan's team. "Jester! Get a move on!" He found the link and started building a bridge back to the event room. "No. I didn't find the orb." A portal shimmered in front of him. "Go, go, go!"

Whelan's team ran through, Sam next. Jester pushed Niall ahead of him as Whelan dived through from his left. Niall let the portal close the moment Jester stepped safely through. His heart raced, every nerve firing a warning he didn't understand. He held onto the residual energy from his bridge.

"Captain Whelan," Towden's aide said from the other side of the protective glass casing. His voice emerged through the intercom. "I have a coded message for you. Message reads: Goliath."

Whelan abandoned pulling off his headgear and swung around to face Niall, his weapon raised.

Niall didn't hesitate, firing an energy wave direct into Whelan's chest with a force that lifted the captain off his feet and threw him back against the glass wall. The shock wave rebounded through the room. Time slowed, this temporal distortion the natural result of his heightened senses. He caught sight of Jester's right arm lifting high, swung around, and managed to block a knockout punch when something stabbed his thigh. A pinprick. Hand crackling with power, he blasted Jester across the room but then Niall's legs gave way.

He dropped, dead-weight, the walls spinning, the floor rising fast, muscles turned to mush. He hit the ground hard.

Sam dropped down beside him, his expression aghast. His mouth opened but Niall heard nothing. He felt tired beyond belief, an unforgiving weight pressing him into the floor. His eyes closed. Shimmering holes in the darkness faded to nothing.

# CHAPTER THIRTY-ONE

He was falling, caught in a vortex. His body jerked; an involuntary reflex to save himself. There was a force pushing on his mind, a pressure he recognized. His heart beat triple time, the flow of blood roared in his ears. Niall dug his fingers into a soft mattress and pushed away with a low grunt, opening his eyes to narrow slits. Grasping his surroundings with a world-spinning turn of his head, he rolled off the bed, reached for his weapon and came up empty. A queasy smell of rubber fed an escalating fear as the grey floor swooped and soared under his nose.

*Biron! Fucking Biron!*

Moving very slowly, he unfolded his tense body into a sitting position, and rested his back against the bed. Long steadying breaths helped to stabilize the spinning walls as he carefully constructed shields to block out the electromagnetic field irradiating the room. His abilities had advanced since the last time Biron pulled this stunt on him. If he couldn't counteract the debilitating effect of the EM field, he might at least be able to manage it.

When he thought he was no longer about to vomit, he took in more details. Ceiling lights well beyond his reach bathed the room in a soft light. Rubberized walls contoured seamlessly into the floor. A wide horizontal window took up half of one wall. A stool was fixed into the floor before it.

*Why? WHY?*

He forced down the raging anger spiking iron hot between his eyes. He needed to stay calm to control his mind's reaction to the force field. He licked dry lips. When he swallowed it was like a fur ball had lodged in his gullet. He needed water. His thirst quickly dominated everything else.

He dragged himself onto the bed and spotted a water bottle set into a recessed shelf. He fell on it, twisting off the lid with trembling hands. The cool liquid splashed over his lips. He gulped down several mouthfuls then poured some into the palm of one hand and splashed the water onto his face. The refreshing feeling helped to wake him up. Holding on to the water bottle, he scanned every inch of his prison. Rubber curving surfaces everywhere. A door in the wall caught his attention.

He opened it and discovered a small water closet incorporating a shower.

*What the hell was going on? What did I do?*

Had they discovered the Asterean's deception to thwart the DruSensi chip? How? When? The Syrian mission had been authorized. Damn it! The DruSensi implant had curtailed his ability to roam the universe at will. This force field stopped everything, cut him off from everyone. He staggered back, the implications gathering and swelling. He had no way of checking on his family, He was totally dependent on Miach and Jose to ensure their safety. When they discovered he had disappeared, what would they do?

The cornerstone of a permanent headache slotted into place.

He stormed up to the window and thudded the side of his fist into the security glass. "What did I do?" he yelled to the empty room beyond. A winking light caught his eye, the fish eye of a surveillance camera. "Show your face, Biron, you fucking, gutless bastard!"

He waited a second. Nothing. Shaking his head, wishing he hadn't, Niall paced up and down the window. Someone would come. He worked through his actions in a logical sequence, searching for something he'd done to warrant such a disproportionate response, a hint of suspicion, something to explain someone issuing Whelan and Jester a coded kill order.

"Because that's what it feels like!" he yelled to anyone bothering to listen. "A fucking kill order!"

They had to know pissing him off would backfire. Towden lectured him on proving what team he was on. He'd put up with their paranoia, the constant attacks on his liberty, the unceasing mistrust, but trust worked two ways. If his own country had turned on him, who did he give his allegiance to now? They were isolating him and it made no goddamn sense. His eyes watered. There was no way back from this.

Gritting his teeth, hands balled into fists, he let rip. "Was it Muhuza?" he yelled. "The man deserved everything he got! I had authorization to do whatever it took!" He swiveled around on his heel, surveyed his new domain, then threw back his head and poured every ounce of frustration into a cry of fury. "Shit!"

He must have paced for a good hour, back and forth, thoughts buzzing, a rampaging anger powering an explosion of energy with nowhere to go. Finally, when his head pounded down to his stomach, he retreated to his bed, hostage to the waves of nausea rolling up and down his body.

He lay staring up at the monotonous grey ceiling, plotting a way to neutralize the goddamn force field that promised to drive him mad. He finished the water, and when he thought he could stand, he used the half-bath. He stank of perspiration and fear. He showered, but had no change of clothes so just put his pants back on. A ravenous pit deepened inside him as his head cleared. He began to think the last traces of the sedative may have combined with the force field and intensified its effect on him.

He scrubbed his hair with his fingers.

How long were they going to keep him waiting?

Another hour passed.

While he slept a fresh set of BDUs arrived through a trap door obviously intended for food. He was being watched.

He dressed in fatigue pants and t-shirt, feeling too wretched to put on his boots, then killed twenty minutes searching for a magnetic anomaly, something he could use to access dark energy. That laser beam he used on Muhuza would slice through the rubber, but probably not the iron steel lining the other side of the wall just visible at the edge of the window. It was a wasted twenty minutes. The force field was his kryptonite, a blindingly simple way to render his superhuman powers useless.

Maybe that's what this was all about—a pointed reminder that he wasn't beyond the full force of the US military. A mandatory retraining—break him down, build him up again. Ensure the fingers of power on the nuclear button reached him too. He'd given away too much, frightened them with laser beams, the ability to make a UN vehicle disappear, portals that descended into the Earth's core slithering across the floor.

He could have been a force for good.

America was the land of the free. The Constitution guaranteed every individual the right to live free of government tyranny. He'd signed his life up to defend that right, that freedom. Risked his life because he trusted that his country stood for the best this world had to offer.

He lay back and closed his eyes.

Senator Biron lay behind this. Did he blame him for what happened to Jacqueline? Guilt warmed Niall's cheeks. He'd sensed a problem. He should have alerted someone. Then when Jacqueline hadn't reported in, Towden might have put two and two together.

"I shouldn't feel guilty! Why do I feel guilty?"

Maybe if he hadn't attracted Muhuza's attention in the first place. Was Biron punishing him?

He launched up off the bed, stormed up to the window, and vented his frustration on the unyielding material. "It was Muhuza's son's life or mine!" His voice began to give way. "An agent's life depended on me. I didn't put my face on the news. Maybe if you'd answered Dayton's call, I could have found her earlier!"

He stopped, waited for a response. Nothing. "Fuck! Will someone please tell me what the hell I'm doing here!"

He splayed his nose and fingers against the window, trying to see right into the near corners of the room. Then a door in the opposite wall opened. He stepped back, drew breath ready to let rip into Senator

Biron. Instead, the sight of the petite woman crossing the threshold stunned him into silence.

Etlinn?

His brow creased. His mind raced. The Vercingetorix did this? But they wanted the orbs more than anyone. Why send Etlinn?

She walked towards him, stumbled midway. She had no aura. Correction, he could see no aura. Niall studied her more carefully. This was a shell of the woman he'd met in France. Her eyes were shadowed and puffy. She looked like she hadn't slept in days.

Days researching him.

A nasty feeling spiraled up his spine, that same sense of foreboding that had haunted him ever since Herecura had opened his mind to an evil beyond his comprehension.

Her jaw shook, her hands trembled. She looked like she might topple backwards if he so much as lifted a finger towards her. She stopped a foot away from him on the other side of the glass. Tears rimmed her eyes.

"I'm sorry, I thought I would be stronger than this," she whispered. Her voice emerged from a speaker embedded in the window frame. "I had to come. You deserve to hear why you've been locked up in here, and you deserve to hear it from me."

"You understand this is torture for me," he rasped. "And it will only get worse."

"Yes, I know. It won't be for long." A sob escaped her lips. Her hand shot up to cover her mouth. Her other hand groped beneath the window. She found a stool and drew it out.

Okay, this was obviously going to take a while. Niall perched on his stool, facing her.

Her eyes dropped to the shelf. When he opened his mouth, she raised a finger. "Wait, give me a few seconds, please."

Watching Etlinn Morgan, his birth mother, physically pull herself together, gave Niall a glimpse of the courageous young woman who had given birth on her own and then defied a powerful organization to secure his future free from a tyranny she no longer trusted. At some point, she must have reconciled her feelings to the Vercingetorix, and he suspected Patrick Morgan must have been the reason why.

She nodded, settled her hands in her lap, and met his gaze full on. "There's a lot to explain."

"Start at the beginning. I've got all the time in the world."

A sad smile tugged at her lips and Niall suddenly wished he'd known her before Patrick Morgan stole his family and put them in mortal danger. As the brief lightness faded back to tension, the band around his chest tightened.

"A while ago," she began, her voice finding a professional calm, "I isolated an unusual strand in your DNA. Analysis identified it as a gene found in Chromosome 15, but closer examination revealed a parasite chromosome wrapped around the affected chromosome."

"Okay, that doesn't sound good. Is it contagious or something?" Niall gestured to the room behind him. "Am I in quarantine? Is this before or after Herecura?"

"Please, I can't explain this piecemeal." She took a steadying breath then looked at him, checking he would let her continue.

He shrugged and tried to keep calm.

"This DNA came from a blood sample provided to us not long after your family was taken. So, nothing to do with Herecura. I've tested this sample a number of times, but I'm constantly developing new techniques. I isolated this chromosome using a quantum splitter microscope. The next time we looked it had gone. I didn't understand why at first, but then I realized that each used sample deteriorated on exposure to the air, specifically to nitrogen. A few days ago, I managed to catch the parasite chromosome disappearing. It transformed its host chromosome into something else, a form of energy."

Niall swallowed. "Go on."

"We needed more samples, for comparison. After you returned to Earth, I sent a request to Russia for samples of Herecura's blood work. We repeated the test on one of those samples. Her blood work gave identical results to yours."

"I thought you said—"

"Herecura isn't the source of this parasite, at least not in you."

Niall heard the tremor in her voice. "Who is?"

"Your father. Kean Morgan."

Niall blinked.

"Kean died recently," Etlinn continued.

"Yes, I remember, the night I returned from Astereal."

"He's your father and so, naturally, I carried out an extensive DNA analysis as part of a full pathology investigation. When the red marrow in Kean's skull stopped producing red blood cells, it set off a chain reaction. We caught the tail end of that chain reaction, a conversion of the chromosome to something akin to electricity that kickstarted a process in Kean's brain tissues. A short while after he was declared clinically dead, his brain erupted into activity. Neuron pathways connecting both short and long-term memory burst into life. The autopsy team measured a significant level of radiation emitting from his skull that lasted seconds before the level dropped again."

Niall closed his eyes, struggling to hold in a building scream fighting to escape.

"Memories?"

"Given Herecura's assertions, this is a logical hypothesis."

"What does this mean? That it's too late? That Balor has Earth's location."

"We've discussed this at length. The Vercingetorix Council, the UN Hideout Council, and representatives of your government."

Niall's jaw tightened. "But not with me? You don't think I had a right to know about these discoveries."

Etlinn flushed. "Yes. I was overruled."

Niall snorted, wanting one perfect moment where he could rearrange the face of every interfering, all-knowing, arrogant sons of bitches who presumed to roll dice with his life.

"I know you're angry, you've every right to be, but please let me finish."

"I'm listening," he growled.

She nodded. "Herecura needed to touch you. It was vital to her. She's now in cryogenic stasis. Kean Morgan never met you. He didn't even know you existed." She hesitated. "Our theory is that this parasite may exist across the universe. Herecura's stated mission suggests it could be a nano search device that infects whomever it happens across. This is speculation you understand. It found Herecura as a small child and based on Pwyll's evidence when he scanned her memory, it affected her personality. A parallel theory is that the same parasite infected Kean Morgan and drove him insane. Mad enough to change the loving father Patrick remembers into a man who raped me."

Niall's head jerked back. "Fuck. That's how it's in me."

"It's part of your DNA make up. Inseparable from your human DNA. It might explain your incredible gifts. If this radiation is able to access the q-dimension, then your mind might be simply replicating the process that occurs on death."

Niall paled. "What about Toby and Lizzie?"

"No, I've just completed a full set of tests, with Tami's permission. There is no sign of any parasite although I would like permission to do a brain biopsy to be sure."

"Shit."

"I strongly advise you or Tami give me that permission. It's in their interests to conclusively prove they are free of this blood agent."

"I need to talk to Tami."

Etlinn nodded. She glanced down at her hands.

"What?"

"Herecura was born a long, long time after I gave birth to you. So, whatever this Balor is, maybe it sensed a connection with you because of this chromosome. From what you've told us, Herecura seemed aware of a mission, endowed with a purpose: to find you. Kean may have just been infected by chance."

"You're suggesting Balor has spies across the universe, agents he can program to do his will."

Niall tried to absorb it all, work through his fear for Toby and Lizzie. However, he analyzed the problem, he kept coming back to this room. "Why lock me up? Why the sudden need to stop me using my powers?"

Etlinn paled, her voice dropped close to a whisper. "The Councils, Vercingetorix and Hideout, believe that your death will alert Balor to your presence on Earth. They are scared that the release of your memory patterns into the q-dimension will draw him... It... here. To Earth."

It took several seconds for Niall to follow that logic to its ultimate conclusion.

"You're locking me up for my own protection! So, nothing can kill me? You can't do that! I'll go mad in here. This force field will drive me mad. So, I don't do risky missions anymore. I'll be more careful!"

"Anything could kill you. You could get knocked down by a car. Faulty electrical wiring, some virus, a heart attack, brain seizure, the list is endless." She gazed at him, a terrible grief ageing her before his eyes. "They know the Astereans found a way around the implant, and if they can't control you, they can't protect you."

"So this cell is my punishment? Isn't that a little extreme? What the hell did they expect me to do?"

"This place is to hold you in one place until—" Her voice crumpled to a whisper hardly audible through the speakers. "Niall, you gave the Council the perfect solution."

He recoiled. "Fuck! A pod! You're going to put me in a cryogenic pod? For how long?"

Tears rolled down her cheeks. "Indefinitely. They've been testing the one they started for Herecura. The one you asked for."

Niall leapt up from the stool. "You can't do that!" He paced the room, thumping the rubber walls with his fist.

"Please don't," she pleaded. "If they think you'll harm yourself the room will be flooded with a sedative."

Niall glanced up at the ceiling vents, cursed viciously, long and hard, and then threw himself against the window. His voice grated against the raw edges of his throat. "Do you know I was once buried alive for months, trapped inside a dead host on Astereal?"

Etlinn gasped and covered her mouth. "No, I didn't." Tears streaked a path down her cheeks. "I'm so sorry. I can't think of another way."

# CHAPTER THIRTY-TWO

The door opened and Niall raised his head carefully, his spiking headache too vicious to ignore. The small portion of meatloaf he'd managed to eat earlier sat heavy in his stomach. The sight of Tami reduced him close to tears. Her eyes shot to the window and then she flew across the room. Niall levered his body up off the bed and put a supporting hand on the wall. He had barely made it to his feet before her nose was squashed up against the glazing.

"What have they done to you?" Her words rang with fear. "Can you hear me okay in there?"

"Yes. It's nothing. Just a headache. Side-effect of the force field." His voice came out scratchy. He worked his way around the room towards her, his knees shaky, but then he would climb Mount Everest with two broken legs to reach this woman. His fingers met hers, a ten-millimeter impenetrable barrier between them.

"I hate them!" Tami snarled. "They're evil and corrupt. Foldane. Our government. The Vercingetorix. All of them."

Niall swallowed down bile. "Yes." He took a shallow breath. "What did they tell you?"

"Everything. About this DNA parasite. That your death will bring monsters of doom upon us." Her voice cracked. "That they're going to put you in cryogenic stasis. For your own protection!"

Blood pumped through Niall's temples. He bit back a whimper of pain. "I'm so sorry. I never foresaw this. I knew something bad was coming... I assumed it was Balor."

Her cheeks flushed with indignation. Her eyes spat fire. "Balor was never your enemy."

263

"No." He rested his forehead against the window.

Her eyes softened, searching his. "Miach's been trying to reach you."

"Ferrite-tiled walls. The only way in or out is through the q-dimension, except this fucking force field is doing my head in. Tami, have they talked to you about the kids?"

"If you mean the brain biopsy, I already gave your mother permission to test them. I'm sorry, Niall. I couldn't risk them being placed in stasis too."

"Hell. How were they with it?"

"Good. Miach insisted he stay with them. He upped their endorphins, they barely felt it, weren't even sore afterward. I had to know, Niall. Etlinn was convinced they would prove negative and I didn't want anyone worrying over whether they were a threat to mankind."

"You did the right thing. Have you got the result?"

"Yes. It was negative."

Relief nearly took Niall's knees out. He gripped the shelf on his side of the window. A lump filled his throat.

Tami's eyes brightened with tears. "Etlinn says it might explain why they don't demonstrate your potential."

"So. You met Etlinn."

"And Patrick Morgan." Her expression darkened. "I slapped him."

"Wished I'd seen that. How'd he take it?"

"Politely. Niall, he wants to see you."

"Didn't think I had any choice in the matter," he muttered, trying to keep his blood pressure down.

"Can't they give you something for the pain?"

"They have. I'm already tanked up on pain meds. They make me sick and drowsy."

She swallowed, the light from his cell dancing in her eyes. "This is such shit!" Her eyes fell on the stool to his side. "Niall, sit down, before you fall down."

She stayed with him as he edged to the stool, like an invisible thread tied them together. "Miach says the Astereans are furious. They're working with Etlinn to find a way to inhibit the death process, but the UN won't approve anything without a cast iron guarantee."

"How long have I got?"

Her eyes filled. "Not long. They know you're suffering down here." Her lips mashed together as she tried to contain her tears and failed.

"Down?"

"Yes. Did you know this place existed?"

"I don't know what this place is." He looked down at his hands, twisted the ring on his finger and tried to calm the herd of buffalo stampeding between his ears. "Tami, where am I?"

"I'm not sure exactly." The way she looked up and around made Niall feel very nervous. "But it's an underground bunker, nearly half a mile down. I had to sign a non-disclosure agreement to see you. Patrick Morgan said a lot of secrets get buried here. They chose the location for its stability. The earthquake risk here is very low." She bit her lip.

Niall's heart thumped so hard he thought it might jump out of his chest. He raised his eyes to the ceiling and squinted at the lights. The earth above his head pressed down on him.

Tami laid her palm flat against the window. "Don't, Niall. Don't think of it that way. Niall? Niall! Look at me."

She shook her head at him. The force of her will reeled him back to her, but a deep certainty settled in his heart. Eons stretched ahead of him. A terrifying certainty swept through him. An urgency born from knowing his days here were numbered.

"Tami," he whispered.

She gasped, shaking her head. Her face contorted with her fear and pain. He had drawn on the dark energy of a universe and now it laughed in his face at his helplessness.

He jumped up and held out against the stabbing pain behind his eyes. "No, listen to me. Know I love you." She nodded. He rested his forehead against hers. "Always, Tami." She nodded again. "You must trust Miach. And Jose. They work well together. Macha, too. Toby and Lizzie need you to be strong."

"What shall I tell them?"

An answer hovered on his lips but the unforgiving ache in his heart stopped him from saying the terrible words. *Tell them I'm dead.*

Patrick Morgan barely recognized the man. On his hands and knees, Niall Kearey looked a broken man, a shadow of his former self. Tami Kearey had brushed past him without a word and now he knew why. Etlinn had thought her son—his half-brother—was holding up well.

No longer.

Forty-eight hours had chiseled deep hollows in Kearey's cheeks and drained him of color. Towden had warned the UN Council this would happen. Then Senator Biron pointed out that when Kearey escaped the force field at the Pentagon, his recovery had been instantaneous. The Council held firm.

Extreme measures would be taken to prevent escape a second time.

Patrick stuck his hands in his pockets and rocked on the back of his heels. "The problem is you scare people."

Kearey shot Patrick a startled look that promptly caused him to grab his head in pain. Patrick frowned watching Kearey force himself to his feet.

This torture couldn't go on much longer.

But then Kearey's gaze met his and if livid fury could blast through bombproof glazing, Patrick knew he'd already be dead.

"And no one's hands are clean. We all went against you—wronged you in some way—and the inherent nature of those who climb the greasy pole to power is never to appear weaker than the stronger person. You have to stay in the fight you see, anything else, and you're gone."

Kearey wagged a hand in Patrick's general direction. "Morgan, what the hell are you talking about?"

"The Vercingetorix remain secret for this very reason. Hitler proved once and for all that outright world domination just doesn't work. Selective persuasion is far more effective."

Kearey froze mid-step. "Adolph Hitler was Vercingetorix?"

Patrick shook his hands in a gesture of denial, appalled by the idea, and that Kearey thought it possible. He despised the Vercingetorix enough already.

"No. God, no! He could have been, the council of the time watched him very closely, but he taught us a powerful lesson. The man created the deadliest human machine ever created. He captured minds and hearts, and yet all his charismatic personality and power, and ruthless indoctrination of the masses, could not prevent the repressed rising to victory. It's the perception of freedom that's vital. The Hideout members wanted that for you—your sense of duty to the US Air Force offered a safety net—but Herecura instigated a ruthless autonomy in your make up, and then you went and flattened everyone's egos with the truth of our existence." He grimaced.

Kearey staggered forward and Patrick steeled himself for the remote possibility Kearey might bulldoze his way right through the window. Instead, Kearey's nose stopped an inch short from being smashed to pulp. "Is there a point to this, Morgan? Or are you here to gloat?"

"Aye, there's a point. I blame myself. I set a chain of events in motion that played to your ingrained paranoia. Now no one's sure how to control you. Balor's become an excuse, a reason to bury a problem too hot to handle and let them sleep at night. They did it for Earth's good, you see."

Kearey reared back then put both hands to his head to hold it still. After a deep breath, he reopened his eyes. "Get to the fucking point, Morgan. You're killing me."

Heat suffused Patrick's neck. Charles Biron had said Kearey would suffer mild discomfort. Etlinn was right; the senator gave slime a good name.

"There's a lot going on behind the scenes. Chinese Intelligence gained full access to the Russian's satellite data on your activities and linked a recent and inexplicable degradation of magnetic components at a uranium enrichment site to you. Powerful corporate interests got hurt, but the main problem is you threaten their entire nuclear defense capability. Naturally, that idea upset the Russians, too. The Hideout members simply don't trust the US not to use you against them."

Kearey shook his head, very slowly and carefully. His whole body sagged.

Patrick hesitated, but the man deserved to know it all. "Opening up a volcanic pit to incinerate Muhuza didn't reassure them, either."

Kearey glared at him. "Foldane authorized deadly force."

"It's the scale of dispatch that's alarming. Protecting national interests gives them added incentive to put you somewhere out of harm's way. In their eyes, keeping the US government from getting too powerful is more important than doing right by you."

Kearey cursed and turned away. The man's struggle to contain his emotions contorted his body.

Patrick held his tongue, inwardly cursing DruSensi for not finding a more humane way to manage the situation.

When Kearey gained enough measure of control to look up, he asked, his voice quiet, "How did you know the implant wasn't working?"

"DruSensi anticipated the Astereans might break the encryption code, so they devised a second encryption level, a system failure alert."

"What will happen to them?"

"To the Astereans? Nothing. We always knew their loyalty to you came first. It proved an interesting test of their ingenuity. They're our ancestors. The Vercingetorix will fight their cause."

"And my family?"

"I promised—" The storm of emotion that clamped his throat took Patrick by surprise. He stopped and cleared his voice of any weakness. "I promised restitution and I meant it. I'm not my father. This Balor thing turned him evil. I remember a good man." Kearey pierced him with almost jet-black eyes and Patrick switched gear. "Like it or not, we're family and that means everything to me. I will protect Tami and your children from any attempt to harm or exploit them."

Kearey beckoned him forward and Patrick stepped closer, still wary of the man behind the screen. "I need to know they will be looked after. If I die, will they get death benefits?"

Patrick nodded vigorously. "Tami will receive a full pension and death benefits within a week of the pod's activation. Your salary will continue for ten years and those funds will be held in trust until the children reach the age of twenty-one. All your property and assets will be put in Tami's name. She will continue to have the bungalow rent-free and there will be a job for her on the island for as long as she wants to work. Your children are my heirs. They will be financially provided for."

"And if they want to leave?"

Patrick realized Kearey was beyond processing the implications of his children inheriting the Morgan estate one day. His half-brother wanted reassurance. "They will be free to leave at any time. I will be available to them whenever they need help; anything they want that I can give. Rest assured, the Vercingetorix Council has pledged not to interfere with your children's lives except to the extent it is requested."

"I want Miach and Jose to be responsible for their security."

Patrick screwed up his face. "Jose, yes. Not a problem. Miach is welcome to stay on the island, but if he wishes to leave, he will need to conform to the procedures in place for all the Astereans."

Kearey frowned. "What about the Morrígan?"

"The Vercingetorix believes the tribe's indigenous status will ensure it remains protected. I will not let them come to harm." He grimaced. "The gryphon, too."

"Then we're done."

Kearey turned away then stopped and looked back and as his haunted eyes met Patrick's, a vision of Kearey trapped in eternal agony slammed up between them. Patrick clawed his face, trying to tear a terrible madness from inside him. The terrifying sensation disappeared. His vision cleared. Warm blood oiled his fingers. Skin clogged his nails. He swallowed, finding it hard to shrug off the panic that shrouded him.

"Jesus Christ," Kearey whispered, his expression horror-struck. "What in God's name did you see?"

Patrick Morgan's terror preyed on Niall's mind. The way Morgan had turned and stumbled out without another word kept Niall at the window on shaky legs for a long time. A guard entering with fresh clothing dragged him from his thoughts. The clang of the outer hatch jolted his raging headache to a fine-edged razor.

"Do I get a last meal?" he asked before the man left. Not that he could eat. Food would be back out before it hit home.

"I'm sorry, sir. You've been designated nil by mouth."

The vice grip of fear tightened. Walls shrank around him. His throat dried until he thought he would choke.

"Water?"

"I'm sorry, sir."

The guard stood there, awkward and uncomfortable, and Niall dismissed him with a wave of his fingers before trying the faucet in the half bath. The dribble of water barely moistened his fingers and he leaned against the wall, worn down and out of ideas. He looked over at the uniform and found a smidgen of fight left to put it on. His boots too.

If there was any chance, the tiniest opening...

He'd barely tied his laces when his ears caught a slight hiss. He rested his hands beside him on the bed. His head weighed a ton. The pillow looked so inviting.

Any shred of hope died as he toppled sideways.

Then reignited as he came to, opened his eyes, and saw Sohan's solemn features.

On the other side of glass.

Niall panicked, jerked his hands up, and discovered he couldn't move. Leather cuffs shackled his hands, feet and neck to the base of the pod. Helpless. The pod closed around him and stretched away in every direction. His head pounded. He had only a small window of glass to the outside world. He tried to launch upright, wrenched his back trying to dislodge his position.

"Niall'Kearey!"

*Sohan?* Niall's vision focused on his former host.

Sohan's face creased into lines of distress. "There is an automatic EM inhibitor in your pod." Niall could see Sohan's lips moving, but his voice emerged out of a speaker by Niall's ear. "If you are trying to telepathically communicate with me, I cannot sense your thought. This will not be for long."

"The Astereans did this?" Niall croaked out, the cuff around his neck placing pressure on his larynx.

"No, we agreed to build a cryogenic pod for Herecura. When you retrieved Uathach's pod, there seemed no reason not to complete the project. It never occurred to us..."

"I mean," Niall closed his eyes with frustration, "the inhibitor..."

"An Earth addition. I am sorry. It is a cruel means of restraint. I have only felt its effects for fifteen minutes and my head aches. I am here with the Asterean engineers who built this particular pod. We insisted on attending to ensure everything works as it should."

Niall strained against the cuffs with every fiber of his body. "Sohan, you have to stop this!"

"The United Nations Council has agreed to let us work with Professor Morgan to identify a way to isolate this agent from your DNA. Niall'Kearey, this won't be like the time your host died. You will not be conscious. Uathach reported a mild discomfort going under, but then nothing. The inhibitor only operates outside stasis. You will feel no pain."

He looked away and Niall's pulse took off. "Sohan, wait." His friend immediately turned back, his expression attentive and Niall grabbed a shallow breath. "Tell Patrick Morgan, Foldane. Anyone. You have to keep looking for the orb. In Syria. Ogmios was there."

"Ogmios?"

"Yes, in Syria. Why was he there?"

"You need to step back, Sohan," a southern voice drawled before Sohan could reply. "Stasis commences in ten, nine..."

271

Sohan vanished from the tiny viewing panel, like someone had pulled him back. Niall clenched his fists and forced the panic down. His mind hunted feverishly for a way out, a shimmer at the edge of his vision, a light in the darkness... tiny sparkles that would transport him across the universe.

Herecura's laughter mocked his panic as a rocking queasiness undulated through him. He heard a slight whine. Light flashed outside, inside. Too bright for his eyes.

*Karma...*

# CHAPTER THIRTY-THREE

Two Years Later

Charles Biron arrived at the Vercingetorix chateau on a glorious day with the burnt colors of autumn lending the normally grey stone walls a warm welcoming hue. He found Sharifah Kalufi and European Commissioner Emile Fitzroy enjoying drinks in the inner courtyard of the secure Council suite. Exotic plants basked in the bright sunshine pouring through an ornate skylight providing a welcome glimpse of blue sky.

Sharifah handed him a glass of chilled Chardonnay. "You look agitated, Charles. Tired."

Charles dampened his aura, but he couldn't mask the shadows under his eyes. "I need to catch up on some sleep." He checked his watch. His plane departed in four hours. His aide wouldn't disturb him for another two hours. If he did, Charles could claim he left the hotel for some fresh air.

Sharifah sank into a soft sofa, curling her legs beneath her, uncaring if she creased the cream silk of her trouser suit. Emile looked equally relaxed in a thin wool sweater and cashmere pants. Charles pressed a button on a control panel and concrete shutters slid smoothly shut. Strategically-placed lamps switched on casting intricate patterns of light and shadow around the room.

"This looks serious," Emile commented, speaking in English for Sharifah's sake. He uncrossed his legs and placed his flute glass of bubbling Kir Royale on the low table before him.

Charles claimed the leather armchair. "What I need to discuss must remain between the three of us. It's vital that Etlinn and Patrick do not get a hint of this matter."

"It is but a proposal," Sharifah agreed. She studied him. "One that is clearly important to you."

Charles paused for effect. "I do not believe there is anything more important than the death of Niall Kearey." He delivered the words nonchalantly, phrasing the sentence carefully, a fait accompli.

Sharifah swung her legs down and sat up. "The cryogenic pod failed?"

"*Non!*" Emile slumped back, his mouth slack. "*C'est terrible!*" Alarm colored his voice. "Suppose this Balor exists?"

Sharifah looked at Emile with horror and Charles raised a soothing hand.

"Nothing has happened to Kearey. Yet. It was your assumption as to the cause of death that I wanted to hear. The current situation has become intolerable. Kearey's wife has been lobbying President Foldane and threatening legal suits for two years now. She wants access to Etlinn Morgan's research and a judicial review on the UN's legal standing for incarcerating her husband in cryogenic stasis. She's obtained a secure hearing at the Supreme Court. When that fails, she'll go public. I know she will."

"The Council will not allow it," Sharifah declared. "Patrick will step in before it gets that far. Etlinn is under enough pressure."

"Etlinn has been working through the night for months on end," Emile added. "She's so exhausted she's making mistakes and having to repeat her work. She only rests to visit her grandchildren. The Council has been considering the problem."

"It's not just Tami Kearey," Charles informed them. "General Towden has tendered his resignation to President Foldane in protest at Major Kearey's ongoing situation. Now the Astereans want to research an alternative solution to cryogenic stasis until a solution to this extra chromosome can be found."

Emile looked interested. "What solution?"

Charles dismissed the Asterean's idea with a wave of his hand. "They have this fanciful notion that Kearey can carry some form of remote cryogenic stasis that is triggered by his death, a temporary solution until his dead body can be placed in long-term stasis. Brilliant, I grant you, but exorbitantly expensive and risky. It's a non-starter, but they are threatening to withdraw their cooperation from the Falcon development."

"So, what are you suggesting?" Emile asked.

"A catastrophic failure of cryogenic stasis." Biron leaned forward and steepled his fingers before him. "There's a strong case to suggest that stasis failure will scramble any energy signal to the q-dimension. Problem solved."

Sharifah bounced to her feet, shaking her head. "No. You cannot be certain of this. There would be an investigation. Anyway, President Foldane would never sanction cold-blooded murder."

"He would sanction the neutralization of a threat to national security and has done several times in the past. However, let's not get into semantics. I do not intend Foldane to have a say in the matter." Charles picked up his glass and sipped his wine, watching Sharifah carefully. "And I do not need to be certain, for I will use the French cryogenic pod. I understand it is an exact duplicate."

Sharifah smiled and nodded her approval. Charles tipped his glass towards her and turned to a hard-eyed Emile Fitzroy.

"How did you find out about the French pod?" Emile demanded.

"You have a security leak, one I'm willing to sacrifice in exchange for your cooperation. DruSensi France can build another pod."

"I suppose I'm here to provide quorum?" Sharifah asked, her eyes narrowing in thought.

"If any of this ever came to light—" Charles began.

"It's not just the risk of attracting Balor's attention. Kearey is the only one who can access the orbs. He cannot die," she insisted.

"Of course not," Charles agreed softly, although he couldn't care less about the orbs, not with Tami Kearey threatening to blow the anonymity of the Vercingetorix into a fond memory. "But we can stop a grief-stricken woman running headlong into personal disaster."

Sharifah's eyes hardened. "Do not presume to manipulate my emotions, Charles. I'm more concerned with steering the Astereans away from a diplomatic crisis."

Charles bowed a tacit apology. Morally and politically, the newly elected Secretary General understood this deception to be the most humane solution available. Sharifah Kalufi promised to rule the United Nations absolutely from behind her gentle smile. He would not underestimate her clear-headed thinking again.

Tami watched Etlinn climb up the steps from the beach. Niall's birth mother looked tired. "I'll put on a tea kettle," she said, ushering the older woman into the cool shade of the bungalow.

Etlinn nodded her thanks. "Where are the children?"

"Toby's at volleyball practice and Lizzie has a violin lesson. They'll be home soon. How's your research? Have you—"

She didn't finish the question, reading the answer in Etlinn's aura. Her empathic sense had matured under Miach's tuition and Etlinn's consuming grief had broken down the barriers between them.

"I'm sorry," Etlinn whispered.

Tami busied herself with making tea. She got down the china cup and saucer she always gave Sheila, Niall's mother, the woman who had brought him up, and the tower of strength holding them all together.

"I do have a reason for my visit today, Tami. When Patrick told me Foldane's latest scheme, I knew I should be the one to tell you. They wanted to send lawyers—"

A shine of sweat coated Etlinn's brow and Tami poured her a glass of cool water before the woman wilted into a puddle. "I'm not dropping my petition."

Etlinn sipped her drink and sat down at the island breakfast bar. "It's not that. Not exactly."

Tami guessed she was about to learn the reason behind that nagging sensation that had been plaguing her over the last few days. She finished making the tea and placed the pot between them. "Tell me."

"President Foldane has reviewed my progress in finding a solution to this extra chromosome. Perhaps I should say my lack of progress. I've talked extensively with Miach about genetically re-engineering Niall's DNA, but all my attempts to alter the sequencing code result in a cascading degradation to neighboring DNA strands. Foldane thinks I should stop."

Tami's hand trembled. Tea slopped over the lip of her mug and she put it down. "You can't!"

"Don't worry. That's not going to happen. President Foldane doesn't dictate what I work on. No one does."

"But he can stop the Astereans in the US working on a solution."

"I don't think he's gotten that far, yet. His concern is more for you."

"Me?"

"Foldane thinks it's unfair you should live in limbo like this. The suggestion is that they legally declare Niall dead. It would allow you to move on. Remarry one day."

"Is he stupid?" Hot pulsating fury filled Tami until she could hardly breathe.

"Emotionally illiterate, maybe, but no, I believe guilt is driving him."

"Is that why they think I'm going through the courts like this? Because I need a man in my bed? Oh my God!"

Tami dragged in some air. Etlinn pushed the glass of water towards her and in some horrible uncontrolled reaction Tami swept it off the counter top. It smashed against a cabinet. Glass shattered everywhere and they both stared at the spreading damp patch in surprise. Etlinn's eyes filled with tears and Tami grabbed her hand.

"These people are sick, Etlinn! Self-absorbed, manipulating cowards! You know what? They're scared I'll go public. Well, maybe I will. Because nothing, *nothing*, will ever make me give up on him! And you mustn't give up on him, either!"

Etlinn's fingers squeezed Tami's in reply. "I'll tell Foldane your answer is an emphatic no, and I'll talk to Miach while I'm here. Maybe, between us, we can think of a new approach to try."

The call Charles Biron had been waiting for came during a last-second alteration to his suit, a suit specially ordered for the announcement of his campaign for the vice presidency.

"My apologies, Alfonso, I have to take this."

His tailor glanced at the clock, his puckered lips clamped around a row of pin heads. He removed them with a surgical skill. "Certainly, Senator, I will be right outside."

Charles waited for the door to shut before speaking into the phone. "Go ahead."

His DruSensi contact kept his message brief. "It is done."

"And the switch?"

"Went precisely to plan."

Charles terminated the call without another word. Relief made him giddy and he rested a hand on his desk for support. Now there was nothing to do but sit back and watch the ripples of his ingenious plan bear fruit. Foldane should thank him. Two years of bullheaded campaigning for Kearey's release would reach a natural conclusion. Towden's aggravating retirement protest would fade into the background and the former general could fish out his twilight years wreathed in self-righteous glory.

Tami Kearey's passion Charles could understand. The general was another matter. A fine career wasted, brought to a premature end while the glittering pinnacle to Charles' political dynasty was only just beginning.

"Alfonso!"

The tailor shot into the room. "Your car is waiting, sir," Alfonso said as he swiftly secured a cuff button in place.

"Leave the rest. It's fine. Has my niece arrived yet?"

"Yes, and with her young beau." Alfonso grinned.

Charles' euphoria evaporated. He suspected Jacqueline had brought Sean Dayton with her to spite him. As the tailor stepped back and admired his work, Charles turned to collect his briefcase. "Until the next time, Alfonso."

"Thank you, Senator."

Charles collected his guests on his way out. "I appreciate this show of support," he said to Dayton, after giving Jacqueline a kiss on both cheeks. He kept their handshake brief.

Dayton managed a terse smile. "I may not support your policies, sir, but to be selected as running mate for the Presidency is an undeniable honor."

Charles inclined his head graciously and gave the boy credit for having the balls to turn up. He suspected the journey from Oregon had been tense. Jacqueline could barely look her uncle in the eye.

"Is there a problem, ma cherie?" Charles inquired.

Her eyes flashed at him. "More than a problem! My boss insisted I come today. I can't believe you went over my head like that." Her voice lowered. "Why can't you let me run my own life?"

"You're alienating the entire geological community, Jacqueline, persisting with this futile research project. You never did understand the value of influence. Fortunately, your superiors do."

"I don't think her research is futile, and her university doesn't either," Dayton growled, his face flushed with anger. "There should be a river. Over hundreds of thousands of years, a massive body of water that reached levels high enough to drown an entire city should have forged a path down to the sea by now. It's not like Crater Lake."

"Yes, I heard you're about to join Jacqueline's research team." Biron smiled a goodnight to his secretary, Nancy. A veritable treasure was Nancy. Never a cross word, unlike his prickly niece.

Jacqueline had changed over the last few years. She'd survived an ordeal that would have crushed many, and despite the aggravation her newfound independence brought him, Charles liked her better for it. He studied the furious Dayton with fresh eyes. Maybe the boy wasn't such a bad match for his niece after all.

"Now we should go. We have a big evening ahead of us."

President Foldane waited for Charles in an anteroom at the hotel. Charles stopped, taken aback by the man's appearance. Foldane looked like he'd lost the election and stumbled over his own grave all on the same day.

"Charles! Have you heard?" Strain and guilt over Kearey had aged the president over the last two years. Now he looked shaky. Unpresidential.

"What? Have you announced my candidacy already?" Biron said with a jovial smile. He converted the smile to a frown. "My apologies, Robert. I take it you are referring to something else. Are you alright? You don't look well."

Foldane grabbed his elbow and dragged him across the room as Secret Service ushered Jacqueline and Sean out. "Kearey's dead," he announced in a hushed but urgent voice.

Charles shook his head with a confident smile. "That's not possible."

"The pod failed! Temperature plummeted and his body degraded beyond recognition. When they realized what was happening, they tried to revive him." The president parted his hands in disbelief. "Nothing left but cryogenic waste."

"Are you sure? Nothing?"

"Yes."

"But that's good."

"Are you mad? What about Balor?"

"The normal chemical process of death couldn't possibly have taken place at those temperatures. Damn, this is what we should have done in the first place." When Foldane's eyes rounded in horror, Biron gestured an apology. "I know, execution would have been totally unacceptable, but fate has played its hand and there is nothing we can do. God, his poor wife. Does she know?"

The president shook his head. "I've asked Colonel Hastor to inform her."

"We should hold a funeral," Charles suggested. "Full military honors."

Foldane brightened. "Yes. Good. That might help." He paused. "Suppose she sues? Unlawful death or something?"

"She can try. See what happens when you go up against the US government on an issue of national security. She'd be tied up in litigation for decades. There's not a sitting judge that will let the evidence see the light of day. Anyway, let Patrick Morgan worry about that."

Foldane glanced at his watch. Color had returned to his cheeks. "Okay. Let's get this announcement over with so we can get those campaign funds rolling in. My Chief of Staff is setting up a series of meetings to manage this nightmare. We'll return to the White House after we're done here. The Astereans will want to know what went wrong. I want to know."

Charles knew the answer to that already. Metal fatigue. A part supplied by a business rival to DruSensi. Now that company would get sued. America, the land of the free and home of the brave, where anyone can sue for any reason under the sun.

Providing the suit did not conflict with powerful interests.

Watching the president pull himself together to face going out on stage, it occurred to Charles that a drawn-out investigation into the cryogenic failure, an investigation demanded and controlled by the Armed Services Senate Committee, would not do Foldane's blood pressure any good at all.

# CHAPTER THIRTY-FOUR

Three Years Later

Sohan studied the onscreen Hubble X-ray image of Proxima Centauri, a dwarf star, and the nearest star to Earth's sun. Colonel Sam Hastor sat beside him.

"Where is this black spot?" Sohan asked.

The colonel zoomed in until the spot became obvious then minimized the image and lined it up against a second image of the same area of space. "This second image was taken by a space probe carrying an Asterean enhanced Faint Object Spectrograph just a few days ago." The black spot was no longer visible and the region of space behind it clearly suggested something solid had been captured on the older image.

Excited murmuring made them look around. Someone in the GBI lab had put on the news. Sohan turned back to Colonel Hastor and tapped the Hubble image. "A stray asteroid, maybe? Or a comet?"

"That was NASA's working assumption," Hastor replied, but his voice sounded unfocused.

Realizing Hastor was distracted by the news feed, Sohan turned back to listen.

"We are getting reports that President Foldane suffered a severe stroke overnight while in residence at the White House," an anchorman reported with due gravity. "Vice President Biron has been informed and is on his way to Capitol Hill."

The colonel looked visibly upset by this news.

"If there is anything our healers can do to assist," Sohan offered, despite his residual anger for the US president. Theirs had become a distant relationship since Niall'Kearey had been forced into cryogenic stasis. A terrible sadness and loss wrapped around Sohan, and guilt, too. Asterean technology may have been cleared by the inquiry, but they should have detected the flawed component that killed the man who saved his people.

"That's very generous, Councilor Sohan," Hastor replied. "I will convey your offer."

Sohan doubted the offer would be taken up. The leaders of Earth avoided direct contact with the Astereans, a setback in the Astereans' strategy to induce a less restrictive integration of his people with the indigenous population. "You were saying an asteroid was the assumption, Colonel? You have additional data?"

The colonel opened up a third file. "This is an image of the interstellar space between our solar system and Proxima Centauri. It was taken by your space probe just a few weeks ago. This object is estimated at one light year away."

Sohan's thoughts leapt to the Asterean fleet that had escaped Astereal's timeflow with Niall'Kearey's help. Was it possible? Had Nantosuelta found Earth's galaxy? After studying the image properly, he realized his hopes were in vain.

"What is it?" Hastor asked.

"I had hoped it might be the Asterean fleet, but there is only one object and it bears no resemblance to our ships." He studied the accompanying data. "It appears to be crystalline, and a strangely artificial shape. What made you connect the two images?"

"What made you think it might be Asterean?"

"Proxima Centauri is just over four light years away. The Hubble data estimates this object to be two to three light years distant. Assuming this is the same object then it must have bridged space in order to be detected one light year away a few weeks ago. Where is it now?"

"It disappeared and reappeared a few days back." Hastor pulled up a spatial map showing the object on the other side of Earth headed out of the Milky Way galaxy. Yet its orientation appeared unaltered, as if the object had turned around and was now pointed back towards Earth. "Houston estimates the distance at half a light year."

A growing trickle of anxiety surged into a full-blown flood. Sohan stared at Hastor, not hiding his alarm. "Bridging the q-dimension does not require a direct course from one point to another. This object is definitely alien in origin, a species capable of bridging space. It's not Asterean. Why did you not show me this earlier?"

"It took a couple days for anyone to make the connection. At the moment this UFO is moving steadily towards Earth. If it keeps jumping..."

"The closer it gets to its destination, the more careful it will need to be selecting its link. Jumping a ship is not the same as Niall'Kearey stepping from Earth to Astereal or from one part of this world to another. Still, it does seem to be taking its time. If this was an Asterean ship, it would have bridged here by now." Sohan closed his eyes for the briefest moment as he considered an awful possibility. Then, controlling his emotions, he met Hastor's concerned gaze. "I am sorry, Colonel. Everything we understood about cryogenics suggested natural brain death could not have taken place, that there simply wouldn't have been time before his brain tissue crystallized and shattered."

"You think this is Balor, then? That Major Kearey's death somehow flagged up our existence?"

"I do not know. Major Kearey died three years ago." Sohan paused, caught by the sharp emergence of grief in Hastor's otherwise faint aura. "Without evidence to show this ship appeared in your galaxy prior to his death, we must consider the possibility that his death triggered this alien incursion into your galaxy. We cannot be certain. Either way, you must alert your president. Urgently." Sohan grimaced, remembering, and they both glanced to the news feed.

President Foldane had fallen ill at the worst time.

Hastor gathered up the papers and rose to his feet. "I'll inform the Joint Chiefs of Staff of your opinion immediately. Sohan, thank you for your assistance. I suspect we will be calling on your people for help very soon."

"Earth is our home now, Colonel. Be reassured, whatever our arguments with your government, we will do everything in our power to assist you now."

Charles Biron stared out across the Rose Garden, wondering whether a God existed after all. First Nicole. Now the threat of Apocalypse. The universe certainly seemed to enjoy punishing him. He had assumed the role and responsibilities of the president's office. For now, he was Acting President, but Foldane's prognosis didn't look good. Charles expected to be celebrating. Instead he faced his first test as leader of the most powerful nation on Earth, an Earth that might not exist for much longer. The event that had no doubt precipitated Foldane's stroke, handing Charles the presidency on a golden platter, had also dropped the bottom out of his glittering new world.

"Aliens..." he muttered.

Behind him, Foldane's Chief-of-Staff gestured for his attention. "The Joint Chiefs are outside, Mr. Vice-President. Also, you just received an update on the president's condition."

"Thank you, Andrew. Show them in."

"Before I do, sir, Councilor Sohan has formally offered Asterean support. He has requested to meet with you."

"I'll see him, but I want an inhibitor field set up. Make the precaution standard procedure."

"Sir, is there a security concern?"

"The Astereans have psychic abilities, Andrew. Secret Service should have implemented appropriate precautions sooner. Show the Joint Chiefs in."

"Yes, sir."

While generals and admirals filed in, their ribbons and brass a display of force, Charles checked his email. "Gentlemen, ladies, take a seat," he greeted them as he scanned the key points in the medical report. President Foldane had suffered a massive stroke; paralysis; indications of significant memory loss and cognitive impairment, all the result of a bleed that had gone undetected for too long with the First Lady out of town overnight.

The timing couldn't be worse. Or better.

"Mr. President, I have an update."

Charles met General Straton's hawkish gaze. Straton despised his Acting Commander-in-Chief, Charles knew that. Unfortunately, now was not the time for change. "Please go ahead, General."

"Based on extrapolation of the front visual, our best estimates put the approaching target at two miles long."

"That doesn't sound good."

"No. NASA has confirmed the target materialized out of nowhere. Previous surveys of the area show no evidence of comets or asteroids. An Asterean assessment of the data suggests an alien vessel powered by an intelligent entity with something similar to Major Kearey's q-dimension bridge capabilities."

Charles sucked in a rapid breath. "The Astereans sent a fleet into space with a bridge-builder on board."

"Councilor Sohan has ruled out an Asterean ship. We're readying all options, but we have to assume the alien vessel has cloaking capability, shielding, countermeasures. You've seen the invasion simulations. We can't win a straight fight. Mankind's best chance is to initiate Response Ohm. Activate underground communication centers, backup systems, evacuate government and key personnel to bunkers, distribute survival kits and rations—"

Charles gestured the man to stop. "I signed off Response Ohm, I don't need a sales pitch. Do it. I'll coordinate with the UN, and contact the Chinese and Russian presidents. I spoke with the British prime minister earlier. GCHQ is taking the lead in coordinating a European response with Germany and France."

The JCS Chief nodded. His jaw jutted forward. "It was a mistake to incarcerate Major Kearey in an ice box. The Astereans should be our greatest ally. Instead they've been dragging their heels across several defense projects. We could have been rolling out hundreds of Falcons by now, not flight testing one."

Charles raised a surprised eyebrow. Straton wasn't prone to pointless recriminations. "The UN Hideout Council took the decision they thought appropriate at the time. But I agree we need to find a new accord with the Astereans. As it happens, Councilor Sohan is making overtures of support."

"Major Kearey died three years ago," Straton persisted. "Now an alien ship turns up. Our working assumption is that Major Kearey's death sent Balor an engraved invitation and that this ship is Balor, or its forces. With Kearey dead, the ship's presence supports the theory that Balor's motive is not personal to Kearey, but an interest in Earth. We need to re-examine whether cryogenic failure could have set off some transmission through the q-dimension or not. We need to validate our assumption on why this alien ship is headed to Earth and what it might represent."

Charles rested back in his chair and steepled his fingers on his chest. Straton raised a pertinent point. His heart hammered inside his chest. He certainly didn't want to reopen the investigation into Kearey's death. His mind sifted through all the permutations.

Why were these aliens here?

Did it matter? Balor or not, a physical on-your-doorstep alien threat was a game changer. *Merde.* Kearey would be an invaluable asset if it came to alien invasion. It had been a mistake to bury him. Charles began to see a path forward. The fear of discovery sharpened his thinking. It was a risk, but Foldane was not in a position to contradict him. Once Charles was safely confirmed as president, he could take steps to ensure Foldane would never be concerned with such matters again.

He chose his words with care. "The aliens aren't here because Kearey's death sent a wire across the universe."

Straton's brow formed a deep groove as puzzled glances were exchanged around him. The JCS Chairman leaned forward in his chair. "Mr. Vice-President, how can you possibly know that?"

"I know because I read the final report into the investigation of Major Kearey's death. Major Kearey is not dead. His ongoing cryogenic stasis was causing problems and President Foldane decided to put his family and the Astereans out of their misery. People needed to get on with their lives, gentlemen. The uncertainty was jeopardizing national security. It couldn't be allowed to continue. I closed that investigation for the same reasons."

Straton rubbed his nose. General Tyler, Straton's replacement as Air Force Services Chief shifted in his chair, his expression turning to a scowl. Major Kearey was Air Force. Biron sensed the mood turn ugly.

"Are you saying Major Kearey is alive?" Straton asked, his voice dangerously low.

"Yes. And I submit that the reason for placing him in cryogenic stasis no longer exists. Major Kearey needs to be reactivated. So, General, I suggest you get to work deciding how best we can deploy him."

# CHAPTER THIRTY-FIVE

*Tami.*

So cold. Light. Too bright. Colors bled through Niall's eyelids. Warm air burned his cheeks. He remembered the Earth crushing him. Rock everywhere. Pressing down on him. He couldn't open his eyes. Got to breathe.

*Breathe!*

Niall gasped air into his burning lungs. More images pounded his mind fueling an overwhelming panic. His ears tuned into a persistent hum. Cool air mixed with the warmth. Some evil spirit twisted a knife in his head.

Memory flooded back. He remembered Sohan's appalled disbelief and Etlinn's tears, the inexplicable expression of terror on Patrick Morgan's face. Most of all, he remembered Tami's devastation.

Fury contorted his fingers into claws.

*Open your goddamned eyes!*

A groan erupted from the burning core of resentment inside him, anger fed by the constant deluge of distrust, and betrayal, and manipulation. Squinting to block out the light, Niall opened his eyes. The rising pod spurred a ferocious attempt to escape. Cuffs thwarted his attempt. His groan escalated into a full-blooded yell of frustration. His head curled into his chest. Every muscle in his body strained with his need to escape.

"Get me out of here!" he screamed. Perspiration dripped down his nose.

"I will, Major Kearey, as soon as you calm down," a gruff voice snapped.

General Towden strode into view. Niall held back a fresh explosion of outrage. He stared at Towden, trying to ascertain the general's role in his incarceration.

The general's stern expression softened. "You're getting out, son. I'm here to explain why, but you're mad, rightly so, and as no one wants you going off half-cocked, we're taking precautions."

Niall's jaw shook with pure anger. "Nothing justifies this!" His gaze followed the length of his body down to his boots. "You gave me no say."

"I agree with you."

Niall jerked the cuffs holding him down. "Then get these things off me."

Towden moved to the foot of the pod and started unbuckling the leather ring around Niall's ankle. "The inhibitor force field is operating until I order it removed. In all honesty, I'm of a mind to turn you loose now and watch what happens, but we have a situation unlike anything we have ever known. I need you to hear me out before you start lashing out. So, here's the deal. I order the force field off and you give me a chance to brief you."

"That's it? We talk. Then I'm free to go."

"Yes."

"Where's my family?"

"Safe on the island. They've been living there ever since you were placed in cryogenic stasis."

Niall scrunched his forehead trying to think. "Ever since?" The general's brow crinkled a lot more than Niall remembered and a hollow pit opened inside him. "How long? How long have I been in stasis?"

"Five years."

Niall inhaled sharply. "I thought something had gone wrong. That stasis hadn't worked."

"It worked." The general finished unbuckling his left wrist and leaned over Niall's chest to work on the last cuff holding him in. "So. What's it to be?"

For a moment, Niall wasn't sure what Towden meant. Then he let his head fall back. He didn't want to fight Towden. He needed to get to his family. "Turn it off. I don't want to move with it on."

Towden nodded. "Okay, then." He looked across the room. "Turn off the EM field and clear the area."

The effect was instantaneous. As the aching pain receded, the world sharpened with his relieved senses. Niall reached out with his mind.

*Miach?*

After a couple of seconds, Niall frowned. Easing up onto his elbow, he looked around the room and then at a slightly puzzled-looking Towden. "Is this room dampened?"

"Dampened? Ah, yes, the walls are ferrite insulated. Telepathy won't work in here. Please, Major, you need to hear me out first. Are you okay to get out?" He offered a helping hand.

Niall shook his head, used to clambering in and out of stasis pods, although that had been when he'd inhabited Miach's body. When he was outside the pod and standing on a pair of very shaky legs, a ravenous hunger hit him. He decided not to explore the q-dimension right now.

"I need food. And water."

Towden nodded down the room. "That I've got covered."

Niall followed Towden to a seating area that had been set up in a corner of the basement style-room. His stomach rumbled at the sight of a covered plate laid out on a table. "Does my wife know I'm out?"

"Not yet. Please, Major, it's best for her that you understand all the facts before seeing her."

Niall just wanted to go. Now. A warning note in Towden's voice held him to his unspoken promise to hear the general out. The general lifted the lid away and the smell of chicken broth dropped Niall into the chair. He drained half a glass of water set beside the mouthwatering food, grabbed a hunk of bread and dipped it in the gravy. Softened, it broke up in his mouth and Niall could not wolf the rich meaty stew down quick enough.

Towden took the chair opposite. "Good? Sohan said your stomach would take solid food."

Niall grunted, his mouth full. The general smiled, but the lightness in his expression quickly faded. Niall swallowed and waved his fork. "Tell me."

The general rested his wrists on the table. His piercing eyes met Niall's gaze head on. "An alien vessel is approaching Earth. Fast. It'll be here in just over a week. Maybe less."

Niall blinked. A wild hope filled him. "The Gobannos?"

Towden looked taken aback then his face cleared. "It's not the Asterean fleet, Major."

"Then..." An all-too familiar dread hit Niall. "Balor?" He sent his mind soaring into space and once again met a wall of nothingness. His urge to escape this room intensified.

"That's the working assumption."

Niall chewed on a piece of chicken. "Wasn't I supposed to die before that could happen?"

He tested his access to the q-dimension. The anechoic chamber at GBI hadn't stopped him linking to Astereal, nor the secure room at the United Nations. He discovered he had the same freedom here. Sparkling holes tempted him. He tuned his mind to detect the implant's tracking signal. Nothing. Perhaps the implant hadn't survived cryogenic stasis.

"It's been suggested that Kean Morgan wasn't the only person infected with this Balor blood agent. The Astereans believe that if comets and meteors were used for transmission, then others might be carrying this extra chromosome."

Niall put down his fork. "Patrick Morgan's convinced this genetic virus changed his father. Turned him bad. He mentioned Hitler."

"Anything's possible. I talked with Professor Morgan on the way over. She's spent the last few years researching Balor's genetic agent, analyzed thousands of samples, the entire Vercingetorix database. She found two matches supporting a theory that comets carry the virus around the universe. Both born in Ireland, both died in the last ten years, Kean's generation. Interviews with their families indicate they both underwent a personality change. She found a third match. A man we assumed had been looking for you for personal reasons."

"Who?"

"Muhuza."

Niall blinked. "Would explain his sociopathic tendencies. How did you get hold of his DNA?"

"Jester's knife drew blood."

Niall remembered gripping Muhuza's head and grinding the bastard's nose into the severed bone of Muhuza's own foot. He shoved his plate away. "I touched Muhuza. Everything was crazy. I wanted to find Jacqueline. Fuck."

"Let's not get ahead of ourselves. We don't know this alien ship is anything to do with Balor."

"I need to take a look."

The general nodded. "Once we're finished up here, I'm authorized to take you to GBI where we can monitor the attempt." He hesitated. "If you're willing. No one's assuming your cooperation, not now. Things have changed for you, Major. You might be Earth's best chance to stop an alien invasion."

Niall lurched to his feet. Stop Balor? He wanted to run. His pulse began to race. "I think you may be overestimating how much I can do. I'll look, but first I need to see my family."

Towden grimaced.

"What?" Niall demanded.

"There's a lot to—" The general stopped, his gaze shifting beyond Niall's shoulder. Niall turned to find Colonel Sam Hastor standing in the open doorway.

Sam's eyes widened as their gazes locked. "Niall?" His mouth opened to say more, but no sound emerged. He glanced at Towden before his eyes tracked straight back to Niall. He tried to point and then Sam's expression transformed as a wide grin broke out. "You never died!" He laughed and punched the air. "Yes! You never died! How the hell did you do that?"

A chair pushed back. Niall glanced to a standing Towden. The general looked unsure how to respond to Sam's unprofessional elation. The import of Sam's words struck home.

"Died?"

Sam strode across the room, his excited expression warning Niall to brace for impact, but then Sam caught sight of the open pod and he stopped in obvious confusion. His face paled. "When? When did you...?" His voice faded. To Niall's surprise, Sam turned on Towden. "His death was all a lie, wasn't it? Did you know?" Anger edged his voice with accusation. "Is that why you retired?"

Niall stared at the general's reddening face.

"It was a lie," Towden said. "But I've only just found out. And I retired because Major Kearey's death sickened me to the core."

Niall exploded with frustration. "Would someone please tell me what the hell you're talking about?"

Sam's jaw tightened, his skin blotched red. He was angrier than Niall had ever seen him, but not at him. "Three years ago, you were declared dead."

Niall blinked, confused. "Why?"

Sam parted his hands. "I don't know. But I can guess."

"Major," General Towden said, his tone solemn. "Both your wife and the Astereans never stopped fighting for your release, but the UN Hideout members were resolute that you had to stay in cryogenic stasis. It would seem President Foldane decided the situation couldn't go on."

Niall shook his head. He could hardly bear to listen. "Oh my God."

Towden stepped around the table. "On President Foldane's orders, an undisclosed unit of the NSA faked a failure of a second cryogenic pod. They blamed metal fatigue, some vital component where failure initiated a catastrophic collapse."

"God, I'm sorry, Niall," Sam said. "I was the one to inform Tami of your death. I believed it to be true. She was beyond devastated. We all were."

Niall couldn't breathe. If they all thought he was dead...

They would have stopped working to bring him back. An aching void opened up inside him. He could have been left in stasis, forgotten, forever.

For a terrible long second, the universe opened up in his mind and then a malevolent purpose crashed through his grief. As the scale of evil took shape, Niall hauled air into his lungs and let his mind follow the link, a need to assess this threat on Earth's doorstep outweighing every other consideration. Within seconds, he clashed with a mental force that put Pwyll and Macha, even Uathach, into the shade. Twisting vines of consciousness reached out for him. His knees buckled and he groped for the chair. This was the same entity he had encountered in his childhood, and briefly in a link from Astereal.

This was Balor.

Niall sensed the entity invade his thoughts.

*No. Balor's servant. His warlord. I am Lugus.*

A hundred, no, thousands of minds reached out to him and Niall whipped his mind back so fast he lost his balance and crashed to the floor, pulling the chair down with him. "It's Balor," he croaked out as Sam dropped to one knee beside him. "Some general of his. An army. And behind them, millions more I couldn't see."

"How do you know," Towden asked grabbing his arm.

Sam got hold of the other and they dragged Niall up. He swayed on his feet, drained of energy, a massive hole in his stomach, and an ache in his heart. They helped him to the righted chair.

"I need to see my wife. I can't operate properly feeling this way. She needs to know I'm alive."

"It's not that simple," Sam said.

Niall quelled him with one furious glare. "How isn't it simple?"

Sam swallowed, his face turning ashen. "Niall, it's been three years. Tami grieved for a long time. She was heartbroken. And then—" Sam exchanged a worried look with Towden.

Niall jumped up and grabbed Sam by the throat. "And then?" Terror exploded from the depths of his belly. "And then?" he yelled.

"Major!" Towden bellowed. The general grasped Niall's wrist, but Niall possessed the strength of fear.

"She and Miach have become close," Sam gasped out.

Niall recoiled and let go. He stepped back and roared. "No!" Sam was ripping his life apart. "No!"

Adrenalin shot his mind into the q-dimension, steering clear of the path to Balor's minions, hunting down the link to the island. Dark energy flowed out of his fingertips, creating a bridge as his mind surfed the island, searching for her. He found her aura, her beautiful aura, tinged with an aching sadness that broke his heart.

A portal appeared without a single conscious thought to bring it into existence. Niall dived through, vaguely aware that Sam followed close on his heels. Niall skidded to a stop mid center in a classroom as the portal winked out behind them. Young kids in school uniform stared at him, their mouths open, but his eyes snapped to the copper-haired vision standing before a screen of moving images.

Tami's eyes grew round. Her hand stretched out towards him. Color drained from her face. Niall stepped towards her, breaking the spell, and she crumpled to the floor. The thud of her head hitting the table turned his stomach.

"Tami!" He crashed his way through desks to reach her, stumbling over a bag in his path and shoving furniture aside in an attempt to catch his balance. Kids screamed.

Niall dropped to one knee, swamped by memories of the night Tami lay on the road with a bullet in her chest and an injury to the back of her head he hadn't detected. Then his attention had been torn in two. This time he forced emotion aside as he gently picked up her wrist. "Tami? Can you hear me? Try to answer me if you can."

Her pulse fluttered strong under his fingers and then her eyes opened.

"Niall?" Tears welled. She began to push herself up.

"Hey, rest up a moment. That was quite a knock you took there."

"Okay, kids, don't be alarmed," Sam was saying behind him. "You! Go fetch a teacher in here."

The door slammed open and Miach filled the door frame. Confusion colored his aura but then Miach's eyes focused on Tami. For a brief second, Niall sensed a wave of possessive love for Tami before Miach's privacy shield shut him out.

Anger surged through Niall but then Sam blocked his path, towering above him.

"No one's at fault here, Niall. This isn't the place and you're scaring the children!"

Niall took a huge shuddering breath, fighting to control the madness filling him. He glanced at Tami's white face and then back at her students. Some stood ready to bolt, others sat glued to their seats. Their young auras pulsated with a mix of alarm, excitement and fear. Niall nodded, feeling like Sam held a finger on the pin to a grenade in his guts.

"Niall?" Tami whispered, her hand clutching at his arm. "You're alive!" Her voice pulled him out of the whirling fog. He gazed into her eyes, relieved to see her pupils normal and fixed on him. Her arms reached around his neck. He wrapped her in his arms and she clung to him as she burst into tears. Her aura pulsated with happiness as she tightened her hold on him and, for long moments, Niall fell blind to everything but her overwhelming love for him.

The scrape of a chair broke the spell.

Tami started. She pushed away from him and looked around her and then towards Miach who stood mute and frozen. "Oh my God." Her brow wrinkled and her eyes clouded with alarm. "We should talk outside," she whispered, her hand cupping Niall's cheek. "Not here."

Niall nodded. He helped her up. There were strands of grey in her hair now grown back to its former length and the pain of loss arced through him at this tangible evidence of five years gone by.

She took his hand, but he noticed the fleeting look she sent Miach and their silent exchange twisted the blade carving Niall up inside. His former host, his trusted friend, frowned but then backed up into the corridor. Tami pulled Niall after her.

In the hallway, Miach was standing down security guards, their weapons raised.

Jose stepped forward from their midst, a huge grin breaking out on his face. "Niall! *Amigo!* Where did you spring from?"

"A long sleep," Niall answered him, his voice a rough growl.

Jose's smile faded as his eyes shifted to Tami, then Miach and back again. ""Hijo de la chingada... this shit is complicated."

"Is there somewhere they can talk?" Sam asked.

"The library will be empty," Miach suggested, his mind still tightly shielded and his aura rigidly controlled. His inner turmoil revealed itself in his eyes.

Niall's anger mounted. Miach had betrayed him.

Jose shook his head. "Not on college grounds."

Niall glared at him. "I'm not here to attack children."

Jose's eyes narrowed with resolution. "But you are here to take what's yours, eh? Niall, this isn't the place."

A pit hollowed out in Niall's chest. He'd no intention of waging war with Jose. He might lose. Niall swallowed down his impatience. He still had hold of Tami's hand, and he wasn't letting go.

Jose stepped towards him, his stance softening. "You need to breathe, Niall."

Tami turned to Miach. "Please, Niall and I need to talk." Her eyes tracked to Jose. "We'll walk back to the bungalow." She didn't give anyone a chance to disagree.

"How's your head?" he asked as she led the way down the hallway, half dragging him along. "Do you feel faint? Sick?"

"A bit achy. I'm fine." Tears tracked down her face.

She picked the pace up and Niall knew she was barely holding it together. She wanted to fall apart in private. With him. Hope soared.

"Sam told me you died. Did he lie?"

"No. That's what he was told. I gather you were making too much noise." He squeezed her hand. "Thank you for that by the way."

She rolled her eyes. "Did you think I wouldn't? For God's sake, Niall, I never gave up on you. When Sam brought us news of your—"

She gasped, turned pale and pushed open the door to the outside where she dragged in some fresh air.

Niall looked around. Tall palm trees scattered a lawn providing desperately needed shade. "You should sit down."

He steered her towards a bench in a secluded corner of the grounds. They sat looking out over the ocean. A fence separated them from the steep cliff dropping down into a lush-green oasis that petered out onto a rocky shoreline. Geomagnetic energy crackled against Niall's skin.

"What a mess," he said, turning the wedding ring on his finger. He sensed a mind reaching out for him. *Lizzie,* his thoughts whispered.

"Yes." Her voice sounded strained. "Who told you?"

"Sam."

"Please don't think the worst! I grieved for you, I never stopped, and Miach supported me through it all. He never tried to take your place, but the pain of losing you was too much, and—" Her face struggled to hold some composure.

Niall couldn't speak for the tightness gripping his throat. He grabbed her fingers and squeezed gently.

More tears dampened her cheeks. "He knows us so well, you see. He has your memories. Did you know that?"

Niall nodded. "Yes, but I never thought..." He stopped, suddenly remembering those odd moments when Miach seemed ready to tear strips off Niall for upsetting Tami in some way or another.

"And he loves the children like they were his own."

"Oh God," Niall moaned.

*Daddy, is that you?*

*Yes, Lizzie. And I love you, and I want to see you, but just give me a few moments with Mom first.*

"Miach grieved for you, Niall, he thought the world of you. Our grief brought us even closer and I got scared I might lose him too."

Niall didn't want to hear it. "This is so fucked up."

Tami stared at him. Her brow furrowed. "How are you here? I don't understand. You didn't die? They lied to me? What changed their minds? Was it President Biron?"

"Can't believe that bastard's president."

"He's not. Not yet. President Foldane had a stroke. He's Acting President."

Niall bit his lip, remembering the reason they'd revived him. Nausea made him sit up and haul in some badly needed oxygen, but the air was warm. Stifling.

Tami grabbed his chin, made him look at her. "They brought you back for a reason. Why? What's happened?"

"There's an alien ship approaching Earth, Tami. That's why they revived me."

Tami recoiled. "Alien?"

He watched her face whiten again. "Yes. Something called Lugus. Balor sent them." He swallowed down a surge of bile.

"How do you know?"

"It told me."

She didn't even question how crazy that sounded. "What do they expect you to do?" She spoke so quietly Niall could barely hear her.

He sensed Tami withdrawing into herself and rubbed her fingers to keep her with him. "I'm not sure. General Towden wants me to assess the threat." A more controlled look this time, Niall decided. "From GBI."

Tami searched his eyes. "And of course, you're going to, aren't you?" Anger mixed in with fear sharpened her voice. "Niall, they froze you in a box! Had you declared dead! Tore your family to shreds. We were lost without you, all of us. They never intended to let you out of that box, Niall. Never!"

"This alien ship threatens all of us, Tami. You, the kids, everyone."

"You're one man! You just came back to us. The kids don't even know you're back!"

Niall looked up. The lump in his throat stopped him speaking. He stood up. Tami followed his gaze.

His children mowed him down. Children? They were full-grown teenagers. Tears flowed down Lizzie's cheeks. She was so slender. Curved. With red hair. What the hell? And Toby! He was taller than his sister, broad-shouldered, with his curly mop hair shaved in a zigzag shape at the side. He looked wired, determined not to let his emotions get the better of him, but happy and bewildered all at the same time.

Niall ached for every moment of their lives he had missed.

Grief, joy, and confusion whirled around him.

"Where did you go? We thought you were dead." Toby stepped back and started to yell. "We had a funeral and everything!"

Shit.

Tami's aura darkened. She was scared. Their future wasn't the rosy white-picket fence dream. The days and weeks ahead loomed messy and full of uncertainty.

Niall grabbed ahold of Lizzie's arms around his neck and gently set her back so he could look into her eyes. "I am so proud of you," he told her. He turned to Toby. "Of both of you. You've survived so much."

Lizzie grabbed his arm. "Don't go again, Daddy," she begged him. "It's too big. You can't fight it."

Niall frowned at her. "What do you mean?" His eyes narrowed. Lizzie had been in his mind. "What did you see?"

Beautiful blue eyes pierced his defenses. "This Balor terrifies you. It's like a black cloud smothering you from the inside."

Tami moaned and Niall scratched at his head, unsure what to say. This wasn't the family reunion of their past. There was no room for pretense anymore. He couldn't protect them from his world. Make believe that everything would be okay.

"I'm going with you," Toby announced, his voice deeper than Niall remembered.

Niall took a good look at them both. Toby's lean wiry body belied the strength of mind blasting out from behind his dark bright eyes. Lizzie had curves he didn't want to see on his little girl and not an ounce of puppy fat. They looked fifteen or so. Not kids anymore.

"I mean it," Toby growled.

"I know," Niall said. Tami shook her head. She looked petrified. A selfish need to keep his children close swept over him. He had missed so much. They would be safe at Groom Lake. It was just a step away. He could have them home for tea.

"No, Niall," Tami hissed, stepping forward. "He's too young. They're safe here."

"Mom, yes. Please," Lizzie begged, "We might not get another chance."

A bell of doom tolled in her daughter's words and Tami gasped. Her haunted eyes shot to Niall's, her body stiff with fear of the unknown. Tami teetered on the edge of a dark abyss and Niall suddenly remembered how close she'd come to succumbing to her terror before.

"We can all go," he said quickly.

*No!*

Niall spun around to face Miach storming out of a portal towards them. So, Miach had found his bridge-building ability. A good distance behind him, Sam, Jose, and several security guards burst through the doors to the school. Niall shifted his stance into defense mode.

"No what?" he countered out aloud.

"You cannot go! Now you want to take her children? You always do this," Miach said, sweeping his hand out at Niall. "Always something more important than looking after your own family. Than your wife! Look at her!"

"That's not fair," Niall growled quietly. Deep inside, a melting pot of anger bubbled. Aware of Lizzie's growing abilities, Niall narrowed his telepathic link with Miach. *You stole my wife. Moved in on my family!* "Tell me what I could have done differently. I didn't choose the last five years. My government shoved me in a living coffin!" *I trusted you!*

*I did not steal anyone! I picked up the wreckage. You were dead.* "I didn't choose our binding, either. You used my body, stamped my memory with your memories." *You made me love them. I had no choice but to love them. She needed me.*

"Stop it, both of you. This is madness!" Tami pleaded.

"If you take them with you, the pain of losing you will be all the greater," Miach said as if she hadn't spoken.

A thick heat washed over Niall. Miach knew what he had seen, the alien threat coming for him. Far too late, Niall shoved up his mental defenses. "You can't know that."

*Balor wants you*, Miach accused. *It sends an army for you. Don't put your family in danger to make you feel better about leaving them again.*

"Niall!" Jose said as he reached them. "*Que paso, amigo?*"

Niall switched his gaze from Miach to Jose. A crackling between his fingers made him lift his hand and everyone took a step back. Jose showed him his palm.

*Daddy, don't be angry*, Lizzie pleaded. *Miach's only scared for us.*

"I won't put them in danger," Niall said, trying to be reasonable, trying to respect Miach's feelings for his family, but there was a possessive quality to Miach's thoughts that lit a jealous time bomb inside his gut. There was something more going on here he didn't understand. "I have to go to Groom Lake. I want my family with me. Make up for lost time," he said tightly, daring Jose, Sam, anyone of them to object to his plan.

*It's fine, Lizzie*, Niall soothed her. *We can work this out.*

Her aura didn't look convinced. Miach looked like thunder had just rolled in.

"They're my children," Niall stated. "Tami's my wife. I'm taking them with me."

"Niall," Jose said, "take a breath, man, you're losing it."

Miach's eyes narrowed. "No. Tami married me. A month ago. You need to stop. Think through what you're about to do."

Married? Niall grappled with the concept and failed. They couldn't be married. Tami was *his* wife. He turned to her and the ugly truth lay exposed in her stricken face.

She began to cry. "Miach saved me, Niall. Please understand. I thought I would die without you. Everything was dark. I wanted to be happy again. I wanted our children to be happy. You left such a hole behind and they found out what he could do. I couldn't lose him, too."

A whooshing noise filled Niall's head, drowning out her words. "You married him?" The idea repulsed him. "What? Did he shape shift back to me? So you could all play happy families? Make believe I wasn't dead!"

Tami gasped.

"No!" Jose shouted. "Watch out!"

Niall turned back straight into Miach's right cross that sent him flying. He pooled all his mental resources into a searing probe that hit Miach's mental shield and shattered it to the four winds. In that split second, Niall raided Miach's mind and his memories. Rage gathered inside him. Lizzie screamed. Toby yelled at him to stop. All Niall could see was Miach making love to his wife, kissing Tami's tears away.

The explosive force inside him burst out.

"I saved your stinking hide! I brought your empty shell of a body back and this is how you repay me?"

Adrenalin surged through him. Astereal jumped into focus. Following the link and opening a bridge happened subconsciously, second nature.

"No!" Miach yelled, as Niall charged. The portal opened on sizzling black lava. Niall sent Miach through on the end of an uppercut that promised a dislocated jaw.

"Miach!" Tami screamed. The portal closed. "Oh, my God! Niall! What have you done? What have you done?"

Niall wasn't sure. Lizzie dropped to her knees and curled over. Niall's heart pounded. A red mist blurred his vision.

Toby launched at him and pummeled his chest. "Get him back! Get him back!"

Niall stood under the onslaught, his mind turned to sludge. As Sam pulled his son off, Tami threw herself at his leg.

"Niall! Please, don't do this. I love him. I love you. I'm so sorry, but, please, you have to bring him back!"

Niall swallowed. The world rushed back into focus. How long could Miach last on Astereal. A few seconds? Ten? A minute?

Suddenly, Jose was in his face. "Jesus, man, if you can get him back, you need to act now."

Niall nodded. Knots twisted his stomach. He felt sick. He had never felt an anger so strong before and its wake left him exhausted but with a crystal-clear vision. He looked around for dark energy. The air sizzled with the stuff. He blinked, tapping a level of power he had never perceived before. His mind flew to the dark presence racing towards them less than half a light year away and a terrible truth opened before him.

Power like his wouldn't be enough.

Tami's grip on his leg tightened. "Niall, please!" She collapsed at his feet.

Niall nodded, and without thinking his mind reached down the link. Astereal had turned into Erta Ale all over, a thin layer of black lava rock melting on a seething planet bed of golden mantle. Miach was nowhere to be seen. Niall swallowed.

*Niall 'Kearey.*

The call was so faint, Niall nearly missed it. And then his mind was racing to the outpost where he had holed up with Herecura, the moon much farther away from Astereal than usual, no longer enslaved to Astereal's gravitational pull but a rogue planet drifting through the solar system and Miach's last hope for survival.

Miach lay face down on the floor. Silent. Unmoving. Niall formed a full-blown bridge, and took possession of Miach's almost comatose mind, keeping the portal open to allow air from Earth to flood the outpost. Tami's grip on his leg loosened. He forced Miach's lungs to drag in air, completed the binding, and then, as he had done many times before, he formed a new bridge back to Earth. To his surprise, his lock hit the Earth's past. What did that mean? Was Astereal's timeflow speeding up? Why? It made no sense. How long had Miach been waiting? Waiting for the toxic air he took with him from Astereal to run out.

A new thought struck Niall. Would he trap Miach in the past? Niall nudged the lock forward, testing his bridge, moving it ever closer towards the present. Maybe it would be better to connect with the past?

Uathach's voice murmured from his memories. Reminding him why he shouldn't try to change the timeline.

Now Niall wasn't sure he had a choice. His bridge from Earth to the outpost faded to a link as Niall focused all his thought into bringing Miach back to the present.

Miach's lungs strained for air. Niall began to panic. He had seconds before oxygen failed to reach Miach's brain. When that happened, Miach's higher order functions would begin to fail and the bridge to Earth would collapse. A shimmering in the air danced before him. A portal formed. Niall locked the bridge and forced Miach to crawl through.

Tami reached him first. "He's not breathing," she yelped.

For the briefest second, Niall felt her soft lips on his, her warm breath filling his lungs, and then with a sharp pain stabbing his heart, Niall broke the link. The portal from Astereal's moon winked out of existence and Niall dispersed the dark energy from his engine safely into the q-dimension. There would be no more crackling anger today. He'd scared everyone too much already, himself included.

Miach coughed, and rolled over.

Tami stroked his back, murmuring soothing words. Jose called for medical help and then silence fell. Niall bit his lip as all eyes turned to him.

He didn't see a way back from this.

# CHAPTER THIRTY-SIX

"Not cool," Sam repeated.

Niall could only hope Sam had exhausted his repertoire of condemnatory clichés. Looking back, he couldn't remember a time he'd seen Sam this angry. An upset, disappointed, disbelieving angry as evidenced by his white-knuckled hands gripping the decking rail surrounding the bungalow.

Niall paced the verandah, too miserable to persist with his grudge against Sam Hastor. Hell, after what he'd just done to Miach, Sam looked saint-like in comparison. Niall couldn't even react to the bird insignia on Sam's chest signifying his promotion to the rank of full colonel.

Five years had gone by. The world had moved on without him.

"Legally, what you did constitutes attempted murder," Sam added.

"Mitigating circumstances," Niall returned, the bitter taste in his mouth revealing the lie. "What are they gonna do? Lock me in the freezer box again? I'm guessing I'll get away with it."

"Yeah, what with an alien entity space hopping our way." The dripping sarcasm in Sam's voice stung. Sam used the back of his hand to wipe sweat of his brow then checked his watch. "We need to get to Groom Lake. Towden's meeting us there."

Niall threw a daggered look at the closed entryway to the bungalow. Tami was inside with Miach, Lizzie, and the island's doctor. Toby was scuffing sand on the beach. Thank God his parents were visiting friends elsewhere on the island. He didn't think he could have handled Tony and Sheila right now. He heard the medic talking, his voice low. Miach lay in bed—in what had been Niall and Tami's bed—an oxygen mask covering his nose and mouth. His lungs coated with a layer of volcanic gases, the stubborn Asterean had refused to go to the island hospital. Niall suspected he wanted to keep Tami close.

Miach fought for more than his life.

Everything had changed. Even Toby and Lizzie could barely look at their father, entombed in shock by what he'd done. His family's torn loyalties hurt, stringing every muscle in Niall's body to the snapping point. Nothing he could say could put things right. He'd driven them away. The best he could do for his family was to protect them from any more pain. Pushing off the wood railing he began to form a portal to Nevada.

Sam put out a hand. "Damn it, Niall, I didn't mean this second. You can't just go without a word."

"Sam, even Jose hates me right now. I fucked up." Niall paused. "I need to focus on the real threat. There's a big, bad nasty coming for us."

"Can't you blast this alien ship halfway across the universe, too?"

Niall flashed Sam a furious look.

"Hey, I'm serious," Sam protested.

Niall focused on his link to Nevada. He scanned GBI's command room. Alerts were going off—his link had been detected. He opened a portal in the event room.

*Daddy! Wait.* Lizzie bolted out onto the deck and into his arms.

Toby appeared on the steps leading up from the beach. "I'm going with you," he said stubbornly.

Niall's heart leapt.

Lizzie lifted her chin. "I'm staying with Mom, but only because she needs me." Her voice softened. "I love you, Daddy."

Niall's eyes moistened. He nodded to Toby and gripped the back of Lizzie's head with its ultra-bright hair, pulling her close. Tropical fruit filled his nostrils. His daughter was all grown up. "I love you, too, sweet pea, more than ever."

Lizzie's thought washed over him like a soothing balm. *Please be careful, Daddy. Come home to us.*

Niall struggled to swallow. Light from inside spilled onto the deck. He looked up to see Tami standing in the open doorway. Her eyes were huge, full of pain. The portal to GBI shimmered in the air. Through his bridge, Niall sensed Security Forces racing to the scene.

Sam stepped up and wrapped Tami in his arms. "You take care, honey. Get Miach well. I'll look after Niall and Toby, as much as Niall will let me."

She smiled bravely and patted his arm. Then she looked over to Toby. "Are you sure?"

Toby's expression said it all.

She bit her lip and Niall grasped her fear. This would be Toby's first real taste of military life—Tami didn't want to lose her son. "I won't let him do anything I would," he said.

She smiled then, a guilty *can't believe he said that* smile that faded like the sun going down. Now all he wanted was to see dawn break one more time. He glanced at the portal, then at Sam waiting. Kissing Lizzie's forehead, Niall set her aside and strode over to his wife.

*His wife.*

He gripped her arms. "I love you, Tami. To the stars and back."

The soft light in her eyes warmed his soul. "I never stopped loving you, Niall."

He kissed her lips gently and felt a new tension in her body. He pulled back. "Later."

Tami brushed hair from her eyes and nodded. Niall backed away, his hand sliding down her arm to her fingertips, not letting go. He blindly gestured Sam and Toby ahead of him, unable to break their gaze or release her hand. Her green eyes captivated him. Impossible to leave her behind. She would be at Miach's bedside, knowing who had done this to a man she loved enough to marry.

Niall had never felt so helpless. How had it all gone so wrong?

She broke first. "You should go." Apology lurked in her whisper.

"Yes." He hesitated. "Will you tell Tony and Sheila I'll be back to see them?"

"Of course." She bit her lip again, on the edge of tears.

Lizzie stepped in close and claimed her mom's hand. Niall had to look away.

Stepping through that portal damn near killed him.

Several weapons trained directly on him stopped Niall dead in his tracks. He raised his hands slowly, assessing the situation, searching for trigger-happy fingers, and acutely conscious that Toby stood with Sam to the side, very still, his eyes wide open with excitement.

"Stand down," Sam snapped at the security team's commanding officer.

"Sorry, Colonel. New standing orders," the lieutenant responded, his eyes shifting to the closing portal.

General Towden walked into the event room and took in the situation at a glance. His eyes rested on Toby. "This isn't a creche, Major Kearey!"

Toby bristled with every part of his body.

Towden smiled and there was a definite twinkle in his eye. "But welcome to the US Air Force, son. Big day, huh?"

"Ah, General, sir," Niall said.

The general belatedly woke up to the guns aimed at Niall and made a dismissive gesture with his hand. "Stand down, Lieutenant."

"Yes, sir!" The security team vanished as quickly as they had arrived. There was a collective sigh of relief.

In the main lab, Max waved at him, a beaming smile on his slimmed down face. Niall nodded back. He had some catching up to do.

Towden glared at Niall. "I just got off the phone with Patrick Morgan. Seems you set their private island alight." His glare switched to Hastor. "You have a report, Colonel?"

"Sir, err..." Sam straightened. "Nothing that can't wait, General."

"Good." Towden studied Niall, his eyebrows joining into a single bushy line of disapproval. "Have you eaten, Major? You had barely a mouthful before."

Niall's growling stomach brought a smile to Toby's face.

"No, sir," Niall replied.

His son grinned more widely. Niall could hardly tear his eyes off him.

"You can eat during the briefing," Towden decided. "Toby, I'll get someone to show you around. I'll issue supervised clearance to GBI and the Asterean facility after your father explains to you what a Non-Disclosure Agreement is and you've signed it."

"General, sir, I know what an NDA is." Toby acted out zipping his mouth shut.

Towden studied him. "Unzipping that mouth means prison. You understand?"

Niall frowned. Toby nodded his head with vigor.

An officer approached them with a printout. Towden scanned it. His eyebrows parted as he glanced back at Toby. "Seems your clearance is already high, Mister Kearey." He handed the NDA to Toby. "Sign this."

The general moved away. Niall waved his hand at Toby for the paper. He scanned it quickly. "Damn."

"I can keep a secret, Dad."

"I don't want you having to keep secrets from your mom and Lizzie."

Sam stepped up. "You can't be worried about this stuff, Niall. Not now. I'll make sure Toby's clear on what he can discuss and what he can't." He handed Toby a pen. "The Vercingetorix take care of their own, Niall. He'll be fine."

"Considering their track record, that's not very comforting."

Toby moved to a table and scrawled his signature with a flourish. Sandwiches and mugs of soup appeared on a table. Niall fell on the food, dunking bread in the soup to aid his digestion.

Sam opened a bottle of water and placed it beside Niall's plate. "They're Morgans, Niall, Toby and Lizzie, whether you like it or not. Patrick and Etlinn won't let anything bad happen to them. That means Tami's protected too."

"Talk about keeping your enemies close," Niall said through a mouthful of food. He noticed Toby chatting with Max. General Towden moved into his glass-enclosed office to take a call.

"The Vercingetorix isn't your enemy," Sam said, sitting down. "That alien ship approaching Earth is. I know you've been out of things for five years, and a lot happened to put you in that cryogenic pod, but you need to adjust your thinking. And fast."

Niall paused, soaked bread midway to his mouth. "I was locked in a box for five years and declared dead, a small detail that fucked up my marriage. I'm lucky to be alive and getting the chance to discover my son again and that's only because I'm Earth's best hope against an alien threat. I know who the enemy is. I also know who I can trust. I will do a job, because the human race needs me to do a job, but when it comes to the governments of Earth, and the Vercingetorix, I don't give a shit."

A scratching at his shields made Niall look across to Toby. His son was staring at him anxiously and a general nervousness pervaded the lab. Everyone appeared engaged in activity, but their auras hinted at worry and distraction. Towden stood looking out of his office, a frown on his face.

Only Sam appeared immune to Niall's consuming rage. "You'd rather do this on your own? Without back up?"

Niall put down the bread and sat back in his chair. "I think I lost my appetite." He saw Max touch Toby's sleeve then point out something on his screen.

"Look, I get how you feel." Sam drummed two fingers on the table. "Hell, makes sense to me now why you hid your abilities for so long." He leaned forward. "But this alien threat changes everything. Earth needs you. Don't waste energy second guessing everyone around you."

"If I do anything, with anyone, it's going to be on my terms. That's as good as it gets, Sam. And don't think that the people who did this to me are going to get away with it. You know what pisses me off? Nature fried Foldane's brain before I could get to him first!"

Sam leaned forward and dropped his voice to a whisper. "So, after you've saved Earth, assuming that's even possible, you're going to track down any and everyone responsible for putting you in cryogenic stasis? Or just those who lied about you being dead? Then what? How far do you intend to go?"

Tension set in Niall's jaw. Sam knew exactly how far he could go.

"Shit." Sam shook his head. He studied his fingers before returning Niall a pointed look. "I get it. They fucked you over. But your burning need for vengeance won't save us. It could destroy us all. You need to get on top of this."

Niall glanced at Toby's anxious face. He sensed the approach of familiar minds and forced his body to relax.

Later.

Right now, he needed the resources of his government. He couldn't afford to be fighting on all sides or lose control like he had with Miach. He needed to face Balor's emissary and determine the threat facing Earth. Everything else he would deal with later. By the time he finished cleaning house of his enemies, there would be no one left to put him in that freezer box. Matter of fact, the box would have to go too. DruSensi and their psi gadgetry were in for one hell of a meltdown.

Sohan and Pwyll walked in, Macha close behind them. They had aged. Sohan sported a trimmed beard dusted with silver. Pwyll looked more seasoned, his face lined with responsibility, but his eyes sparkled with pleasure and his wide smile competed with his broad shoulders. Macha had changed the least. The artificial lights jumped out of her golden square pupils and her translucent skin glowing as pale as her silver aura showed off the triangular eye pendant hanging around her neck.

She ran up to Niall, and gave him a warm hug. Her thought murmured in his head. *We know what happened with Miach. You went back for him. Remember that.*

And then her thought was gone. She stepped aside and let a beaming Sohan in. He and Niall shook hands.

Niall clapped Pwyll on the back. "What did you think of the Grand Canyon?"

"I never saw it in person, but they couldn't stop me from remote-viewing the canyon." Pwyll looked uncomfortable, but he didn't hold back. "Security tightened after you were put in stasis." *We used the Falcon project to earn back some trust.*

Niall frowned, but said no more, turning instead to greet a clean-shaven Max. Klotz had lost a ton of weight. Toby stood beside him. The unlikely duo seemed to have struck it off.

"Good to see you, Major."

"And you, Max. Didn't recognize you."

"I have a plan. Involves a boat. Decided it was time to get fit."

Niall grinned. "Good for you."

Max grinned back. His eyes brightened.

Towden emerged from his office. "Let's get started," he barked. "Lieutenant, lights, please."

Niall stepped back as a holographic projection of the approaching spacecraft materialized in front of him. He frowned. Walked around it. It looked familiar. His emotions had overwhelmed him during his earlier contact with the ship. He remembered that alien mind rifling through his head. Dangerous. He'd let his guard down. Given the aliens even more reason to head to Earth.

*What do they want with me?*

"A routine study of the Centaurus constellation picked up an anomaly between two and three light years away," Towden briefed. "The unexplained phenomenon was later matched to an object at one light year distance, but still in the direction of Proxima Centauri. Our evidence indicates the object appeared out of nowhere in both instances. The same object then jumped to the other side of our solar system, half a light year from Earth and in the direction of Orion's Belt. If it jumps again it could arrive at Earth in a matter of days. Maybe hours."

Niall listened to Towden, but his son caught his attention when Toby slipped off his chair and went down into a squat, craning his neck to see under the ship. Niall's breath hitched and he nearly got down on the floor with him. "Excuse me, General," he said instead.

Towden paused, his eyes flitting to Toby.

"Raise the visual," Niall requested. Max touched a data pad he was holding and the holographic ship rose into the air until Niall could step under it. "Higher."

A memory teased at him. Niall's throat went dry and he grabbed the bottle Sam had opened before he choked.

"Major?" Towden asked.

Niall swallowed a mouthful of water then wiped his lips. "I need to get closer. Feel it. Something about it. I'm sure I've seen this ship before."

"There is nothing like this vessel on Astereal, Niall'Kearey," Sohan said.

"It wasn't from Astereal. I'm not sure..."

"Hold tight, Major," Towden said, "you'll get a chance to check it out again very shortly. This alien ship is steadily moving towards Earth, faster than anything we've got."

The visual disappeared and was replaced by a simulation of the vessel's passage through interstellar space.

"Maybe it doesn't want to jump into something close up," Toby commented.

"That's NASA's conclusion, after consulting with the Astereans," Sam said. "Big vessel. Get it wrong. Hard to stop."

"The UN Office for Outer Space Affairs is concerned at the general presumption of aggressive intentions," Towden informed them. "They're asking how we can be sure it's Balor."

"This ship is Balor's," Niall said. He looked at the others. "I remote-viewed the ship earlier. Made contact with a mind on board. Said his name was Lugus *and* that he was Balor's warlord."

"He?" Pwyll asked.

"He, she, it..." Niall shrugged.

"I informed Vice-President Biron of your initial impressions, Major Kearey," Towden said. "He ordered GBI to monitor your next remote-view. EM output, chemical analysis of your reactions, that sort of thing. I thought Pwyll and Sohan could validate your observations, and Macha could verify your emotional response. Macha informs me she can um, tag along for the ride."

"If that is acceptable to you," Macha hastened to add.

Niall nodded. "It's fine." He sent her a private message. *You can update me on what's been happening with you.* Macha didn't respond, smiling at Toby instead. Niall realized his son was watching them strangely. *Can you hear me, Toby?*

Toby's eyes widened. He grinned at Niall and nodded. A surge of pride filled Niall that he directed at Toby until the boy's ears turned pink.

*Your children are progressing well,* Macha told him. *I have kept in touch through Miach.* Niall's bubble of joy deflated and Macha's tone hardened, her thought tightening into a private exchange. *You charged Miach with taking care of your family. He had no way of knowing you were alive.*

*I never asked him to fall in love with my wife!*

Macha frowned at a flicker of rage he could not suppress. She nodded at Toby. Niall's stomach lurched at the look of distress on his son's face. *Damn.* He was grateful when Max flicked a switch that lit up the Event Unit from where Niall had explored Groom Lake's past.

"I've reconfigured the remote-viewing column for four. The helmets are advanced versions of the DRUMSI unit."

"Can't wait," Niall muttered.

"I swear on my life there are no hidden extras," Max said quickly.

"You'd better be right. Be a real shame to put all that hard work to waste," Niall replied, his voice clipped.

"I am. I triple checked everything. Nothing invasive either. We have wireless sensors to monitor blood gas and chemistry. They just stick to your arm."

Niall nodded reluctantly, willing to take Max at his word, not looking forward to the scrutiny.

"Are you ready for this, Major Kearey?" Towden asked. "Everything's set to go."

"I'm good, General."

Niall took a seat opposite Macha, Pwyll to his right. They sat in silence as Max fine-tuned the monitoring equipment in the tight space. Chatter filled Niall's head.

*President Biron refuses to see any Asterean without dampening precautions,* Sohan said. *Macha, too.*

Pwyll scratched his nose. *Senator Biron started to distance himself after you rescued Dr. Klotz. I believe he has something to hide.*

*What about Foldane?* Niall asked.

Sohan replied. *I met President Foldane a couple of times before your reported death. I always thought he regretted the decision to place you in cryogenic stasis. After your death there were many accusations until a fault was established. The general mistrust had the effect of keeping us out of the loop. The cover up was very convincing. Relations became fraught and I have not seen President Foldane since.*

Niall glanced at the general watching them from outside the thickened glass. *Towden has no problems with any of you. Nor has Colonel Hastor.*

*I did meet Patrick Morgan a few months ago,* Pwyll said. *He hid it well but he was worried for his wife.*

*Etlinn?*

*Your death, your reported death, devastated her. She went into reclusion for several months.*

Macha's mind nudged Pwyll aside. *Lizzie brought her out of it. After you went into cryogenic stasis, Etlinn visited Tami. She stayed on the island for several weeks. She and Lizzie became quite close. Both your children are very talented.*

"I can tell you're chatting, you know," Max interrupted. "Just to report monitors are operating normally."

"Major? Status?" Towden barked out.

"Ready, sir. Searching for a link now."

He navigated the q-dimension easily. Macha, Pwyll and Sohan traced his link. Better do a proper recon this time. He shielded his mind tightly, leaving a sliver of a channel open for the others.

*What are you looking for?* Macha asked.

Niall surfed around the ship, committing the crystalline lines and random protrusions to memory. *It looks almost natural. Freeform. No weapon arrays.*

And yet its dark ugliness and a thrumming sensation chilled his blood.

"Max, report," Niall ordered.

"Um, you're showing elevated levels of adrenalin, Major. Everyone else is reading normal. What's causing that?"

"I'm not sure. Irrational fear," Niall replied. "I don't identify any obvious weapons, General."

"Confirmed," Pwyll said. "Try reducing your shielding, Niall'Kearey."

Niall opened his eyes and found Toby monitoring his status with Max. "Toby, I'm expecting a bad reaction, but I'll be fine." His son gave him a thumbs up and a confident smile. Niall stopped worrying about him and focused on opening his mind slowly.

Nothing.

Relief washed through him. He barely heard Macha's protests, or Towden's demands for an explanation. He felt almost giddy. "He's not hurt," Toby was insisting.

"That's correct. I'm fine," Niall croaked. "Whatever I encountered before, it's not here now."

Niall's studied the shiny rock-like substance. The radiation field interacted with his consciousness and that sense of deja vu struck him anew.

"We have not seen this gravitonic isotope before," Pwyll stated.

"Has Dr. Biron arrived yet?" Towden asked. "I had her flown up from Bolivia," he added as an aside.

*Bolivia?*

*She's running a research project at Lake Titicaca,* Sohan replied.

"ETA in five minutes," someone responded.

Niall sensed something more, a force beyond the ship's hull. "Patch me through to her," he said.

"Do it," General Towden ordered.

"Jacqueline?"

"Um... hello? Is that Major Kearey? Wow. It's so good to hear—"

"Later. Remember when I replicated a magnetic field? What was that? Point seven Tesla?"

"Yes, that's correct."

"This feels a hundred times that."

"What does?"

"The alien ship."

"What's its shape?"

"Long, cylindrical, half a kilometer diameter, close to two kilometers long. Hard to say without a reference."

"Can you see inside?"

"Maybe. If I adjust the link. Pwyll, why did you call it a gravitonic isotope?" Niall asked.

"The ship exhibits gravitational wave annihilation. Anti-gravity generation derives from dark energy. If this process reaches critical mass it releases subatomic particles your scientists call axions." Pwyll sensed Niall's confusion. "Look for the radiation imprint the gravitational wave leaves behind."

Niall thought about this suggestion for a second, decided he hadn't time for games, and raided Pwyll's mind. When he saw the rippling energy radiating from the ship, he adjusted his conscious mind to view a wider energy spectrum from the perspective of the q-dimension.

*That I have not seen before*, Pwyll confessed with some awe.

Space around the ship compressed and expanded in a gentle rhythm gradually diminishing to stillness over a radius approaching hundreds of miles.

"Now why don't I like the look of that?" Niall asked.

"The axion's magnetic dipole can accelerate gravitational reversal," Pwyll explained, "and it's very dangerous near gravity dependent matter, like a planet. If something goes wrong with a ship's anti-gravity generator the reaction can spiral out of control, destroying the ship and anything in its path. Right now, the hull's decay could be normal, or the product of a reaction with dark matter particles in space. However, if the rate of decay alters, say from proximity to Earth's sun, or contact with Earth's atmosphere, and reaches critical mass, it could set off a chain reaction."

"You're talking about the gravitational equivalent of a nuclear fission bomb," Niall said. "A super charged meteorite set on a course for Earth."

"I am more concerned about what the hull is protecting inside. It may not be an accidental meltdown causing the reaction. It could be deliberate."

Niall battled an inner revulsion. Where had the alien consciousness gone? This *Lugus*. Balor's warlord.

"Major," Towden growled. "Can you extend your link to inside the alien ship without compromising your safety?"

Niall drew in a ragged breath. "Yes, sir."

"Proceed."

Extending his mind through the isotopic crystalline hull reminded Niall of forcing his way through mountain rock all those weeks ago. No, not weeks. Years. He began to perspire. In a coffin. Like Herecura. Trapped and at the mercy of a black hole. Had she died? Given him away to Balor with her dying memories?

*Niall'Kearey. Focus*, Macha berated him, but it was the strength of the magnetic forces buffeting him that fixed his mind on the job at hand. It skittered his mind into a blinding swirl of...

*Fuck.*

*Energy. Dark energy.*

He shifted onto the edge of his chair and gripped the armrests to stop him launching up. "It's a magnetic engine. The whole goddamn ship's an electromagnetic engine focused on generating gravitonic isotopes from dark energy. The magnetic forces are incredibly strong at the hull, decreasing towards its center. Perhaps the isotopic nature of the hull serves a dual purpose, containment and safety valve all in one."

The energy scratched at the edges of his mind. Distracting him.

"Get out of there," Sohan yelled, his mind withdrawing. Macha moaned then also backed out from his mind.

Pwyll stuck with him long enough to scream, *Close the link!*

Niall didn't hesitate. He shut the link down and took several calming breaths before opening his eyes.

Macha stared at him, wide-eyed. "What could create such a thing?" she whispered.

"Can we destroy it?" Towden demanded. "Neutralize it?"

Jacqueline Biron walked into the command room. "General, sir. This ship sounds like an antimatter containment field similar to that used at CERN several years ago."

It seemed like only a few days ago since Niall found Jacqueline shocked and battered in a shipping container. Five years had made her strong again. A sense of relief filled him.

"What sort of destructive power are we talking about?" Towden asked.

Niall looked to Sohan and then Pwyll.

Pwyll grimaced. "A lot?"

"Niall'Kearey, you understand dark energy better than any of us," Sohan said. "Compare it to what you know."

Niall swallowed. "Like a black hole in a bottle. Destroy that ship and the dark energy will annihilate the space around it."

Towden glowered at him. "You can't funnel the energy somewhere safe? During Operation Hideout you drew dark energy from the galactic center of the Milky Way."

"I took what I needed to create and stabilize the bridge between Astereal and Earth. This is a massive imbalance, an overload of energy from the start. I'm not sure where I could put it, or if I could control the rate of dispersal." There had to be a way. General Towden expected a solution. The pressure fogged up his mind. "I'll think of something."

Towden's expression soured. "So, what's its purpose? Who's driving the thing?"

"No one I could detect," Niall admitted.

"I concur," Pwyll added.

"It's remote controlled," Toby said.

Towden spun around and looked at him. Then he snapped his fingers. "Of course, it is. It's the equivalent of a nuclear-tipped alien drone."

"That suggests this Lugus warlord is remote-creating bridges through space." Niall felt sick.

*What does Balor want? Why me?*

He couldn't deny the obvious any longer. It had been there with every contact. Balor evidenced a fanatical fear of anything with the potential to oppose its dominion over everything it touched.

"It thinks I'm a threat. It detected my mind and thinks I represent the evolution of a species that challenges its supremacy. What more have you learned about Balor?" He turned to Jacqueline. "Did you find the third orb?"

"No. Sohan persuaded the Vercingetorix to keep looking. The Council negotiated an archaeological dig with Syria, but we didn't find an orb. Then all hell broke out over there." She hesitated. "A lot has happened."

Niall glanced at Max. "You know about the Vercingetorix?"

The scientist nodded. "Yeah, they upped my clearance a few months after you died. My research lucked out big time. Put me back in the good books."

"What research?"

"Factors that might affect the Asterean's response to Earth's geomagnetic field."

"Can we do this later?" Towden said.

"With respect, sir," Niall intervened, "I need to know this."

Towden looked surprised, then grunted. "Go ahead, Dr. Klotz."

A deep crease joined Max's eyebrows. "Well, how much do you know already?"

Niall's patience wore down to a thread. "Pretend I don't, Max."

Max winced. "Okay then. Well, I was reviewing the visual recording you took of Astereal to prove its existence. The sky there was lilac. Here it's blue. It occurred to me that Earth is subject to a range of radiation. Stands to reason that the cosmic radiation in our part of the galaxy is different to Astereal's, and depending on the season, geomagnetic storms and the like, some parts of Earth are more exposed to higher energy radiation than others."

Pwyll nodded. "Our scientists confirmed that your galaxy is more active with higher energy radiation than our own and Earth's geomagnetic field is generally not as effective at screening it out."

Max drew Niall's attention to an onscreen map. "See here? Nevada is closer to the South Atlantic Anomaly. After you, um, disappeared, I got approval to move a test group of adversely affected Astereans to a facility further north. Ninety percent of that group recovered a modicum of telepathic ability. That's when I got full clearance. Genetic analysis has discovered that many coded families in the Vercingetorix have a natural EM resilience to this radiation."

"Dr. Klotz has an interesting theory," Sohan said.

Max's chest swelled. "It's possible," he declared, his eyes alive with his excitement, "that evolution of the human race has stumbled upon a way to counteract this higher energy, a natural immunity if you will. Shit. You could be the first Asterean descendant able to fully utilize the potential of the human brain."

"There's a second possible explanation for Major Kearey's unique abilities," a feminine voice added.

Niall swung around to discover Etlinn Morgan standing beside his son, her hand resting on Toby's shoulder. Niall's heart thudded. The sight of his birth mother stirred emotions he couldn't deal with right now. His throat tightened. "Go on."

"We named the genetic marker in your DNA, Balor 24."

Niall flinched. Etlinn's discovery of Balor 24 stole five years of his life, hijacked his family.

"A twenty-fourth chromosome?" Toby said.

Etlinn gave him a look of approval. Grandmother and grandson exchanged a look that spoke of familiarity and affection.

Niall battened down a surge of resentment beneath his privacy shield. *Pwyll, check her story out. Discreetly.*

Pwyll's nod of assent was barely noticeable.

"The marker isn't a true chromosome, but it might as well be," Etlinn answered him. "I doubt this marker is solely responsible for your father's ability, Toby, but it is a likely contributor. I suspect the answer to be an amalgamation of evolution, as Dr. Klotz hypothesizes, and this marker." Her voice quavered as she looked at Niall, her eyes misting. "It's good to see you, Niall. I could hardly speak when I got the news. We all thought..." She swallowed, taking a moment to compose her expression. Her eyes fell on General Towden and hardened. "The Vercingetorix is seeking answers from your government."

Towden's eyes darkened. "I was as surprised as you, Professor Morgan," he growled.

Niall's stomach twisted. This had to stop; he didn't need any more drama today, and random dots were joining up in his mind. "The high radiation might explain why Balor hasn't ventured into this region of space before, at least not as far as we know."

The general's eyes shifted from Etlinn to him. His glowering expression lifted. "It might also explain an unmanned drone."

"It wasn't unmanned the first time I contacted the alien ship," Niall reminded him. "I didn't imagine this Lugus."

Sohan nodded. "It is entirely feasible that Balor's warlord can link to the alien ship just as you linked to Astereal."

"Yes," Pwyll said, his eyes narrowing in speculation. "The magnetic source containing the anti-matter can equally shield the ship from outer radiation, thereby protecting a transient crew from any ill-effects."

"Cool set up," Niall said, mulling over the options. "Send out a drone as reconnaissance, weapon and homing beacon all in one, link to it as the situation demands. Turn that link into a bridge and the ship transforms into a platform for invasion."

"What's its mission?" Towden demanded. "Acquire or destroy you? Or annihilate Earth?"

Niall felt that deep void opening up beneath him. The distinction made a difference. He did know that ship emanated raw destructive power. "I didn't see a targeting system, sir." His stomach growled, his energy levels dropping fast and dulling his mind. "I'm hungry. I have to eat. Get some sleep."

Towden peered at him and nodded. "Okay. Get some food and rest. Freshen up. Then we'll see where we're at. Your old quarters have been made available to you. I'll let you know if anything changes."

Niall nodded.

Etlinn stepped up before he could move. "Niall?"

The uncertain wariness radiating from her aura ratcheted up the tension inside him. He couldn't deal with Etlinn, too much unresolved emotional baggage to work through.

"Not now," he said, his tone gruff. He tried to sidestep her, but her hand reached out. "What is it with you people?" he snapped.

Her color blanched at his tone and her hand fell away. "Please, you have to understand," she said, her eyes overly-bright. He saw her fight to keep her emotions under control, but her aura betrayed her pain. "With the data we had available, there seemed no alternative to the cryogenic pod. When you died..." Etlinn's voice caught, forcing her to clear her throat before she could continue. "I didn't see much point in continuing my research. Your children saved me and I turned my attention to identifying the source of this alien marker, for them. Please, won't you hear me out?"

"I already know about Muhuza. General Towden briefed me on your research."

"I understand, but there's something else you should know."

Niall quashed an irritable urge to lash out. Etlinn was intent on unburdening herself and he needed to learn everything he could. Plus Toby was watching, listening to every word, and the protective streak coloring his aura wasn't for his father.

*Etlinn Morgan speaks with honesty, Niall'Kearey,* Pwyll murmured in Niall's mind. *I do not read an ulterior motive.*

Niall made his decision. "We can talk while I eat."

Etlinn's eyes widened. He'd surprised her. Relief flooded her features. Then she smiled at him, and Niall suddenly knew who Lizzie had inherited her dimples from. "Thank you."

# CHAPTER THIRTY-SEVEN

Taking Etlinn's elbow, Niall steered her towards the Asterean village, clasping Toby briefly to his side so his son knew to tag along. Toby's excited interest in the hi-tech military base lightened Niall's mood. The strapping lad matching his strides had matured so much, but the little boy he remembered was still in there.

In the end, Toby slowed them down, for Etlinn's benefit.

"Toby!" Etlinn exclaimed, with a look of surprised delight. "I heard that. You caught me unawares."

Niall frowned. "I got nothing."

"You weren't supposed to," Toby said with a wide grin. "The last time Maimeó stayed on the island, she showed Lizzie and me how to keep our conversations private."

His children called Etlinn 'Grandmother'? Niall flashed Etlinn an irritated glance. She shook her head, silently asking him not to make a scene over it as Toby's smile faded.

"Telepathy is harder here than on the island," his son said. "Is that because we're closer to the South Atlantic Anomaly?"

"Probably," Niall said, going along with the diversion. "I couldn't remote-view Washington DC from Bolivia. You wouldn't know that. Remember when we stayed in the Morrígan village and Miach went to Washington DC?" Niall hesitated. Toby had witnessed him nearly kill Miach earlier that day. Too late now though. He powered on, determined to show that he had his feelings back under control, hoping no one would realize they walked alongside a smoking powder keg. "We found our minds could meet at the edge of the anomaly. I used to listen out for Macha that way." Niall threw the boy a quick look.

329

Toby seemed unperturbed, or adept at hiding his feelings.

An upsurge of love for his son caught Niall unawares. Toby's cheeks reddened, but his aura danced. So, his son hadn't been able to ignore that. Niall looked at Toby's aura more carefully. The complexity of the colors startled him.

"Teenage hormones, Niall," Etlinn murmured, seeming to read his mind, even more disconcerting.

They reached the arboretum. While Toby absorbed the existence of an underground oasis, Niall fixed his eye on the self-service restaurant. Leading the way, he grabbed a plate.

"Help yourself, Toby." Niall eyed a blood-red sirloin steak. Saliva filled his mouth. He could practically taste the juices as the hole inside him intensified to a roaring ache.

"Perhaps you should eat something more easily digested," Etlinn suggested.

Nope. Miach had never had a problem on Astereal. Niall selected the steak, a baked potato and then grabbed a plate of apple pie, custard, and some sugar packets. Etlinn's lips twitched, her aura lightened, and when she shrugged, Niall's irritation melted away. His birth mother sat on the Vercingetorix Council, had been instrumental in putting him into cryogenic stasis, but there was undeniably something about her that he liked. Toby liked her. That had to count for something. She *had* protected his family. Her insight could be helpful.

"Let's sit up there." Niall indicated a private balcony overlooking the fountain, and the milling Astereans.

An air of excitement filled the space and several smiles beamed their way. His presence had been noticed, but no one disturbed them. Niall suspected he had Pwyll to thank for that. Once seated, he wasted no time tucking in, savoring his first mouthful as if it might be his last.

Toby copied him. "It's okay here," he mumbled through a mouthful of French fries.

Etlinn picked at a green salad and Niall sensed her aura turn inward. "What is it?"

She shook her head. "The psychic potential here is overwhelming."

Niall hoped she hadn't detected Pwyll's probe.

"The Vercingetorix Council has started sending non-telepaths to the Asterean facilities," she added.

"Any reason?" he said carefully.

"Charles Biron is demanding security changes to protect our interactions with the Astereans."

Toby stopped chewing. His eyes flipped from Niall to Etlinn and back again.

Etlinn glanced at her grandson, hesitated, and then seemed to arrive at a decision. "DruSensi has been unable to establish contact with the chip implanted inside you."

"Yeah, well, seems it didn't survive the cryogenic freezing."

"Expectations are that it should not have been affected."

So... the Astereans had done more than check the cryogenic process worked as it should when they put him under, and Etlinn was telling him the V knew that now.

She nodded; her expression meaningful. "Your Asterean friends are very loyal to you. More independent than we mistakenly assumed."

Niall detected no overt threat and kept his voice soft. "The word that's important here is 'loyal'. Perhaps it's time this world stopped thinking of the Astereans as an investment property and started treating them as valued allies."

"You believe Earth will get the chance?"

"Dad will save the Earth," Toby declared, his earnest brown eyes testing Niall's resolve to keep his emotions together. "He just needs to work out how."

Etlinn couldn't hide her doubt, even from Toby, and Niall couldn't blame her. He carved up his steak as if it held the solution to all their problems. His mind rattled through all the different ways he could send Balor's missile to oblivion. Opening a bridge inside the vessel and dropping a nuke inside would be catastrophic this close to Earth. Dropping it into a portal leading to a distant sun seemed the most viable option and yet, he couldn't shift the feeling he'd seen the answer already.

"I feel like I've seen this ship before," Niall said slowly, working through his memories. "It was dark." There had been a gateway. *Bolivia.* A Sun god. Nausea filled him and Niall lurched to his feet, shoving his plate away with a force that made Toby drop his fork and Etlinn stare at him open-mouthed.

Time slowed and the clatter of metal on the table cut across the memory unfolding in his mind. He looked up at a looming dark shape that crossed the sky. Something had preceded it, he remembered. A shooting star. Or...

The blood drained from Niall's head, the answer he needed preordained—impossible to deny or evade. Faint with horror, he grated out, "Excuse me."

He headed for the restroom, rebounding off a wall in his haste. Inside the restroom, he stumbled to a basin, hit the water faucet and splashed cold water over his face until the heat thudding through him ebbed away. His nausea settled, but his hands shook uncontrollably. Bloodshot eyes stared back at him from the mirror. The door creaked open and, in the mirror, Niall saw a pale-faced Toby stop just inside the door.

Niall straightened, turned around and forced a calm note to his voice. "I'm fine, Toby."

"You don't look fine." Toby's deepening voice cracked. "You keep leaving us, Dad. Mom can't go through that again. Whatever you thought of, don't do it. There has to be another way."

"Shit," Niall whispered, running his wet hand through his hair.

"Why does it always have to be you? Why can't we all be normal like other people? What you can do, it's not right. Jesus, Dad! You sent Miach to a volcano on the other side of the universe!"

"Watch your mouth, Toby."

Toby's voice raised a notch. "Watch my mouth? Don't you get it? Miach could have died!"

"Yes. I shouldn't have done that," Niall said, his voice a strangled mess. "I... just..."

"Mom did nothing wrong."

Niall closed his eyes. This conversation had been bound to happen. He should have prepared better. When he opened them, he saw a young kid chewing his bottom lip, his forehead creased with the effort of keeping his eyes dry. Once upon a time, Toby would have run his emotions into the ground as fast as his little legs could carry him. Now he faced them and Niall couldn't be prouder.

"No, Mom did nothing wrong. But it hurts, Toby, to see the woman I love with a man who knows me inside out. Miach has my memories. It feels like this huge betrayal. Intellectually, I know I shouldn't blame him. He thought I was dead. He acted on his feelings for a woman I made him care for. I asked him to protect you all. He did everything I asked of him, but it hurts, Toby, to see them. Like that."

"Mom loves you, Dad."

"I know." The words choked Niall's windpipe. He couldn't let go that image of Miach and Tami. Together.

No. Don't think about it.

Niall steadied his voice. "I'm sorry for what I did, and that you had to see it. But I won't let what happened distract me now. I won't allow my feelings to get in the way of dealing with this threat to Earth. To us all."

Toby nodded, the muscles in his neck bulging as his eyes glistened.

"I'm glad you're here," Niall said, stepping towards him, inviting Toby in.

His son met him halfway. Niall clasped him tightly, ruffling what he could of Toby's hair into the unkempt state he remembered. Then he grasped his son's shoulders and pushed him back far enough that he could look deep into Toby's solemn brown eyes.

"I need you to be strong, Toby. But most of all, I need you to remember we all choose the path of our lives. You must choose the one you believe to be right," Niall thumped his own chest, "in here."

Toby nodded, even as his aura screamed, *No.*

Only then did it really hit home. Toby could read Niall's aura too, and the boy knew that his father was body-shaking terrified of the inescapable path that stretched ahead of him.

"I can do this, Toby. I can save Earth."

The answer lay in the past. But what about Earth's future? What about the next drone? What other nasties did Balor have at his command? This was only round one.

Niall searched the fear lurking in his son's eyes and felt that overpowering need to chase the bogeyman away. "I made you a promise once, Toby. I swore never to stop working to get you home. And I kept that promise. Well, today, I'm making the same promise. While there's breath in my body, I will work to get back to you." He tightened his grip on Toby's shoulder. "I swear to you."

"Since when did Major Kearey start dictating attendance at the UN Security Council?" Charles Biron demanded. Wiping spittle from the corner of his mouth, he launched out of his chair and paced the Oval Office. His temple pulsated with anger driven by the fear licking at his innards. His heartbeat thudded in his chest.

General Straton's stony face gave nothing away. "I understand he has a plan to neutralize the alien drone headed this way."

Charles threw the Joint Chief's chairman a sharp glance, but let the general's evasion slide. "And that's good, but the Astereans aren't part of the decision process. They don't need to be there."

Andrew, the President's Chief of Staff intervened. "Secretary General Kalufi has already agreed to his demands, sir."

Charles fumed silently. He knew why. Etlinn Morgan had her husband's ear and Patrick Morgan practically owned the UN. It didn't help that making President Foldane the scapegoat for Kearey's faked death had infuriated Sharifah Kalufi. She couldn't say much without incriminating herself, but she wasn't taking orders from the newly confirmed US president either.

Mutiny set into Charles' lower jaw. "Then explain to Madame Kalufi that the Astereans' telepathic ability presents an unacceptably high security risk to every member of the Security Council. The United States of America will attend via a secure comms link or not at all."

His declaration put a dent in Straton's impassive demeanor. "Mr. President, Major Kearey asserts that the Astereans cannot read the minds of non-telepaths. If they could, then Major Kearey would not have been taken unawares by his security escort after rescuing your niece—"

"Major Kearey is *not* Asterean and there are a number of Astereans whose telepathic ability is exceptional enough to break through the strongest of privacy shields. It will take the Astereans more than a few years to prove that their stated intent to integrate with the human population does not hide a more ambitious agenda. Think about it. Their very presence at a UN Security Council denotes their extending influence in matters of governance." Charles thumped the table. "Earth is our world. They are guests. No more."

Straton's eyes blazed as he pointed skyward in a sweeping arc. "That alien ship is a far more dangerous threat to the human population than the political ambitions of the Astereans. Sir, we need their experience! Their insight!"

Charles snorted. "Insight? The Asterean civilization barely made it past medieval sword play! Their EM pulse grenade is a middle grade science project. What can they offer to protect Earth against this missile? They've resisted overt weapons development for five years, and the aliens could be just hours away. If they jump again—" He stopped. Stepped back from the edge of panic. Straightened his tie. "What does Kearey intend to do?"

Straton grimaced. "Major Kearey refuses to divulge his plan."

"Are you telling me he's out of control?"

"I'm telling you that the President of the United States of America needs to be at this meeting."

Charles snapped his mouth shut before he said something he'd regret. If he couldn't avoid the meeting, he could take sensible precautions. He turned to his aide. "Get Secret Service in here."

# CHAPTER THIRTY-EIGHT

A flurry of snow chased Niall and General Towden into the United Nations' Visitor Center. After checking Toby in for a guided tour, Niall and General Towden met up with Colonel Hastor in the main foyer of the Conference Building. UN police surrounded them at a discrete distance. Sam's expression conveyed skeptical reticence as he handed Niall the security devices mandated for delegates' use by the US Secret Service.

Niall rolled the miniature ear plug between two fingers, suspicious of anything that came out of the DruSensi Corporation. "Personal EMR shields?"

Sohan stamped snow off his shoes and studied the specifications supplied with the little shields. Niall loosened his tie and removed his overcoat, the foyer uncomfortably warm in contrast to the sub-zero temperatures outside. The Arctic blast cutting deep across North America had blanketed New York in three feet of snow.

"Well?" Niall said, his tone sharp with irritation, and worry. If Biron distrusted him this much, he had an uphill battle ahead of him.

Sohan looked up, unruffled. "The EMR personal shield breaks up telepathic waveforms. It's a privacy shield with a limited range. I could stand next to someone with one on and it won't affect my ability to communicate, but I won't be able to detect their thoughts."

Niall put the sample ear plug in his ear and switched it on. *Sohan?*

Sohan frowned at him. "I am receiving something. It's more like static."

Niall tried Macha next. Nothing. "Can you contact Macha?"

Sohan's face stilled and then he nodded. Niall turned the device off.

*Macha?*

*Why are you shouting?*

*I'm not shouting. I'm not even speaking. Where are you?*

*Our car just pulled up outside. I do not like this snow.*

*I'll see you in a moment.* Niall took the ear plug out. "Makes you wonder what Biron's so desperate to hide," he said to Towden.

The general's nostrils flared with quiet disgust. "So, are you okay with these devices?" Towden asked him.

"Yes, sir. We'll do the Asterean inquisition another time."

Towden's eyes actually gleamed with humor.

"If your leaders feel threatened by our abilities, these shields may assist our cause," Sohan suggested.

"Maybe," Niall conceded. *Not gonna help you get your own way in the future, though.*

When Sohan didn't respond, Niall double checked the EMR shield was properly switched off. It was. Looking up, he caught Sohan's smile. Niall narrowed his eyes. *You wanted me to do that.*

*There is more to induco than telepathic ability, Niall'Kearey. A simple pause; a well-chosen word; a precise intonation, all these can induce the desired train of thought. The ability to read an aura is more important. The EMR shield will not hinder Pwyll's ability to discern deceit from truth.*

"When you two have finished," Towden growled.

Niall winced. "Sorry, sir. We're in agreement. The ear plugs will not be an issue. A dampening force field on the other hand..."

"The UN Secretary General has given her personal assurance that you will not be inconvenienced by any security measures, Major."

The main doors opened letting in an icy draft.

"Should have ordered Arctic gear," Towden grumbled.

Macha and Pwyll hurried in. The Morrigan Queen looked swamped by her coat and scarves. She shook off a light dusting of snow causing Pwyll to sidestep an icy shower.

Niall recognized General Straton approaching from the direction of the Security Council Chamber and automatically straightened.

"General Towden, Major Kearey," he boomed. They shook hands as Towden completed the introductions. Macha's warm smile suggested Straton had instantly gained her trust. General Straton's stern demeanor relaxed, his eyes alert with interest as he scanned Macha's alien features. "I'm delighted to meet you at last, ma'am."

"Call me Macha, General Straton. I am only sorry we meet under such urgent circumstances."

"Yes, we must get on." Straton smiled at Sohan and Pwyll and then he faced Niall. "I'm not ashamed to say it's a relief to see you alive, Major." His expression darkened. "Despite appearances to the contrary, the military has your back. I don't know what plan you have up your sleeve or even if I'll like it, but you won't be alone in there."

Niall's tension eased. "Thank you, sir."

"We're ready to start. I'll show you the way."

Walking into the Security Council Chamber, Niall was taken aback by the amount of space. Rows of chairs looking down on the main circular conference table sat empty. The seats encircling the conference table were fully occupied. A huge mural on the far wall toned in with the gold and blue decor.

"The UN Secretary General is chairing the meeting," Towden murmured.

Niall recognized Sharifah Kalufi from his meeting with the Vercingetorix Council five years ago. She rose gracefully to her feet, the passage of time barely discernible in her face. He focused on her aura until it sharpened and detected mainly anxiety and relief. He swallowed hard. All their hopes rested on him. They wanted him to wave a magic wand and make the evil disappear. He wished it were so simple. The dull ache in his heart throbbed.

*Niall'Kearey?*

*I'm fine, Macha. Please don't smother me.*

Her mind withdrew, but she stayed close to him as they walked forward.

"Welcome to the Security Council, Major Kearey," Sharifah said, inviting them nearer. "We all know why we meet today and I have no intention of wasting time on preliminaries. This is a closed session. I have personally vetted that every person present has the appropriate clearance. You may speak freely. There are no secrets in this room."

Niall opened his hand to reveal the little EMR shield and Sharifah sighed, her expression one of apology.

"Let me rephrase that. There are no classified secrets in this room."

"I understand."

"Thank you. Your companions may take seats, Major, and then you have the floor."

Niall stopped at the gap leading inside the circular table and directly facing Sharifah. He took a few moments to identify the other members present, glad that he'd paid attention to Hastor's briefing on Security Council members. President Biron nodded to him, his face set in an amiable expression Niall knew masked the politician's true feelings. He also recognized the new President of the European Commission, Emile Fitzroy. Etlinn and Patrick Morgan sat behind him. The Vercingetorix was out in force. Etlinn smiled, but her eyes were anxious. She wouldn't feel any better once he'd outlined his plan.

He spotted Jacqueline and raised a questioning eyebrow at her.

She nodded, blushing when heads turned in her direction.

"You all have my report on the drone headed towards Earth," Kearey opened, taking the pressure off her. "I've checked on it periodically over the last twenty-four hours. Twice, I've sensed an alien presence. The other times, the drone has been deserted. I believe the aliens can link with the ship, either as a remote-control mechanism or potentially to board it and turn the drone into an alien invasion platform."

"Is that the alien's intention? To invade Earth?" President Biron asked.

Niall's hackles spiked. He forced down his dislike of the man. "I can't discount alien invasion," he said to the group generally, "however I believe Lugus, the alien who connected with me on my first contact with the ship, is here for me." Niall reddened, not understanding how he had become such a risk to Earth, but unable to ignore the certainty growing inside of him.

Balor had been searching for him since that first contact in his childhood.

Sharifah shook her head. "Major Kearey, I have read nothing in your report to substantiate this statement beyond doubt. There has been much conjecture and Professor Morgan has provided supporting evidence for Herecura's wild claims and your own conviction that this Balor is seeking you, but what makes you so convinced this alien ship is specifically here for you and not for Earth? You make it sound as if we could hand you over to the alien ship, then sit back, and watch it fly away!"

Niall held her gaze and Sharifah Kalufi's expression slowly altered to one of belated shock.

"I can't say Balor won't come after Earth," Niall said slowly, "and that ship is designed to destroy worlds, whole solar systems, not one person, but there *is* something you do not know, that isn't in the report." It felt like everyone in that room held their breath, but Niall's attention remained focused on the woman candid enough to speak the obvious out aloud. "I have seen this alien ship before. Fifteen thousand or so years ago. On Earth."

Sharifah recovered her poise. "Explain."

"When I searched for the orb at Lake Titicaca, I was forced to return when a meteor fell out of the sky. It was preceded by what looked to be a shooting star."

"I have read this report. I think many of us have," Sharifah said. "Go on."

"I now believe that shooting star was me, and that the meteor was the alien ship."

The room exploded with noise, a cacophony of anger, disbelief and denial. Niall stayed silent, pointless to shout over them. Let the implications speak for themselves.

Straton stood up, his bulk dominating the room.

341

"Quiet, please," Sharifah called then nodded to Straton. "Please, General, speak."

Straton waited until order had been restored. "Major, your reports indicate the alien drone carries dark energy on the scale of a black hole."

"Yes, and I have no way of dispersing that much dark energy unless I drain it by creating a bridge across space and time. We do know that the alien ship that hit the Pacific Ocean fifteen thousand years ago had only enough dark energy to lift the continental floor and flood the whole region."

"You can't know that!" President Biron protested.

"I can. History tells us what happened. I'm telling you what caused it," Niall replied.

Biron jumped to his feet, his face contorted with disbelief. "You want to tamper with Earth's timeline? Again?"

Niall fought off his doubts. They were the product of fear. He knew what had to be done. "I preserved the timeline bringing the Astereans and Morrígan to Earth. This is our only chance."

Fitzroy raised a hand and Biron sat down.

"The Chair recognizes the President of the European Commission, Emile Fitzroy," Sharifah announced with a pointed glare at Charles Biron.

"Thank you, Madame Chairman. Major, why can't you steer the alien drone across the universe, even into the past of another galaxy? Why bring it back to Earth?" A perplexed frown drew his eyebrows together. "Why do you need to cross the universe *and* time? Isn't one enough?"

"I'm not sure I can access the distant past so easily, and taking the alien ship across space alone is not enough to drain this amount of energy. I do know the link from Astereal to Earth. Astereal's timeflow is shifting out of alignment with Earth, and I know I can bridge fifteen thousand years into Earth's past from Astereal's solar system because I've done it before. I've accessed this region of Earth from Astereal before. It makes sense I would do this. It explains what happened fifteen thousand years ago and we know our planet survives."

"You will be killing a civilization," Sharifah pointed out. "Many lives will be sacrificed."

Sharifah's words opened up a raw wound. Niall carried the Paladins' deaths in his heart.

"The people who died have already lost their lives. I knew this Paladin line would die out when I placed them there. They knew it too. We have no choice. If I don't do this, an alternate timeline will form and it will be as if the world we know never existed."

"What are you?" Fitzroy snarled. "The architect of humankind? Do you think you're God or something? Playing with our lives this way?"

Niall's fist clenched.

"President Fitzroy, you are out of order," Sharifah snapped. "And Major Kearey, unless you want to give credence to President Fitzroy's slur, I suggest you dampen that energy field you're emitting."

Niall glanced down at his glowing hand. *Shit.* He carefully dispersed the energy he'd harnessed and his hand returned to normal.

Silence reigned. The delegates looked shocked. Dammit, he shouldn't have lost control.

*You knew this meeting would be difficult, Niall'Kearey,* Macha murmured in his mind.

Pwyll slipped in. *I detect fear behind their anger.*

*I know, and that's no more than I expected.*

*You are the problem here,* Macha pronounced. *Accept your destiny, and your path will be clear. They will have no choice but to follow.*

Macha had said something very similar when he had evacuated the first of her people to Earth.

"Major?" Sharifah prompted him.

Niall turned to Straton. "I'll need the test Falcon, General. I haven't time to learn how to fly anything else."

Straton didn't blink. "Have you time to learn to fly a Falcon? I understand Earth's magnetic grid is very different to Astereal's. We've made several modifications."

"I'll manage."

"How can you be sure the alien drone will follow you?"

"Only that it already did, sir."

Straton's expression darkened. The Chairman of the Joint Chiefs of Staff glanced at Towden.

Towden straightened. "Sir, the full plan is news to me, too. However, Councilor Sohan and Dr. Jacqueline Biron have been researching some points of interest on Major Kearey's behalf."

Sharifah turned to Sohan. "Councilor, we would be pleased to hear your thoughts on Major Kearey's proposal."

Sohan rose to his feet. "Thank you, Madam Chairman. There are several factors pertinent to the choice of Lake Titicaca, the first being that it sits below sea level where the geomagnetic field is relatively weak."

Sharifah raised her hand. "You are incorrect. Lake Titicaca sits two and a half miles above sea level."

Jacqueline rose to her feet. "It does now, Madame Chairman, but my aunt, Nicole Biron, umm... Uathach... collected several papers theorizing that a geological disturbance flooded the area and then uplifted the entire region along pre-existing fault lines, adding to the Andes Mountain range we know today. Major Kearey's report on his visit to Lake Titicaca included data supporting the theory that the basin forming the lake once resided at sea level."

Sharifah glanced to Niall. "I recall this. You heard the ocean. Described a sea-fishing industry."

"Yes," he replied, "and as a result, Dr. Biron has spent the last few years researching the area."

Jacqueline nodded. "Very recently, we found sea-fossil evidence supporting Major Kearey's observations. I am now convinced that Major Kearey settled the Paladin refugees on land much closer to sea level than we initially believed."

Charles Biron sat up straighter. Relief tinged the president's aura, relief that turned to pride.

"I see." Sharifah's brow creased with concentration. "Proceed, Councilor Sohan."

Jacqueline sat down as Sohan picked up his explanation.

"Thank you. Targeting the ocean minimizes electromagnetic output, but Earth's rotational axis means your planet's geomagnetic field is weakest across the South Atlantic. This anomaly extends across South America and into the Pacific Ocean. However, the lower altitude of the inner radiation belt will help reduce the spread of dark energy across the globe. It is significant that the inner belt in this area shows an unusually high proportion of Compton electrons, a bi-product of higher energy waves, and possibly a lasting result of this alien drone hitting Earth. In summary, I believe that the Pacific Ocean off Peru and Chile is a good location to curtail the damage to Earth."

Jacqueline Biron stood up again. "Madame Chairman, the uplift of the Andes Mountains including the region of Lake Titicaca has never been explained. A meteor crash is one possible cause, but a more plausible explanation would be a bomb generating an equivalent EMP field strength exceeding 200,000 volts per meter below the detonation."

Niall's heart began to race. If he didn't disperse enough energy, if he missed his entry point to Earth, or hit land instead...

The delegates looked even more appalled.

"I have to follow the link to Lake Titicaca from Astereal," Niall said. "It's the only way I can be sure I form a portal so close to the surface that the alien drone has no time to take evasive action."

"How can you be sure it will follow you?" Fitzroy demanded.

"I saw it. I remote-viewed the past and I saw it."

Fitzroy threw his hands up in the air. "C'est tout à fait absurde!"

"No more so than dropping aliens into the past and that worked out," Patrick Morgan said softly.

The room stilled.

*Interesting*, Pwyll spoke in Niall's mind. *Patrick Morgan and Sharifah hold the real power here. They are the ones to persuade. Fitzroy believes you are dangerous, but he feels powerless to stop you.*

Niall watched how Emile Fitzroy slumped in his chair, the way his jaw set into an angry line.

"Madame Chairman, there is more that can be done to contain the impact on Earth," Sohan said.

"Continue, Councilor Sohan," Sharifah replied, quelling what looked to be an interruption from the US President with a single shake of her head.

"Dark energy drives the expansion of the universe while gravity is what holds it together. The magnetic fields required to contain it must be enormous. The collapse of those fields and the release of the dark energy will result in the huge explosive force Dr. Biron has described in terms of a nuclear event. To mitigate the explosive potential, we need to provide the dark energy with a slip route into the ocean *before* the containment field collapses. This can be achieved by using a fission bomb to break through the hull of the ship seconds prior to the main detonation event and at a point where it will not result in the instantaneous collapse of the containment field."

"How will this charge be placed?" General Straton asked.

Niall answered. "On entry into Earth's atmosphere, I will set the Falcon on an automatic heading into the ocean, eject and sky dive to Earth. The computer will adjust speed to ensure contact with the alien drone on entry into the water. The detonator will be programmed to explode on impact with the alien ship."

"What will you do then?" Sharifah asked.

"Return to the present, ma'am. Macha and Pwyll will maintain a telepathic link with me to Astereal and then back to Earth's past. Macha helped me retain my link back to Earth during Operation Hideout."

"An unauthorized link," President Biron pointed out.

"Does that really matter now?" Sharifah asked him. "Major Kearey, Macha has not proven she can retain a link with you into the past before, at least, not as far as I know."

A risk Niall tried not to consider too much. "That's correct, Madame Chairman, she has not. This may be a one-way mission."

"A suicide mission?" Sharifah asked with a slight frown.

"I hope not."

"I see." Sharifah glanced at a pale-faced Etlinn. "Did you know of this, Professor Morgan?"

"Major Kearey has conveyed to me that the mission will be dangerous."

Macha rose to her feet. "Madame Chairman, I have watched my people step through from Astereal into Earth's past, a time thousands of years before the events at Lake Titicaca. I could follow that link, and I experienced a telepathic connection with my people until the portal closed. We have never done this before, and even with Niall'Kearey retaining his link to the present through Astereal, the risk is considerable. It *is* Earth's best hope."

Niall decided to put an end to the discussion. "Look, if the link fails, and I'm still alive, I will have to learn how to work my way back."

"And how much damage to our timeline will you cause on the way?" Fitzroy demanded.

Niall blinked. "Excuse me?"

"Perhaps we should start looking for evidence of your existence in Earth's history? Have we even done that yet?" Fitzroy looked around wildly. Expressions from the other delegates varied from shock to mild disbelief.

Niall glanced at Pwyll. *What the hell?* Pwyll shrugged.

Sharifah rose to her feet, her eyes flashing, and Niall sensed that if Fitzroy wasn't wearing an ear plug, she would be privately roasting him.

"President Fitzroy, Major Kearey is offering to risk his life for Earth. An alien ship is headed our way. We face the unknown. Earth faces possible annihilation! Fortunately, all available data suggests the alien's interest is in Niall'Kearey. If this holds true, then Major Kearey will be leading the alien drone to a faraway galaxy. This has to be a desirable objective. If he then establishes a link to Earth's past, history tells us his mission succeeded. I agree we need to discuss this further. In the meantime, I propose the Security Council authorizes the US military and all Earth's resources to prepare for this course of action. The mission will not proceed until the Security Council grants President Biron full authorization to act on Earth's behalf. Now we will vote."

# CHAPTER THIRTY-NINE

"Sharifah Kalufi said 'fortunately'," Jacqueline fumed. "Like she didn't even care."

Niall wished she'd give it a rest. He couldn't afford the distraction. He scanned the UN foyer for Toby. When he turned back, Jacqueline was frowning at him.

"Why aren't you mad?" she demanded. "These people ruined your life!"

"I am mad," Niall said quietly. "I'm furious, but I can't afford the luxury. I allowed myself to get angry already and nearly killed a man, although God knows Miach deserved it!" Jacqueline flinched and Niall reined back his raging emotions. Dealing with his anger had gotten harder. The thought that Balor's gene might be the reason why didn't help. Was it changing him? Like it had Kean Morgan, and Herecura? Muhuza? Niall swallowed. No, he was nothing like Muhuza. His DNA hadn't changed, but his world had. He focused on Jacqueline. "Stop worrying about me and work on where I should dump this alien drone. I need a bird's eye view of the coastline, landmarks. There will be no second chances at this."

She nodded, her face pale.

Sam Hastor appeared beside them, his slight frown and shake of his head aimed at Jacqueline and a clear warning that she should back off. He looked at Niall. "We've got clearance to leave for Groom Lake straight away. Where's Toby?"

Niall spotted his son entering through the main entrance with a tour guide. He waved at Toby who pointed Niall out to the guide. The woman smiled and left.

"The Falcon simulator's been booked out to you for as long as you need it," Sam continued as Toby sauntered over. "You could log a few hours this afternoon. The others are waiting in a private room down here. We can bridge out."

The grin on Toby's face told Niall he was sharing a private joke. He high-fived his son. "Lizzie?" he asked.

Disappointment creased Toby's features. "You heard us?"

"No." They fell in behind Sam and Jacqueline.

"So, how'd you know?"

"Toby, you two have been conspiring since you were in diapers. I think I know. Is Mom okay?"

Toby's expression clouded over. "I think so. Lizzie says she walks on the beach a lot."

Damn. Niall held it together, but the ache in his gut dragged on him like a ball and chain. "And Miach?"

"When he's not asleep, he's meditating. That's bad. Can't usually shut him up."

Niall stopped dead. Toby even walked on a few steps before turning back with an anxious glance. The pain in Niall's chest intensified. Miach had been happy. *With my family.*

"You okay, Niall?"

Sam sounded far away when he was only a couple of yards ahead. A vicious jealousy hammered for release making it hard to say, "Yes." Toby's shrinking aura reminded Niall his own feelings were also on show. He strengthened his privacy shields and forced a smile to his face. "Just something I meant to ask Etlinn. I'll call her."

"If you need to—" Sam started to say.

Niall raised his hand to stop him. "No, it's all good." The skepticism in Toby's face made him say more. "Your mom and I just need a bit of time to work stuff out," he said to Toby. "When I get back, we'll talk. Properly."

"You promise?"

"Yeah. I promise." Niall could feel the bore of Sam's gaze. He looked over and the rebuke in Sam's eyes grated worse than nails on metal. Niall's eyes narrowed. Sam didn't believe he'd make it back. "Want a turn in a Falcon simulator?" he asked Toby.

His son shrugged. "Sure."

A quiet discomfort descended over them all. Niall got them back to Groom Lake on automatic pilot, racing through the motions, employing familiar links through the q-dimension, routinely harnessing the energy needed to bridge. It would be good to get into the cockpit of a falc'hun again, connect with planet Earth.

A car waited for Sam and Niall up top. Their security escort took Toby's presence in their stride. General Towden must have cleared the way for him.

They headed towards two distant hangars glinting under the sun's brilliant rays. The buildings formed part of the black projects complex, a source of magnetic disruption that Niall had noticed during his first authorized link to Astereal. For him, that first official contact with an off-world planet had been several months ago, and yet the event felt like years ago. In reality, it had been. Five years of enforced exile had stolen so much—his wife, seeing his children grow. He couldn't even call their home his own. Not now. The knowledge of Miach's presence taunted him.

And for what? It hadn't stopped Balor from finding him.

Now it had found Earth and somehow Niall doubted Balor would stop there. Evil like that needed to possess or destroy everything foolish enough to cross its path.

Would this mission be enough? What other option did he have?

*I saw my future. Dare I change it?*

He closed his eyes and willed another solution to reveal itself. None did. The relentless course of time drove him onward, his actions never fully his own, enslaved to fate.

"We're here, Dad," Toby said.

Niall opened his eyes, surprised to discover the vehicle pulling up between the two hangars.

An Air Force instructor awaited them. He saluted Colonel Hastor and nodded to Niall. "I'm Major Jackson, Colonel. I'll be instructing

Major Kearey." His coal-colored eyes raked Niall from head to toe. "We only let the Astereans or our Top Gun graduates with a high psychic rating try out a test Falcon. Needless to say, there haven't been many and the last one barely escaped with his life after going into tail spin. He ejected at forty thousand feet and broke both legs on landing. This latest version is the only one left until more roll off the production line. I looked up your flight record, Major. You're only qualified for whirly birds and you haven't logged any hours in years, although those years were redacted."

"Major Kearey's psychic rating is exceptional and he has flight experience in an Asterean falc'hun, the details of which are classified," Sam responded.

"I see." It took a split moment for Sam's words to sink in and then Jackson's expression brightened and his back straightened. Intense curiosity filled his features. His gaze shifted to Toby.

"This is my son, Toby," Niall said. "I promised him a turn in the simulator. What problems are you having with the Falcon?"

Jackson's attention focused back on Niall. "The Astereans' design uses a gravitational dipole to drive the falc'hun forward with Earth's geomagnetic field actively contributing to the potential energy difference. Deviation from a prescribed grid reduces thrust and altitude, increasing mass and their backup fuel system proved surprisingly clumsy."

"It was a last-ditch addition."

Jackson shot Niall a curious look as he entered a code into the security pad. The door opened and he led them into a building-sized room, its ceiling crisscrossed with catwalks several stories above their heads. "A variant of their sky city technology overcame initial inertia and provided auxiliary boost. For those who can actually fly the thing, a Falcon has the versatility of a Harrier jet with super-sonic speed. It's the dark matter tech and the interplay with the geomagnetic grid that makes the pilots testy." He eyed Niall with a dubious expression. "Main problems occur off grid, or when the geomagnetic field alters unexpectedly. But boy do these hummers fly. I've never seen anything like it."

The instructor showed them into a white room and escorted them over to a sophisticated simulator at its center. A control room was visible through a large window at the third level. Jackson opened the access door into the machine. "The Astereans have made significant improvements to the Falcon's fuselage and skin. It can withstand Earth's radiation belts. Re-entry isn't a problem. Submersible as well. Climb in, Major. We'll be upstairs monitoring your progress. I can direct you from there."

Niall climbed steps to a realistic-looking cockpit. He climbed into the pilot's seat and an overhead canopy descended into place. He buckled up and put on the headgear. Familiar-looking instruments swept the control board before him. Jackson's voice emerged from a speaker. The instructor worked through a series of questions, his reticent tone disappearing as Niall produced the correct responses.

"Okay," the instructor conceded. "You have the basics covered. We'll try a controlled take-off. You're going to stall at first. The system will abort if it gets too bumpy."

A runway displayed on the cockpit window and Niall's heart rate accelerated with his excitement. He activated the gravitational engine and sensed a magnetic turbulence from the wingtips to the rear of the simulator. He watched the mass distribution readout drop as reverse inertia came on-line.

Sam's voice emerged from the radio. "Any adverse reaction?"

"Negative," Niall replied. It had only been on Earth that his body's magnetic antenna had struggled with the EM output as his mind grew more attuned to the radiation around him. He did not recall any of his hosts experiencing a problem when flying falc'huns on Astereal and he felt just as comfortable now.

"All electrical and propulsion systems use Asterean shielding to prevent cross-interference," Jackson advised, providing the likely reason why.

Or maybe his body had adjusted over time.

Niall physically felt the Falcon responding to the magnetic stimuli, the simulator demanding the freedom to lift through the gravitational dipole pulling it forward. Niall released the braking system and eased the throttle forward. The Falcon shot off so fast he nosedived with a bump.

"You got it off the ground," Jackson said. He sounded surprised. "Let's go through the takeoff sequence again."

Niall actually learned more watching Toby wrestle with the simulator than he had during several simulated flights of his own. Major Jackson happily set Toby up for another launch, his earlier pessimism laid to rest by Niall's easy handling of the Falcon's systems.

When Toby wiped out his Falcon for the fifth time, Niall leaned towards the mike. "Toby, remember when you taught me how to juggle?"

"Yeah?"

"You're the ball. The Earth is you."

There was a slight pause. "Oo-kay."

Niall smiled. "Set him up again."

This time Toby got off the ground before stalling.

Jackson shook his head, smiling. "Hey, would you look at that! The boy's got potential."

Niall's smile turned to a frown. Perhaps it had been a mistake bringing Toby to GBI. His eyes had been opened to a world of possibility. He should talk with Toby. Warn him that when you joined up, the military owned you.

An outside presence touched his mind and Niall straightened. *Lizzie?* His mind expanded to reach her. *Hi, sweet pea. I can hear you.*

*Dad? I wasn't sure I could reach you.*

Her thought was tinged with distress. Niall glanced at Toby on screen. His son was hopping his virtual Falcon down the runway, apparently oblivious to his twin sister's call. Their instructor was chuckling, but in a good way.

*Don't say anything to Toby*, Lizzie warned.

*What is it, Lizzie?*

*I'm worried about Mom. She's won't stop watching the news about this alien ship.*

*It's on the news?*

*She hasn't moved from the TV for three hours. Miach shouldn't be up yet, but it's like Mom's frozen, and I can tell he's worried. Please, Dad, you have to do something.*

On screen, the Falcon came to a shuddering stop, but still in one piece.

"Toby, we're going home," Niall said into the mike, telepathing his words to Lizzie.

"What? Now?"

"Now. It's important."

"Niall?" Sam asked.

"Now!" Niall said, prompting a frown to cross Major Jackson's face. The officer glanced between the colonel and his supposed subordinate, but Niall didn't give a shit about protocol anymore. "Thanks, Major Jackson. I'll be back for the test flight."

Jackson's frown deepened. "I'm not sure that—"

"General Towden will be in contact, Major," Sam chipped in. "Thank you for your help. You're dismissed."

Niall had a link home before Jackson had left the building. Toby appeared, his expression a turbulent mix of mutiny and concern. His eyes widened as a portal appeared in the room.

"What's going on?"

"Mom needs us," Niall said.

Toby's expression twisted with misgiving. "What you gonna do?"

Niall dialed down his emotional output. "I'm going to talk with her."

"Is Sam coming?" From the tone of Toby's voice, he wanted Sam with them.

Niall glanced at his son's godfather. Sam looked hopeful and Niall guessed he'd been ordered to stay close by. "Not this time, Toby." When Sam shook his head, Niall flashed him a warning look. "I'm through with the personal escort, Colonel. Just let me know when the test flight has been set up."

Sam hesitated, but then he nodded. "I'll be in contact. Try to take it easy, yeah?"

Niall didn't reply. He stepped onto the deck of their family home and marched through the front door, Toby trailing behind him.

Lizzie ran up to give Niall a hug. Tami sat on the sofa watching the TV. Her head turned from an amateur's picture of the distant alien drone to Niall then back again. Her pale face whitened in profile. Then she stood up, wiped her hands on her shorts, and faced him.

"Kids, why don't you give us some space?" Niall said. He squeezed Lizzie's hand. *Honey, don't worry. You did the right thing.*

"Miach's resting." Tami's voice cracked on Miach's name. She sounded defensive. Tears welled in her eyes. Niall stepped towards her, but he stopped when she stiffened. She glanced at the TV and then back at him. "How will you stop it?"

Niall ran a hand through his hair. Physically, a few steps separated them. In truth, a ravine of heartache and the unknown lay between him and the woman he loved.

Niall shielded his eyes against the sun turning the ocean blood-red. The aftershocks from his attack on Miach ricocheted on, chipping away the crumbling bedrock of his life.

Tami placed a fresh beer on the table between them and retook her chair. "I let Tony and Sheila know you'll be over."

"Thanks." He studied her profile, her gaze fixed on a point somewhere down the beach. They both walked a knife-edge of emotions, but Tami had lived the loss of five years and she couldn't easily reverse the damage. "I don't blame you for being angry."

Her arms wrapped around her stomach and after a few moments she said, "I've never seen you like that before." The words emerged from deep inside her, rough and torn.

He dulled the edge of throbbing regret with another slug of cold beer, its bitter taste too much like the self-reproach castigating him inside. His third bottle. Better than hitting the hard stuff. He wiped froth off his upper lip. "I was beyond angry. They took everything from me...

even my family it seemed. You're my wife and I love you so much it hurts. I thought Miach was my friend."

Her eyes snapped to his, glittering with emotion. "He was... is... sweet Mary, give me strength. Niall, Miach never stopped being your friend! You were dead! We both thought you were dead!" She whipped out a scrunched-up handkerchief and buried it into her tearing eyes.

Niall wanted to comfort her, to make things right, but his entire being was knotted with frustration and the green rage, all mixed with the fear he'd lost her.

He cringed. *I can't lose you. I can't.*

Too scared to say the words out loud, he sat there in silence. She had witnessed him pitch Miach onto a volcanic rock in a fit of jealous rage. His throat constricted so tight he couldn't speak.

Tami re-emerged from her hanky, her eyes rimmed with red. "We decided you'd want me to find happiness again, that you'd want Miach to help me raise the children." Her words carried a hefty punch. Tami's lips thinned. "Macha said you wouldn't want me to spend my life grieving."

Niall turned the ring on his finger. His eyes traveled to her hand and his heart leapt. Tami still wore his wedding ring. "Macha was right," he whispered. "All I've ever wanted is for you and the children to be happy. In many ways, I know you did the right thing, but Tami, I'm not dead, and for me, barely two days have passed since they put me in stasis. You've always loved me so much, it shines out of you. It's hard to accept you could love anyone else." The hurt exhausted him. "I can't switch off my feelings for you."

Her hand stretched out across the table towards him. "I don't want you to."

A familiar presence touched Niall's mind. He stiffened. Tami looked towards the bungalow. The double doors opened and Miach's bulk filled the space. He looked paler than Niall remembered, his breath wheezing in his chest.

Niall rose to his feet. "I'm not here to cause trouble."

*I know. We need to talk.*

Although Miach's thought was strong, his fingers clutched at the door frame, burn dressings on the palms of both hands. Tami jumped up to help him. Niall watched the tender way she guided Miach to a rattan armchair, the easy familiarity between them, and he saw the guilty look Tami flashed his way. Jealousy surged through him, a toxic mist that made it hard to see reason.

"What you did..." Miach rasped. The Asterean shook his head, his aura depressed with disappointment. "It was wrong."

Anger submerged an upsurge of guilt and Niall opened the floodgates to his fury and dumped the emotional fallout on his rival.

The older man hissed, whitened. "I see," he said, his voice low and taut.

Tami's face creased with concern. "What? What is it?" She turned on Niall, her eyes flashing her ire. "What did you say to him?"

Niall rammed up his shields and her mouth dropped open.

Her eyes narrowed. "I don't believe it. I may not know your thoughts, but I know when you're shutting me out. Always trying to protect me—" She stopped. Her searching look turned to apprehension. "You've decided what you're going to do with that ship out there. Haven't you?"

Niall found his breath and fought to contain his emotions. He couldn't keep losing control like that. He would destroy them. "Yes."

She stood, hands on hip, demanding to know. "Well?"

*Tell her the truth.*

Miach's thought dropped like a rock into Niall's mind, batting his shields aside like they were matchstick thin and spreading chaos in its wake. Niall glared at him. Miach knew him better than anyone. His former host had so much of his memory, had access to his mind and emotions, it was pointless to try and deceive him.

He composed his expression to answer Tami. "I'm going to lead it away from Earth."

"Lead it where?" she demanded.

"First to Astereal, and then into the past. To Lake Titicaca. You see, it's happened already. That alien ship is the event that destroyed the Paladin civilization I put there during Hideout."

"Lir's might! It was you? You destroyed them?" Miach's face turned a mottled red.

A thundering filled Niall's ears. "Yes."

"And knowing they will die, you will fulfill this destiny, too?"

Niall's fists balled. "That ship is carrying a fucking black hole! If that ship blows, or hits Earth before I can drain most of its dark energy payload, there'll be nothing left of this solar system. I can deplete the vessel by leading it into the past, but if you've got a better solution to save Earth, *and* preserve the timeline, then please, tell me, 'cos I'm all ears!"

Miach opened his mouth to speak, but no sound came out.

Niall's jaw clamped so tight his ears popped. He shook his head, partly from anger, but mainly because he knew Miach was as stumped for a solution as he'd been, right up until the moment he'd remembered where he had seen that ship before. The lack of options scared him, trapping him in this q-dimension rat run with only one door out.

Niall turned to Tami. She stood rooted to the spot, caught in a wheel of perpetual dread, her brow tense and tears welling. He tried to soften the blow.

"Macha and Pwyll will follow my link to Astereal and then into Earth's past. They'll help me find my way back. It's not a one-way trip. I will come back."

Her eyes flicked to Miach, the brief action betraying the strength of her feelings for the man who now shared her bed. The sick feeling midriff intensified. Whatever happened, no one was emerging from this mess unscathed.

"If you want me, Tami," Niall said softly, the gentle cadence of his voice dragging her attention back to him, "I will be here. You're my wife. Lizzie and Toby are our children. This is our home." Niall's eyes swept across to Miach, cold and hard. *I'll never give her up.*

*I am not taking her from you,* he responded. *I will be here though, whenever she needs me. Unless you intend to finish the job you started earlier?*

*Don't tempt me.*

Tami's sob made them both start. "Stop it! Both of you!" She launched to her feet, nearly tripped over a chair, and stumbled into the house.

"Mom!" Lizzie cried out from inside.

Miach threw Niall a cold look and went in after her.

Niall swallowed hard and picked up his beer. "You can come out now."

The shadows moved and Jose appeared out of the darkness.

Niall glanced his way. "You know, I didn't bring you here to protect them from me."

Jose grabbed a beer out of the cooler, popped the lid and gestured towards the bungalow. "Yeah, because that went so well."

Niall gave a laugh to frighten the dead. "I don't need any more lectures."

"I don't lecture. I kick your stupid ass. *Amigo,* what are you doing? The woman loves you and you frighten her away! You're all hurting so much no one is listening. Miach hurts and not just because you barbecued him on a volcano. Tami's so scared she gonna lose you again she's clinging to the one person keeping her sane. *Amigo*, she fell to pieces after you died. Then Miach got his mojo back and Tami started thinking they would take him away, too. That's when Patrick Morgan stepped in."

Niall closed his eyes. "Morgan."

Jose dropped heavily into the rattan chair and gulped down some beer. "Yeah. He's the one who suggested they make their thing official." His gesture made clear their *thing* could not be defined. "Made it easier for him to fight Miach's corner with the Council. Tami wasn't sure. Macha talked to her. I talked to her. Man, it seemed a good idea at the time. Now it's tearing her up with guilt."

"You're saying the marriage is a sham?"

Jose shrugged. "You need to start listening. She loves you. That never stopped."

He took another swig of beer and Niall mirrored his action in old-age tradition. Fight together. Drink together. Live to fight another day.

Jose smacked his lips with satisfaction. "So... you about to kick some alien culo? Or have you met your match this time?" He cast Niall a sideways look. "'Cos I only got a six-pack left and if the world is gonna end, I need to get to the store pronto."

Niall chuckled. "A man who knows his priorities."

Jose tipped his bottle to Niall. "We aren't the ones trying to take over the world. Shoving you in a freezer box. Don't let your shit blur the difference between friend and enemy."

A high-pitched wail of a violin started up somewhere in the bungalow, the notes flat and squeaky. Jose's beer stopped midway to his mouth. Within seconds, the complex melody faltered.

Jose groaned and rose out of his chair. "While you were dead, we've been stuck here listening to that racket. Every day. Chinga su puta madre!" He took his beer with him.

Niall listened to his friend's uneven clumps hitting the steps to the beach as he stared out over an ocean silvered by moonlight. He needed a few moments before he headed over to reunite with his parents. At least Tony and Sheila would be over the initial shock of discovering their adopted son never died. He inhaled the salt air on a warm sea breeze, his thoughts whirling. He felt displaced, at odds with the entire world. He had become the interloper in his own home. Jose was right. Asserting his claim this way could only drive her away. Tami loved him. He needed to let her come to him, her way.

It had always worked before.

# CHAPTER FORTY

Niall gripped onto a handhold as the Combat King's flight crew checked his pressure tri-wing suit and oxygen supply. He didn't strictly need the oxygen for this training run, but he would need it when he faced the drone. The rear exit door opened revealing clear blue sky and a distant horizon of green. An airman tapped Niall's shoulder and gave him the thumbs up. A stream of information emerged from his ear piece.

"Approaching Serra do Araca."

"Brazil Air Traffic Control grants permission to enter exclusion zone."

"Mission Control testing. Lima Six, do you copy?"

"I hear you, Mission Control," Niall replied.

"Good luck, Lima Six."

"Thank you, Control." Niall tightened his gloves and took a calming breath of clean air. His pulse was steady, his head alert. He double checked his helmet and the oxygen mask. His heart skipped a beat. This training jump came with a twist.

"Altitude at 13,000 feet. Air speed 200 knots. Windspeed 12 miles per hour north-east."

"Copy that." He walked forward, holding the safety lead.

"Drop zone, in three, two, one."

Niall jumped and spread out his arms and legs, keeping his back arched until he stabilized and his heart had rejoined him. "Mission Control. Free fall in progress," he reported. He scanned the Amazon Forest below, searching for the sandstone ravine where he would catch his ride to the Morrígan village. Information crawled across his visor. "10,000 feet. Adjusting course for wind speed. Target area sighted."

363

"Copy that, Lima Six."

For a brief moment, the exhilaration of free fall obliterated everything else from Niall's mind. The sun warmed his back. Earth stretched out before him, an endless horizon, the weaker magnetic field barely visible in this part of the world. The wide blue tributaries of the Rio Negro, dotted with islands of green, wound their meandering way to the majestic Amazon River.

Freedom.

He had carried out several HALO jumps in his time, many from far higher altitudes, but this was his first solo in a wing suit. He wanted the moment to go on forever...

An uplift of air jolted him back to reality. Niall adjusted his position to regain control and aimed for the ravine. Yerit met him astride Kestra a few miles into the gorge. The gryphon flew ahead, her enormous wingspan providing Niall with an unexpected uplift.

Niall reported in and then focused on Yerit as Kestra's speed altered to match his. She dropped very slightly, slowed until he could see the intricate layers of her feathers and the scars on Yerit's back. Kestra continued to drop as Niall released the leg section of his wing suit and clamped his knees against the gryphon's flanks. Yerit swiveled and grabbed Niall's left wrist the moment Niall connected solidly with Kestra's back. Kestra dipped under Niall's sudden weight then straightened.

"Contact made," he reported. The air billowed out the material between his arms and side nearly dislodging his seat. Niall tucked his elbows in and tightened his hold around Kestra's belly.

"Copy that," Control spoke in his ear piece.

Yerit looked back at him, his alien eyes twinkling with good humor. "You fly good for a dead man, Niall'Kearey," he yelled, the wind almost whipping his words away.

In greeting, Niall opened his mind to his fellow warrior for whom words could never convey his complex emotions. Yerit and Choluu had cared for his children on Astereal, taken them into their hearts and home. Their generosity had been instrumental in reuniting two cultures which had been at war for the equivalent of centuries.

His and Yerit's telepathic connection tended more to the empathic so Niall pulled off his oxygen mask to shout in Yerit's ear, "Macha tells me you and Choluu have a son! Congratulations!"

"He is—"

"What?"

Yerit held up four fingers then pointed to a prominent cliff face. "We work there."

Kestra landed heavily on the ridge, perhaps thrown by the double weight on her back. She tossed her head irritably and all but threw them off. They watched her take to the sky.

Yerit grimaced. "She angry when Macha gone."

"Let's hope this works then. Gonna be a nasty bump if I get this wrong."

Yerit bared his teeth, a wry grin of sorts. "This place bad. You need create grid." Yerit opened his mind as he swept the ground clear with his booted foot then lay down. Niall gleaned the meaning behind his words by watching Yerit manipulate the magnetic field around him. The Morrígan drew on dark energy to magnify the forces below him. Max had demonstrated Lenz's Law with a magnet and copper piping. This was something else. Yerit remained stationary. His mind altered the electromagnetic forces. Niall shook his head in admiration when a horizontal Yerit lifted into the air.

"Okay, it's not enough to repel the magnetic field. I need dark energy to increase the potential difference."

"Is easier when falling. More..." His eyebrows rose in question.

"Flux," Niall supplied.

It should have been easy. An hour later, Niall had barely raised his arm without considerable effort. He wasn't ready to risk jumping off a cliff. He lay on the ground looking up at the blue sky while Yerit sat in meditative silence.

Finally, the warrior stirred. "You need leave Earth."

Niall contracted his pelvic muscles and sat up. "What?"

Yerit waved a hand. "Where you go. Between worlds."

"The q-dimension?"

"Body here. Mind there. Mind more powerful."

Niall lay back and let sparkling holes form at the edge of his vision. His link to Astereal shone bright. His mind sensed the ominous presence of the alien drone and his heart accelerated in his chest. He forced away the negative vibe and found the place where his mind could see through walls—a place where time slowed.

He had been in this place many times, aware of every detail of his physical surroundings, a seeming eternity available to assimilate and assess the possibilities. His subconscious had been practicing this for years. He'd put it down to instinct, a psychic gift he didn't want to think about too carefully. This place between worlds had saved his life again and again.

Should have appreciated it more, learned to master his mind's potential a lot earlier, before an unseen enemy chucked a goddamn black hole into Earth's backyard.

He gathered the magnetic forces needed to manipulate the dark energy and created a miniature application of the gravitational potential that powered the Falcon.

"Good," Yerit said, breaking Niall's concentration.

Niall hit the ground with a jarring jolt. "Ow!"

Yerit stood over him, his hand outstretched. "Now you jump."

Niall threw a passion fruit to Yerit and Choluu's little boy. The chirpy kid squealed as the makeshift ball landed squarely in his hands and then mysteriously fell between his fingers to splatter across compacted dirt-floor. The touch of Macha's familiar mind burst through Niall's amusement as Choluu's laughter transformed her son's dismay into a smile. Niall's mind surfed up to meet her at the edge of the South Atlantic Anomaly.

*The alien drone jumped, Niall Kearey.*

Nerves crawled to life throughout his body. *How far?*

*At its current speed it will reach Earth in two days. General Towden requests you return to GBI. Now.*

"I have to go," he said, rising to his feet. He wrapped Choluu in his arms. "You always made the best stew. Please don't ever tell me what goes in it."

Her gentle aura encased him, imbuing him with her strength. "Come back to us, Niall'Kearey."

He kissed her forehead. "I will." Niall turned to Yerit. "Thank you."

The warrior did not return Niall's smile. Sadness lurked in his eyes. "Too much think. Is bad. Instinct better."

"I hear you, my friend."

Niall traced a link through the q-dimension to GBI, struggling to find the will to make the connection. He looked back at the newest family member in his mother's arms, and then at Yerit standing shoulder to shoulder with his wife, and imprinted the image in his memory. "Be well."

He stepped through his portal and a sense of displacement swamped him as a hi-tech military base replaced the warmth of Yerit and Choluu's forest home.

General Towden greeted him. "Major Kearey, this way."

Towden walked faster than usual. Niall barely had time to throw Max a thumbs-up. He did hear Max whoop and Niall bet Max would soon be researching historical cases of levitation.

"The Falcon is being prepped for your test flight as we speak," Towden advised him. "You can change at the tower. Air Traffic Control has a flight plan prepared. It's a narrow window. We've closed down several international airports across the world. Stick to the route and you won't encounter any air traffic."

He threw Niall a glance. "You should know that the general population is beginning to panic. UFO spotters rival NASA and it's impossible to prevent speculation. The UN was concerned that the sonic boom created by your test flight would incite further alarm so President Biron announced we're testing a space worthy weapon capable of destroying the alien ship during the next hour."

"I think my son wants to join the military."

Towden shot him a knowing stare. "What happened to you won't happen to him."

"How can you be so sure?"

"He's got Patrick Morgan looking out for him." At Niall's skeptical glance, Towden added, "Colonel Hastor told me. Hastor's up top by the way, waiting to drive us."

Major Jackson met all three of them at the control tower. Niall glanced at the pristine unmarked Falcon absorbing the rays of sunlight hitting its sleek, black skin. It rested on the runway, surrounded by engineers checking every screw and bolt. Jackson saluted Towden and Hastor before nodding to Niall. "Major, this way. We'll get you suited up. How did you find the wing suit?"

"Worked fine."

"How did you land?"

"Carefully."

Jackson was still scratching his head when Niall emerged refreshed and suited up. "A few pointers," the instructor said. "The Falcon's loaded with an unarmed missile to replicate the weight you'll be carrying. Avoid the stratosphere. We haven't time to repair any damage. This is a training flight only. Oh, and you have an audience of Top Gun pilots." Jackson glanced at Towden. A sly grin lightened his features. "The general here asked me to delete your simulator flights. They have no idea."

# CHAPTER FORTY-ONE

George Towden entered mission control where a screen showed the interior of the Falcon's cockpit. The lower half of Major Kearey's face was visible through the space helmet headgear. An oxygen mask hung off to one side. Kearey's expression displayed professional concentration as he ran through the pre-flight check sequence. The general spotted Colonel Hastor with the instructor and moved over to listen, prompting several pilots in flight gear to jump to attention.

"At ease," he directed.

The mission director looked around, and nodded. "General, welcome to the tower."

"Pretend I'm not here."

"Yes, sir."

The man wouldn't forget. No one forgot the presence of a four-star general. He could leave, monitor proceedings out of sight, but Kearey no longer trusted the system not to turn on him and, for whatever reason, Major Kearey still held a measure of respect for Towden.

General Straton understood that. It was why he'd hoisted Towden out of retirement. *"Earth's survival may well depend on one man. He needs to know we have his six."*

Watching Kearey work over the past couple of days, his family life in chaos, Towden knew his coming out of retirement hadn't been needed. A code of duty pinned that man together, a steel core that would not yield for anything, or anyone.

As Kearey taxied the Falcon down the runway, the noise level dropped. Slouching backs straightened. Eyes fixed on the monitoring screens. There wasn't much runway. The Falcon possessed the technology to vertically lift from a standing position.

Hastor caught Towden's eye. The Colonel looked nervous. He had his phone to his ear. He finished the call and moved towards Towden. They moved to the back of the room.

"That was Patrick Morgan," Hastor began.

"And?"

"A powerful contingent is building behind a Security Council resolution to order Major Kearey to lead the alien drone to a distant world, preferably in another galaxy."

"Doesn't surprise me," Towden admitted. "The question is, would Kearey agree?"

"They need leverage to force his agreement. Morgan's concerned. He's increased security at the island."

"Damn." Towden tracked Kearey's progress on screen. A verbal countdown commenced in the background and he lowered his voice. "His family isn't the only target. Major Kearey considers Macha and Pwyll both vital to his mission. Increase security across base, and alert Captain Whelan. I don't want any unauthorized personnel within ten miles of GBI or the Asterean village."

"Captain Whelan? Sir, is that wise?"

"The president re-assigned Whelan's team to GBI. They already had clearance." Towden hesitated. Whelan and his team had been following orders when they ambushed Kearey on his return from Syria. Kearey knew that. Still, maybe Hastor had a point. "Tell Whelan to keep his team out of Kearey's way. No need to make it an issue."

"Sir." Hastor straightened and left the room.

Towden watched the Falcon's wheels leave the runway, its nose slightly elevated.

One of the watching pilots shook his head. The pissed off roll of his eyes summarized the general air of pending doom. "This is crazy! He'll never hold that bird steady once she takes off."

"Silence, or leave," the director snapped, cutting off a rising murmur, but not before Towden caught a flash of green notes exchange hands.

A heart-stopping air of expectation swept the room. When the countdown hit zero and the Falcon shot forward and up, the Director's head jerked back as if surprised.

"One-eighty knots," Kearey's calm voice reported.

The Falcon shrank to a dot in the sky before disappearing and the room burst into life. Heart thumping, Towden released the breath he'd been holding as whoops and hand claps punctuated a general outbreak of congratulations. Even the director relaxed his dour expression. No one there had expected Kearey to make the launch.

Except one. Major Jackson looked a very happy man. Towden hid a smile. He'd collect his cut later.

Niall followed the flight plan long enough to get a feel for the Falcon's capabilities. Just like in the simulator, he remained insulated from the super-magnetic system propelling the Falcon forward. He was moving too fast to get a visual on Earth's geomagnetic field, but he could sense the magnetic flux on the horizon. He focused on improving his ability to predict the grid, taking the Falcon close in to mountain ranges, assessing the ship's response to the changing fields.

"Mission Control. Overriding auto-systems."

"This is Mission Control, Lima Six. Do not, I repeat, do not override auto-systems."

Niall grimaced. "With respect, sir, switching to manual, in five, four, three, two, one."

"We lost auto-control, sir." There was a high-pitched note of panic in the controller's voice.

"Lima Six!" the Director yelled. Niall banged his ear piece then turned down the volume. The man's voice faded. "Get those auto-systems back online!"

"Mission Control," Niall said calmly. "I have orders to test this aircraft for a specific mission and that's what I intend to do."

He steered the Falcon towards a cliff and let it slide against the energy vortex there, using the spiraling forces to spur the Falcon in an unexpected direction.

"What the hell was that?" someone asked.

Niall ignored the question, concentrated on the magnetic forces filtering through the Grand Canyon coming up. He sensed a path through the twisting ravines and flew the Falcon down the weaving line. Another part of his mind found his link to Astereal, gathered energy, and began to build a bridge, keeping the portal a mile ahead of him at all times.

"You're losing altitude, Lima Six. Climb to ten thousand feet."

"Negative, Mission Control."

Niall entered the canyon at a speed exceeding eight hundred miles an hour. For ten glorious minutes he put the Falcon through a series of twists and turns. He had bounced falc'huns off Astereal's magnetic grid for fun. Now he wanted to discover the Falcon's limitations. When he descended to fifty feet off the ground, Mission Control stopped chewing off his ear. Probably holding their breath.

He stabilized his bridge to Astereal before he ran out of canyon.

*Macha?*

Her mind snapped into focus. *I see your link,* she responded.

Pwyll's mind brought a wave of excitement. *This is cool!*

*Temperature's good from where I'm sitting,* Niall replied. He veered left, skimming an outcrop of rock. Pwyll's thoughts emanated confusion and the corner of Niall's mouth twitched.

*Cool?* Niall teased him.

*I am trying to integrate with your world.* There was a minute pause. *Awesome?*

Niall grinned. *We'll have you Americanized yet. Before you know it, you'll be married with two point five kids and driving a minivan.*

Niall sensed Pwyll's increasing bewilderment and refocused on his task. *Are you locked on?*

*Yes, I have your link.*

*Cool. Don't let it go.* Enjoying Pwyll's indignation, Niall said aloud, "Going offline, Mission Control. Keep the lights on."

"What the—"

Niall shot through the portal and emerged above a planet on fire. He slowed and allowed the Falcon to drift at will as he got his bearings. The Falcon's systems ran at quarter strength without Earth's gravitational pull holding it down. He matched speed with a nomadic asteroid, darting around it until he understood the Falcon's capabilities in space.

Then he searched for a link back to Earth, into Earth's past.

This was the moment of truth. He needed the divergent timeflows to see the way clearly. It was close. Unbelievably close. He could see the palace, then the Gate of the Sun. A little more into the future and he could see a wall of water crashing down over the palace. He shouldn't be surprised. His entire plan rested on the inevitability of this link's existence.

He had already witnessed his own future fifteen thousand years in the past.

The risks loomed large in his mind, creating a terrible pressure in his chest that physically hurt.

*Many will die, Niall'Kearey.*

Pwyll's thought echoed around Niall's mind.

Macha's mind surged down his link. *This is your timeline, Niall'Kearey. If you choose it.*

Niall's eyes narrowed. This mission held no place for doubt. *If I don't, what new timeline will unravel? I can protect Earth now by preserving its past. Balor's drone has to go somewhere. If Balor thinks I'm beyond his reach—*

*Balor has found Earth already,* Pwyll argued. *Sacrificing the Paladin civilization will not change that.*

*You think this is wrong?*

*I want you to be sure. Maybe you could look into the future.*

Niall checked his instruments, mulling over Pwyll's suggestion, his attention gradually drawn to the magnetic forces swirling out of Bacchus. On a whim he flew towards the dark star, driven by a sudden need to see Herecura's pod with his own eyes, but the forces were too great to risk the Falcon, and he coasted to a stop while still at a safe distance. His mind surfed past the debris orbiting into the black hole's cavernous mouth and homed in on the cryogenic pod. Its systems worked and its occupant lived.

A tomb for the living.

Icy fingers gripped him, a crushing vice of panic. He had been buried alive. Incarcerated in a box. Shame surged through him and he began to overheat. Temperature sensors began to wink on and off, a red alarm that only exacerbated the shame washing through him. *I can't leave her like this. She deserves better.* The compulsion to free her became irresistible.

*No,* Macha shot down the link. *Niall'Kearey! Stop!*

Niall raised his shields to drown her out. He gathered a minute ball of dark energy inside Herecura's pod and contained it within a magnetic sphere. With no escape, the pressure inside his engine increased exponentially until Niall released the energy.

Fast.

The explosion could be seen across Astereal's solar system.

Silent. Final.

Macha had fallen quiet, but Niall sensed her shock. Pwyll's too.

*You didn't see what she had become at the end. Her mind was a mess. She wanted this.*

Silence. He swallowed.

*Miach is concerned about you,* Macha said.

Niall's vision blurred. Red spots blotted out the starscape. He channeled his fury down his link. *Don't go there.*

Macha didn't back off. Instead, she countered his rage with an equal measure of concern.

Niall flinched and took a deep inhale of oxygen. His head cleared. *I saw what happened to the Paladins... to their descendants. I'm not making this decision lightly, but Uathach showed me numerous alternate timelines arising from even the smallest decision. I wanted to go back and change the past, but there was no way to predict the outcome of my actions. If I start chasing my future now, I'll never stop.* Impatience tinged his thought. *I thought you understood this.*

*I do—*

She fell quiet and Niall's stomach churned. He'd disappointed her.

*No, but I admit your anger troubles me.*

Frowning, Niall redirected his link back to Earth's present then spun the Falcon around to face the open portal, an oval of azure blue. As he accelerated out of the narrowing Grand Canyon and back onto his original flight plan, Niall slammed the lid on any further doubt. The past was in reach. The drone ship would be destroyed, and Earth would survive. The Paladins had always known their fate.

He would do this alone if that's what it took.

"Mission Control. This is Lima Six. Accelerating to Mach 10 at five thousand feet. Back on flight plan."

"Where the hell have you been?"

"A minor detour, sir. I'll include it in my report."

# CHAPTER FORTY-TWO

Charles Biron straightened his tie as the make-up girl applied more powder to his nose.

"You're ready, sir," she said.

"Thank you, Janie. An excellent job."

"President Biron, we're ready for you in the Oval Office."

His cell-phone vibrated in his pocket. Biron checked the caller ID and frowned.

"I'll be one moment," he told Janie. Closing the study door on her and the organized chaos invading the White House, he pressed Answer. "Emile, *qu'est-ce qui sa passe.*"

"Kearey's out of control."

"You have other problems. Amy Tighbuck called me. The FBI is connecting a financial paper trail between the terrorist attack that devastated Kearey's home town and the attack on Dr. Klotz."

"A trail that went dead four years ago. I have a fall guy set up."

"You should never have told me about it."

"You could have reported your concerns to the Council at the time. That moment has passed."

Charles pressed a hand to his chest. Fitzroy had stacked a house of cards under his presidency. Moving to his desk he opened a bottle of Foldane's pills and swallowed one dry. "What do you want?"

"Kearey has the Security Council on a rope," Emile said. "Authorizing his plan is a formality to save face. He can't be allowed to dictate policy again."

"He's the best protection Earth has." The words stuck in Charles' craw, but he couldn't avoid the truth and he didn't like where Fitzroy was headed.

"You know what you have to do."

Charles paled. "And what about the next drone?"

"There won't be."

"How can you possibly know?"

"We have your wife."

Biron sat down heavily. "My wife is dead."

"Come see for yourself."

Charles Biron walked into the Oval Office, his mind reeling. This was his first televised address to the nation, and by extension, to the world. The US and Presidential flags stood proudly, one on each side of his desk. He spoke to stem the escalating panic, and his words, thrashed out by the UN Security Council, would be echoed across Earth by the world's leaders. Instead, thoughts of Nicole, dominated his mind.

Not Nicole, but Uathach, High Brighid of Astereal.

A traveler from the future.

He had to speak to her. Fitzroy said she was a mature woman, the same age as when he met her. DruSensi satellites detected her arrival in Paris two years ago.

He turned to his Chief of Staff and dropped his voice. "Andrew, get me on the fastest jet we have in one hour. Not Air Force One. I need to be in France tonight. Incognito."

Andrew's eyes rounded. He gestured to the cameras. "Mr. President, is that wise? You need to be here."

"It's not up for debate," Charles snapped. Heads turned them and Charles plastered on a genial smile. Out of the side of his mouth, he snarled, "Get me on that plane."

Niall watched Biron's address to the nation in the GBI control room. When a picture of his own face filled the screen, the cardboard cup of coffee he was nursing imploded in his hand. He barely noticed the hot liquid scalding his skin. The picture grew to show him in dress uniform.

"*Merde!*" Jacqueline grabbed some napkins, threw him a handful, and started mopping up the spillage. "Can someone get some ice?"

Niall turned to Towden. "I thought I was officially dead."

Towden shook his head, his jaw set in anger. "You were."

Charles Biron's voice continued in the background. "Major Niall Kearey is a decorated officer with abilities that are symptomatic of an evolving trend amongst the general population in neuro-magneto control, abilities traditionally described as psychic, or supernatural. Now science is proving those abilities to be flashes of the human brain's untapped potential."

"What's he doing?" Niall murmured.

Biron's eyes glittered, his chest puffed out with pride. "Major Kearey's abilities are so advanced that he made contact with an alien species on the edge of the universe. A momentous achievement. Historic."

Niall felt sick. Exposed.

An airman put a bowl of iced water in front of him. The cold lessened the burning sting and chased away his nausea.

"This isn't the speech agreed by the United Nations," Towden said. "I saw a transcript."

"That contact has proved fortuitous," Biron plowed on, "for we are not alone. The evidence is undeniable. The alien ship approaching us is an armed drone with the ability to short cut space. There is no intelligible life on board. Now, with the technological advice of our new alien allies we have developed a defense capability that will jump the alien ship to another part of our galaxy where it will be harmlessly destroyed. At this time, Major Kearey is the only pilot we have capable of carrying out this task. It is personally very dangerous, and we pray for his safe return.

"The people of Earth face a new era, a time where we must set aside our fears and prejudice. The future of the human race depends on our embracing the idea that extra-terrestrial aliens exist and that our emerging human potential enables us to stand tall among those whose technological prowess appears to dwarf ours. We are a resilient species and these are exciting times in the course of human evolution. We need to reach out to our alien allies and welcome them to Earth. Five years ago, President Foldane introduced you to Operation Hideout. For security reasons at the time, the full truth could not be revealed, but now is the perfect opportunity to demonstrate that our alien allies stand beside us. I ask you for your trust, your patience, and your prayers. Major Kearey is a true hero, an American who demonstrates the very best of our military forces. I wish him God's speed."

Niall's jaw clenched as the president stared proudly out at them all. "Bastard!"

"Why did he do that?" Jacqueline asked, her face pale. Her cell phone rang. "It's Sean... Hi, honey." Her face creased into a grimace as she glanced at Niall. "Yes, it's true. I'm sorry I couldn't tell you." She paused. "I only found out a few days ago."

Niall pointed at his chest and she nodded before walking away a few steps.

"Yes, it's good news." She paused. "I don't know."

"Major Kearey?"

Niall turned with a start. "Sorry, General."

Towden dismissed his apology with a shake of his head. "Son, I don't know what President Biron is thinking, and this has taken me as much by surprise as you. If there's anything I can do?"

"I'm more worried about my family, General. My parents. I need to see them."

"Of course. We'll make sure that happens. I need to consult with General Straton. Assess the repercussions from President Biron's bombshell. But first," he indicated his office. "Patrick Morgan's on the phone. He wants to meet with you."

A jack hammer pounded Charles Biron's head and it wasn't from the dampening field Fitzroy used to stop the High Brighid accessing her formidable abilities. It was the aching sorrow that had afflicted him all those years ago when the woman he loved had changed. Watching her drift away from reality, lost in her own world, insensible to his pain... It shamed him then and it shamed him now, but he had abandoned her.

His ambitions hadn't room for an ailing wife with dementia, or whatever it was that had afflicted her. She held him back. At first, he'd endured the looks of pity, but then, as patience wore thin, it became harder to ignore the masked sneers of derision. The political establishment feared mental illness. Nicole stymied his presidential ambitions. Her death had boosted his career.

Looking at her now, his Nicole, even more beautiful than the day they had met on that *belle soiree* in Paris, Charles knew he had thrown aside his greatest asset. No other woman could ever live up to her.

And yet he knew now, she had used him.

He pressed the intercom Fitzroy said would disguise his voice.

She looked up from her studies, still, alert. "Qui est là?"

"You are learning to speak French," he replied in his mother tongue.

"So, I have a new interrogator."

"Interrogation? No." Charles paused. "You have been badly treated?"

"I am a prisoner. This dampening field is very uncomfortable."

"Yes. I am sorry. I hope we can change that. What is your name?"

"Nicole. Nicole Boutin."

"What are you studying?"

"The French Revolution. Your people do not like to be ruled."

Charles laughed. "That is true."

Her head tilted and she closed her book. Charles sat up. He had piqued her interest. He felt a lightness of spirit that had lain dormant for too long. He had always enjoyed Nicole's easy intellect, her insightful observations. She had never felt the need to dominate the conversation, and yet, when she spoke, he had paid attention.

"What is it you want?" she asked.

"You come from the future?"

"My captor has often told me this."

"Are you trying to reach a point in the past?"

She hesitated. "What I want is to start my life, on Earth."

"Tell me of the future. I need details, Uathach. Yes, we know who you are and I know that you want to preserve the past, to secure Earth's future for the human race and the Astereans. I want that, too, but I can't let you continue your journey until I know Earth has a future."

She nodded slowly, taking her time to reply. "Very well. You have been honest with me. I will tell you as much as I think will be safe, but I fear I cannot tell you much. I did not stay long in the future. It was broad daylight. Paris was so... busy... I could hardly breathe. There was a café near the Eiffel Tower. I went in and ordered an espresso." Her nose wrinkled at the memory and an aching pang tightened across Charles chest. Nicole had never enjoyed coffee, preferring a herbal tea. "No one paid me any attention. They were more interested in watching Couleir."

"Couleir?"

"A Frenchman. You call it a tennis match. If he won the game, he would win the Grand Slam." Her eyes took on a reflective look. "It was a very exciting game."

Biron got out his cell phone and looked up the name. Relief left him breathless. France did have a young tennis protege, a Marcel Couleir. Fifteen, and already a junior tennis champion. He could not possibly win the Grand Slam for a few years yet, suggesting Balor would not return. If he did, Earth had time to prepare.

"Did he win?"

She hesitated. Then, "Yes."

"Why didn't you contact Major Kearey?"

"You know a lot about me."

"Yes."

"I could not sense his presence. Do you know where he is?"

Charles wondered how much to tell her. He needed to be careful. "He seeks the orbs in the past. We have not found them all."

"We?"

"The Vercingetorix. We reached an understanding. Tell me, what did you do? In the future."

"I could not pay, and I realized I was in the wrong time. There was so much noise." Her voice trailed off.

The mistake seemed to concern her. Charles considered the inconsistency. The High Brighid should have landed in the past. Astereal's timeflow had been aligning with Earth's, moving steadily towards the future. Kearey's link had always been grounded in Earth's slower timeflow, or linked to the powerful mind of the Morrígan Queen.

The High Brighid had been acting on her own recognizance. She clearly had the ability to bridge space-time.

If they had never met, never married, what would have changed? A deep sense of loss penetrated him at the thought. No, don't think about that. Work it through. Without the orb, Kearey would have had no bargaining power with the Vercingetorix. He would have remained on the run, his abilities growing all the time.

Better to keep him close.

A new thought struck. Nicole had collected theories regarding Lake Titicaca's formation. Could she have foreseen this event? Collected clues for Jacqueline to find? High Brighid Uathach had seen Earth's future. She might know more than she let on. She had allowed the Paladins to settle in a place that would one day be flooded. Did she know that Major Kearey would be the source of their destruction?

Nicole's beautiful jade eyes gazed towards him, as if she could see right through the one-way window. Her intelligent strength pulled him in.

*We would never have married.*

Biron made his decision. He had what he needed to know. Earth had a future, a place where people could drink espresso in a café; a world where a Frenchman would win the Grand Slam; and a time when Major Niall Kearey did not exist. The little details mattered. Understanding what you didn't know mattered more.

Outside, he rang Fitzroy. "Let her continue her journey. Remind her she needs to reach farther back into Earth's past to evade detection by DruSensi. Do not give her any further information."

"You're sure?"

"Yes. I've decided Kearey is right. We need to preserve the past."

"And what about that other matter we discussed?"

"We also need to secure our future. Consider it done." He took out his cell phone and checked his contacts list. He found the name he was looking for. Whelan.

# CHAPTER FORTY-THREE

"What do you want?" Niall demanded of Patrick Morgan. "More blood? Haven't you taken enough from me?"

Morgan looked taken aback. His eyes narrowed and he appeared set to counterattack with equal venom when Etlinn stepped between them.

"Niall," she protested softly. "Please, I know you have your differences, but Patrick is on your side."

"Differences? He endangered my family, nearly got them killed!"

"And I've cared for them for the last five years!" Morgan countered angrily.

Niall's fist clenched. "You married my wife off to my best friend!"

"That's not fair," Etlinn protested. "We thought you were dead."

Morgan waved her down and met Niall's gaze head on. "Whether you accept it or not, protecting your family is my priority now. That's what I've been doing and that's why I'm here." He glanced around the small grey office, empty but for a table and chairs. "But not the only reason. I wanted to warn you. When I visited you before your cryogenic stasis, I had a vision. Clairvoyance is one of my gifts—a random one. Be nice if I could control it."

Niall remembered Patrick looking like he'd seen Hell waiting for him. Abruptly stepping back from confrontation, he pulled out a chair for Etlinn and waved Morgan to another before taking a seat for himself across the table.

"Okay, I'm listening."

Morgan's eyes reflected the turbulence in his aura. His powerful presence reached across the table between them. "You were trapped," he said, struggling to get the words out. "In terrible pain. It never stopped."

"So, not your Hell, then? A little unjust, don't you think?"

Morgan winced and Etlinn's mouth tightened. "Niall, please."

"Etlinn, it's fine." Morgan took a deep breath and returned Niall's assessing gaze. "I assumed this hell was the cryogenic stasis."

"And yet you allowed it to go ahead."

Morgan didn't blink. "Yes."

"Sibling rivalry runs deep."

"It wasn't that."

Etlinn leaned forward. "Niall, even I thought cryogenic stasis the only humane way to safeguard Earth."

"All I've ever done is to safeguard Earth!"

"And it's taken this insane plan of yours to make me realize just how far you'll go," Morgan said. He stopped and focused inward. "Niall, I've seen what will happen to you. Suppose my vision was meant as a warning. That taking Balor's ship into the past will lead to nothing but pain. You've never done this before. On Astereal, you stepped back a few Earth months. Here, you've remote-viewed farther back, but you've never actually stepped into the distant past. Even if you can pull off this mad stunt you've got planned, you could still get trapped there."

His hands splayed out on the table. "Why not take Balor's ship across the galaxy? Crash it into an uninhabited planet. Blow up a few rocks. Astereal even! At least you know you can get there and back again. Before you say no, we've been considering the possible outcomes. So South America gets a different coastline. Maybe the Paladin civilization dies out later on, or maybe it survives. Maybe it will shape a new South America in more ways than geography."

Niall stared at him in disbelief. "You want to risk Earth's present to save me from some eternal damnation?"

"We're not sure this solution will save Earth. You could be wrong."

"Shit! I don't believe this!" Frustration, doubt, made Niall's voice louder than he'd intended. Etlinn bit her lip and glanced to her husband. Niall curbed his irritation. "We have an alien drone about to hit Earth with enough energy to destroy the solar system just hours away. I know what I saw."

Morgan sighed. "It's not your decision."

Niall blinked. "That's where you're wrong. It *is* my decision. I've told you what needs to be done. You can try to stop me stealing that Falcon. Put me under, back in stasis, anything. But you can't stop that alien drone without me. And right now, I'm more worried about Biron's latest stunt."

"His speech?" Morgan queried.

Niall nodded.

"We had no idea President Biron was going to say that," Etlinn said, her eyes flashing. "The Security Council approved a different statement that did not mention you. Charles' motives are selfish. By exposing you and the Astereans, he's consolidating his authority as president. He's looking towards the next election. People always remember who told them the truth first. If you don't make it back, Charles Biron will lead the United States in national mourning, and the Astereans will need his political protection more than ever. He's making a bid for leadership of the Vercingetorix Council, and he has considerable support among the coded families. He would be the first democratically elected president with coded powers. He knows our every secret and he's a shareholder of a large portfolio of Vercingetorix assets."

"Maybe the world should know about the Vercingetorix, too," Niall said.

"Perhaps you're right," Patrick Morgan retorted. "Why not create a two-tier society? Those who are coded, and those who are not. I can see the riots now. The witch hunts. The jealousy. And everyone will know your children are special. Different."

Niall's jaw tensed.

"Patrick, please," Etlinn said, not hiding her annoyance. "Leave Toby and Lizzie out of this."

"No, Etlinn, this is why we're here. Kearey spent his whole life hiding his superior abilities. He understands exactly what I'm talking about." Patrick thumped the table. "Once the Vercingetorix goes public, the coded families will be forced to band together, or be picked off one by one. It will be civil war. Sharifah would so offend the religious sections of her country she'd be forced into exile. Everything she's achieved for women in her country would be wiped out.

"Psychics are tolerated now only because the majority of the world believes they're harmless crackpots. Imagine the reaction in North Korea? The slightest hint of a trance would be punishable by execution. The moment the world realizes these people possess 'unnatural' power, war will break out. It will be us against them. We've earned our influence. We provide energy, jobs, financial security. Behind the scenes, we bail out bankrupt countries, and topple dictators. We will destroy anyone who threatens our anonymity."

"And the money it brings you," Niall pointed out, but deep down, he knew Morgan painted an uncomfortable truth.

"Charles Biron understands our vulnerability more than anyone," Etlinn said, her voice deceptively soft. "He is holding you up as a poster boy for all those with an advanced ability. He hopes to portray our kind as saviors for the world. He is betting that indisputable evidence of extraterrestrial life will persuade developed countries to look upon us with favor."

"It won't work and we need to protect Lizzie and Toby," Patrick declared. He focused his gaze on Niall. "With you exposed there are factions of the Vercingetorix who won't hesitate to exploit the children of a world-wide hero, dead or alive. We need to hide them. A witness protection scheme of sorts. New identities. Fake fingerprints. A secure home, at least until they are old enough to cope with their legacy." His eyes bored their message home. "Both mine and yours."

Niall's stomach took flight.

Etlinn's eyes gleamed. "I control their DNA samples. I can have them destroyed and alter the records, so if anyone runs a DNA test on them for whatever reason in the future there will be no match found to Elizabeth or Toby Kearey. We can protect them, Niall."

Niall heard the words, but Etlinn's voice sounded distant. A rushing noise filled his ears. His family couldn't take anymore.

"But we need to move now, while the world is distracted," Patrick added, the sudden richness of his Irish brogue a sign of his urgency. "If you want us to, that is. It means uprooting them from the island. I know the children are happy there, getting the best education..." He paused. "I need to know what you're thinking. We need to move fast to get this done, before the Vercingetorix realize your children offer the perfect cover to hide behind."

Niall couldn't get off the treadmill. He wanted time to stop. He wanted to catch breath, and think. "Where? Where would you hide them?"

"Etlinn's grandparents owned a small island off Scotland. Treska. It has a beautiful house and its own loch. It's accessible only by boat. It was passed down to a distant cousin. She's very trustworthy, but getting on in years and needs help. Your adoptive mother has medical training so Sheila would be a godsend for her. Tami could manage the estate and act as a companion." Patrick hesitated. "I can arrange for DruSensi's portal detection system to be offline, but there is still the Russian satellite system out there. One is bound to be covering the northwest hemisphere."

"I can knock out all the satellites covering the northern hemisphere," Niall pointed out.

Patrick frowned, half nodding in thought. "The Russian satellite should be fine, but the DruSensi satellite network supports some strategic intelligence infrastructure. The whole world is already at a heightened state of alert." He paused. When Niall did not respond, he leaned forward. "If we do this, we need to move your family tonight. Jose and his family, too. Without your family their position on the island would rapidly become untenable."

Fragmented thoughts tumbled around Niall's mind, connecting and then spiraling apart. Biron's speech; the alien drone; discovering his wife had married a man who knew him inside out; Patrick and Etlinn's portrayal of a race uneasy with its own evolution; the impending death of a civilization by his own hand... *Tami hates the cold.*

"What about Miach?"

"There's plenty of room on Treska." Etlinn's eyes creased with concern. "Niall, I know this is difficult for you, but Tami's barely coping as it is."

Her words hit Niall like a hammer blow. "You think I should step aside?"

"No, but the President of the United States might as well have stated you're headed off on a suicide mission. This isn't the moment to fight your corner."

Niall rubbed the aching tension behind his eyes. "God, it never ends."

"It's worse than that," Patrick said, his voice gruff. "I don't believe you're going to make it back from this one. You need to get your house in order."

# CHAPTER FORTY-FOUR

Tami listened without uttering a word as Niall explained Patrick and Etlinn's plan. While Sheila and Tony quizzed Etlinn about her cousin and the Outer Hebrides isle, she carefully compressed the bubbling panic in her upper sternum into a nugget she could contain inside of her and began to mentally list the items they couldn't leave behind.

Luisa reached out and squeezed Tami's hand. They shared a brief glance, no words needed. Jose and Luisa were the closest friends Tami had in the world. She thanked God they were here. She looked at the others. Jose projected a blank canvas, attentive, but giving nothing away. Miach leaned against a wall, stubbornly refusing to sit down, his aura shooting off angry sparks. She wished Miach hadn't helped her finetune her psychic intuition. Niall's pain was so raw she could hardly look at him.

"Hannah McCloud has been a reclusive for many years," Niall said.

Tami plucked at a loose thread in her dress. The decision had already been made. Niall wouldn't suggest this if he didn't believe it necessary. She would go anywhere in the world to protect her children. It hurt too much to think beyond that. Keepsakes, she decided. Photo albums. Her mother's memory box. She could buy art supplies, but there were several of her pictures she could not bear to leave behind.

"Lizzie, go pack your violin and clothing you want to take with you. Lots of warm clothing."

"No electronic devices," Patrick said. "We'll get you new ones."

Tami nodded. She would have to start her photography business over, develop a new style to be safe. She looked at her son. "Toby, you

391

too. Miach, we have four suitcases in storage. Would you find them, please?"

Questioning faces turned to her. All except Miach. He pushed himself straight and then moved to the rear of the bungalow. Good. Better to keep him occupied.

"We're going then?" Luisa asked, her tone resigned.

"Yes." Tami refused to look Niall in the eye, afraid she might break.

Jose took Luisa's hand. "Niall isn't suggesting this for fun." He turned to Patrick. "How long do we have?"

"The satellites will be offline in one hour. Niall will deal with the Russian one."

The room erupted into a hub of activity. Tony and Sheila left first, closely followed by Jose and Luisa. Lizzie burst into tears and ran out of the room, Toby close behind her. Niall cast Tami a mournful look, but then he followed their little girl. Tami began to breathe again.

"I am so sorry, Tami," Etlinn said, moving to sit beside her.

"No, I'm grateful."

Patrick stirred from where he had been hiding in the far corner. Tami looked at him and was stunned to see his eyes shining with unshed tears. The painful blockage in her throat thickened.

"I've caused your family so much pain," he said. "I wish I could make this easier for you."

Tami waited a second before responding, just in case her heart softened. It didn't. "Don't bother hoping I'll forgive you, Patrick. I tolerate you for Etlinn's sake. That's all."

Etlinn patted her hand and jerked her head towards her husband. A few seconds later, they were alone. "I don't blame you, Tami darling," Etlinn said. "I haven't forgiven him either, but he means well by you now."

"I can't decide who we're running from. Charles Biron? The Vercingetorix? Or the whole world?"

"All of them. And it's not right to keep running—it's horribly wrong—but the children need space to grow. To discover themselves."

"It's not so bad. I love Scotland, even when the wind is biting and you feel you will never be warm again." Tami smiled as treasured memories brought her to the edge of tears. "Did you know the children were conceived there?"

Etlinn's eyes widened. "No, I didn't." She grabbed Tami's hands as the precariously-built dam holding Tami together breached. "Don't, pet, please."

"I don't know what to do," Tami whispered. "It shouldn't be possible to love two men so much. I feel so torn. All of the time. Miach makes me feel safe. Niall creates this ball of terror right here." Tami pressed her naval. "It's always been there. I handled it for years. The not knowing. A sense that his world was a lot bigger than mine. He made it all worthwhile. But it's different now. He's changed."

Yet her feelings for him had not.

A sixth sense made her turn her head. Niall stood in the doorway, his eyes dark, every visible muscle tight with tension, his jaw holding back his grief. Tami couldn't move, or speak. She sat there, rooted in dismay.

Etlinn's face drained of color. "Niall."

Tami struggled for breath. Walls pumped in and out.

"I need some air," Niall said, his voice a bare scratch against the dull roar rushing through Tami's ears. The door slammed shut behind him.

Miach appeared. "Go after him, Tami. Make him understand. I'll take care of the packing."

Tami nodded and stood up, too fast. She closed her eyes until her head stopped spinning then she drew in a long breath. "Excuse me, Etlinn. I need to persuade your son that I love him." She paused. A loose end glued her to the spot and she swung around to stare at a surprised Etlinn. "What Russian satellite?"

Niall spotted Patrick walking on the beach and turned in the opposite direction.

Tami's words haunted every step. He filled her with terror.

She was right. He put the world before his family far too often and it had brought them nothing but pain. That would have to change. First, he would destroy the alien drone. After that...

His mind stalled.

*Shit.*

"Niall! Wait! Please."

He swung round. Tami raced after him, barefoot. Her sandals dangled from one hand while the other fisted around the hem of her white sundress revealing tanned well-toned legs. The rays of the setting sun lightened her hair to the color of gold. Part of him wanted to run, before he wrecked their crumbling relationship anymore. The hurt side, the angry and betrayed side, stood fast.

"I'm sorry," she said, pulling up short before him, her eyes imploring him to listen.

Niall watched her catch her breath, hating this chasm of uncertainty between them.

Tension creased her eyes. "What I said back there, I can't deny its truth, but nothing's changed between us! The world's changed, yes. *We've* changed! You're not the dutiful, brave, heroic American officer I married, and I'm not the military wife waiting at home, ignorant of where your job takes you and what you do. Your powers affected us well before those bastards took you from us. You became this national security risk, a bone for Earth's governments to squabble over, and it's changed everything."

Tears streamed down her cheeks. "What you can do... you put us in danger, now the entire human race, but always me and our children. When you're alive, I'm scared! All of the time! But when you were dead, I wished I was dead too, and that feeling, you know, it's all-consuming, turning the day to night and night to Hell. I loathed the person it made me. Lizzie and Toby deserved better!"

Anguish twisted her face and, letting go of her dress, she wiped her nose with the back of her hand.

Niall could not speak for several moments, terrified by where her words would take them, heartbroken for her pain. He swiped tears away from his eyes and Tami bit her lip. She looked out across the ocean crashing on their island paradise, but then her gaze returned to him.

"Say something, Niall. Please!"

Her voice implored him for a response, something, anything, but his thoughts had frozen. Their whole future hung on his next words. The hurt carving him up inside became unbearable and he blurted out, "You said nothing's changed." Frustration carried him forward, seared his voice. "How the *fuck* has nothing changed?"

Her lips mashed together. She looked at him, shaking her head. "The reason it hurts so badly, and the reason you *scare* me so much, is because I love you. *That's* what hasn't changed." She threw her hands up in the air and her sandals went flying. "None of this is our fault! It's not Miach's fault! I have never been unfaithful to you, Niall, even when I thought you were dead. It's the God's honest truth. I can't undo the decisions I've made, or how I feel about Miach. Over the last three years he's kept me sane and I can't help loving him for that, but that will never come close to what I feel for you. You're my first love, Niall, my husband, the father of my children. You're the man I want in my bed, the man I want to hold in my arms..." She wrapped her arms tight around her chest, choking on her words, trying to hold herself together. "But now you have a decision to make."

Blood pounded through Niall's veins. This woman held his entire world in her hands. He would bend all of time and space to be with her.

Her hand reached out and pressed against his heart. "You can choose to trust in me, trust in our love, and everything we've shared together, or you can let your jealousy and rage suffocate us, throw it all away. You choose. Not me. I chose long ago, and I may regret the terrible times, and I may curse you for your powers, and I may hate you being enslaved to your duty when that puts your life at risk. *But...*" Her voice cracked. "I will never *ever* stop loving you!" Her lips curved into a gentle smile. "It's hardwired into my soul." She took her hand from his heart and placed it against her own.

Stunned beyond words, Niall stepped forward and wrapped her in his arms while he gathered his thoughts. The fresh apple scent of her hair comforted him in a way no words ever could. "We need time," he whispered. "We're on a rollercoaster and everything is moving too fast. When I get back, we're going to sort this mess out. I'll find a habitable planet on the other side of the universe where no one will ever find us. We'll be the modern-day Swiss Family Robinson in space. You, me, and the children!"

Tami's muffled laugh rumbled against his chest. She looked up at him, her beautiful blue eyes glistening with unshed tears. "That is the craziest idea I ever heard. I love it, but I love you more. I'll go wherever you take me, Niall Kearey, as long as you're there at my side."

He kissed her then, a loving embrace full of passion, tenderness and promise. A soul-destroying pain eased deep inside his core. He dug his fingers into the skirt of her sundress, bunching and pulling the material up high until he touched soft skin. Her aura glowed. She pulled out his shirt...

General Straton stared at the revised estimate for time of impact. "One hour thirty?"

"It jumped."

"Alert Air Control. We need that Falcon prepped and ready to go in twenty. What's the status on the armed missile?"

"It's on-site."

"Sir, we just lost a feed from the DruSensi network."

"Get it back. Get me the president. And where's Major Kearey?"

Niall's mind orbited Earth. Morgan's plan relied on his influence with DruSensi. Not good enough. This time Niall didn't bother mimicking a solar flare. He targeted a pulse of electromagnetic radiation directly at the gamma plus sensor situated on a second DruSensi satellite. He bombarded the Russian satellite in passing.

Jose paused in his packing. "*Esta bien loco, cabron.* You got that look, like you just dropped somebody off on top of a volcano."

"Yeah. Gonna take the lot out."

"Not planning on coming back?"

"What's Biron going to do? Arrest the man who saved the world?"

"Never underestimate Biron. *Es un vibora, bien malo.* The *cabron* ain't gonna kiss your ass."

"All the more reason then."

In less than a few minutes, Niall systematically wiped out every portal detection sensor north of the equator thereby increasing the potential search grid for his family. He savored a grim satisfaction before a crawling urgency distracted him from the moment.

"Jose, you ready?"

"We're ready," Luisa answered him from the door to their bedroom. She carried their youngest, now five in her arms. Handing the boy over to Jose, she walked to over to Niall.

"Come here." She wrapped him in an arm-crushing hug then kissed him on both cheeks. *"Dios te bendiga y la virgen te acompaña."* The blessing brought a lump to Niall's throat.

"Just to focus your mind, Major," Jose added, "that violin makes it to the other side, *I'm* kissing your ass."

Niall grinned.

He sent the Pérez Navas tribe through to the Hebrides isle ahead of the others then dropped in on his parents. If he stopped to think, he might explode. Throwing bags through a portal kept his hands busy. It didn't fill the aching void cutting his life out from under him.

His cell phone rang. General Towden.

Niall's mind raced. Had he missed one? If the DruSensi network had picked up his portal for Jose's family... He could zap the lot. Blow them out of the sky.

It would be too late.

His whole body broke out in a cold sweat.

He accepted the call. "Yes, sir?"

"The alien drone jumped. It's within spitting distance and the Security Council has made its decision. The Falcon is being armed and will be ready to launch in fifteen minutes. You have a go."

Niall's pulse slowed to a steady throb. His mind cleared. "How close exactly?"

"Get out a telescope and you can see it coming."

"Copy that. I'll be there in five."

His rushed embrace with the parents who had raised him only sharpened his sense of growing loss. Tony and Sheila had barely stepped through to Scotland before he was running back to the bungalow, his boots barely touching the sand.

*Miach! The drone is here. You have to go now.*

*We are ready.*

Niall had his third bridge to Treska formed by the time he bounded up the steps to the deck. Patrick and Miach started throwing luggage through. Niall could see Tony on the other side grabbing the bags to make space. To his left, Lizzie's face crumpled.

"Come here," Niall said, his voice rough as he drew his beautiful daughter into a bear hug. "I'm sorry, sweet pea. I thought we would have more time."

"Daddy, please be careful."

He wiped the tears off her face, kissed her forehead, and turned to his son. "Toby," he rasped.

Lizzie moved aside. It seemed like only a few short months ago he could hold them in his arms and hug them both at once.

Toby stared at him with shining tears in his eyes. "No one's got a dad like mine, Dad."

Niall laughed, but when Toby hugged him, the pride in his son's aura hit Niall like an electric bolt. Over Toby's head, Niall met Tami's wide-eyed gaze and knew her heart was breaking. Niall's vision blurred.

He gave Toby a pat on the back and ruffled his hair, then moved towards her. "I'll be back," he said, hating to leave her this way, so quickly. "Then we'll have that talk, find that deserted planet, and sail away."

She nodded, her copper hair glowing from the light pouring onto the deck from inside the bungalow, those incredible eyes holding his, a transparent portal to her heart. An explosion of love built up inside him, but then her gaze shifted to Miach watching them.

"It will be okay," he whispered.

"I love you, Niall." The words sprung from her lips.

Niall caressed the corner of her mouth with his thumb. "I know you do. I love you, too. Forever and always. Nothing... no one... will ever change that."

A rush of love colored her aura, enriched by passion, tinged with grief. She moved closer and lifted her chin. Niall claimed her lips with the desperation of a parched man.

Gentle words accompanied her tender kiss as they parted. "Forever and always. To the stars and back. I will wait for you, Niall Kearey. Trust me."

"All I want is for you to be happy," he whispered.

She parted from him slowly, her fingers squeezing his before letting him go. For long seconds he could not pull his eyes off his woman, beautiful in her anguish, but then the frantic activity around them stopped. The luggage was through.

Patrick Morgan cursed his phone and looked up. "Kearey, you need to go."

Niall nodded then turned to Miach. "I will be back."

His former host, a man Niall had entrusted with his family, with the love of his life, inclined his head. "I wish you well, Niall'Kearey."

The spoken words revealed the depth of the chasm between them. Miach's mind was closed to Niall now. Dumping Miach on Astereal had destroyed the deep understanding and trust that had existed between them. Their friendship had been incinerated in the flames of a burning planet and suffocated by the toxic fumes of jealousy.

"I'm sorry, Miach."

A wet shine filled the older man's eyes and then his mind opened, extending Niall a hesitant tendril of understanding, and hope. Revealing the complex truth.

Miach and Tami's relationship had never been consummated.

*We came close once, but it proved too soon. It was never an issue. Her love for you drew us together. I could not change that love any more than I can stop breathing. I do not stand between you and your wife, Niall'Kearey. Know that I am here for her in her time of need when you cannot be here. Trust that Tami and your children will have my protection for as long as I live. Never think I take her from you.*

The simple honesty of Miach's open mind defused Niall's anger, but the jealousy and insecurity that sat in the pit of his stomach would take more than time to heal. Tami knew him well. This was his choice. He needed to choose their future. The past could not be undone. Every choice he had made since awakening to his destiny, every action he had taken, served that singular truth. Miach had earned his wife's love and her heart was huge and impossibly loyal.

Unable to trust his voice, or his thoughts, Niall could only nod.

He watched them go, his heart aching beyond endurance when his children gave him a final brave wave before stepping through to their new home. Tami turned at the last moment. Her aura shone bright with a declaration of true love.

And then they were gone.

Hidden on the other side of the world. His wife. His children. And the doppelganger he should never have saved. He blinked back tears, hating that he could think such a terrible thought.

"Niall," Etlinn said, her hand resting on his arm. "Go. We will stay to settle things here." She touched his cheek. "Come back to us. I pray for your safe return."

Niall squeezed her fingers as he pulled her hand down. It was all he was prepared to give. "Pray Balor wants me more than Earth."

Emile Fitzroy thumbed the intercom. "Uathach." His prisoner looked up, her expression wary. "All the satellites are down. I don't know why, but if you're going to continue your journey, you should do so now."

He terminated the force field securing her room. Instantly, her chin lifted. She stood up, her body radiating an energy Emile hadn't realized was missing. Permanent lines in her forehead smoothed.

"Has something happened?" she asked. Light appeared at her fingertips.

Her recovery was incredible. Charles Biron had been wise to restrain Major Kearey so carefully.

"Yes, and you need to continue your journey. Go back farther than you did before. You don't want your portal to be detected again."

"I understand." She took a few seconds, searching for something Emile could not see and then her expression relaxed. A portal formed before her.

"*Bon voyage*," Fitzroy said.

She looked straight at him through the glass and smiled. "*Au revoir, Monsieur Fitzroy.*"

# CHAPTER FORTY-FIVE

Colonel Sam Hastor paced up and down, one eye on the engineers swarming around the Falcon triple-checking every bolt and wire, the other eye on his watch. Where was Kearey? *Dammit*! Had the second hand stopped working? He noticed Whelan drop down from the cockpit then walk towards an exit. The captain looked back and there was something furtive about the movement that held Sam's attention.

He contacted General Towden by phone. "Sir, I just saw Captain Whelan. Is there a problem?"

"President Biron ordered a final security sweep of the area."

"I see. Sorry to have troubled you, General."

Towden disconnected the call and the general's words should have been final, but Hastor couldn't shake that expression on Whelan's face from his mind. Why would Charles Biron be personally concerned about security? Area 51 was the most secure site on Earth. A thudding anxiety set off a griping pain, a flare up of an old ulcer. He jogged after Whelan.

"Captain?" he yelled as he burst through the door into blazing sunshine.

He spotted Whelan talking to Jester. Hastor slowed to a walk as the pair threw him a salute.

"Is there a problem, Colonel?" Whelan asked.

"What were you doing? On the Falcon?"

"Last minute security sweep, Colonel. We've got orders to make sure nothing goes wrong. Do you know where Major Kearey is?"

"No." Hastor controlled his rising tension.

"You should get TomTom to check that bird over," Jester said. "All due respect, Captain, but TomTom's better qualified to spot anything out of place."

Whelan's eyes flashed for less than an instant, but Hastor noticed the slight frown that creased Jester's broad forehead. "Sure," Whelan said. He tapped his communicator. "TomTom, get your hiney over here and give the Falcon a quick once over."

"On it," TomTom's voice responded. "Although my hiney has..."

Hastor closed his ears. Conscious of the time, he walked back to the hangar and discovered Niall changing into the specially designed wing suit for the mission.

"You're cutting it fine," he said, then remembered where Niall had been. "How was it? Is Tami okay?"

"No. She's not okay. She's terrified and putting on a brave face. That son of a bitch Biron has put my family at risk again."

Niall fixed his headgear in place and carried out a quick communications check then finished zipping up his suit, his movements hyper and his eyes tense.

Sam leaned in close. "You didn't, you know, do anything stupid?" he ventured and immediately wished he hadn't when Niall slung him a furious glare.

"Like Charles Biron exposing me and my family to the whole world? No, sorry, simply can't compete." Suspicious eyes skewered Sam inside out. "Did you know he would do that?"

"No, of course not. No one did."

Sam exhaled softly when Niall's mouth relaxed. He decided to tread lightly. Niall was living in a pressure cooker.

Niall laced his boots. "Forget it. And Tami and I will be fine. Everything will be fine."

Sam wished he could feel so confident.

His boots hooked into the all-black suit, Niall glanced up. "Give me a status update."

"The nuke's on board." Sam gave Niall a quick rundown including Whelan's security search then handed him over to the chief engineer who wanted to go over some preflight checks with him.

"Good luck, Major," Sam finished.

Niall acknowledged his words with a nod, but his attention was already with the Chief.

Sam hesitated, wanting to make some gesture for this mission, shake Niall's hand, but he doubted Niall would welcome the sentiment and, anyway, the moment had passed. He made his way to the control tower where Macha and Pwyll waited to establish their telepathic link with Kearey. The memory of Whelan's face dogged him every step of the way. Before he could consider the wisdom of what he was about to do, Sam called Biron on his private line.

The president answered almost immediately. "Colonel? This had better be good."

"Sir, I'm sorry to trouble you. You ordered Whelan's team to redo a security check? Is there a problem I should know about?"

There was a minuscule pause, not one Hastor was used to hearing from Charles Biron.

"Just a guilty concern following my speech."

Hastor could hear a background babble of noise. A voice speaking French. "Mr. President, are you in France?"

"I had urgent business to attend to. I'll be monitoring the situation from Air Force One. It just landed. Has something happened, Colonel? I assume there's a reason for this call?"

Sam took a deep breath, certain Biron was holding back on him. "Yes, Mr. President. I believe the security team has been compromised."

"*Merde!*" Biron lapsed into a stream of excitable French before seeming to catch himself. "Do not overstep your mark, Colonel Hastor. I have complete confidence in the security team." The phone went dead.

Sam frowned at his phone. Then he pulled open the door to the control tower and climbed the stairs. He joined Macha and Pwyll. Towden was deep in conversation with the Mission Director.

"Something's wrong," he said, keeping his voice low. He explained his disquiet then looked at Pwyll. "If someone wanted to ensure a successful mission, but make sure Major Kearey didn't make it back, what would they sabotage?"

The Asterean nodded. "One moment." He went quiet for a good two minutes.

Sam's skin began to crawl. He glanced at Macha, disconcerted to find her strange square-shaped, golden pupils studying him. Could she see into his mind? Did he have an aura?

Pwyll stirred. "Colonel Hastor, we have an Asterean engineer who advises that the simplest method would be to jam the ejection rocket safety pin after all the checks have been completed."

"Damn."

"You truly believe someone would try to sabotage this mission?" Macha asked.

"Not the mission."

Horror darkened her eyes. Anger washed through in its wake. "I will warn Niall'Kearey."

"I could be wrong," Sam admitted. His chest tightened and the power of his emotions rushed through him, loud and impossible to ignore. "Macha, please, there's something more."

The Morrígan Queen listened, inclined her head, and then fell silent.

Niall's mind surfed into space, found the alien drone, and knew they had run out of time.

"Commencing launch sequence," he advised the tower.

"Copy that."

This time there were no arguments. He ran this mission. No one else.

Macha's thought hit him without warning. *Colonel Hastor has reason to suspect the ejection seat has been sabotaged.*

Niall absorbed Sam's warning while calmly completing the launch sequence. Macha also conveyed the intensity of Sam's plea for forgiveness and the strength of his need for Niall to survive this mission and return safely. Too much to process.

*Don't let me go, Macha.*

*Niall'Kearey. Hear me. Do not torture yourself with what you could not know. Do not lose your way in the pain that follows hard choices. Trust your instincts.*

*I hear you.*

*I will not let you go.*

The Falcon took smoothly to the air and was entering the stratosphere when Pwyll's mind joined Macha's.

*Niall'Kearey. I can connect you directly to an engineer who may be able to help.*

*Go ahead.*

The excited Asterean overflowed with information. Every possible scenario flooded Niall's mind. Niall nearly slammed up his privacy shield on Pwyll's link.

*There isn't much room in here,* he pointed out. *It's not like I can start rummaging around on the floor to look.*

He extended a small sliver of his consciousness to explore his immediate surroundings as he simultaneously found a link direct to the drone and created dark energy to feed his bridge. He shot through a portal avoiding Earth's stratosphere and pulled the Falcon to a halt before he slammed into the drone's nose. Then reversing the dipole gravity field, he accelerated back to match the drone's speed.

His pulse rate went into overdrive. He didn't need this sabotage shit. He flew nose to nose with a monster whale, a grey barnacled whale that watched him. He couldn't detect any eyes, but every bone in his body knew the predator had scented its prey.

*Call me Ahab.*

*Niall'Kearey?* Pwyll queried him.

*It's a book. Moby Dick. You should read it.* "Contact made, Mission Control."

"Copy that, Falcon One."

Macha's soothing presence flooded his mind. Then to his surprise, Niall detected Yerit's pride in his human warrior friend and Choluu's generous spirit wishing him well. Pwyll's mind opened too, extending out on numerous channels. Sohan's quiet confidence calmed Niall's nerves. Miach sent promise of a friendship he could trust, and reassurance that his family felt welcomed on Treska. Lizzie snuck in, tearful, loving him, and then Toby. His son held his mother's hand and Niall was hit by such a mix of Toby's pride and Tami's love that a tear blurred his vision.

Behind them all, an ocean of Asterean goodwill overwhelmed him with a tidal wave strength.

*No more, Pwyll.*

In a moment there was only Macha and Pwyll, their link strong and holding him on course. His vision cleared.

Outside his mind, his world was a cold and deadly silence. The chill of space was a lonely place to be. Quiet. Beautiful. The spiraling arms of the Milky Way undulated before him, rich and sparkling, marred by an alien threat that did not belong in his world. Despite the hardened insulation of the cockpit, Niall could still sense the gravitational disturbance outside his protected shell. It reverberated through the q-dimension. The drone moved steadily towards him.

Towards Earth.

Niall broke into a cold sweat. Could he be mistaken?

If he'd misjudged Balor's interest in him...

And then a new presence rolled in. Balor's servant. *Lugus.* A trickle of pure fear slid down Niall's backbone. The alien's aura was distinctive. Chilling. A malevolent presence that echoed the fears of his childhood and so overwhelming Niall nearly missed the drone's sudden acceleration.

Increasing reverse thrust, he angled off Earth's path by a fraction of a degree. The drone adjusted to his course, its slavish response unnerving. Niall strengthened his shields against the mind probing his purpose here.

*You'll never have me, Lugus.*

Silence.

He tried again. *To come so far. All this effort when I have the whole universe open to me.*

*You cannot hide forever.*

What the hell? Niall bit his lip. The alien's command of his language made no sense. He probed the alien mind's defenses, seeking a way to burrow inside. What once worked on an unprepared Charles Biron now hit a protective wall denser than anything the Morrígan had established on Astereal. He tried a more direct approach. *Forever is a long time. What do you want?*

With me?

Lugus did not respond. Then something smashed into his privacy shields, demanding access to his mind. The shock wave reverberated through his consciousness. Niall threw off the attempt, and shifted course another degree, hoping to distract the alien. When the drone moved with him, Niall reversed the polarity, swung the Falcon into the shifting gravity well and shot off at Mach 2. The drone accelerated in pursuit. To Niall's alarm the two-kilometer ship was impressively responsive, but it was a subtle disturbance in the q-dimension that set his blood racing.

He explored the source, his mind entering the drone just as he had the first time, flying the Falcon on automatic, retaining his open channel to Macha and Pwyll. The matter containment field inside the drone was changing. He used the magnetic flux to his advantage. If he could bleed the sucker dry...

"Got to go," he warned Mission Control as he rapidly formed a link to Astereal and opened it with dark energy supplied by the enemy.

The drone snapped at his tail as he shot through the portal then accelerated. There was no time to think. Astereal dominated his view-screen filling the cockpit with a fiery brilliance before disappearing as he veered towards Bacchus. It was a risk, but closer proximity to the time-warping dark star would help him lock onto Lake Titicaca, and the past.

He rotated his head, trying to get a visual on the drone. It emerged out of his portal and turned hard in his direction. The tangible evidence of its personal interest intimidated Niall so much his hands began to shake. He fought to keep control of the Falcon. That's when he realized someone was missing.

*Macha! Where the hell's Pwyll?*

*I have you,* she responded. *Focus your mind. Your plan is working. Your instincts have not served you ill. But consider this—Astereal serves no purpose now. Send it there.*

*No. I won't risk the timeline.*

Pwyll interrupted. *Niall'Kearey? Colonel Hastor arrested Captain Whelan.* Pwyll's thought conveyed urgency.

*Talk fast,* Niall ordered.

*General Towden ordered me to probe Whelan's mind. The idea terrified Whelan and he admitted sabotage... says the catapult manifold valve has been blocked... that he was under presidential order to protect the timeline.*

Niall couldn't deal with this. The Falcon raced through Astereal's solar system at Mach 100. At this speed he would fly within Bacchus' range and struggle to escape its hold. On his console, the drone steadily caught up with him.

Niall found his link back to Earth.

*I see it,* Macha assured him. *Remember, Niall'Kearey. Trust in your instinct.*

Niall had no choice. He had no time for sightseeing, to second guess his timing. He traced back through the centuries and zeroed on the first lock that jumped out at him. It had the draw of a homing beacon. Only then did he realize the source was his own mind.

His presence from Earth's future, remote viewing Lake Titicaca's past in search of an orb.

Completing the circle.

Samsara, Tupac had called out, repeating the old woman's instructions to him, again and again. Unable to let the memory of the little boy go Niall had looked the word up. In many languages.

Samsara: the continuous flow of life.

A circle of time repeating over and over.

An existence echoing the past.

*Samsara.*

Niall locked onto his own mind from five years ago and plundered the dark energy sent by an unknown enemy to destroy his world. Wherever that world happened to be.

Earth was little more than collateral damage.

His portal opened and Niall shot through sending back a last whispered thought to Macha. *Don't let me go.*

# CHAPTER FORTY-SIX

He burst out above South America. The Falcon's guidance system automatically matched landmarks and plotted a course. Niall let the Falcon have its head. He could barely think. His head pounded. He breathed in deeply, grateful for the steady flow of oxygen filling his lungs, but the sense of nausea only worsened. Panic set in. His hand reached for the ejection handle. His fingers curled around it.

That sixth sense saved him.

The knowledge there was still something left for him to do.

The drone.

His mind steadied as the Falcon cleared the inner radiation belt. He leveled off, all the time decelerating. The drone emerged behind him.

Niall battled his mind for control. He didn't understand. The cockpit was hardened. Hardened from electromagnetic flux, but not from contact with his own mind.

Concentrate! Niall grabbed the firing control, placed his thumb over the firing button, and locked weapons onto the pursuing target. He waited for the automated weapons system to zero in on the preprogrammed spot where the matter containment field was weakest.

*Concentrate!* Nothing else mattered. The nuke had to detonate inside the drone's hull. He needed only a tiny hole to allow a perfectly placed missile to pass through.

The cross hairs blinked at him. An alarm intensified the longer he took. He pressed the button.

He sat there for a brief second, in an ejection seat primed to fail, on course for the Pacific Ocean, off the Peruvian-Chilean coast of ancient South America, with an unexplained, evil entity bent on destroying him hot on his tail. Nausea made him gag. His mind went blank. No Morrígan Queen spoke up to kick him out of his funk. His contact with Macha and Pwyll had been severed.

His fault. He'd lost focus.

Think.

*Think!*

There had never been anything to suggest he would make it back. His mission would succeed whether he lived or died. Fucking Balor didn't care whether Earth survived or not. His unknown nemesis would both lose the battle and win the war.

To hell with that.

His hand went for the ejection seat handle. What had Pwyll said? Manifold valve? Gas. Piston. Explosive. His neck crawled. Time slowed. Niall gripped the handle and let his subconscious out to play. In Sedona, he had sensed the earthquake coming. In Somalia his inner sight had detected a telegraph wire out of nowhere. Intuition saved his life countless times.

*Trust your instinct.* He could almost hear Macha's voice.

He didn't need an ejection trigger.

*He* could set off the explosive.

Niall confirmed his speed. Nine hundred miles per hour. Energy spurted from his fingers and set off an electrical cascade under his chair. Niall braced as the cockpit canopy blew backwards. His seat pulled his legs in close. He pulled his arms in tight. A terrific force pushed him back and Niall rammed up his privacy shields as his seat shot upwards. The alien couldn't be allowed to detect he had abandoned his ship.

It could still spot him. Change course.

Unable to move his head under the incredible G-forces he prayed the rocket system lifted him clear of the massive drone ship tailing him.

The wash of the drone's passage caught his seat at the top of its arc. Before he could free himself, the seat with him strapped inside started tumbling over and over. Earth, sea, and the night sky rotated around and around, increasing his nausea. He fought to control his breathing, stabbed for the button on the midriff strapping that would release him.

He made contact. His straps retracted, his seat spun away, its base clipping his head in passing. And then he was falling. He couldn't focus, stars inside and out. He nearly passed out from the shock wave caused by the alien drone entering the water.

The main event was still to come.

Had he bled enough dark energy? He couldn't tell. His brain felt ready to implode.

*Go home*, he willed his mind from the past. *I can't do this while you're here. Go home.*

His mind cleared. As the churning sensations eased, he arched his back. Arms and legs spread-eagled he slowed his descent enough to properly deploy his wing suit. An uplift of air nearly sent him spinning out of control, and then he was speeding towards Peru's coastline, and a little boy fleeing for his life in terror.

He didn't think it possible, but the ocean moved at a furious pace, his night vision goggles casting an eerie green hue on the frothing waters forging across the ancient palace. The Gate of the Sun disappeared under water. Niall fought to retain enough altitude to reach the terrified aura of light still several meters distant. Yerit had taught him enough to slow his descent.

The boy looked up, saw Niall hovering over him, and screamed.

*Samsara*, Niall sent to him, his mind searching for somewhere to go. He was in the past. Holes shimmered everywhere, nothing familiar. Too much choice. *Decide, goddammit. Now!*

His thoughts raced as he swooped down. He had visited only one other place in the past from Earth. Syria.

The orb.

Ogmios!

The raging waters rushed up to meet him. Tupac disappeared. Niall hauled oxygen into his burning lungs. He couldn't hear anything over the thudding double beat of his heart pumping on an adrenalin high. He didn't take his eyes off the spot where he had last seen the boy.

A hand appeared out of the murky froth.

The link jumped out at him.

Niall seized the hope of salvation and grabbed Tupac around the waist. With the boy's piercing shriek in his ear, the frothing waves drenching his suit and pulling him down, Niall and his small companion washed through the portal on the crest of a tsunami. They hit the Syrian Desert with a thud. Hard. Salt water carried them forward, engulfed them. Niall closed the portal shut with an explosive bang as he failed to control the release of dark energy from his bridge.

He realized he couldn't feel Tupac against his side. The water drained away. He sat up and pulled the oxygen mask off his nose. "Tupac!" he yelled, scanning the desert with his night goggles. A flicker of aura drew his attention. "Tupac!"

He stood up and promptly collapsed as a stabbing pain arced up his leg and through his hip. He spat out the horrid taste of salt in his mouth. It made no difference.

*Goddammit!*

He forced himself upright and dragged his injured foot alongside him as he hopped towards the tiny bedraggled form lying across the puddled sand. White hot pain in his ankle nearly stopped him, but losing Tupac now would hurt a helluva lot more.

As he reached the unconscious boy, guilt dropped Niall to one knee. He touched the boy's black hair. "Tupac," he whispered.

He bent down and listened for the sound of breathing. Nothing. Wiping his finger clean on his suit, Niall swept Tupac's mouth clear then turned the boy onto his back and began to pump his stomach gently. Water dribbled out of the boy's mouth. He pinched Tupac's nose and gently performed CPR, mentally counting the ticking seconds. One minute passed.

*Come on, Tupac. Fight, little one.*

He stopped, listened, and then Tupac coughed up more water. "Good, Tupac. Cough it all up."

Praying it hadn't been too long, Niall placed Tupac into the recovery position and checked for broken bones while trying to keep the boy's head still.

He couldn't feel any damage, but then he didn't exactly have an X-ray machine. Then it hit him. He could go one better. He extended his mind and found the place between Earth and the q-dimension where he could see everything. Broken bones included. Tupac had none. He was fine. Niall's own ankle was fractured, just millimeters off the healed bone from the previous break. Another clean break. His boot held the bone in place. He'd been lucky.

Lucky?

He needed certifying.

He looked up and wondered where he could find help. As long as it wasn't Ogmios. He could sense the Asterean's mind somewhere to the west. He would try the settlement to the south.

The little boy's coughs turned to hacking sobs. Niall picked him up and wrapped him in his arms, sharing his body warmth as he soothed the frightened child with soft words.

"It's okay, you're safe. Samsara, samsara."

Slowly, the violent heaves shaking Tupac's body eased until the boy slept fitfully in Niall's arms. Niall kept watch, using both his eyes and his inner vision to look out for predators and hostiles alike.

What a mess. He may have saved this little boy, but he'd killed Tupac's people to save his own. He didn't even know if Tupac had family. He'd watched the kid run around the town, seemingly independent, but then so had many other children. Tupac's mother, father, maybe sisters or brothers, all dead now.

Niall winced. *His* Earth, *his* future, *his* family, had to be safe. Any other alternative didn't bear thinking about after this. Unbidden tears wet his eyes and mashed his lips together, refusing to give in to indulgent despair. *Stop second guessing yourself and figure out a way home.*

Tupac stirred and Niall shifted to retain his balance, biting down a moan as a burning white fire shot up from his foot.

What now? He was completely unprepared. He hadn't anticipated the impact of his own mind's presence here in the past. With the exception of a nuclear bomb and his penknife, he hadn't packed a weapon. Dark energy at his fingertips had made him cocky. Anyway, twenty-first century weaponry would only invite attention he didn't want, although if Ogmios dared to show his face, Niall would happily bring an impromptu lightning display out to play. The murdering scum had showed no mercy to Succellos and Niall had a young boy to consider, an orb to find, and nothing would stop him finding his way home to the future. He couldn't shift the disturbing notion that one black hole in a tin can was only the beginning of Balor's campaign against him.

One enormous and terrifying question teased him. Why?

# CHAPTER FORTY-SEVEN

Niall laid the sleeping boy on the sand. The rising sun and the building warmth suggested it was summer in this ancient region of modern-day Syria. He sliced the inner lining of the leg sections of his wing suit into two keffiyeh-style scarves then placed one over Tupac's head to shield his face before tying one around his own head.

He had just finished tying the twisted cord he'd fashioned to hold it in place when Tupac sat bolt upright, then jumped to his feet. He pointed at Niall, shouting unintelligible words.

*Tupac. Enough.* Niall sent the thought directly into the boy's mind.

Tupac's eyes widened and his jaw dropped. The boy struck such a funny pose, Niall chuckled, inspiring Tupac to new heights of voluble indignation. When tears spilled onto Tupac's cheeks, Niall's grin faded.

"I'm sorry, kid. You're right, it's not funny." He scrunched his nose up and shook his head. "Bad samsara."

Tupac's tears vanished. He stared hard at Niall before walking right up to him. Before Niall could realize his intention, Tupac drew back his foot and kicked Niall's broken ankle. Hard.

"Ow!" Niall yelped, overbalancing and landing on his butt. "What the hell did you do that for?"

To his surprise, Tupac didn't laugh. If anything, he looked even more stunned.

"It's okay," Niall said, riding out the fire shooting through his foot, but a storm of disbelief and terror broke across Tupac's face. "No! Tupac! Wait!"

Too late, Tupac was off running across the desert.

*Shit.* Niall grabbed the boy's scarf and stuffed the wing sections inside his suit. Collecting up his headgear, Niall dragged himself up and began hobbling across the desert. A stabbing agony accompanied each jarring step. He could have done with a shortcut through space, but the distance was too close. "Tupac! Wait!"

Tupac kept on running. Niall caught up with him an hour later. The kid sat on a small outcrop of rock overlooking miles of desert. He sat, shoulders hunched, his head resting on folded arms.

Niall swallowed, beyond tired, his body feeling like a husk sucked dry by the desert heat. Waves of pain racked him. He felt baked and exhausted. His misery did not compare to the desolation radiating from this little kid. The stony ground looked a long distance away. He gingerly lowered himself down then nudged Tupac with the scarf.

"Put it on."

Tupac shook his head. Niall softened his tone. "Kid, it's for your own good."

The boy sighed, glanced at Niall's keffiyeh and then his black eyes met Niall's. Niall smiled, raising his eyebrows a little to encourage him. Finally, Tupac accepted the material and planted it on his head. Niall produced some more twisted material and helped Tupac tie it down.

"Good," Niall said. "Now we find water. I happen to be good at finding water."

Scanning with his mind, Niall located numerous clumps of brush growing along what looked to be a dried-up stream. "Here, help me up," he ordered, giving Tupac his hand. Tupac gamely took some of Niall's weight and Niall held in several curses. He began limping west, not needing to look back to see whether Tupac followed him.

As they came in sight of the dried-out stream bed, Tupac ran forward, shouting excitedly and pointing. Niall stopped and watched the boy grab a stone and study the rocky silted soil before starting to dig. When Tupac showed no sign of stopping, Niall eased his way to a rock and carefully lowered himself down. It could be a mistake. He might not be able to get up again.

Tupac dug like a demon possessed. Niall might have stopped him, but he sensed water not far below and they wouldn't survive long without it. Instead, he scanned the rocky desert farther afield and discovered Ogmios closing in on them.

Now an old man, the former Asterean Councilor relied on a twisted branch to keep him upright. His scraggly beard reached his chest. He paused, as if sensing Niall observing him from afar.

*Niall'Kearey. I ask for a hearing.*

Niall tensed.

The Asterean's head tilted. *I have been expecting you. I've paid my dues for Succellos. The High Brighid made sure I did not escape justice on your side of the universe. Now I live out the rest of my days in exile.*

*Why should I believe anything you say?*

*I am giving you unfettered access to my mind.*

Niall didn't hesitate. He scaled the lowered shields of the Asterean's mind, set siege, and bonded with the man. As Ogmios lost control of his body, he collapsed to his knees. Niall felt his pain and shoved out Ogmios' hand to stop him busting his head open on rock. Then he made Ogmios draw a shuddering breath.

*Lir's sea, have mercy! I am not used to this.*

*Mercy? The same mercy you showed Succellos? And the Morrigan? You forget. I saw dead Morrigan butchered on your orders.*

*I can give you the orb.*

*What? You're going to bribe me to spare your miserable life? I don't need you to find the orb.*

Ogmios fell silent. Niall sensed a growing horror and quickly ramped up his privacy shields, but Ogmios had already glimpsed the truth.

*If the information you seek about Balor is on the orb, I can help you find it,* he tempted Niall.

Niall's inner laugh was bitter. *After what you did, why should I trust you?* Ogmios rallied up a bid for control of his body and mind, but Niall refused to be thrown out. *Uathach told me about your sister. Show me!*

His prisoner moaned and then Niall was in a barn watching Ogmios' father remonstrating with a group of Morrígan. They had been caught foraging the harvest. Suddenly, a Morrígan yanked Ogmios' arm back and yanked him outside, forcing the father and several laborers to back off. Out of nowhere, a little girl flew into the melee, armed with a metal wrench she could barely lift above her shoulder. The Morrígan focused on her father swung around to meet the approaching threat. Everything happened very fast. The back swing of the Morrígan's sword sliced off the little girl's head. Blood spurted everywhere. Ogmios screamed. His father turned deathly pale then dropped to his knees beside his daughter. The Morrígan all stared in horror before running for their lives. Yelling farmhands raced after them in hot pursuit.

Ogmios had run to his sister's head and picked it up. He tried to reattach the grisly remains to its body, but he could barely see, the gory detail obliterated by the blur of his tears. Niall's angry condemnation of the former Councilor eased. That one horrific senseless moment had scarred Ogmios for life; transformed a young innocent boy into a pit of hatred.

He remembered to let Ogmios draw breath and discovered the old man on his hands and knees, weeping into the desert sand.

Ogmios fought for control of his mind and Niall could not withhold it from him any longer.

*I waited years to take my revenge,* the Asterean said, his voice trembling from the force of long-buried emotions brought back to life. *I still remember the celebrations when you killed their Queen Nuada. You drove the Morrígan back from our lands. You hated the Morrígan, too.* Outrage edged his thought. *You have no right to judge me.*

*I misunderstood the Morrígan,* Niall admitted. *I heard the stories of pillaging and attacks by Morrígan on the Asterean and I never questioned what argument had brought them to that state.*

He had helped banish the Morrígan to the Southern continent and his shame would always haunt him. Succellos had been the only one prepared to listen to the Morrígan's side of the story.

*You bullied a good man seeking only to learn the truth,* Niall accused Ogmios, *and when that didn't work, you murdered him.*

*He was consorting with the enemy. The Morrigan were attacking our sky cities.*

*You should have taken your concerns to the High Council.*

To Niall's surprise, Ogmios subsided, his inner defenses down.

*Yes, this I accept. But you must accept that I have served the punishment meted out to me by the Council. I served my time and am now exiled from my people.*

*Then how do you know of the orb?*

*It stands out strong in your thoughts. I suspect the village you sought exists in the future, but your mind sensed me.*

Niall remembered this. He had homed in on the memory of a familiar mind.

*I think I know where the orb might be,* Ogmios continued. *The Astereans you settled on this land constructed a temple many months walk from here. I will show you the link. I can see my way, but I cannot summon the energy to form the bridge. This world, your Earth, is different, but you can.*

*What do you want in return?*

*To have my exile commuted. I am old, Niall'Kearey. I wish to die with my people.*

Niall suddenly woke up to his physical surroundings. He stared into Tupac's curious eyes and felt a small hand touch his cheek.

Ogmios' voice whispered in his mind. *Niall'Kearey?*

Niall considered his options then sighed. *Find us. I will think it over.*

He let Ogmios go and blinked. Tupac burst into a stream of unintelligible noise, pointing behind him and then Niall understood. Tupac had found water, clean-looking water. It bubbled up out of rock and trickled along the sun-bleached bed.

"Okay!" Niall smiled and patted Tupac on the shoulder. Bracing for the pain, he got back onto his feet and limped towards the stream. The water tasted pure, but he didn't want to risk the boy. While Tupac collected brush, Niall got out his knife, sliced off a small section of his t-shirt then pulled out a fire steel rod from his knife's leather sheath. Minutes later, he was adding kindling to the flames within a small circle of rocks. Tupac stopped to watch.

"More," Niall said with a shooing gesture. He picked up and shook the kindling. "More."

Tupac spun around and darted off. Niall watched him for a second. The kid was amazing.

He looked around him for a suitable rock and then decided the one he was sitting on would do the trick. The underground stream held a small amount of magnetic flux, enough to generate a few blasts of dark energy that he hurled at the stone until he'd formed a hollow.

Tupac ran back, shouting in alarm.

"It's okay," Niall said showing Tupac the rock. As Niall fed the fire Tupac skipped back and forth, filtering water through Niall's t-shirt into the newly-formed container. Niall wore his gloves to drop a couple of heated stones into the water.

Ogmios reached them shortly after sunset. Niall had tracked his progress, and had to acknowledge Ogmios' stubborn resilience. When he shuffled up to the fire and let out a heartfelt sigh, Niall held out his hand. "Give me your bowl."

Ogmios dropped a leather pack to the ground, rummaged inside, then handed over a carved wooden bowl. Niall scooped up some water and handed it back. He watched the man who had killed Succellos drink it down. Ogmios' hands shook so much that the precious water dribbled over the bowl's sides.

Niall could not have kept his mind closed enough for Ogmios cast him an angry look. "I killed one man! You killed thousands of Morrígan in your time on Astereal. You just destroyed the last of the Paladin. Many would call that genocide. Or perhaps, having given life, you believe you have the right to confiscate it again."

Niall rammed up his shields, stung by the comparison. "I did it to save the future!"

"Does the boy understand that?"

Tupac frowned, perhaps sensing the newcomer referred to him.

"No of course not."

Ogmios stuck out his chin, belligerent, accusing. "I paid for my crimes."

Niall glowered back. "Don't test me, Ogmios."

"Balance is the natural law of the universe. Good must be paid for with bad. There was always going to be a price for saving an entire world from annihilation. Deep down, I suspect you know this."

Niall stared at him hard, taken aback by the fierceness of Ogmios' challenge. He hadn't destroyed the Paladin civilization out of vengeful hatred, but still a flush of doubt heated his ears. He changed the subject, his voice aggravatingly hoarse. "Where's the orb?"

Ogmios took a few moments to simmer down. "I can take you to Ceo. She's the daughter of the leader you placed here. She will know." He laughed sourly. "You will receive a hero's welcome. They will probably throw a feast in your honor. The man who saved us all."

Niall's hackles rose at Ogmios' bitter tone. "Don't bother. I'll find them myself. Shouldn't be too hard."

"The settlement split up. We are two generations further on, different groups spread far and wide. You hate me so much you cannot accept my help?" His shoulders drooped. "My bones ache. My spirit is tired. If you cannot bear to appeal on my behalf then find the decency to kill me now."

Niall studied the dying fire. Soon they would run out of firewood. Tupac needed food. Water. He had discovered links to several nearby settlements, but none to the world of Niall's time. He looked at Ogmios with a conciliatory gaze. "I need a scholar on temporal bridges."

Ogmios grimaced. "Few exist. Even Succellos' skills were limited to visions of the future. After Succellos, Nantosuelta understood the subject best, but she mainly studied the theory. Of course, Uathach possessed the natural ability, but she always disapproved of tampering with the timeflow."

Niall snorted. "Tell me about it." He threw more brush onto the embers and poked the fire with a stick. The temperatures were dropping fast. "Nantosuelta went with the Asterean fleet. And Uathach is dead."

Ogmios nodded; a reflective gesture more than anything else. "I remember being told Nanto had left us. Then I cannot help you." He paused. "The High Brighid is dead? She was supposed to go to your time. What happened?"

Niall wondered how much he should share of the future with a man who formed part of Earth's past, a man already aware of the orb's existence, and now of its importance. "It doesn't matter."

"Mmm... I suspect it does." Ogmios sighed, his posture carrying the look of a defeated man. The light from the fire flickered on his face. His eyes lost focus and Niall sensed a link forming in the Asterean's mind. "Babylon," Ogmios said, showing him ornately carved openings hewn into rock. "A city in the making. Ceo is an insightful leader. She will want to help you."

Niall stared at stone terraces of cascading plants and waterfalls. One of the seven unknown wonders of the world. Some even doubted Babylon had ever existed. The sight of the lost city filled him with awe.

"I never agreed to help you," Niall pointed out softly.

"I know," Ogmios replied. "I have much to atone for. As do you. We are kindred spirits, you and I. Deny it or not as you wish."

# CHAPTER FORTY-EIGHT

Slightly disbelieving, Niall pressed the spot Ceo indicated and then stepped back as the huge stone swung smoothly aside revealing a simple shelf. His heart jumped to see the orb sitting just where Ceo had promised it would be.

"Unbelievable," he said to her. "You're sure there are no hidden death traps in this place."

The Asterean elder looked confused. "My father hid the orb very carefully, Niall'Kearey, just as the High Brighid instructed him. He did not design this place to kill anyone. He planned that I would be the last to know of the orb's existence. On my death, my body would be sealed in this crypt, buried in the foundations of a temple to the gods." She smiled at Niall's startled look. "The natives of this world are very superstitious. They would never defile a place of worship."

"Nothing lasts forever, Ceo, but I can safely say that Babylon will become the stuff of legend. You are creating a beautiful legacy to the Asterean people." Niall picked up the silvery globe that encased the orb he sensed within its confines. "Thank you, Ceo. I mean that. I'm sorry to be so cryptic, but this orb may hold vital information to help us fight off an enemy in the future."

"I understand."

"Will Ogmios be a problem for you?"

She shook her head. "He shared his mind. He wants to die in comfort. Who can blame him? There is no one here who has more cause to deny him this than you. We will respect your wishes to grant him clemency. What will you do now?"

"I need to work that out."

"You and Tupac are welcome to stay with my family. The healer would like more time to work on your ankle. She could have done more for you on Astereal, but our abilities are limited on this world."

Niall shook his head. "I can walk on it. It will be fine."

"If you need someone to care for Tupac, my son and his betrothed will happily take him in."

Niall hesitated. Tupac would be happy here, but it would be a wrench to leave him behind. "I'm not sure what my plans are yet. Maybe when I've discovered the orb's secrets."

Ceo smiled. "Take as long as you need. No one will disturb you here. Should we expect you for evening meal?"

Niall smiled a yes.

When her footsteps had faded away, Niall opened the globe casing and touched the shimmering orb inside. Data spilled out, filling the tomb with wondrous light and images, a delicate spider's web of information. Fortunately, Sohan had shown him a hidden search facility. When Niall entered the name Balor, information spun out across the open crypt.

His heart jumped and he started to read.

Niall ramped up his privacy shields and knocked on the door to Ogmios' room.

The door opened a crack then opened wide. Ogmios looked surprised to see him. "I did not think I would see you again," he said.

Standing back, the old man let Niall in.

Niall looked about the spacious room. Hard to believe nothing this sophisticated city had ever been discovered in his time. He wanted to know what had happened to Babylon. So many civilizations had vanished on Earth in just thousands of years perhaps he was deluding himself thinking he could or even should preserve the civilization of his time. What would be left of his Earth five thousand years on from his generation?

Balor had survived hundreds of thousands.

"Tell me about the tapestry hanging in the College, the one depicting the War of Ages."

"This is to do with Balor?"

"Yes."

Ogmios gestured Niall to a seat. Preferring to stand, Niall noticed the careful way Ogmios lowered himself into a chair at a square wooden table. Although frail with great age, now he was cleaned up with his beard neatly trimmed, Ogmios looked more like the haughty, closed Councilor Niall had met and distrusted on Astereal. The man's experiences on Earth had changed Ogmios. His aura had mellowed and Niall sensed no hidden agenda. Ogmios had grown beyond political games and yet, Niall did not trust him.

He watched the older man's eyes dim in memory. "The tapestry you saw on Astereal was not the original. It was the last of many replicas depicting an historic account of love and war. 'War of Ages' is just one ancient title attributed to the tapestry. I cannot testify to the accuracy of its subject, or say if giants with one all-seeing eye are based in fact or are simply the product of a fertile imagination."

"Macha inherited a pendant, an eye inset into a triangle, from her mother, the Queen Nuada."

"You suspect a connection?" Ogmios shook his head. "The design could simply be the remnants of an earlier time. Long ago, the Morrígan and Asterean shared the city of Navan. They certainly knew of the original work."

"I know they did." Agitated, Niall began to pace the room. "I remote-viewed Astereal earlier today."

Ogmios' aura brightened with interest. "And?"

"Navan looks awesome. For a brief moment, I saw Morrígan and Asterean living together in harmony, but when they sensed my presence, a wall went up."

"You present an unknown threat. You had a child's mind when you first visited Astereal, no threat at all." Ogmios studied him. "What of the timeflow?"

"Astereal and Earth seem to be in Alignment."

"That makes sense."

"Why?"

"The records of time flow divergence are sketchy, but it is recorded that High Brighids could travel the cosmos, certainly before the time of the Great Divide." Ogmios let out a bark of surprise and pointed at him. "You intend to go to Astereal!"

"The orb didn't answer my questions. I stand more chance getting the information I need in Astereal's past. If not, I can always return."

"You hope."

"I get a better sense of Earth's time flow from a distance."

"So, what do you want from me?"

"When our minds bonded, I glimpsed a memory of the night you killed Succellos."

Ogmios blanched. "Please, I have paid for my crime."

"What did he say? Don't make me force it from you."

"Succellos was rambling. He made no sense. Not at the time." Ogmios frowned. "It was a long time ago. I need to remember his precise words." After a few moments, his expression settled into quiet satisfaction. "Succellos said..." His words emerged slowly, weighted with the passage of a lifetime. "He said that Macha could be trusted."

"That's it?" Disappointment turned Niall's mouth dry. He walked forward and planted his palms on the table. "Think, Ogmios! Why would he say that?"

Ogmios waved his hand for quiet. "I intuited his meaning, but it made no sense. He meant Macha was not her mother."

The memory of his bloody duel with the former Morrígan Queen chilled Niall's thoughts. Nuada had refused to die, and he really did have to rip out her heart to kill her, no doubt fueling the fantastic myth Ogmios had drawn on to justify butchering Morrígan dead by the hundreds.

"Something to do with Nuada's blood," Ogmios continued. "Something he meant to tell you."

"Nuada's blood?"

"Before Sohan, Succellos was our foremost expert on the Morrígan. Nuada's remains were taken back to the College. Analyzed. I recall reading a report that her genetic code was infected by an unknown parasite."

Niall rocked back on his heels. "Why was I not told this?"

"You did not visit Astereal again for many seasons. The moment of interest passed."

No one had realized the significance. Balor's virus would explain Nuada's aggression, her determination to rise up again and again, except she had not touched him, she had touched Sohan.

Kean Morgan sired him. Nuada tried to kill him. Herecura to seek him out. Finally, Muhuza.

All of them, demented.

"That is all I know," Ogmios declared. "Do you know what Succellos was trying to say?"

Niall nodded. "I think he wanted me to see past my prejudice—he was a wise man." Although Niall doubted Succellos understood the significance of Nuada's affliction. If he had lived, Niall might have discovered his heritage sooner. He gazed down on Ogmios and steeled himself to finish what he had come here to do. "I'm sorry, but you know too much and I have to protect the future."

The older man's eyes widened with fear quickly eclipsed by an instinctive horror. He pushed back as Niall directed an electromagnetic pulse directly into Ogmios' defenseless brain. As the left side of the Asterean's face sagged, Niall moved around to catch a slack-mouthed Ogmios before he hit the floor. He carried the frail almost weightless body to the soft pallet that was his bed.

"You got your wish, old man, to die in comfort. Ceo's people will care for you well. It's more than you gave Succellos."

Niall let the magnetic forces of the mountain range flow through him, assessing the surrounding flux before turning to Ceo.

"Yes, this will do. Thank you, Ceo. For everything." He would miss her, and her family. They had welcomed him with open arms and he couldn't be more grateful.

"We will take good care of Tupac, Niall'Kearey," Ceo said, giving the young boy a gentle squeeze of his shoulders.

Tupac burst into a furious spiel of protest, his hands gesticulating wildly as his eyes welled up with a distress that exceeded Niall's expectation.

Niall dropped down to one knee, put the orb down beside him then caught Tupac's upper arms firmly. "You will be happy here, Tupac. These people will look after you, love you." His voice cracked. His world was messed up, his family in turmoil. So much to fix. He couldn't bring back a child, or abandon him on an alien planet. "This is your time, Tupac."

"No, no. Samsara, samsara!"

Niall's throat seized up. Tupac's anguish killed him. "I'm not sure I understand your samsara," he said in a hoarse whisper.

"I think he means you are connected," Ceo offered.

"You see, Tupac? Ceo understands you far better than I do."

"Niall'Kearey, please! I be good. No trouble," Tupac pleaded, his lower lip quivering.

Niall gazed at him helplessly. Tupac reminded him of Toby in so many ways. The turbulence Tupac stirred in him almost changed his mind. "I'm sorry, Tupac. This is your home now."

The boy dismissed his tears with a swipe of his hand. "I hate Niall'Kearey!" he yelled before turning away, his stance cold and angry.

For a moment, Niall could not get up. He remained stuck on one knee as Tupac ran from him and back to the growing city of Babylon. Ceo's young nephew bolted after him. Tupac's sorrow packed a powerful punch. He should have said his goodbyes at Babylon then sneaked out and saved the kid this misery.

With heavy heart, Niall forced himself up, collected the orb, and found the link to Astereal in his mind. Focusing on the square in Navan, he created his bridge and as he stepped across to another world, Tupac's anguished face burned a resting place in his memory.

# CHAPTER FORTY-NINE

Niall watched the widening gulf between Morrígan and Asterean spark a torrent of angry words he struggled to follow. In the stone Council Chamber, the members of Astereal's High Council stood on their feet, their auras thick with the black rot of fear. There was an undercurrent here Niall didn't understand and his pulse raced, every sinew of muscle wound tight to the point he almost forgot to breathe.

"Balor will send Formorri—" Cetheru protested.

"No one disputes the danger," Valen said, cutting the Morrígan Councilor off. Opposing voices drowned out his authoritative voice. Anxiety creased the High Brighid's brow and he threw Niall a furious look.

Niall rose from his stone bench. "I didn't come here to cause trouble between you—" His words dried up as a stunned silence preceded a wave of rebuke headed his way. The people of Astereal's past had received him graciously, but with a reticence he wasn't used to, not on this planet.

Impatience edged Niall's tone. "There is no record of Balor's presence in this galaxy before my time. You have nothing to fear. But Asterean legend tells of an exodus that brought your kind to Astereal. I need to know where you came from. Tell me what you know so I can use this knowledge to protect Earth in the future!"

"You cannot reach your time! This Earth of the future! Knowledge will not help you," Cetheru countered. Large eyes in an enormous head bore into Niall, the hints of gold in his square pupils flickering to black. Talons extended from four digits before retracting again. The Morrígan's aura radiated his mistrust.

"Reaching my time may take longer than I had hoped—"

Valen shook his head. "A bridge to your world, your future, will break the timeline you seek to protect. It is inevitable."

"No—"

"You will die," an elderly Morrígan warned.

The High Brighid grimaced. "Trantor speaks with truth, Major'Kearey. All is connected. The body belongs with the universe of its birth. A bridge across time cascades degeneration when cells shift out of phase with the natural timeline." Valen's eyes shifted to Cetheru as the Morrígan gestured towards Niall. Their auras intensified with dissension, and Niall grasped in an intuitive leap that Cetheru knew Niall withheld information from them.

They all did.

"The Ancient Prophecy is vague," Niall explained. "I must be careful how much I reveal—"

Cetheru rounded on him. "You ask us to destroy our world. *This* knowledge you *have* revealed!"

"Let him speak, Cetheru," Valen intervened.

Cetheru's mouth formed a snarl. His taloned finger stabbed towards Niall. "We have always been safe here. At peace." He redirected his fury towards Valen. "The Morrígan do not exist in his future. He claims to be the one to save us, but he will destroy our kind and save yours. Balor has been stricken from our hearts and minds for good reason. We do not speak of Balor and that is the way it will remain."

Niall lowered his head in defeat. He stood on a small island rising precariously out of a torrential river that one day would form the majesty of the Fel, the last habitable place on all of Astereal to succumb to a sea of lava. Overhead, a radiant sunset cast its spell across the violet sky, setting the crystal spires of Navan afire. Behind him, Astereal's second moon crested forest-fringed hills forming the geological footprint for the mountain ranges of the future—a distant future that lay beyond his reach. He had been here several moon cycles and the aching chasm in his heart deepened with every passing day. The link to Earth never changed. The distant future eluded him, and he could find no clue of his existence in Earth's accessible timeline, nothing to guide his way back to his time, his people.

*I need to go home.*

His promise to Toby bore down on him. His children needed him to come home, and the thought of Tami turning to Miach for comfort soured his mouth and darkened his heart. No, she loved him, she had promised to wait. If he returned to the point in time that he had left, there would be no paradox. If he left for Earth now, and kept moving, never staying long enough to disrupt anything...

What if he returned years *or even decades* too late? What if Miach got his chance to worm his way into her bed? What if he was written off as a dead man, a martyr who saved the world? Eventually she would succumb to her love for Miach. There was little Niall could do to stop it from happening—except to get his ass home as fast as possible.

The unexpected opening of a portal broke the dark path of his thoughts. Valen conjured up bridges so casually he made Niall feel clumsy in comparison, but then Astereal's magnetic grid was strong, an abundant source of energy for the sky cities to come.

"Did I disturb you?" Niall asked carefully.

"I think all of Navan sense your numerous attempts to reach Earth." Valen dusted off his blue tunic that dropped to his knees. Loose white pants swamped his sandaled feet. Current Asterean fashion reminded Niall of traditional Indian dress. The austere robes of Uathach's time had not yet infiltrated the High Council.

"I thought maybe I could establish a bridge to Earth from a point in Astereal's future."

Pale blue eyes studied Niall. "I see." His awkward pause prepared Niall for bad news. Valen expelled a gruff sigh. "The High Council continues to debate your request to study our records of Balor."

"I never intended to cause dissent."

The High Brighid harrumphed. "Your vocabulary has improved quickly during your time with us."

His pointed tone set Niall on edge. "Your language hasn't changed much," he replied carefully. Judging by Valen's expression, the High Brighid expected more. "I grew up on two worlds and I must have absorbed more Asterean than I realized."

"Cetheru has noticed your knowledge of the Morrígan language is limited."

Niall's pulse jumped. "I had less contact with the Morrígan." His tone came out evasive and Valen raised a disbelieving eyebrow.

"The Morrígan have drawn their conclusions." The High Brighid shook his shaven head. "You claim Astereal will die, that you are the one to offer salvation. Well, all must come to its natural end."

Niall didn't hide his confusion. "I've told you everything the Ancient Prophecy allows me, and no more."

"We have never heard of this Ancient Asterean Prophecy. Not until now."

Niall's stomach dropped. He couldn't have gone back more than fifteen thousand years on Earth. He had hit Astereal further back into its past than he'd thought possible. "You never said. Why didn't you say?"

"We needed to decide if we trusted the prophet."

Niall closed his eyes as his world shifted once more. Prophet. He was the prophet, the doomsayer. He tried to recall his precise words since arriving on Astereal. He had given away so little. It didn't matter. He had told them that Astereal would one day fall apart under the pull of the dark stars and that the Astereans would find refuge on planet Earth. He met Valen's knowing gaze.

"Samsara," he said on a sigh. Tupac had been right all along.

"Precisely. There is no escaping the circular nature of truth. What will happen has happened, or you would not be here." Valen studied their surroundings as the final rays of Astereal's sun disappeared, chased by the promise of a moon hovering below the horizon. The sky turned a dusky hue. "Why are you here?" Valen's right hand signaled the river.

"This island is where I crossed over from Astereal to Earth, as close as I can work out. I hoped... that maybe..."

"The timeflows are in alignment. You can return to your Earth of the past. Live out your life quietly."

"I came here to learn about Balor. You have to understand. I've sensed a presence." Niall shuddered. "A mind I'll never forget—"

Valen held up a hand. "Stop, Major'Kearey. Your emotions are leaking, and it is important this discussion remains private."

As Niall fortified his defenses, the High Brighid gestured to a shimmering portal that effortlessly materialized with the flick of the High Brighid's hand.

"Let us return to Navan. There is much I have to tell you."

To Niall's surprise they emerged inside the College library. The place was eerily deserted, almost as if Valen had prearranged a private sanctuary. The High Brighid walked across to a hanging tapestry that bore only a vague resemblance to the one Niall had seen hanging in the College of Navan's future. They studied the escalating scenes of carnage. Niall translated the title. *War of Ages.* Not much hope on offer in this depiction.

Valen traced his fingers along a silvery filament that wove an undulating path from one side of the tapestry to the other. "Your memory of Balor's touch gives credence to everything we know of Balor. He is a monster, an entity that feeds off the memory stream."

"Memory stream?"

"The memory stream is a... place, a dimension that collects the conversion of sentient energy from one realm to the next."

Niall frowned heavily, reminded of something Etlinn had said. "We have a theory that an energy burst from the brain's neuron paths can send a message back to Balor, but it only seems to affect those with a genetic mutation." He paused—Valen looked distracted. "High Brighid, is something wrong?"

Valen placed a hand on Niall's sleeve, a gesture of caution. "Strengthen your shields." Turning on his heel, he walked over to a cabinet and pulled out a leather-bound folder. Bringing it back, he opened it to an illustration of a brain notated by mathematical formula.

"We believe death initiates a transfer of energy between dimensions, a burst of energy encapsulating a lifetime's learning and knowledge. Short term memory is converted first. Useful information. It is said the Formorri routinely raid the stream for strategic information on enemy movements. Of course, the energy dissipates naturally, but it is speculated that the stream retains an echo of every memory."

Niall couldn't hide his doubt.

Valen frowned with disapproval even as his aura bespoke indifference. "You must remember this is in Balor's universe. Here it is very different, or Astereal would have been discovered by now. It may be that this genetic mutation you mention diverts the normal flow of energy in this universe, and somehow activates the mind to access the memory stream."

"I don't understand," Niall said. Valen threw him a warning look and Niall dropped his voice as he contained his growing sense of dread. "Are you saying Balor is from another universe?" At Valen's nod, Niall's panic mounted. "Then how can I find him?"

"You cannot. Balor is consciousness. You need to attract his attention, but the attempt would be futile, suicide. The only language Balor understands is dominion over all. The Formorri are his weapon, designed to impose his will throughout the universe. *His universe.*"

"Go on."

"We always believed escaping to this universe put us beyond Balor's reach. Our ancestors stumbled upon Astereal by chance." Valen nudged at Niall's mind. "If you wish me to trust you, you must trust me to do what is right with the knowledge your mind grants me."

Natural caution battled with Niall's need to know. Need to know won. He flinched as Valen trawled through Niall's memories, darting down neural paths and raking over painful wounds. The cataclysmic images of Astereal's destruction turned the High Brighid pale. He staggered towards a chair.

Despite his grey pallor, Valen's aura reflected not a hint of his inner turmoil, spurring Niall to match the High Brighid's mental discretion. The Asterean leader explored Niall's knowledge of the Ancient

Prophecy carefully, and then traced the events that had brought Niall back to Astereal's past.

*I see.* Valen's thought came across strong and sure. *The cycle must not be broken. The High Brighid of your time was correct in this regard. I see this now.* A dip of his eyebrows spoke of a new respect, but one tinged with horror. Apprehension crawled under Niall's collar. Valen leaned forward, creating an air of mystery. *The knowledge of how we came to this world has been passed down the line of High Brighids and no other to reduce the risk of discovery by Balor. You must protect this secret both with your life and in your death.*

The Asterean's mind invited him in, but Niall sensed Valen's reticence.

*Tell me,* he pressed Valen. *On the island you said, 'what has happened, will happen'. My very presence here is proof of that. I came for this. I need to know.*

Valen's mind wrinkled with indecision. *The High Council is concerned your knowledge could alter the timeline... if it enters the memory stream.*

*I won't let that happen.*

*Our future tells me this.* Still Valen hesitated. *Tell me what you intend to do.*

Niall's mouth set into a grim line. "Find a way to stop Balor."

"You cannot do this without undoing your past. Destroying Balor will alter the future timelines of two universes. Your existence came into being when Balor's mutation infected your father. Your existence enabled our migration to your world. Our people altered the path of human evolution. All would unravel in an ever-expanding paradox."

"I understand this, but I can stop Balor in the future, if I understand what I'm dealing with. He has to have a weakness. Dammit! You have to tell me. I saved your people. Help me save mine. Both our races are threatened, together, on Earth. Our two peoples' fates are tied. It doesn't matter how much time separates us."

Valen bowed his head and sighed. "Yes, and that is the conclusion of the High Council, the majority view." He nodded at Niall's look of surprise then got up and walked to the wall-hanging, the *War of Ages.*

Niall followed him, puzzled. The Council had seemed so emphatic in its opposition.

Valen pointed to a swirling constellation woven into the star background, but his eyes stayed on Niall. *Bacchus is the link to Balor's universe.*

The thought pooled in Niall's mind.

*The dark star?*

It made sense—the amount of dark energy in a black hole had to be colossal. "Uathach knew nothing of this," Niall said, choosing his words carefully.

"Your knowledge indicates that much of the events that led us to this planet have been lost over time. The Morrígan and the gryphon are both products of Balor's experiments, hybrid mutations of different species, including our own."

"I knew this about the gryphon, but not of the Morrígan."

"Balor mixed our ancestor's code with that of the Formorri and made it vulnerable to radiation. The Morrígan on Astereal do not resemble the Morrígan that came here, the radiation in this galaxy altered them. The pure Formorri gene breaks down outside of their universe before stabilizing in another form."

"So, they sent a drone instead," Niall said. Max had theorized that the radiation in Earth's galaxy was different to Astereal's, and the Morrígan's genetic code had quickly regressed on Earth. The gryphons died out altogether. Kestra would be the last. "Balor has found a technological means to access our universe. Or at least this Lugus has. Is Lugus Formorri?"

"Based on the mind I glimpsed in your memories, yes."

Valen led Niall to a small alcove where the High Brighid settled into a comfortable winged chair. "Balor needs the Formorri to retain control of his universe, but do not be fooled, he will sacrifice his servants without pause. He may have sent a drone this time, but he would not hesitate to send his agents the next, even though it would be a death sentence for them to spend any significant time in this universe. Devout servants, the unquestioning fools consider their sacrifices to Balor a blessing."

Niall took the seat opposite. He leaned forward, resting his arms on his knees. *How did the Asterean and Morrigan find this world?*

*A fortuitous accident. Morrigan rebels on a flight of gryphons helped a group of Astereans escape a Formorri prison. When their escape was detected, one of the Astereans built a bridge. He was weak, but with the Formorri closing in, no one stopped to think. Unsurprisingly, their bridge began to collapse, but one of the Morrigan, a powerful bridge builder, glimpsed Bacchus. He transferred the bridge through the dark star to Astereal. The Formorri never followed. They probably assumed all had perished in the initial link.* "This world has proved safe from the Formorri ever since."

Niall's brow furrowed and then a terrible realization shook him to the core. He straightened. "Even if Balor doesn't know about Bacchus now, in my time he's found a way through. I have to go there! I need to find a way to stop Balor reaching this universe ever again."

Valen's silvery blue eyes held Niall's gaze. "The High Council believed you would decide this, and your past suggests we continue to live free from the Formorri until this future Alignment, but you cannot take the data orb with you. It is too dangerous. If it fell into the wrong hands it could lead Balor to Astereal before your time. Neither can you leave it here. You must hide it deep in the q-dimension where only you can retrieve it."

"Is that possible?"

"Yes. If a bridge collapses, anything in transit is trapped. I can teach you how to protect the orb from the forces of time and space. Only High Brighids possess this knowledge."

Niall frowned. "Uathach didn't know this."

"Are you sure?"

"There was a bridge that collapsed. People died. Uathach wasn't sure what would happen. I accessed her mind often. I shared her grief. Her helplessness. She didn't know."

Valen nodded. "Then I will ensure this knowledge dies with me." His piercing gaze gripped Niall's attention. *From the moment of your arrival, I knew you heralded a change in the natural order. I saw it, but...* Valen's apprehension stole through Niall's mind. The High Brighid struggled with his decision. "I fear if you take this step, there will be no turning back."

Niall bowed his head. He wanted to go home. He longed to cherish the woman he loved. Return his children their father. Still, the universe continued to thwart him. Deep inside he knew Valen was right. There could be no turning back. He could only go forward.

"This is my chance. To stop Balor from destroying everything I love."

If he didn't take it the consequences were unimaginable. How far would he go to preserve his world? A world he might never see again.

His mind reached out to Valen. *I have to go through the dark star.*

A seed of determination blew into existence. From the stars of another universe to Earth, a way home existed somewhere and he would find it. Then close it behind him. Whatever it took.

# CHAPTER FIFTY

Astride a pair of obsidian-colored gryphons, Niall and Valen chased the second moon east to the Central Rift. He and the High Brighid of Astereal retraced the journey Niall and Uathach would one day travel at a distant point in Astereal's future, a flight that had changed Niall's life. The Lir'Mara glittered on the horizon, a silvery crescent of ocean that in the centuries ahead would form a physical barrier dividing the Morrígan from their Asterean cousins.

The wind tore at Niall's face. Muscles contracted beneath him as the gryphon's powerful wings sliced the air. Tension, trepidation, and fear honed his awareness to a razor-sharp edge.

Past and future merged into one.

Uathach's revelation of his destiny had been a small link in a larger chain. Neither he nor Uathach knew then that saving the people of Astereal from extinction involved steering the course of human evolution.

The ramifications rumbled on.

Valen's mind opened, inviting Niall in. *The Central Rift is the source of a magnetic vortex that is channeled along the Varal Meridian. We have barely begun to tap its potential.*

Niall kept his thoughts private. In the future, those same forces would support a web of sky cities. He had tutored Valen on the Ancient Prophecy, and he trusted the High Brighid to conceal the full truth from the generations to come, but Niall had to believe he wasn't the architect of every detail.

Valen pointed to a precipice overlooking the Rift valley. Niall nodded his understanding and led the way. Their gryphons landed with skillful precision on a rock protrusion that led skyward, a fanciful pathway to heaven, or to another universe. Niall swung his leg over his gryphon's back and slid to the ground—an untidy dismount that did the job. He strode to the pinnacle of a granite-like outcrop and looked across the valley. They were at a dizzying height and his body thrummed to the inner pulse of the spiraling forces emanating from the planet's core.

Magnetic forces at war—a never-ending tug of war between Astereal and the wrenching pull of the dark stars that surrounded this doomed world.

Valen stepped up behind him and gazed out across the rift. "I think you have enough space to play," he said, his droll tone making the corner of Niall's mouth quirk up. "You won't find a better position to access the forces you need. Remember bridging a dark star takes you to another universe. It's not like opening a portal to Earth."

"I'm ready. Your ancestors made it. I will, too." Niall studied the landscape. Orange-pink colors tinted a lilac sky, a sunset as vivid as any he had seen across the Pacific Ocean from the tranquil beach he once dared to call home. "This place reminds me of Earth." The poignant memories blocked further words. Taking out the rolled-up wing sections, he reattached them to his wing suit.

When he straightened up, Valen pointed east. "Bacchus is there."

Niall forced aside his sense of loss and tracked Valen's finger to the sky. He opened the front of his wing suit and took out the data orb safely locked inside its protective casing. "Let's get the easy bit over with." He scanned the q-dimension with his mind.

"Do you sense the rippling tides?" Valen asked.

Niall let his mind drift through a random hole. The longer he hovered inside the q-dimension, the more he began to see outside it. "Everything feels so close, and yet so distant at the same time."

"You must keep watching, but not too hard. Let the natural rhythm of the universe slip into view."

On Niall's journey to the Central Rift with Uathach, colored light had marked the sun's crossing with Bacchus. Now, far back in

Astereal's past, the dark star shimmered somewhere on the edge of his mind. Niall lost track of time, watching... waiting. The longest time he had spent in the q-dimension had been exploring cosmic holes under Nantosuelta's tutelage. He had connected with Balor, the contact reducing him to a quivering wreck. He felt Balor's existence now and, with a sense of shock that resounded down to his boots, he realized that his connections to Balor had always been through Bacchus. He had discovered the secret of the dark star in his childhood, just never realized its import, or the fact that he toyed with a portal to another universe.

"I sense Bacchus now." The rhythm of the dark star reminded him of the gravitational forces emanating from Balor's drone, but different, dragging the matter of the universe into a vortex from which nothing could escape.

"Good."

Niall tested his sense of Balor, relieved to discover he did not feel that terrifying debilitation that had always afflicted him before. Instead, Balor's presence pervaded everything, but too dispersed and unfocused to be a threat. This made sense, if Balor had not discovered the dark star's secret, and him, until much later in the future.

"Do not let Bacchus unbalance you," Valen said, misunderstanding Niall's distraction. "See past its presence."

Niall's mind drifted, darting every now and again after a wisp of movement.

*You see the rhythm*, Valen approved. *Nudge it with your mind, just like you create the magnetic sphere to trap the dark energy of the universe. You want to create an enclosed bridge, one that has no start and no end.*

Blood pounded through Niall's veins, the rush intense and necessary. He tapped an unimaginable tidal wave powering the expansion of universes. A circular portal materialized before them, an indescribable cushion of... something. Niall let instinct guide him. He pushed the orb inside, snatching his hand away when the portal wrapped around the silvery globe and disappeared, taking the orb with it. Gone from

447

physical sight, Niall observed the data orb with his mind. It sat there, an alien object inside the q-dimension, protected from the buffers of time and space.

"It will be safe. Only you can retrieve it, whether now or some time in your future."

"It's like a magic trick. My son... he would love this." The pang of remembrance hit hard, sharper than Niall could ignore, and he gasped in an intake of air.

Valen cast him a look of concern. "Are you sure you should do this? You will be farther than ever from your home."

Niall did not answer him. A warning prickle at the back of his neck caused him to scan the horizon towards Navan. His inner eye pulled away from the q-dimension and he pointed at a V-line of dark specks closing in on their position. His mind swept towards the approaching army and bounced off a barricade of shielding. "Morrígan."

"Cetheru leads them," Valen intoned. His eyes turned opaque.

Niall picked up the High Brighid's call for help, but any aid from the Astereans would arrive far too late. He turned to the Central Rift and swept the magnetic forces into a swirling vortex that expanded across the valley. The resulting tidal wave tore into the ranks of gryphon and wreaked havoc. The regimental advance faltered.

"Help me," he ordered Valen.

The High Brighid followed Niall's lead and called lightning down from the dark clouds gathering overhead. The air rumbled angrily, a threatening sound that promised worse to come. Caught in the turbulent forces of wind and magnetic energy, gryphon clipped wings and tumbled over one another sending Morrígan falling to the ground. Their bodies dropped like stone out of the sky and Niall prayed they knew Yerit's trick to soften their landing.

Valen clawed at Niall's sleeve, his face riven with anguish. Tears brimmed in the older man's eyes. "We're killing them. *This* is why you do not speak Morrígan. Everything stems from our actions in this moment. We shall never again be at one with our Morrígan cousins." His voice turned accusing. "You are both our savior, and our demise."

Niall's mind shifted perspective. Valen's words echoed down the ages. Astereal's history unfolded, stretching far into the future, and it was like the universe kicked him in the teeth.

He created the discord between Asterean and Morrígan.

*I caused it all. The Ancient Prophecy. The Great Divide.*

No! Not true. Everything stemmed from Balor.

His own timeline wouldn't exist without Balor. Balor wouldn't be in this universe without Niall. Niall wouldn't have been able to save the people of Astereal without Balor's genetic trickery flowing through his bloodstream.

His mind spiraled into circles at the unfathomable paradoxical consequences arising from his actions, from his very birth. Without Balor's corruption, his father would not have raped his mother.

It always came back to Balor, any other alternative unacceptable.

Consequences be damned. Balor had to be stopped. Earth and the Asterean refugees deserved a chance, and if Balor's creation could be turned against its maker to give them that chance, then so be it.

Niall turned and gripped Valen's shoulders. He had to shout over the thunderclaps ripping across the Rift. "Your future was cast from the moment I arrived." Forks of lightning stabbed deep into the valley. "I still have a chance to save billions. Billions, Valen! They are your descendants!"

Valen's vocal cords bulged. He knew this, had witnessed the truth through Niall's memories. Resolve settled into the lines of his face. "Then finish this!" he shouted back. "Go! Now!"

Niall's eyes swept across the mighty forces he had unleashed on this beautiful planet. The answers he needed lay on the other side of that dark star, the gateway to another universe, his future preordained by a birth of blood tainted by Balor's malevolent genetic disease. He gathered his engine as elements and rift combined, drawing on an incredible magnetic flux that blew his mind.

An enraged thought broke his concentration. *Major 'Kearey!*

Cetheru.

Niall looked back at the Morrígan battling the elements to reach him. To his right, the High Brighid had his hands raised to the mother of all storms as he threw hail and lightning and tornadoes into the path of the Morrígan leader.

Cetheru blasted each deadly assault aside with his own formidable mind. *Major'Kearey! You will destroy our world! I have seen it. Don't do—*

With a storm raging around him, and a tempest inside his head, Niall blocked out Cetheru's pleas and focused on his growing portal; a shimmering vortex that passed directly through the center of a dark star, a black hole into the great unknown. The path through Bacchus lit up his mind like a flare, guiding him to a distant place. An enormous portal writhing with a rainbow of light stretched out across the valley. His mind sensed land... water... an alien world, but habitable with an atmosphere that supported vegetation not dissimilar to plant life found on Earth or Astereal. Valen had told him Balor's universe abounded with M-class planets and he knew what to look for. He had searched this galaxy for habitable worlds for the Astereans and instinct told him this world would not kill him.

"Major'Kearey!" Cetheru yelled, his words whipped away by the gale. The Morrígan fought past everything Valen could throw at him. "You will destroy us!" His arm raised high and a bolt of lightning ripped the sky dead ahead as Cetheru began to fight fire with fire.

The electric concussion strafed Niall's body and set his head spinning. His mind hovered, in a place outside reality, where everything could be seen. The churning forces spelled out a timeline Niall had witnessed either first hand, or during that long-ago evening on Astereal when Macha drugged him with baya root and immersed him in the history of Morrígan generations.

His mind's eye sat outside Astereal's timeline and saw across the Great Divide between Morrígan and Asterean to centuries of war and needless suffering. Alignment existed as a mere speck of hope in the future as the contorting forces of the here and now coalesced into a singular point.

A crossing from one place to another.

A shimmering in the dark.

The Rift pulsated back and forth, fluctuating mayhem, straining to contain the portal between Niall's universe and Balor's.

A sick dread filled Niall and his mind snapped back to Astereal. He grabbed Valen's arm. "You know, don't you?" he yelled. "You know what will happen if I do this!"

The High Brighid stared at him, his face riven with the terrible truth, his eyes liquid pools of sorrow for the future of his world. *When our ancestors came through Bacchus, the resulting time flux made it impossible to escape this solar system, and they were forced to settle here.*

*Time flux?*

*Traveling through Bacchus reversed the magnetic forces within the dark star. The consequences either side of the dark star are impossible to predict, but for a long time our ancestors could not escape this world.*

Niall's fingers dug into the High Brighid's arm. Cetheru's gryphon closed on their position. *And what will happen when I cross over? Tell me!*

Valen gazed out to the distant alien vista, dark, forbidding, and devoid of visible life. The wind dropped to a whisper as Astereal stilled before the terrifying forces that temporarily held her captive. "You will alter our timeflow, Niall'Kearey, and disconnect us from the universe. It is why you are here. You sow the seeds of our future."

Niall closed his eyes.

When he crossed the dark star, he would alter the flow of time. Maybe he had destabilized Bacchus, set Astereal on a path that led to a future Armageddon. Or maybe, by accelerating the timeflow, he had given life to many more generations of Asterean and Morrígan than would have been born if they lived on Earth.

Destiny paved his future, but he chose to walk its path.

*I am not all-knowing.*

Opening his eyes, Niall shifted his grip into an arm hold. Valen returned Niall's gesture, his fingers strong. The High Brighid's wise old eyes conveyed acceptance of his people's fate. The thumping wing beats of Cetheru's gryphon and the Morrigan's triumphant cry broke the spell. With one final squeeze of farewell, Niall released Valen, filled his lungs with air, and took a running leap into the abyss.

Cetheru swooped down on his gryphon. A downdraft nearly knocked Niall off course. A vicious beak snapped shut just inches from his feet before Valen bowled the gryphon aside with a powerful gust of wind.

Tucking his arms in tight to his side, Niall targeted the portal, gathering speed as he fought a rising gale to fly into the yawning void climbing towards him. The flap of wings grew louder behind him.

Niall's heart burst in his chest.

He was alive, he controlled a dark star, held the power of galaxies at his fingertips, and the knowledge brought him nothing but pain.

He chose everything and controlled nothing. Balor and the Formorri had driven him towards this moment. His former life was over. He left behind his world, his family, and the woman he loved to forge an uncertain future of interstellar war, all to preserve a past filled with death and destruction. All else paled by comparison to his true enemy. Balor reduced Foldane, Charles Biron, Sam, and the Vercingetorix to irritants littering his way. Balor, the destroyer and enslaver of entire worlds was a threat to this universe he could not leave unchecked.

His only advantage was the certain knowledge that Balor did not yet know the man who came after him. This early attack in the timeline gave Niall a chance to take the war to Balor. A terrible anger took root at Niall's core, a fierce rage he would need to sustain him through the unknown, long enough to make a difference to the fate of his world, his universe, and his loved ones.

As Niall plummeted through the portal closing between him and Cetheru, one thought swept aside all others.

*You made me what I am, Balor.*

*You gave me this terrible power. Now I come for you and your dark creation will be the weapon that destroys you.*

Count on it.

# THE END

Continue Niall Kearey's journey in *Elecion Forces*,
the next volume in the *War of Ages* Series and sign up for
future book news at cerilondon.com

.

# ABOUT THE AUTHOR

Ceri London writes a blend of high-powered science fiction and thriller
filled with charismatic but believable characters that
show the human psyche at its best and worst.

Her exciting *War of Ages* series confronts the military mindset with hard
science, metaphysical powers, and political intrigue to uncover an
ancient truth that spans space-time and more.

*Rogue Genesis* started this mind-bending ride and readers can explore
the *War of Ages* world to their heart's content
in the follow up books, *Destiny Nexus* and *Elecion Forces*.
The fourth and final book in this series will follow soon.

cerilondon.com

# ACKNOWLEDGMENTS

The more I write, the more I appreciate my wonderful friends and family who have helped me, first with writing *Rogue Genesis*, and then steering me straight with its sequel, *Destiny Nexus*. Some I have met through writing this series and I thank them for their ongoing support and honesty.

I must thank Debby and Travis for reading *Destiny Nexus* in its fledgling form and giving me the benefit of their experience and initial reactions. I am particularly grateful to Travis who has provided ongoing support throughout with content and line editing. He never fails to offer his honest and insightful opinion and has generously provided feedback, edits, and advice on the cover and story description.

I thank my father for his proofreading and my beta-editors. Readers have Terrie to thank for an ending that is not as dark as it would have been, and I also thank David for advising on pace. My grateful thanks to Marcha, firstly for simply enjoying my work without reservation, and secondly for helping me keep the science within the bounds of speculative credibility. Grateful appreciation goes to my brother, Paul, who confirmed my other beta's reactions, sometimes using their exact words, which was a little eerie, and to my other brother, Richard, for his encouragement and advice on the cover.

There are so many others who have answered the odd question, advised me on different aspects, it is impossible to mention them all, hard to leave them out. Thank you all.

Finally, my love and thanks once more to my wonderful patient husband and my two lovely daughters. They put up with me, keep me supplied with food and clean clothing, set the alarm clock, pay the bills...

Made in the USA
Monee, IL
07 May 2025

17042341R00267